FREEDOM STATION OCCOQUAN

A novel by

Cris Alvarez

War is not simply the killing of people,
it is the eradication of ideas.

Cristobal Alvarez
Arlington, VA
http://www.crisalvarez.com

United States • Canada

FREEDOM STATION OCCOQUAN

ISBN 978-0-6151-6267-6

First Printing: September 2007

Printed in the United States

O ne half-hour before the break of dawn, while the sanguine rays of a new sun made ready to cut the night open, a beast of the new age edged forward along a narrow dirt path. The dark limbs of the forest hung over the trail like a double-file of shadowy mourners giving obeisance to an approaching perdition. In the year 2022, the juggernaut that was man's war against himself still commanded reverence.

But this green and brown camouflaged beast that possessed such grave influence made little sound as it advanced. Its hot engine purred softly while gentle twigs broke with pitiable submissiveness under its rubber wheels. The beast's eyes, if one listened closely, buzzed imperceptibly, though their sudden appearance would undoubtedly precipitate incongruous shouts of terror in warriors.

They were two, glowing-white, glass-shelled lamps aimed low at the ground being traversed. Those eyes, marvels of science designed somewhere safe and secure by geniuses in bleached lab coats, maintained a gaze compact, focused and deadly. In fact, each individual part of the beast had been designed with rapturous devotion to a singular, cruel purpose. The hunt was its mission. So, this well-crafted beast crawled quietly towards its game while in its open belly, three individuals not so perfectly formed, shared its curious hunger.

The jeep's front passenger abruptly raised his hand, paused, then pointed into the distance. Under a pine tree, one thousand feet away, a figure, the docile prey, sat simply in a chair. The jeep pulled closer and stopped exactly three hundred meters from that solitary soul. An electronic rangefinder, a miniature face glowing green inside the belly of the beast, helpfully provided that precise reading.

From his position in the passenger seat, Special Agent Conrad Greis, wearing night-vision goggles and army camouflage fatigues, carefully raised a sniper rifle to his right shoulder. The air though still was thick with moisture from a recent downpour. Conrad's damp undershirt slid reluctantly over skin but he did not pull at it. Comfort as a priority held a distant second to the lust of the kill.

Conrad instinctively pressed his rifle stock into the front of his right shoulder and wrapped his hand around the grip. His right eye sought and found the beautifully clear picture provided by the rifle's night-modified telescopic sight. The goggles and the sight, additional miracles of modern science, absorbed both ambient light and infrared light and provided an almost clear picture of the woods through which the jeep moved. The sitter remained oblivious and pre-occupied with his book. The beast was good at what it did and so were its masters.

A cloth strap, attached to both ends of the rifle swung loosely inches beneath the rifle barrel. Without taking his eyes from the scope, Conrad wrapped the strap around his left triceps and wrist. He tightened the makeshift loop sling against his arm and pushed the butt of his rifle more securely against his shoulder. In this position, he felt as one with the rifle.

The jeep's other two crewmembers, the driver and the back seat passenger, both also clad in army camouflage fatigues and wearing night vision goggles, sat silently and unmoving. Conrad took a shallow breath and with his right hand, quietly opened his door. He raised his head from the scope and slid his legs over the doorframe. The ground was moist so when he shifted his weight to his feet, he dropped his center weight slightly to compensate for the slickness of the clay earth.

Conrad looked through the sight again and began to kneel for a better shot. The target was a man sitting in a chair and leaning forward over a book he held with both hands. An easy shot. But as the view from his scope dropped with his body, Conrad saw that a low wall of bushes in front of the target would obscure his aim if he shot from a kneeling position. Halfway into the kneel, he stopped and rose back to a standing position.

Conrad's pulsing blood sounded in his ears. He smelled nothing strange in the air. The wet earth sucked at his feet as he adjusted his footing. The picket man, still seemingly unaware of Conrad, remained hunched over the book cupped in his hands.

Conrad leaned sideways against the jeep to brace himself and concentrated on taking slow breaths. He raised his scope's crosshairs from the target's chest to the target's head. The man's head, uncovered and with a mop of shaggy hair on top, moved slightly back and forth. The man's goggles were lying on the ground by the side of his chair. His focus was the book.

Conrad, letting the air out of his lungs, focused briefly on the beating of his heart, and then slowly and firmly, using the meaty part of his finger, pulled the trigger of his rifle. The gun kicked slightly, the shot muffled by a silencer on the gun barrel, and the picket's head exploded with a soft thwack. The book dropped to the ground and the target leaned forward and slid out of his chair.

Conrad lowered his rifle, quickly slid back into his seat, and nodded at the jeep's driver. He slipped his sniper rifle into a vertical sheath attached to the left side of his seat and took hold of an X8 assault rifle lying in the empty space between himself and the driver. The jeep bucked slightly, moved quietly forward, one hundred and eighty meters closer to the picket's body, and stopped.

The jeep's driver, Department of Homeland Security Assistant Special Agent David Bronson, put the jeep into park without turning off the engine. He took hold of his own X8 rifle and stepped out of the driver's side of the jeep. He slowly scanned his surroundings as he moved. The body of the man Conrad shot lay unmoving in the grass. The forest was still silent.

Conrad and the jeep's third passenger, DHS Assistant Special Agent Angelina Velazquez, Lina as her peers had nicknamed her, both slowly stepped out of opposite sides of the jeep. Nearly simultaneously, each dropped to one knee, placed their rifles against their shoulders and, with their backs to the jeep, covered the flanks. Conrad scanned the area and saw nothing but stillness in the surrounding bushes and the trees.

Dave, six-three and oversized, took slow and cautious steps towards the picket, walking like a man ready for a surprise to jump out at any moment. He eventually moved behind the ragged line of low bushes that sat between the dead man and the jeep. A few minutes later, walking casually and with caution apparently thrown to the wind, Dave Bronson returned to the jeep.

He shook his wide head and his deep voice rumbled. "Nothing but the dude and his chair. He had this cell phone. And this bible." Dave held a muscular arm out towards his superior. In the large man's hand the phone and field bible looked like they belonged to a child's toy action figure. Sweat covered the bare areas of the big man's face and wrist.

Conrad and Lina lowered their rifles and stood. Conrad slid his infrared goggles to the top of his helmet and took the phone from Dave's hand. He looked it over without opening it and placed it on the jeep's dash. Conrad placed his rifle on his seat and took the bible with both hands.

He turned the pages until he found the ones splattered with bits of the picket's brain and blood. Matthew 18:7 was underlined.

'Woe to the world because of offences! For it must needs be that offences come; yet woe to the man by whom the offence comes!' Conrad calmly flipped to the inside front cover. Joseph Crunt. Monash church. Conrad closed the book and grabbed a microphone radio attached to the jeep's dash.

"Eagle, over," he said into the mike. Static. Ten seconds passed.

A nasally voice answered. "Yes sir."

"Eagle. We touched a picket a half-mile ahead of you. We'll wait here. Pull to me and once we're together we'll advance in column until we're a quarter mile from the target, over."

"Got it sir." Eagle, otherwise known as Army Sergeant First Class Meeks, coughed and the encrypted communications line went dead.

Conrad Greis pulled his goggles back down over his eyes and surveyed the wooded area around them again. He saw nothing else to interest him. He grabbed the overhead crossbar of the jeep and swung back into his seat. Dave and Lina took their seats as well. Conrad looked back at Lina.

When her body wasn't covered by fatigues and gear, she was a tall, slender, dark-haired woman. Lina was of Mexican descent and had the deep brown skin of a mestizo and beautiful almond-shaped eyes that Conrad saw in his mind's eye. She was an average looking woman but a constant flashing anger in her eyes and her physical training had given her a firmness and strength that most men found hard to resist. Conrad lifted his goggles from his eyes. The horizon behind her was changing from black to a dark blue. Conrad Greis smiled and, for a moment, enjoyed the colors of the sky.

Agent Velazquez broke the silence. "How do you feel about this team sir?" Her voice was smooth and firm and Conrad enjoyed the sound of it. It was so musical and measured she had used it to win a high school state singing competition many years ago. Well before the Civil War. Conrad realized he hadn't been quick to answer her and he looked side to side slightly embarrassed. Dave flicked a glance at Lina.

Conrad squeezed his eyes shut and silently cursed himself for losing concentration. "You mean the auxiliary team?" he asked. Lina nodded and kept her eyes steadily on Conrad.

"I'm worried about platoon sergeant Meeks. Seems a little green. His squad leaders are pretty solid. I'm not sure why one of them isn't leading instead."

"Politics sir?" Velazquez asked. She pushed her lips together.

"They are from Washington," Dave said, his voice mocking the statement. Conrad nodded in agreement to the sentiment but said nothing. Dave was an ex-cop from Cleveland who had seen his share of violence and office politics. At times, Conrad didn't know which bothered the man more.

Dave's squirmed around in his seat, one obviously not made for a man his size. "Can I smoke sir?"

"No." Conrad squinted at Bronson. There was no smoking during operations, not while the sun was down, and Dave knew it. "You need to quit those things Bronson. You're getting operationally lazy."

"Operationally--?" Bronson grunted and looked forward. He shrugged and ran his finger along a small U.S. flag imprinted on the front of the jeep's dashboard. "I thought we had the freedom to do whatever we wanted." He lifted his chin and grinned at Conrad.

"Cut it Dave." Conrad turned his head back to Lina. "They all seem solid enough. My worry is that one of them starts shooting before negotiations finish."

Lina nodded but said nothing. She scanned the horizon with her goggles.

Conrad continued. "As for today, I'll stick Deevers with Fam. You'll go with Buerhle, Bronson you'll be with Mackey and I'll hang by Tomars."

Dave chuckled and scratched his crotch. "It's so funny. I can't even imagine the meeting where the President let DHS begin leading DoD operations, sir. The SecDef must have shit a brick when he got the instructions on that."

"That's history Bronson. Don't even worry about it. They'll follow our instructions."

Dave spoke softly. "Two years ain't enough time to integrate DHS and DoD like that. Or make them follow our instructions." He quietly hacked up a clot of phlegm from deep down in his throat and spit over the side of the jeep.

"Well," Conrad said as he pulled his goggles down and turned to look forward across the darkness "Meeks doesn't seem the type to try anything funny." He paused and scratched his knee. "I've got a handle on it Dave."

Dave looked out across the woods and gruffly placed his rifle across his waist. "Just don't want to get killed," he said low and maybe to himself.

"You know sir," Lina said, "I still don't get all this politics stuff. You get an order you follow it. Right? No questions. What's wrong with these army guys?"

Conrad twisted quickly in his chair to look at Lina. "Damn I like your attitude soldier. And I won't forget you said that."

Lina lifted the body of her rifle close to her mouth and blew two short, sharp breaths over the barrel. She rubbed it with the sleeve of her uniform and shook her head slowly at Conrad.

Dave laughed and looked at her through his rear-view mirror. "You are quite the exception V. Quite the exception." Dave looked at Conrad. "Any air support sir?"

Conrad looked at the cell phone hooked to his belt and shook his head. "Nothing."

"Good way to run a counterinsurgency program."

"Come on Dave. You know we're strapped for resources. The Kansas problems are keeping the helos tied up pretty good."

"I thought it was the Arizona situation holding things up right now."

Conrad ignored the statement. He tapped a few buttons on his phone and became agitated by a series of dots he saw on the small screen. "Why is the long range finder on?"

"It's not," Dave said. "I turned it off when we left Fort Denning."

"It's on."

Dave flipped open a panel on the dashboard and frowned. "I swear I turned it off." He typed a code on a small keyboard next to the panel he had opened. The dots on Conrad's cell phone changed appropriately.

Conrad trusted Dave completely. He didn't continue the questioning but he became worried that the rebels might have intercepted the signal that U.S. military units used to let their headquarters track them. The signal was normally turned off immediately before engagements. Yet the picket had been entirely unaware of their presence.

Dave sighed. "Here they are." He pointed his thumb back behind them.

Cris Alvarez

The steady hum of four armored combat vehicles became audible as a Stryker commander's vehicle followed by three Stryker infantry carrier vehicles rolled in on the bare, dirt path that stretched out behind Conrad's jeep. Conrad shook his head as he angrily noted that all four Stryker's had their top-mounted .50 caliber machine guns pointed straight ahead. The vehicles stopped in column and moments later, Meeks, wearing his camouflaged army battle dress uniform and toting an X8 rifle, came around from behind the lead Stryker and approached Conrad. Meeks had a wide, almost flabby face, and a small hooked nose. He had a broad forehead and despite his youth, he was balding.

"Sir," Meeks said without saluting.

"Helmet Meeks. Keep it on."

Meeks' eyes flicked around. "Oh, oh sure sir." He quickly donned his helmet. He gave a sheepish smile and pulled a map out of a side pocket on his pants. He unfolded the map and held it open in front of Conrad.

"Your long range finders are on. Turn them off now."

Meeks looked even more confused. "But we turned them off at-"

Conrad double-checked his phone. "They're on now."

While Meeks quickly relayed the order to his drivers over his shoulder communications unit, Conrad pulled a penlight from his chest pocket and nonchalantly pointed at the Strykers. "Your guns. They need to cover all four points Meeks. Your vehicle straight ahead, number two covering the right flank, three the left and four the rear."

Meeks gulped, smiled tightly and forced a chuckle. "At least, I got my command vehicle right l-t."

"Fix it." Conrad leaned over the tactical map of western Northern Virginia and pointed the pen light at it. "There's our target. You can see they have the one dirt road leading to the building but there are clear fields approaching it along the hills surrounding its location. We're going to move in a file along this route," Conrad moved his finger along the map from their present position to an area near the specified building, "spread into line here and then pull up at the top of the ridge where we'll stay in line with our rears pointing at the target. Your command vehicle will be the pivot point and position at the left flank. I'm going to put my jeep to your left rear."

"Trust the maps?" Meeks asked.

"They're fine."

"Yes sir. Then we negotiate with the bullhorns once we get there?"

Conrad flashed his light up to Meeks face. He wasn't sure if that tone was neutral or suggested some sort of sarcasm. Meeks looked puzzled. Conrad dropped the light down to the map again. "We'll get moving once the sun breaks the horizon. Until then stay tight."

"Yes, sir." Meeks began folding the map as he walked back towards his command Stryker.

"Meeks," Conrad said.

"Yes sir?" Meeks said turning back towards Conrad.

"How's Deevers doing?"

"Your liaison?" Meeks shrugged. "Fine I guess."

"You guys giving him a hard time?"

Meeks spoke without expression. "Isn't being DHS a hard enough time as it is?" Meeks paused. "Sir."

Bronson covered his mouth to stifle a strong belly laugh. He shook his head at his steering wheel.

"Wait for my order to move," Conrad said. Meeks saluted and jogged back to the rear of his Stryker.

"Boy, no respect, sir, no respect," Dave said.

"They'll get used to it," Conrad said.

"It's been two years."

Conrad punched Dave in the shoulder. Then the cell phone Dave had taken from the dead picket began to ring. The phone played a mournful religious tune while it blinked green. The phone flashed like an overgrown lightning bug sitting in the darkness. Dave and Conrad stared at it until it stopped.

"Pizza's ready," Dave said.

"We'll stick to the plan," Conrad said. He laid his head back on the headrest and looked up at the stars blinking out of existence in the western sky. "Watch the picket for any movement."

The three DHS agents peered into the darkness and waited for the sun while the four squads of Department of Defense auxiliary troops, an army platoon assigned to support DHS operations against rebel Americans and other heavily armed crackpots, sat in their Strykers, lit cigarettes and drank from cold coffee canteens.

Cris Alvarez

2

F rom the top edge of a grassy ridge that ran more or less along an east-west axis, the ground sloped steeply down and north towards a wide sun-drenched valley. Three-quarters of a mile from the ridge, in the center of that wide, idyllic sweep of ground stood a three-story concrete building protected on all sides by a four foot high stone wall. The wall was in turn surrounded by the Virginia wildflowers and scattered oaks that covered the valley. An array of broken-down cars and trucks littered the interior and exterior of the compound.

Conrad looked up towards the sky from his position on the ridge. Birds sang in the pine and maple trees around him. It was mid-afternoon and the day was hot. Conrad ran the back of his hand across a sweaty forehead. Flies and gnats buzzed about searching for a taste of his skin. The smell of gunpowder and diesel fuel wafted along a warm breeze that came up from the valley.

Conrad shook his head. He was dwelling on the scenery and it bothered him. He gathered his wits and peered again through his electronic binoculars, slowly adjusting its settings to get the clearest view possible.

Armed men frantically moved back and forth within the compound's yard and inside the building. Men who looked just like the men Conrad worked with every day. Brothers, neighbors and friends. But these busy brothers were focused on the wrong thing. They were focused on the vehicles positioned opposite Conrad – on the north side of the valley.

Conrad's Strykers sat on the ridge, one mile from the rebel position, as decoys. Occasionally, the two-man Stryker crews fired bursts from their vehicle's machine guns towards the rebel compound. They had been instructed to distract and scare, not to actually shoot anyone or anything in the compound, until the proper time. They were causing confusion and that put Conrad at ease.

Behind Conrad, the ground sloped downwards but not as sharply as the front side. The noise of thirty-six soldiers, anxiously attending to their weapons and backpacks, drew his attention from the fortified house. A few of the men behind Conrad stifled coughs.

Guns clicked like beetles as the men fiddled with them. One leg was numb. Conrad shifted himself slightly on the grassy ridge to ease the pressure on it.

Meeks moved from a position below Conrad and slid close to him. Meeks peered over the ridge line. "See them l-t?"

Conrad didn't look directly at Meeks. Instead, he looked back at the house. "Yeah. I see them. What little gunfire there is...is focused on the decoy team in the woods to the north."

"So when are we going?" Meeks sounded impatient.

No doubt the other men were impatient too. Conrad knew their joints were getting stiff and their rears were getting overused. He turned his head to look at Sergeant First Class Meeks and those prominent jowls of his. Civil war had taken the best and left the rest to clean up the country. Men like Meeks were better left behind a desk than a gun but that's what the nation had.

Conrad rolled on to his back and looked at the sky. He closed his eyes. "Get the men ready to move. Assault gear only."

Meeks gave the order. The men rose to their feet, equipment clattering around as they gave a collective groan of relief. "Those fuckers hung my cousin." That was Corporal Litle's angry voice. Conrad opened his eyes and looked down the hill at the men moving below him.

One of them, Sergeant Buerhle, saw Conrad's look. "Keep it professional," Buerhle said to Litle. Buerhle accompanied his words with a light punch to Litle's shoulder. "It's not even the same fucking people." Litle growled back and said nothing.

Conrad understood Litle's feelings about these operations. Litle wasn't too keen on the personal freedom law codes passed by the Feds and the states over the last few years but Litle was more intent on two more immediate and visceral needs - revenge and protecting the political integrity of the nation. The same reasons that motivated most of these men. It was the same reason that motivated Conrad. Without a nation unified, the future would be chaos. Who could honestly deny that? But Conrad also believed in the new rules. They made sense to him. They made sense to most Americans under the age of forty.

Conrad closed his eyes again and pressed his bare hands against the hard ground. He let his fingers become close and intimate with the grass underneath him. Radio traffic crackled from his shoulder mounted communications device. He blinked and pulled his air filtration system off the front of his neck and over his mouth. He took a few deep breaths of filtered air, pulled the cumbersome device off his mouth and rested it on his neck again. He raised his right hand to his face and with one finger, he scratched at the wet dirt embedded in the thin wrinkle lines of his forehead. He and his men had been at this location for almost the entire day and the grime of the valley had settled nicely on them.

Over the comm unit, Conrad Greis heard more screams and yells from angry rebels directing their verbal venom at the vehicles deployed to the north. They screamed, "Praise be to God" and other such things which made Conrad's eyes roll. He wondered if they thought it was God's will that they be so well armed too. He had heard those sentiments spoken many times, many years before.

Conrad closed his eyes and for a moment he was back, crouched against the hot sandy hills of Iraq. He was operating in the triangle. A dangerous area alive with insurgents. His platoon had a small group of the enemy trapped in an abandoned building. The insurgents originally thought they had the jump on the U.S. troops but Conrad was not a foolish officer.

He always acted with confidence and he had always won. But for one single moment then, with the odds on his side, he didn't think he could win. He didn't think that they could win. He didn't think anyone would win. People would just lose. It was a no-sum game. No winners, just losers. The Americans, the Iraqis, the insurgents, the Muslims, the Christians, the Kurds. The Sunni, the Shia, everyone one of them a loser.

"Sir, sir. We're in position. When do we go?" a sergeant asked.

"Just a minute. Just a minute."

Conrad could let them surrender. He could wait them out no problem. They were in an isolated area cleared of obstructions with nothing but that four story building in the center of a nine hundred meter radius circle of land. They could wait these sitting ducks out and try to get them with a minimum of bloodshed. But who wanted that? What would that buy anyone?

"Squad one?"

"Check sir."

"Squad two?"

"Aye sir."

"Squad three?"

"In position."

"Squad four?"

"Right on sir."

Four squads and not one could answer like any of the others. A unified army of free individuals. A smile crept across his face. Freedom.

"Okay. On my fire. Squad one, two, and three forward while four covers. Go in hard. They'll be confused and they'll miss and we won't."

Conrad lifted his rifle over the sand ridge and aimed at the window where the main stream of gunfire came from. He pulled the trigger and a grenade flew from the launcher attached to his rifle. It crashed through the window and exploded inside. His men rushed forward, along protected positions, firing well-aimed shots. Smoke began to drift out of the shattered window. There would be cheering and drinking and singing that night.

Conrad blinked tightly and he was back again in the present. Facing insurgents again, sixteen years later, on American soil. Fundamentalists of a different brand. Mostly Christians, fundis, with a few of a non-religious breed mixed in. They all fought the same way though. Hit and run tactics, blending with the population and taking advantage of opportunities while slipping away unseen from danger. But they had a good tip this time and Conrad had bagged this bunch in their low, three story fort-like home.

It galled Conrad. They took advantage of the freedoms that the American government now provided to all American citizens. They abused that freedom and used it to hurt and kill innocent people. That's why Conrad had to have zero mercy with them. That's why his superiors approved of those sorts of extreme tactics. Let one slip and the others will follow and soon the U.S. would be back again in the mess it had recently escaped from. A vision of his ex-wife and his two sons flashed before his eyelids. He wished he had a photo handy, something he could kiss for luck, but to protect his family's identity he never brought one during an operation. If the enemy ever got him...well they were willing to go to extremes.

"Sir?"

Conrad widened his eyes. Meeks was looking down at him.

"Sorry. Thought you were falling asleep. The men are ready."

Conrad tapped his shoulder device. "Deevers, over."

"Sir. Go ahead."

"What's the word?"

"No go sir."

"Roger." Conrad bit his tongue. Nicholas Deevers was the newest assistant special agent assigned to Conrad's Occoquan Freedom Station. Nick was a Boston native and had been at Conrad's field station for six months now following a few good years of working with the Orlando police department on some hairy situations. The twenty-six year old man had a great resume. A liberal activist who majored in peace studies and conflict resolution in college and he was very aggressive about it. He was also very aggressive about his professional condition. Conrad's superiors had insisted that Conrad give Deevers the lead negotiator role as quickly as possible. Conrad had reluctantly acquiesced - he didn't like young negotiators - and now he'd have to chew the butts above him for this. Nick Deevers wasn't working out too well for many reasons.

Conrad peered through his binoculars at the vehicles to the north. Nick was up there with the Strykers to negotiate from a position of strength. Not only were the Strykers good decoys but they also served as props to provide the proper intimidation factor. "Tell me clear Nick."

"Lieutenant. They refuse to surrender."

"Don't call me lieutenant Nick. It's a nickname. Only the army guys call me that."

"Yes sir."

"It's been eight hours of negotiations hasn't it Nick?" Conrad felt like he was admonishing one of his sons.

"Something like that sir."

"It's been eight hours seventeen minutes. Be exact on this."

"Right sir. Got you. Sorry."

"That's seventeen minutes over the stated requirement for negotiations. Out." Conrad looked at his watch and then pulled a field map from his waist poach. Meeks did the same.

"All right," Conrad said, "all of you take a few swigs of water. Hydrate, hydrate, hydrate. Anyone fall out from lack of water will answer to me personally." Four staff sergeants moved up close to Conrad and Meeks. "Mackey, take your men around the left along the Charles Creek. Buerhle take your men along the trees here on the right. I'll go with Tomars and his men up the middle along these fields. Morales you keep your men here and monitor the valley.

Watch for any surprises and keep your machine guns focused on the building. I'll hang back for fifteen minutes while Mackey and Buerhle move up the flanks then we'll move up. If I get attacked before this point," Conrad first pointed out a landmark on the map and then he pointed out in the field in front of him, "keep moving and do not attack until you are nine o'clock and three o'clock with them. Got it?"

Meeks and the four sergeants nodded but no one spoke. Conrad looked at each of the men staring back at him.

"Prisoners sir?" Mackey asked.

Conrad's throat tightened. Here was the moment of truth. They had been sitting in negotiations with this bunch for over eight hours. That was the legal requirement before issuing a no prisoners order. With the state of the country today, the country's law enforcement and military personnel did not have the time or resources for stretched out negotiations. Action must be decisive and swift. Conrad knew this and he accepted the wisdom of it. The barbarians were at the gates of America and there was no reason to suffer rebel fools gladly.

That's the attitude it took to defend the area around Washington, DC. That was the attitude needed to defend all of the major urban centers of the United States. New York, Chicago, Los Angeles, Saint Louis, and the two dozen other cities that were the main population centers of the nation. Before Conrad, the Washington, DC suburbs and exurbs were a hotbed of rebel activity. Now the rebels of this area had been reduced to a bunch of wild dogs running from spot to spot until they were cornered in little out of the way areas of Northern Virginia like this one. It was a tough and terrible kind of war but Conrad was a soldier.

"Shoot all armed males on sight, regardless of whether they surrender or not. Bring unarmed adult males to me."

"Aye sir, yes sir, will do," they answered in series.

Conrad looked at his watch again and spoke into his shoulder device. "We're at eight twenty-two, acknowledge."

"Give me another thirty minutes sir."

Conrad growled. "What are you after Deevers?"

"Shouldn't we, uh, let them have a little more of a chance to give up first?"

Conrad knew the rest of his men were listening to this conversation. Some grinning, some frowning, depending on their

Cris Alvarez

taste and constitution for this type of work. They didn't look at Conrad directly now but they were listening.

"They've had their opportunities all ready, don't you think Deevers?"

From the throng down the hill came Dave's voice. "Aw, come on Lieutenant. Let's get this over with and forget about Nick." During operations, Dave was a man like the grim reaper. He did his work well and wanted to do it fast but he never seemed happy about it. Lina stood next to Dave just as grim faced but she didn't speak. She was that type of agent.

Nick hesitated between his words. "Yes sir I suppose they have." Conrad hoped that Nick didn't hesitate between operational movements too. Then again, that would be the perfect excuse to let him go.

"Okay," Conrad said. "You all know procedures. Now that they've forced us into forward action, there must be no mercy taken. Don't give it a second thought. We have presidential authority for this. We've warned them multiple times already and they know that we mean it. They're no strangers to this. They know what happens."

"But sir," Nick said.

Conrad was shocked at this persistence. "Enough Deevers. The line has been drawn and we will stick to it. If I receive reports that you hesitated in your duty, you will be separated from the Department. Understand?"

"Roger, sir," Nick snapped back over the radio.

"Out. Okay people. On my fire. Hit them hard. Now-" A tap on his shoulder interrupted him. Dave had moved close and was pointing north. Something hovered in the sky far in the distance. Perplexed, Conrad lifted his binoculars to his eyes. A Chinese-made Jaysing military assault helicopter floated stationary like a vicious hummingbird waiting to feed.

"Air support?" Dave asked.

"Fuck no," Conrad said. "We didn't load any Spikers did we?"

"No." Dave sounded dumbfounded. "That's a rebel chopper?"

"Yeah. Hm. Maybe he thinks we have a Spiker. Hopefully he'll stay back."

"Should we abort?"

Dave was no coward. He simply knew proper procedure. "No," Conrad said. He turned to the men. "The chopper is red. Don't give it a second thought. It'll stay away."

The men squirmed with a touch of fear among them.

Conrad barked his next order. "Let's move out!"

Buerhle and Mackey's men crouched and trotted forward, along the flanks, with Lina and Dave moving behind their specified charges. When Buerhle and Mackey had moved far enough ahead, Conrad waved Tomars forward. He and Meeks followed behind Tomars' men.

They crouched and jogged forward, maneuvering behind concealing cover the entire way. When they got to a tree line one hundred and eighty meters from the house they dropped to their stomachs and began crawling forward. In thirty more minutes, Tomars, Conrad and the other men were in position behind a low ridge in the land. They hadn't been seen yet.

Conrad peeked over the ridgeline and looked over the building ninety meters in front of them. He sighted his rifle-mounted grenade launcher and watched as his popper slowly arced up and on to the building's roof. It impaled itself there and in five seconds an explosion ripped half of the roof off. Bits of concrete exploded into the air like confetti.

Suddenly, heavy machine gun fire ripped the air behind Conrad's troops. Conrad's head and body spun to the left. A platoon-sized crowd of men, perhaps as many as fifty, was crouching two hundred and seventy-five meters in the rear of his position. Another heavy machine gun joined the first and then the rest of the rebels joined in the staccato symphony with their own automatic weapons.

"Down," Conrad shouted but he said it out of instinct. All his men were flat on the ground already.

"Morales," he said into his communications unit.

"Sir," came the response.

"Do you see them?" The rebel guns came in heavy. Conrad's men tried to return fire but they were on lower ground and mostly kept their heads down.

"Not really. They have good cover."

"They're two-seven-five meters to my rear flank. Seven o'clock to my position. Move forward carefully and shoot what you can. Don't get in our line of fire."

"Roger."

Conrad turned his attention to his Strykers. "Sergeant Fam."

"Sir," responded the head of the Stryker crew.

"Put your M4s," referring to the machine guns mounted on the Strykers, "on the ambush behind me." Conrad knew he was working with the extreme effective range of the M4s but it had to be done. "Close the distance if possible."

"Roger," said Fam.

The M4s joined the symphony and their bullets ripped up the ground and the rebels behind Conrad. He tapped his helmet hard with his knuckles. Maybe that'll shake up this foggy brain of mine he thought ruefully.

The ambushers were decimated by the Stryker gunfire. The rebels in the compound fired at Conrad's men too but it looked like the majority of their force had joined in the ambush. The government troops mopped up the men behind them before turning their attention back to the compound. Conrad checked the horizon. The helo was gone.

They United States resumed its attack. Rifle grenades arced from the perimeter of the wide partial circle his men formed around the building. The grenades embedded themselves into the roof and the upper walls. The building tore apart as the grenades began exploding. Responding gunfire was thin and sporadic. After two minutes of softening the building, Conrad and his men rose and charged the husk of a building.

The dirt in the fields Conrad and his men dashed through was mixed with ash from old fires. This area had been razed before. Fresh grass grew here and there but the ground was still mainly dead. Nearly three years of hellish civil war had seen to that. The continuing guerrilla activity kept death hanging around. Conrad's job and the job of other Freedom stations heads like himself was to convince the grim reaper that it was time to leave the United States alone. They did that by exterminating problems faster than the reaper did.

Conrad also happened to do it a lot better than anyone else, which is why he had command of the most important station in the land. His station, Freedom Station Occoquan, existed to eliminate rebel activity in the region south of the nation's capitol, Washington, DC. Conrad was proud of the job he had done of clearing most of Northern Virginia of its rebel problem. He liked working himself out of a job.

In thirty minutes, Conrad and his men finished the operation against the Occoquan Patriot Committee. Eighty-seven bodies of the Patriot Committee lay twisted in the ruins of their home. Fourteen young prisoners, boys under the age of eighteen and the surviving women and children, were taken.

As Conrad expected, not all of the military age males had been killed on sight. Three wounded men were brought to Conrad. A dozen soldiers stood nervously close by. Conrad knew they were all wondering the same thing.

"Sir." Conrad turned. Staff Sergeant Morales stood grim faced behind him. Conrad knew the look.

"Three dead, six lightly wounded."

Conrad lowered his eyes. "Who?"

Morales gulped. "Meeks, Litle, Suarez."

Conrad nodded and wondered about all the negative things he had thought and said about Meeks.

Morales leaned close and whispered in Conrad's ear. "Litle took friendly. An M4 round."

It happens, Conrad reminded himself. War is chaos. The costs are known by those who fight.

Conrad turned his attention back to his prisoners. He had them lined up against a wall while they called loudly to Christ and God to protect them. Three of Conrad's auxiliary soldiers quietly lined up five meters from the three men and double-checked the working condition of their rifles. Conrad waved them off. They looked at him and then each other and hesitated to move from their positions.

"I'll take care of this," Conrad said. They shuffled off to join the other soldiers who stood thirty feet back.

Nick, Dave and Lina stood with the soldiers. Dave and Lina were just as dirty as the men they accompanied on the assault. Conrad was proud of that. Nick was nearly clean but he couldn't blame that on the man. Negotiators rarely got as dirty as the men who did the front line fighting.

"Get me the vid," Conrad said to Lina. Conrad's command jeep was parked next to the four Strykers. Lina went to the jeep and pulled a video camera from a pack sitting in the rear of the jeep. She quickly set it up on a tripod facing the three men lined up against the wall. They had their hands clasped and their heads bowed as they mumbled prayers to themselves.

"Swing it here first," Conrad said.

Lina turned the camera towards Conrad. He removed a small slip of paper from his back pocket and loudly read the presidential order which authorized the immediate execution of these men. He looked at them and felt a pang of guilt. He took no pleasure in the executions but he took full responsibility for them. This isn't revenge, he told himself.

He looked back at the soldiers watching him. Those young men didn't need the memories of doing something like this. When he was done reading the order, Conrad added, "May God have mercy on your souls."

He lifted his rifle and Lina swung the camera back to the three trembling men. One, a thick set middle-aged man with gray stubble over his face, stopped praying and pointed a finger at Conrad. Then he pointed his finger at the sky. "He'll get you," the man bellowed.

Conrad paused a moment before gunning them down with rapid succession kill shots. He stepped closer to the bodies and put one more bullet into their heads before turning his back on them.

Some of Conrad's men crossed themselves, some murmured prayers from the Old Testament and a couple said prayers from the Koran. Conrad ordered the dead rebels buried, paper and electronic documents collected, and the house demolished.

The battle had been won. Mission accomplished. Beers all around. Despite casualties, the United States was victorious again. As the building came down and the dead were being buried, Conrad meticulously prepared his three men's bodies for transport.

3

C onrad shaded his eyes from the sun as he squinted up at the twenty-foot high concrete wall that loomed before him. A few pillows of clouds hung in the blue sky above. He looked left and right along its length and sighed deeply. He would have liked a sturdier wall wrapped around the perimeter of the eight hundred acre Occoquan government compound. Something actually built to keep out more than just men and wild deer.

He looked to his left again. A tall metal gate set into the wall served as the compound's front entrance. From the gate, a paved road ran to Route 123, the main road that served the area.

Up and down 123, two steady streams of light traffic flowed. One went north towards Fairfax, fourteen miles away, the other moved south towards the river and the city of Woodbridge two miles away. About twenty-five miles northeast of the compound was the city of Washington, DC. The city Conrad was paid, and felt privileged, to protect.

He imagined a circle thirty to thirty-five miles in radius with Washington at its center. Along the edge of that circle, scattered rebel groups hid in the woods and probed for opportunities to hurt that proud city. But they were become less and less of a danger with each passing month. The reports he saw each day from DHS headquarters confirmed that his work was going well.

Conrad looked at the gate again. It was shut but unlocked. A uniformed DHS agent stood, tall and silent, in the sentry box situated on its left. Right of Conrad, on the wall, a large five foot diameter discoloring blemished the otherwise evenly-colored tan surface. Seven weeks ago, a rebel bomb had blown a hole in the wall and repairs had been hasty. The quick fix of bricks and concrete had been buttressed by a support made of wood and metal sitting inside the compound. Conrad made a mental note to double check the soundness of that inner structure.

As he stood with his hands on his hips, Conrad glanced at the large white metal sign that was attached to the wall near the sentry box. It read "Occoquan Federal Center". More than two dozen bullet holes peppered its surface. Conrad shrugged and headed for the front gate. He had to make sure his personnel were focused on security during these hot periods, times when the rebels were feeling particularly vengeful. But the compound was as secure as could be considering the available budget. Mental note seventeen. Push budget issues with HQ today. He'd have to make a few calls.

He passed through the gate and nodded at the guard in the sentry box. Inside, the center itself was made up of the refurbished buildings of the old Lorton Penitentiary. The prison had started as a progressive institution. President Theodore Roosevelt pushed its development in 1909 as a place where lawbreakers could be rehabilitated by working the land and raising farm animals. A breath of fresh air for the lost and troubled.

Conrad recalled a curious fact he had recently learned. The irony still amused him. In 1917, about one hundred and seventy suffragists were brought to the facility. Women who had been arrested for marching in front of the White House to promote women's rights. They were rounded up and tossed into Lorton for their actions, for their expression of freedom. Conditions were less than ideal for them and the article he had read stated that the poor treatment they received at the prison helped get the woman's vote in 1920. The prison had grown through the decades until being closed in 2001.

Ironically, this federal center also had a history with national security. The prison had hosted one of about three hundred Nike missile sites scattered across the country. These missile sites were established as a last line of defense against air attacks against U.S. cities. Nike site W-64 was co-located with the Penitentiary from the 50s to the 70s. The launcher facility later became a rarely visited cold war museum. But once the prison was closed in 2001, the entire compound had sat empty for years, patrolled by bored security guards and visited occasionally by film crews, until it was converted into a barracks house in 2017 during the civil war. Three years ago, in 2019, it was converted into the Occoquan Federal Center.

The facility's nine main office buildings, all of them colonial revival red-brick buildings and two stories high, included offices for DHS investigative offices, DHS uniformed services, the army, and the Bureau of Prison personnel who manned the jails south of the main buildings. The old guard towers were manned too but most often by remotely controlled robotic guns that shot plastic bullets. If the guards manning the security cameras pushed the right buttons, those bullets became thoroughly lethal.

Barbed wire and broken glass lined the top of the concrete wall that encircled the station. Underground tunnels crisscrossed underneath. So much protective material but what he lacked was personnel. The most important thing and yet it wasn't in the budget.

He looked at his watch. 7:42 a.m. It wasn't his responsibility to spend time checking the center's security but it made him feel better to know how things stood. It was the ghost of the army officer in him that demanded that sort of diligence.

Conrad passed through the center's long rectangular parking lot. To his left and right were twelve converted barracks that extended away from the parking lot and which served as offices now. At the end of the parking lot was the two story red brick building that housed his DHS office. It was more Greek revival than colonial - Greek-columned and with heavy stone lintels above modern doors and windows. There were dozens of additional buildings, long barracks and prison houses, small administrative offices and storage sheds, on the compound but it was the one in front of him that was his pride and joy - the Occoquan Freedom Station.

With his foot resting on the first step, Conrad paused. He liked the fact that his office was stately in form. A pleasant reminder of the founding fathers and of historic Occoquan nearby. The town was over two hundred and seventy years old and still retained some of its history. The building inspired memories of happier and safer times. Easier times. That sleepy little town of Occoquan was a welcome relief from the confining rigors of evening life in Georgetown, Washington, DC.

Conrad continued up the steps and through the building's sliding double doors. He nodded at the uniformed officer working the reception desk. He walked up one flight stairs, emerged in a wide hallway and strolled through a set of sliding double doors into his division offices. A plain reception desk stood between him and the main area of the division's common room. A three-foot high metal-slated security partition ran parallel from the end of the desk to the wall. A narrow gate was set in the center of the partition.

Office doors lined both sides of the common area. The back of the room was dominated by a large window that provided a view of the grassy rear of the compound. Blocking Conrad's view of the outside was a grim-faced Dave Bronson and two unknown men in suits. Three of his agents, Lina, Nick and Blounts, sat huddled around a table at the back of the room.

"Sir. Good to see you." Dave Bronson's face lacked its usual smile.

"What's up?" Conrad asked. He pushed aside the metal gate and walked into the common area. The gate clanked shut loudly behind him.

One of the two gray suited men stood quickly. "Agent Greis? I'm Agent Ridenauer. This is Agent Yablount." He gestured noncommittally to his still seated companion. "We're the debriefers."

Conrad sized up the two men. They were standard government issue federales. Yablount tending towards the tall, thin and blonde but not quite markedly any of those. Ridenauer to the short, stocky and dark-haired type but not quite any of those either. DC by day, DC by night kind of fellas. Conrad snorted through his nose. "Why the glum faces?" he asked.

"This." Bronson lifted a copy of the front page of the Washington Post. The headline read "Rebels Executed in Virginia Raid."

"So?" Conrad said. But he knew what this was about. He dropped his head and put his hand to his forehead. He had been getting a lot of headaches lately. That wasn't usual for him. Through nearly two decades of security work, he had always felt tension but in the last year, the headaches had been coming too frequently. Maybe it was finally time to see a doctor about them.

"This was supposed to be a classified operation," Ridenauer said. "How'd the papers get a hold of it in two days?"

"Hell if I know," Conrad said.

"And on top of that," Yablount broke in, "you only gave the rebels eight and a half hours to negotiate."

That comment really pissed Conrad off. Why don't you two go in the field? he yelled in his head. But he answered calmly. "The regs state that six is the minimum and eight is the maximum time allowed."

Yablount and Conrad stared at each other. Yablount's jaw continuously clenched and relaxed. Conrad's was doing the same. He narrowed his eyes, tempting Yablount to say something stupid, but Yablount remained quiet.

Ridenauer spread his hands out. "Come on Agent Greis. We know the regs. You know the regs. Heck everyone knows the regs. But you let them have more. It's sensible and who does it hurt. Otherwise we get shit like these news stories."

Yablount spoke now. "Your negotiator says he asked for more time but you refused his request."

Dave turned to look towards the rear of the room and Conrad's gaze followed his. Agents Velazquez, Deevers and Washington still sat, watching the heated discussion. Conrad was only slightly relieved that his fifth assistant agent, Milway, was out working the field. He pointed at Nick and motioned him over with his finger. "Let's take this in my office gentlemen." Conrad turned to lead them. Dave moved a step forward.

"Not you Dave. Deevers. You come in here."

Conrad unlocked his office door and swung it open. He held it while the three men trudged inside. He closed the door firmly behind him.

The office reflected Conrad's personality. Three piles of work were neatly stacked on his desk. The room was comfortably air-conditioned. Two patriotic posters and five commendation letters and awards decorated the walls. The walls on which they hung were clean and white and the floor was covered by a thin, maroon layer of carpeting. The wooden furniture around his desk was worn but he liked the feel of nostalgia it gave the office. Satisfied with the office's ordered appearance, Conrad finally spoke. "What the shit is this about?"

"We just told you," Ridenauer said. Conrad and the other two men stood around the desk with arms crossed.

"Bull shit. I've conducted operations like this before without problems. No one's complained about me sticking to the regulations on negotiations."

Yablount spoke. "Okay. You're right Greis but the President, well the executive office let's say, is getting really bad press on stuff like this. We're a liberal nation now. People don't want to see all this bloodshed and killing. They look like executions."

"They are executions," Nick said. He looked glumly at the floor as he spoke.

Fucking politics thought Conrad. Do I do my job or not he wondered. Conrad looked up and scratched the back of his head. "Is this the problem?" Conrad asked. "You guys stick me with a bleeding heart negotiator, he complains and next thing I know you guys are feeding me the greasy stick."

Ridenauer firmly rubbed his palms together "Listen. I'll level with you."

"Uh-huh. Please do," Conrad said.

Cris Alvarez

Yablount walked towards the large window that overlooked the prison buildings and grassy fields that took up the space between Conrad's building and the concrete wall in the distance.

Ridenauer opened his palms towards Conrad. "DC was hoping that a more compassionate negotiator would soften you up a bit Greis," he said.

Conrad looked at Nick.

Nick looked back at Conrad with his eyes wide. "I totally respect you sir."

Conrad nodded. He wasn't sure if he believed that. "I see. I see. Why not just replace me?"

"Cause they say you're good," Yablount said. He spoke to the glass without looking back at Conrad.

Conrad didn't respond except to cross his arms again.

"They also say you follow orders," Yablount said, again to the glass.

"There's another problem here though Greis," Ridenauer said.

"Yeah?"

Ridenauer coughed into his fist and scratched at his arm. He looked at Yablount.

Yablount had his hand on his hip, the end of his jacket draped behind his wrist. He was still turned towards the window but he was looking back at Ridenauer now. Then Yablount looked at Nick. "Agent Deevers, you'll have to leave."

"Oh, sure." Nick hesitated, looked around and then left the room. No one spoke as he closed the door carefully and softly. Yablount stared at the glazed glass of Conrad's door. He didn't speak until Nick's shadow disappeared from view.

"Moles," Yablount said.

"Moles?" Conrad asked.

"This story came out with too much detail and too soon. That shouldn't have happened."

"I haven't read it yet, I can't comment."

"Well we can," Ridenauer said. He pulled a toothpick out of the front pocket of his jacket and began picking his back teeth with it. He sucked on his teeth between digs. "It ain't good."

"What the hell can I do?" Conrad said. "I conduct the security routines of these offices according to the precautions dictated by DHS and according to my budgetary restraints."

Ridenauer peered at his toothpick. "We don't think that anyone from the outside stole the information."

"Right. Moles."

"You don't agree," Yablount said. He went back to admiring the view outside. Ridenauer pulled a wooden curved-back chair out from under the front edge of Conrad's desk and he dropped into it with a grunt.

Conrad walked closer to the window but opposite the side at which Yablount stood. "It's hard for me to distrust any of my men," Conrad said. "It's a lot easier to believe that someone hacked into our computer systems or got an e-mail from the rebels while we had them penned in."

"Jeez. You field guys are all alike," Yablount said. He turned and pushed an accusatory finger at Conrad. "Lucky for you and this country, some of us can be objective."

Conrad shrugged and scratched his crotch. "Okay, okay." He shrugged and held his palms out. "So what am I supposed to do?"

"Don't talk to reporters."

"We don't." Conrad gave Yablount a close-mouthed smile.

"Keep a close eye on your men."

"And women." Conrad lifted one finger emphatically.

"Yeah, yeah smart guy," Ridenauer said. He chuckled. "Cute woman too."

"Feet off the desk tough guy," Conrad said. Ridenauer had thrown one foot onto the edge of Conrad's desk and had it resting on a brown folder. Ridenauer grunted and dropped his foot. The file folder came down with it.

"Aw shit," Ridenauer said. "Sorry." He bent over and tried to even out the papers that had slipped lose.

"What other obvious precautions do you want me to take?"

"I think you get the idea," Yablount said. He glared at Conrad and then turned his head back to the window.

"You keep staring at it so hard, you're gonna crack it."

Yablount looked back with disgust on his face. To Conrad's amusement, Yablount even sneered slightly. Ridenauer banged the folder on Conrad's desk to straighten the papers in it and laid it down. "Well we've got to do the de-briefing on the op anyway."

"We'll do that in the common room," Conrad said.

"Think that's a secure location to discuss the operation?" Yablount said. He faced Conrad and crossed his arms.

Conrad took a deep breath and his chest rose and dropped rapidly. He wasn't amused any more. His eyes clouded over slightly. His hand went to the holster under his left armpit and he grabbed for his gun. Yablount looked at the holster and frowned. Conrad looked down at it too. His hand was on it as though he were trying to grip an invisible gun. But the holster was empty. The gun was in Conrad's drawer.

Conrad shook his head and dropped his hand. The haze over his eyes disappeared but his equilibrium felt slightly off. The floor swayed slightly under his feet. His heart raced. What the hell is going on he thought. He had never before experienced a combination of sensations like that outside of combat.

Ridenauer took a step towards Conrad. "You okay pal?"

Conrad didn't answer.

"Well?" Yablount asked.

Conrad blinked and the sensations were gone. He looked Yablount squarely in the eye. "Is my office secure? Well it better fucking well be or we might as well give this whole game up." Conrad walked quickly to his office door and pounced on the door handle. He swung the door open. His four assistant agents jerked their heads up to look at him.

"Well everyone." Conrad bit his tongue and swallowed the invectives he wanted to lay out there. "Let's get down to business."

4

Yablount and Ridenauer wrapped up their bullshit about protocol, procedures and political considerations and finally called it a morning. They collected their belongings, gave cursory farewells and retreated from the common room. Conrad leveled a malevolent gaze at their backs as they slipped through the double doors and out of the reception area.

His eyes left the door and dragged across the faces of the four assistant special agents at the table with him. Bronson, Deevers, Washington and Velazquez were all too busy typing or stylusing information into their portable electronic notepads to notice Conrad's disgust.

Dave abruptly looked up. He playfully wagged the stylus he held between two meaty fingers. "What if the papers call?"

"Same as usual. No comment."

Lina looked up from her own notepad, her dark red lips pursed. Conrad glared at that angrily puckered mouth but its sensuality offered no consolation to his anger. Conrad looked to her eyes when she finally spoke.

Her words came in a rush. They were an attack on a perceived enemy. "Why do the paper's push us for classified information? They know it's our jobs if we talk, don't they?"

"They know Lina." Conrad tapped his stylus on the edge of the desk and leaned back. "They know." Her excited anger broke through him. He relaxed. He calmed at the thought of women, relationships, affection. He thought of Mary.

Lina's dark eyes widened and she smacked the table with her palm. All four men jumped in their seats. "Then to hell with it. We should arrest the reporters." Agent Washington chuckled. Conrad smiled at him.

Like Lina and Nick, Agent Dwanell Washington was in his late twenties. But he had eight months in Conrad's division to their six. Washington, otherwise known as Blounts, had for years sported long dreadlocks with blond tips. Six months ago, Blounts decided that his hair was too much trouble to take care of and cut it off. Now he had a leopard's pattern of blond circles over his cropped dark hair.

Blounts had come in from the San Luis Obispo Police Department after seven years of work there. Like the rest of these youngsters, he wanted to work national, make a name for himself and maybe make a difference. Maybe. He was tall and thin and used to be a surfer back under the sun of California. Now he just jet-skied on the Potomac.

Blounts turned his infectious smile towards Lina. "V. The center's not big enough to hold all the journalists who want to ruin our careers."

"No. I'm serious," Lina said. "There must be something we can get them on for making our lives hell." She maintained a stern visage in the face of Blounts' glowing grin.

Dave lazily turned his head to look at Lina. "I second that V."

Nick shook his head and pushed away from the table. "Come on people. They're just doing their jobs."

Blounts smiled. "Yeah. It's no biggie. California news was all about exposing police corruption. That's their paycheck. Just roll with it."

Dave glanced over at Conrad. Conrad nodded his head lightly in response. "They have the right. Know what? Those calls remind me of freedom. So I just smile 'em off."

Blounts stood up and emphatically pointed at Conrad. "Chief knows the deal. He's been around." Blounts walked to a table pushed up against one wall. He reached for a stack of overturned Styrofoam cups, took one and flipped it over. He slid it into a large black coffee and pushed the espresso button.

Angelina snorted through her nose. Her face was red and she looked like a bull ready to charge through the phone at the next newspaper fool that called her. "Chief. You really believe that crap?"

Conrad crossed his arms, took a long, deep breath and exhaled loudly. Talking with his people, he was feeling better by the minute. "Sure I do." He looked the four over. Moles. Could be them. Could be the guys in the field. Could have been any of the army guys. What do I know? "Make sure you lock your keyboards and lock your files away when you're not working with them."

"Damn it," Dave said. "What a piece of-"

Lina looked at her watch and cut in. "Sir, I need a signature for a search warrant I'm trying to get approved by the court. It's a tight situation. I have eight hours max."

Conrad rubbed his eyes. "All right, let me see what you got."

Lina reached down and pulled a sheaf of papers from a black briefcase that sat on the floor next to her. She handed an affidavit supporting the warrant and the warrant itself to Conrad. Nick and Dave rose and joined Blounts at the coffee table.

Conrad noted their departure from the table without comment. "Where's the approval form?"

"Here sir. I thought I'd let you read the documents first." Lina pulled another sheet of paper from her briefcase.

"Why didn't you do this electronically?" Conrad read the documents as he spoke. He didn't bother to look at the incredulous expression on Angelina's face.

"Software's acting funny sir. Didn't want to waste time fiddling with it."

"Your formatting is a little off on some of the paragraphs. And some of the preparatory language is wrong. I personally don't care but the courts get antsy when they see that."

"I'll fix it next time, sir." Her voice was tight. Conrad smirked. He pursed his lips to pull that smirk back before Lina noticed it. He failed.

"Did I write something funny sir?"

Now Conrad couldn't help but grin.

"No, no Lina." Her inexperience and impatience charmed him. He loved her attitude but if she wanted to get anywhere in law enforcement, if he wanted her to get anywhere, he'd have to grind that impatience out of her.

He looked up to see her glaring at the papers in his hand. Of all his agents, she hated paperwork the most. Naturally, she loved fieldwork the best.

He prodded her a little for the fun of it. "Lina. I know you don't appreciate all the intricacies associated with this paperwork."

"Can't this wait sir? It's urgent."

"Now is as good a time as any. You have time. The court's just on the other side of the parking lot. And do it electronically."

Cris Alvarez

She didn't answer. She squeezed her lips together and her face became a deeper shade of copper.

"What's on your mind?"

"Sir. I have experience with this. I'm not some bumbling greenie."

"But you don't appreciate it do you."

She looked down at the edge of the conference table and her lips squirmed around again. Conrad glanced at the men around the coffee table. Nick said something about the basketball playoffs.

Conrad turned his attention back to the woman seething in front of him. "I know you're experienced Velazquez. Four years with army military police. Four years on the Arlington County police force. Decorated and all that. I know you're good in the field. But you need to be good in the office too."

Lina stretched her words out. "I know that sir." But she said no more and kept her gaze on the table. The thumb of one hand tapped the wood. She wanted to explode. Her chest was heaving up and down under her cotton blouse. Her shoulders rose and fell with each deep measured breath she took. She glanced at her watch.

Conrad's impatience abruptly returned. Lina was not a pair of tits. She was a tough agent whom he had ultimate responsibility for. His voice boomed. "You know that but you don't appreciate it! I've been doing this shit..." He paused, slightly embarrassed.

"Excuse me sir?" Lina's head came up. Her lips weren't jumping anymore. She looked confused, embarrassed as well.

"This shit. You heard me. I've been doing this government paperwork shit for going on twenty-two years now. I resisted for the first eight until about your age. Then I understood. 2009. I was twenty-seven. A year older than you are now, right?"

"Yes sir."

" I had been assigned by the FBI to investigate the Hollywood Boulevard bombings. You know the ones."

"I was thirteen when it happened. I was living in San Diego at the time." Her eyes narrowed and she looked humbled. "It's what got me interested in this work." She paused. "Sir." Lina leaned forward in her chair.

"Good. Then you'll appreciate this." Conrad rubbed his chin in thought. "Of the eight bombs that exploded, more or less simultaneously between Vine Street and La Brea Avenue on the

Boulevard, the one at the theater yielded the best clues. Fingerprints, DNA, that sort of thing."

"Yes of course sir. You had some decent video surveillance of the suspects too."

"Yeah. We thought we had them nailed pretty good. So a few weeks after we had gotten our case together, we slapped some search warrants together. Good factual basis for approval and all that. But we screwed up. One of the agents I worked with listed the home addresses of the suspects in the affidavit but didn't list the homes as the places to be searched. It was alluded to and assumed in the affidavit that this vital piece of information was clear enough. We were going to search their residences for evidence but we were working too fast for our own good. The defense team successfully argued that the evidence should be tossed since the affidavit did not properly support the search warrants. I should have caught the mistake but I was too busy working another aspect of the case. It was a bullshit defense but that was no excuse for not being thorough."

Lina nearly brought her palm down on the table but stopped short. "All that shouldn't matter. The fact that you proved who the terrorists were should be the prime consideration."

"But it did matter. It mattered to that judge and to every judge along the chain of appeals. So the evidence was tossed, two of the seven suspects were freed and then three years later, those two were behind the bombing of the Poplar Street Bridge over the Mississippi.

"That's just," her teeth and lips nearly said fuck, "stupid sir."

"But Velazquez. That's not what matters." Conrad leaned forward in his chair. "The process matters on how you get to it."

Lina leaned back and threw up her hands. "It's a waste of time sir and I hate it."

"It has a flip side V."

"I know, I know, you get your case done hassle free if you do all that crap."

Conrad shook his head. "It's more than that V. If you do all of that right, if you do all the paperwork right, then the people you work with and under, your peers begin to assume you do everything right and they grant you leeway when sometimes they normally wouldn't. If you keep your underwear clean all the time, then one day, they just stopping looking to see if it's dirty."

Lina raised her eyebrows and a curl played at the ends of her lips. "Are you suggesting that once I master the paperwork I can start doing things the wrong way?" The red in her face drained a little.

"No. I guess that sounds like what I just said but what I mean," he played with that word, "is they just stop getting in your pants and your work becomes a whole hell of a lot easier."

Lina's enthusiasm died. "I'll have to see it to believe it sir."

Conrad nodded. "I guess so. You may not realize it but this office of mine gets a lot less flak than the other offices do simply because of my reputation with paperwork." Conrad tilted his head. "Well it used to."

Lina twisted her mouth sarcastically. "I guess that's something to be proud of sir. Can I submit that warrant?"

Conrad gave up. "Get Milway to help you fix the problems and bring it back to me when it's ready."

"That could take a half hour sir." She looked at her watch. "Assuming he even gets back soon."

"Then you'd better hurry on doing what you can." Conrad held the papers out to Lina. The sound of her chair sliding back on the wooden office floor set Conrad's neck hairs on end. She snatched the papers from Conrad's hand and ferociously walked to her office. Nick glanced at Conrad before following her in. He closed her door behind him.

Conrad chuckled but it was a bitter sound. Looking for a piece of ass Nick? What he needed was more married agents.

Conrad rose, clasped his hands together and stretched towards the ceiling. Something clicked in his left shoulder blade and he winced in pain.

"I heard that," Dave said.

Conrad eased around the conference table and walked up to Blounts and Dave. The big man was busy making a second cup of coffee.

Blounts leaned back against the coffee table. "Yoga could help," he said. "Loosen the tendons. Even at your age."

"Even at...how old are you again Blounts?"

"Twenty-seven sir."

"Ever had a forty year old foot up that twenty-seven year old ass of yours?"

"If I ever get the privilege of having a foot up my ass sir, I'd hope that it'd be the foot of someone as esteemed as you." Blounts gave Conrad a theatrical bow and headed to his own office. Dave pulled a ceramic mug from the coffee machine and held it out to Conrad.

Conrad shook his head. "Goddamn. I shouldn't feel this old at forty. Maybe I need my own piece of ass sometime soon."

"What?" Dave pulled the coffee mug back towards himself.

Conrad thumbed towards Velazquez's door. "Those two." He took the mug from Dave.

Dave smirked. "Thought you was getting funny or something sir."

"Want to hear something funny? What do you do if you get shot in two places?"

Dave shrugged. "Uh, keep still and apply pressure?"

"No. You don't go back to those two places." Conrad chuckled and sipped his coffee.

Dave grinned and patted Conrad's shoulder. "You need some new jokes chief."

A sharp buzz sounded from the unit speaker mounted on the wall just above the reception desk. A uniformed officer rushed to the double doors from the hallway outside. He waited for them in frustration and slid through before they were fully open. He stood just inside the doors grimacing. He ran a hand through his blonde crew cut.

"Well?" Conrad asked.

"Agent Greis. Sir. We just got word that Agent Milway was hit on Sudley. Near Manassas battlefield. Rocket propelled grenade blew his car off the road."

Conrad put his mug down. "Shit. How bad is it?"

Dave took a step towards the exit but Conrad put his hand on Dave's chest. "You. Watch the house. I'll see to this."

Dave gritted his teeth. "Fuck!"

Blounts charged out of his office. "What about Milway?" He grabbed his jacket off the coat rack. "I'm going with you!"

"Goddamn it," Conrad said. "No one's going with me." But he felt terrible saying that. Milway was a veteran of the office and mentored Blounts when the youngster first showed up. They had developed a strong respect for each other though their styles were completely different. "I'm the only one who's going," Conrad said emphatically.

Conrad took his jacket off the coat rack and walked through the security gate. He stood in front of the uniformed officer until he got tired of waiting for the man to speak. "Well? Which hospital?"

The officer blinked. He ran his hand over a sweaty forehead and through his hair. "Sir. Agent Milway died. He's at the medical examiner's office."

"No!" yelled Blounts. Lina's door opened and she and Nick stepped out.

Conrad looked at Agent Milway's closed office door. The back of his skull floated away and his thoughts left with it. He felt insanely calm. He rubbed his nose and said, "I have to call Lisa."

5

A broken streetlamp flickered, creating a strobe effect within the enveloping dark of the early evening. Wet streaks of light cut the asphalt and thin pools of water, murky soups of grime, oil and gravel, mirrored the mad optical vibration until a car, any car would do, scattered those sedentary will-o-the-wisps across the pavement.

7:45 p.m. and he was late as usual. A vision of pristine, well-groomed loveliness waited, sat very still and rigid, on the bus bench. The two objects, she of the billowing dress and it of the perfectly arranged slats, were perfectly in sync with each other and with the sharp-angled mall towering over them.

She wore a loose white dress, modestly cut high near the neck. Naturally, the dress fell prudently below her knees. Her medium-length brown hair was pulled back into a bun and her pale skin blended nearly imperceptibly with her outfit and the concrete sidewalk.

Lisa Woodley raised her hand lackadaisically when her eyes caught sight of Conrad's black Mustang. Conrad carefully drove through the crowded street that ran parallel to the sidewalk where Lisa sat waiting. She climbed into the car without a word or look for Conrad and crossed her long and shapely legs.

He looked her up and down but she might as well have been back on the bench. She looked straight ahead without moving. Conrad nodded in thought. There was nothing to be said to break the stalemate unless he was willing to swallow his pride.

Her breaths were slow, deep and measured. The sounds of the street were muted by the rhythmic waves of her audible annoyance. Conrad went over a pothole a touch too fast. The car tugged slightly.

"Watch where you're going." Her voice was sharp, smooth, controlled.

Conrad's senses reacted. His body thrilled at being the object of her emotions regardless of her intent. "Don't be a-" He caught the word mid-tongue. It wasn't time yet in the game for that kind of language.

"A what?" Her retort cut neatly through his forehead.

He chewed on one cheek and checked the rear-view mirror. "I've had a tough day. Let it go."

Her voice softened. "I've had a tough one too." Then she channeled the energy of her anger into listing the litany of her day's problems.

It took a tough thirty minutes to drive through the evening traffic to his apartment. She complained unceasingly in a calm, resonant voice the entire time. Conrad exited the Whitehurst Freeway and came into east Georgetown. His apartment building, the Dominion Arms, was only a couple of blocks away. On the street, traffic was still heavy.

Finally, he slowed, turned and drove past a security guard down into the Dominion Arms' heavily secured underground parking garage. Three levels down, frustration building on frustration, Conrad eventually found a parking space. Lisa and he exited the car and walked across the parking chamber. Their footsteps echoed through the narrow confines of the garage as Lisa continued complaining. They took the elevator up to his apartment level where the coconut deodorant smell of the hallway air blended conveniently with the lime green color of the hallway carpet.

Once inside the apartment, Conrad told a few jokes to lighten her up. After cooking her a chicken parmigiana dinner, they made love in his bedroom. She looked at the ceiling from the start and when he entered her, she barely responded. Her hands rested lightly on his back through out. At the end, she betrayed him with a faked orgasm. When he was done, he rolled over and dropped the used condom in his trash basket.

They stared at the smooth white ceiling. Jazz played softly in the living room. Milway, the dead Milway, looked down from that blank canvas above and blinked. Conrad squinted and blinked the image out of his mind. He swallowed a lump in his throat. "What's the problem Lisa?"

"You." Conrad glanced over at her. She still stared at the ceiling. Did she see Milway there too? She looked over at Conrad and then swung her legs over the edge of the bed. She bent down, snatched her dead white panties and bra and hurriedly put them on.

She walked to the sliding glass door that led to his balcony and opened it. A cigarette packet was lying on a sleek, black bureau positioned near the sliding door. She pulled a cigarette from the packet, snatched the silver lighter laying next to the packet, and lit the cigarette. She leaned against the threshold as she smoked and looked out across downtown Washington, DC. The lights of the city's other high-rises, and perhaps the other men and women who just finished making love, stared back at her.

Conrad looked back to the ceiling. It was nothing but plain white again.

With her arms crossed, Lisa turned and put her back against the threshold. She alternated looking at Conrad and looking at the darkness. She finished the cigarette and flicked it over the balcony and into the night. "Okay. It's time we break-up."

Conrad's chest tightened. "Why?" he asked without caring about the answer.

She glanced down and looked up again. "Because you're not the man I thought you were."

Conrad stayed in bed with his hands folded behind his neck. He inhaled deeply and exhaled slowly. "And what kind of man is that?"

"An honest one. "

His face warmed. He slung his legs over the opposite edge of the bed and sat with his back to her. "Explain."

"You don't do drugs or anything wild. You're a good clean cut man despite everything the law would let you get away with if you wanted to."

Here it comes.

"But the people you associate with. The things you tolerate. It," she paused and Conrad raised his head to look at her reflection in the mirror hanging on his wall, "it's disgusting. And I don't care if it's legal."

"You're talking about Melissa."

"For one, yeah. And other things. You don't have a problem with the sheer hedonism people in this city exhibit do you?"

"They've been through a civil war. Get over it."

"Always excuses. Never any accountability."

Conrad turned himself towards Lisa. She moved towards her clothes and bent over to pick up her dress. Though she was an average sized woman, her prosperous breasts hung low when she bent down. Conrad felt the thrill of sex again. She was a workout fiend and watching her calf and back muscles tense quickly under the influence of her anger made her look that much better. Then he remembered how stiff she had just been in bed and the thrill ebbed just as quickly.

She sat on the edge of the bed, and began rolling her stockings on. "It's been three years. From what I can tell, those sodomites need to re-learn their moral values if they want a better life."

Conrad got off the bed and walked around it to face her. He didn't care that he was stark naked. She glanced up and down his muscled and scarred body and he felt proud. She tightened her mouth and went back to putting on her stockings.

"Just because I don't do something," he said, pointing his thumb at his chest with emphasis. The smell of condom lubricant mixed with her scent drifted from his fingers to his nose. He took a deep breath and continued. "Doesn't mean that I think other people shouldn't do it. I don't do drugs but I don't want to stop other people from doing them. I'm not gay but others can be. Understand?" He had shouted the question and felt good doing it. "Just because I believe something doesn't mean I expect someone else to believe the same thing."

Lisa spoke gently and in a patronizing tone. "But there's such a thing as believing there are issues worth fighting for."

"You mean positions worth forcing other people to take."

"Make it sound bad. Go ahead."

"You want to know what makes me feel good Lisa? That this country is closer now to the ideals that the founding fathers proposed two hundred and fifty years ago than it has ever been."

"Oh, you're a historian? Those men were Christians too and they would definitely not have been happy to see things as they are now." Lisa stood and pulled on her dress. Her breasts slightly resisted the dress and Conrad watched the struggle. She turned away from him and continued speaking. "These new laws are not freedom. They're a hell for all Americans who actually have values."

"The only hell is the one that religious freaks are causing for the rest of the country."

"That's easy for you to say. You're job is to fight them so naturally you'd think that."

"I believe in what I do."

She looked back at him and down at his crotch. "Can you put some clothes on? I'm tired of seeing your disgusting thing swing around while you yell at me."

"I'm not yelling." Conrad picked his boxers off the floor and slipped them on. "And you're the one dumping me remember?"

Lisa paused and her face became blank. For a moment she said nothing. Then she pushed her face against her palms and began sobbing. Her chest jumped up and down and she sniffled from inside her hands.

"Now what?" Conrad asked.

Lisa looked up. "I'm just so sad that I spent so much time on a man who seemed like he was worth marrying, but then I find out all this stuff about you in one week."

"So it is all about Melissa."

"There's more."

"She's a damn good friend, an old one, and I won't let some new girl ruin the good things I have in this world."

"It's been building. I'm not dumb. I started seeing." Lisa ran the back of her hand across her nose and sniffled again. Her mascara had streaked across her face and in the dim light she looked like a mad hyena.

"So you'd rather we were back in 2000s?" Conrad asked. "When people had less freedom than they do now?"

"Those were good times. People were sane and we had a damn good president with values."

"Uh-huh. How about the 1960s then? What about before desegregation?"

"You're twisting what I'm saying. You know I don't have a problem with black people!"

"How about 1900 when they hated Japs and Chinese or 1880 when they were massacring Indians?"

"Stop it! You're making it sound like I'm a racist when all I believe is that some fundamental things are right and some are wrong - gays, drugs, all the criminal immigrants."

Conrad chewed on his cheek while Lisa spoke and frowned. She was in a lather.

"Who cares about American families now?" she asked. "The Democrats don't."

"There are plenty of families out there," Conrad growled. "Shit. Gay couples are taking care of half this country's war orphans.

"Oh Conrad. I shudder to think what sort of values they're teaching those poor children. It makes me want to cry for them."

"Have you ever talked to gay couples or talked to their children?"

"Do I need to? I've read and heard enough about their lifestyles. I don't need to meet them."

"Well obviously you won't meet them will you?"

"You know what really infuriates me. That we fought a civil war for the sake of fags and junkies!"

Conrad nodded his head. "You know who else was pissed at the old rules? Gun owners, business leaders, and everyone, including Republicans, who were sick of the way the government kept scaling back our privacy, all in the name of fighting terrorism. They gave up using warrants!"

"You sound like you wanted a revolution!"

"Do I? When did the rebellion start? It didn't start when the Republicans were in power. The shooting started when the Democrats had the presidency and did something that a radical element of the Republican party opposed. Try and deny that. I know what happened. I was a Republican at the time."

"So that's it? You're guilty about having been a Republican?"

"Fuck that. I'm not beholden to any political party Lisa. I'm beholden to an ideal. That's what guides me now."

Lisa shook her head and picked up her purse. "Fuck you too." She looked hard at Conrad. "You sell-out."

Conrad was shocked. The second phrase he'd heard plenty of times. It was the swearing he was startled to hear. He decided to get nasty. "Would my work still bother you if I were executing Muslims instead of Christians?"

A look of panic swept across Lisa's face. "What would I have against those...Muslims?" she asked.

"I don't know. Muslims tend to be a little more brown than Christians. And their clothes look funny too," he added without bothering to restrain the sarcasm in his voice.

Lisa wiped her face and regained her composure. "I said it already. It's through. I'm done." She sobbed again, once, and stood erect, almost looking down her nose at Conrad. "And to imagine I let you have sex with me." She glanced at Conrad's crotch and his scrotum receded from the look she gave.

"Don't call me again," she said as she walked to the front door.

"I won't."

Lisa looked back at Conrad. "You're nothing but a...a heathen." She opened the door and slammed it behind her.

Heathen? That was a new one. He turned and walked to the open balcony. The wind blew lightly across the vertical surface of the high-rise. He stepped out to feel the shifting pressure of the breeze on his face.

The night was cool. The building lights, the streetlights, the lights of the traffic all blinked randomly. The living city went through its motions. The blast of a car horn rose to his ears. One and a half miles away, the rotors of two patrol helicopters rhythmically pounded the soft air hanging over the White House. Invisible to his eye, their menacing sounds drifted off to the southeast.

And what are you accomplishing Conrad? Holding the line?

Would his political ideals always be the priority? All other parts of his life dropped along the road he walked, like emptying a heavy rucksack of supplies never really needed. How depressing it was to happily pack for the long trek and then to discover that all those good things you brought with you didn't matter in the face of the true obstacles you would face.

He closed the balcony door behind him, shutting out the inside world, and leaned against the railing. Was it time for him to finally accept the truth of his life? Standing up for the rights of men is a lonely fucking business.

6

T he speaker at the podium had started strong but the audience of three hundred became restless as the lecture dragged on. The room felt stuffy, someone at the front coughed loudly. Conrad had positioned himself in the last of the room's fifteen rows of steel and plastic chairs in case of such a dilemma.

He looked at his watch. For the first fifteen minutes, Conrad's patience had held, but after that, he no longer felt capable of listening to the procedural nuances of dealing with foreign non-combatants captured on U.S. soil. He stood and, as unobtrusively as possible, slipped to the back of the lecture hall. He softly opened, then closed, the heavy door behind him.

Out in the tall, expansive hallways of the DC Convention Center, business-suited professionals rushed by, some alone and some in groups. A large white billboard mounted on a wall nearby read 'Welcome to the 2022 gathering of the Association of Federal Law Enforcement Professionals.' Conrad moved away from the lecture room door and anxiously looked for a building exit. That billboard made him uneasy.

The 2009 Hollywood Boulevard bombings he had investigated presaged American disappointment in the military. Conrad had sensed the shift in America's mood then and this worry had pushed Conrad to crack that case and others like it as quickly as he could. People had begun to wonder what the hell six years in Iraq and Afghanistan had done if terrorist bombs were still going off in the U.S. But the U.S. military maintained a presence in the sandbox even up to the Second U.S. Civil War of 2017.

Fourteen years of occupation had caused a huge drain of American money and men. Nearly a majority of Americans, a mix of conservatives and liberals, had gone from disliking the military to actually hating it. Isolation and a renewed focus on internal security were the current year's grand motivators of political action. There was no more energy in the American citizen to save the world. The catch phrase now was "save the nation".

Conrad moved quickly through the gleaming white faux-marble perimeter of the Convention Center. Security was everywhere. Ironic Conrad mused. Someone would think that the National Conference of Law Enforcement Officers wouldn't need a high level of security attached to it. Weren't they their own best security? Or were they all too busy socializing and getting drunk?

Finally he found an exit door that didn't have a huge crowd around it. Grateful over the simple discovery, he stepped outside into the intimate warmth of a humid May day in Washington, DC. Close by, a confused looking Virginia national guardsmen stood at a nearby intersection helping a DC police officer direct traffic around the Convention Center.

Despite the guardsman's vaguely menacing appearance, the drivers around him yelled and blared their car horns. He was a pimply-faced young man wearing forest-green military fatigues that were slightly over-sized. His rifle was slung over his shoulder with the barrel pointed at the ground.

Conrad grunted and pulled a cigarette pack from a pocket inside his suit jacket. He popped out a paper tube of tobacco and touched it to his lower lip. He narrowed his eyes at the boy made a man by government direction.

A lot of people didn't welcome the sight of a national guardsman anymore. A little tension always gripped Conrad when he saw them too. He lit his cigarette and watched the guardsman standing, nearly uselessly, next to the police officer who did the real work of directing a heavy line of traffic. Conrad took a strong pull on his cigarette then took it out of his mouth to stare at its red tip.

He recalled 2014 vividly. He was still with the FBI that year, investigating the major bombings that hit the country every three or four months. He was all over the place, coast to coast, making good collars and missing just as many. There were a lot of terrorists around then, both foreign and homegrown.

It was an ugly year. A Democrat, Johanna Avery Reed, had been president for two years and she had been trying to juggle a country that had gotten sick of twelve years of Republican rule. Conrad spat on the ground. People made it so easy on themselves to figure out problems, didn't they? Democrats good, Republicans bad. Democrats bad, Republicans good. Fucking party politics while bombs went off across the country. He had been a Republican up to that point, but not a political dog.

Then all hell broke lose over what seemed to be, in his opinion at least, the least important of issues at the time. The Supreme Court found a South Dakota law that essentially abolished abortion to be constitutional. In 2014, every state was suddenly free to make most abortions illegal and many did. The economy was in shambles, gas prices were sky-high and the occupation of Iraq and Afghanistan continued while bombs were blowing the tops off U.S. buildings. But the politicians on both sides put all of their energies into fighting over the issue of abortion.

Suddenly the major, "liberal" cities of the U.S. exploded in riotous opposition to these new abortion laws. Conrad remembered being called to investigate domestic bombings of both conservative state capitol buildings and abortion clinics. Rural towns formed illegal patriot committees to intimidate anyone objecting or protesting the new laws outlawing abortion. Invisible battle lines were being drawn between states, cities and communities. Church turned against church.

Finally somebody, no group took real responsibility for the act, started a massive fire that destroyed much of the U.S. Congress building. Rioting exploded everywhere and the National Guard, made up of boys just like that youngster on the street corner, was called out to quell the biggest civil upheaval in the U.S. since the civil war of 1861.

"Conrad!" The voice was deep and familiar.

Conrad finished the last bit of his cigarette and dropped it to the concrete sidewalk. With the tip of his left boot, he ground the stub into oblivion.

"Still smoking those cancer sticks?" asked the same voice.

"Hey Brown, how are you?" Conrad stuck his hand out and firmly gripped the meaty paw of the stocky woman who had approached him. Melissa Brown of the Alcohol, Tobacco and Firearms division. She wore thick, black boots, a long heavy denim skirt and a light blue dress shirt. She was never one for fashion or DC professional dress. Dark, heavy frame glasses rested on her thick nose and her medium length brown hair was pulled back in a tight ponytail. Not a strand was going to escape that hair band.

"Doing well," she said. "Could be better. A lot of unregistered firearms out there."

"Well they made plenty for Iraq. Someone had to sell them somewhere after the war."

"Which war are you talking about?" Melissa gave a weary smile.

Conrad curled one end of his lips up. "Learn anything interesting in there?"

Melissa gave a husky, heavy cough and laughed. "Just meeting some old friends. Good ones too. Not your usual bullshit kind of acquaintance."

"I'm sure they think the same about you." Conrad smiled. Melissa was a loyal person. Big too. At six foot two, she had two inches on Conrad and she weighed probably a good two hundred pounds. It was mostly muscle but Conrad could see a bit of softness in her neck now. They were both getting old.

"How are the kids?" Conrad asked.

"Both of them are good. Salls still stays at home and watches them. But they'll be off to college soon and then she and I will, I promise you this, we will finally retire to French Polynesia." Melissa swept her hand into the distance wistfully.

"Wish I could say the same."

Melissa put both fists on her hips. "About retirement or the kids?"

"Both I suppose."

"Mary still has the kids?"

"Yeah. They're still kicking it in high school but over in Fairfax now."

"They should be in college soon though, right?"

"Let's hope."

Melissa smirked. "How are you holding up? Meet anyone new?"

Multiple car horns broke the normal sound of traffic. A city bus was blocking the intersection and the guardsman was yelling at the driver.

"No chance, Conrad said. "Too much rebel activity in this area."

"For the last two years?" She smiled broadly and spread her arms out. "That's why you can't meet anyone?"

"It's not like Seattle, Melissa. Things aren't so calm here."

"All right, I won't question that. But it's not a good excuse."

"I don't need a woman right now. I had Mary for sixteen years so that'll do me for now."

"Hell, I couldn't go two years without a woman."

"Screw you." Conrad guffawed loudly and the guardsman looked back at him from where he was standing near the bus. "What the hell do you think the kid's telling that bus driver?" Conrad asked.

"These kids," Melissa said. Her eyes turned to the young guardsman. "You think they know anything about what real trouble is like?"

"It only ended three years ago. He might know."

"Look at him. Baby face. He was probably still in training when it finished." Melissa rubbed her left forearm. A thin, jagged scar ran across the spot she rubbed. Conrad knew that scar bothered her plenty.

She had been a lieutenant colonel in the Marines during the Civil War, a reservist called back to active duty, and she took a good shot in the third and final year of the civil war, right as it was ending. She got a purple heart for it and a nice promotion in ATF soon after. But they knew each other further back. They had both been in the sandbox fifteen years ago. She had saved his life there and that was something a person never forgot.

"Woman, you don't like those young kids do you?" Conrad finally said.

"I don't like anybody Dibs." Conrad smiled at the mention of that old army nickname. He kind of liked it better than lieutenant. When he was younger, much younger, he was always saying "I got dibs" for everything and then he got dibs on being called dibs. That was courtesy of Melissa.

"Hell if you don't," he said.

"Hey," Melissa yelled towards the young guardsmen.

He looked confused for a moment before narrowing his round eyes at her. "What?" he yelled back. His voice was high-pitched and unsure of itself. The kid was also smaller than Melissa even with his boots and gear on.

"Stop waving that gun around or I'll report you to your sergeant."

The guardsman's gun, his X10, was presenting to the sky. He dropped its nose immediately so that it was pointing at the ground.

Melissa burned holes in the young man with her eyes. "Don't you know how to carry a carbine?"

Without a word, he turned away to look ahead at the traffic the policeman was directing. The DC officer gave the boy an extended sidelong look before resuming his traffic duties.

"Jesus Christ," Melissa said. "Where does he think he is?"

"Want to go back inside," Conrad asked. "This humidity is killing me."

"Sure. You going to the Wireless Communications Encryption talk?" she asked.

"Yeah. Exciting stuff."

"You got that right Dibs."

They walked through a set of automatic doors and breathed in the refreshing blast of cold air that hit them. The hallways of the center were still filled with government types wandering to and fro. Small and large groups of suited people chattered and laughed. They all looked clean-cut and squared away. All progeny of the now little thought of military. They had switched agencies and titles over the course of their lives, gone from military to civilian life, but they were much the same as they always were.

"Coffee?" Melissa offered. She pointed at a table sitting outside a set of interior double doors. Melissa glanced over Conrad's shoulder as they walked towards it. "That's funny. Don't look back."

"What is it?" Conrad said. When Melissa gave an instruction, he followed it. She was a tough broad but that's not why he listened. He listened because she knew what she was talking about.

"You've got a tail. A pretty shitty one at that."

"Really?"

"I saw him through the doors when we were outside. He wasn't very good at surreptitiously watching you."

"Hmm. SAT word. Nice. What's he look like?"

"Government. Gray suit, short blonde hair. You being investigated?"

"Not that I know of."

"You'd tell me wouldn't you?"

"Yeah. Of course. You'd have to be a character witness if anything happened to me."

"For the prosecution?"

Conrad chuckled. "So you think I've got a government tail? Goddamn it. It's not me. It's my office they're investigating. I've heard rumors about counter-intel folks working the freedom stations. I'll need to check this out."

"Why not just confront him now?" Melissa asked.

"You want to slip and grab him unawares?"

"Sure. It'd be fun." She grinned at Conrad. He waited at the table while she made her way down the hall. He turned and casually took a look at a man matching the description Melissa had given. The tail was trying to look natural by leaning against a large cement pole and looking at a distant group of people but he looked awkward doing it.

Watching from the corner of his eye, Conrad saw Melissa walk slowly behind the pole and then grab the man's shoulder. He jumped and tried to tug away from her, but she held on and said something. With the acoustics and the distance, Conrad couldn't make out what they were saying but he stayed put. Melissa was smiling at the man whose face had become ashen. He looked confused.

Melissa and the suit exchanged a few more words and he handed her his wallet. She flipped it open, looked at it and perceptibly relaxed. She handed the wallet back to blondie and let him go. He looked over at Conrad, dipped his head and scurried out the front doors of the Convention Center. Melissa watched him go and then walked heavily back to Conrad.

"Well?"

"FBI. You're being watched."

"Did he say why?"

"No. And I didn't press him."

"Feel comfortable talking to me still?"

"Dibs, I ain't afraid of nothing, not even the FBI. Let's go hear that talk."

Conrad looked back at the sliding doors but the man was gone. He looked back at Melissa who was still grinning at him. They wandered off to find the encryption talk.

7

Hearing about the merits of JS10 data encryption techniques for wireless data gave Conrad the intense desire to punch the topic presenter solidly in the face. Actually, every sound – a cough, a murmur, a sneeze – made Conrad fighting mad. It was simply the presenter who happened to be making the most noise.

Conrad's mind drifted from a perceived frustration to the real one. The fucking FBI. Who do they think they are? Why would he, of all people, possibly be under suspicion. He was the agent primarily responsible for the sharp decrease in terrorist activity throughout Northern Virginia. He was the person defending the government. He was the tip of the spear. Did somebody actually believe he was with the fanatics? He barely even went to church anymore.

Conrad impatiently squirmed in his seat and tapped his foot on the floor. Heads in the crowd turned towards him and glared. When he noticed Melissa eyeing him curiously, he stopped fidgeting. His armpits became damp and he tugged at his collar. The speaker at the front buzzed on, excited by his own voice.

Conrad needed to get out of there, somewhere with more space and less people. He took a deep breath to relax his escalating rage and almost immediately felt his chest tighten. Within seconds, his neck and jaw were just as stiff and getting worse.

Conrad elbowed Melissa in the ribs. She looked at him reproachfully and frowned when he motioned towards the exit with his head. They made their way down the narrow aisle of space between two rows of chairs, silently mouthing sorry to each person they passed.

Once in the hallway, Conrad tugged at his sweat-stained shirt. "I thought they had air-conditioning in this damn place."

"So what's up?" Melissa asked. She had her arms crossed as she leveled a heavy gaze at Conrad. "I was actually enjoying that."

Conrad nodded. "Yeah, he was good." He paused and rubbed his face and then he blurted his words out. "They got one of my agents Melissa. Ambush."

"Another one?"

"Uh-huh." Conrad's stomach turned a few circles at the thought of Milway's wife and young children. Milway had started at the Occoquan Freedom Station only a few months after Conrad had been handpicked by the Deputy Secretary of Homeland Security to head it. Conrad and Jim Milway had coped with seeing seventy-four agents maimed and twenty-eight killed over their three years at the Occoquan station. Other Freedom stations around the country, those in less hostile areas, had suffered far fewer losses. Jim was a brother in arms, a brother in blood to Conrad.

"Shit, Conrad." Melissa shook her head and looked away. "I don't know." She shook her head again and scowled. "You don't need this crap."

"Well there's no use in me giving it up. I'm already divorced." The joke tasted bitter in his mouth and he immediately regretted making it.

Melissa unfolded her arms and grinned with one side of her mouth. She punched Conrad lightly in the shoulder. "Don't go getting sorry for yourself Dibs."

"So what if I do?"

"All right. You deserve it I guess. We've lost a few agents too you know. It's always tough. But no one goes into this work blind."

"I know. I know. But it still stinks so bad."

Melissa sighed deeply and they both stood in silence for a minute. "What are you doing about the ambushes?"

"I'm not sure. This part of the country is still crawling with rebel sympathizers. They're drawn to the capital. How can I weed out the problems? They're everywhere watching my people." Conrad realized he was talking with his hands. He dropped them to his sides. "I need to relax."

Melissa shrugged. "Eh."

"Milway was an old-timer too. Seventeen years, eight with me all told. He knew the business and still they got him."

Melissa nodded and looked down at her shoes. "I don't know Conrad. Sometimes partition seems like it might have been the right idea."

"Secession? Fuck that. There'd be a third civil war. Too many people from both sides too close together, too filled with hateful memories and too damn well-armed."

"Borders can work."

"No. We've got to stay and stay between them until everyone just starts thinking calmly again."

"In about fifty or sixty years you mean? People don't forget seeing their family bleed, Dibs."

Conrad stabbed his finger in the air. "Well they need to. And however long it takes, it's worth it."

"And poor shlubs like you and me can do all the dying for everyone else's security."

"Isn't that how it always is Melissa? Hey we get the glory too." He smirked sarcastically.

Melissa nodded. "Yeah. Sally did go for the Marine uniform all right. Guess I can't complain too much." She laughed loudly and slapped Conrad on the back. Conrad looked down and she dropped the smile. "Sorry. I thought some joking might help out."

"It does," Conrad said quietly.

Two security men, guns drawn, rushed past them.

"What the fuck is that?" Melissa asked. The people around them began making more noise and moving towards a commotion.

Melissa hit Conrad on the chest with the back of her hand. "Come on. Let's check this out."

They hurried behind the crowd as it moved down the hall. When the group rounded a tall column, they all saw, high up over the hallway, a frantic maniac standing on a long, narrow, free-swinging beam held from the ceiling by steel cables. The man was shouting something but the noise from the crowd made it difficult to hear his words. Conrad moved as close as he could.

"Bow down and be humble," the man said. He shouted his words and waved his hands in sweeping motions. A shaggy white beard and a mane of white hair bounced as he spoke. He wore blue jeans, dark shoes and a black priestly robe that hung down to his knees and bounced along with his of hair. Underneath his feet, the narrow, blue platform he stood on, one of a series of decorative beams hanging from the ceiling, swayed like a slow, lazy pendulum. He kept slipping as he paced back and forth, but somehow he maintained his balance. "Rejoice in the Lord and you will be saved. Continue on this path and you will be damned."

"Get down you freak," someone yelled.

"Come on before you hurt yourself," another added.

"We're not going to catch you," a third person said and some in the crowd laughed out loud.

"You know your crimes," the robed man continued. "You will tremble before the Lord when judgment time comes. You are all traitors to yourselves and to this country." He emphasized his words by alternately crouching and standing as high as he could on the balls of his feet.

"One of your people?" Melissa asked.

"He's not Monash," Conrad said. "At least I don't recognize him as one. Damn, won't someone get him down?" Conrad looked around. Security guards in the crowd were looking up too and a couple more stood on the fourth level walkway. An overhang extended from the fourth level walkway towards the platform but didn't quite reach it. Conrad surmised that was how the old man got on the platform.

"I'll be back," Conrad said.

Melissa frowned. "You'll miss the show."

Conrad jogged down the hallway until he found a stairwell. He bounded up the stairs, two by two, until he got to the fourth floor. He flew through the exit and came out onto the walkway near the overhang. The crowd below was getting bigger.

The two security guards standing near the overhang simply stared at the robed man as he preached to the crowd. Conrad ran past the guards, jumped onto the overhang, and ran across it towards the narrow platform. He leapt towards the beam and grabbed it with both hands while in midair. It swung sharply and the old man had to extend his arms and arch his back to keep his balance. The crowd bellowed and people pointed at Conrad.

"Sir," one of the guards behind him yelled.

"I'm a law officer," Conrad shouted back. He immediately realized how ironic the comment was. He huffed and grunted as he pulled himself up and over the top of the beam. He ignored the security guards' yells to return to the walkway. He also ignored the yells from the crowd when he stood up and walked towards the preacher.

The cables holding the swaying platform to the ceiling were thin. From this vantage point, Conrad saw that there were seven beams in a row with twenty feet of space between each. Conrad regretfully noted that each beam was only about twenty inches wide. Why am I up here again? Oh yeah. I'm a good guy and felt the need to be a hero.

Conrad held a wire as he walked forward and when he had to let go he extended his arms out to the side to balance himself. He kept his eye on the beam as he walked gingerly towards the preacher.

Then the preacher startled Conrad by spinning gracefully to face him. "Repent, repent. Woe to he who does me offense. For he will be punished."

Conrad lunged at a wire in front of him, grabbed it with his left, and reached out with his right. "Come on buddy. You made your point." Conrad looked down at the anxious crowd. "No need to fall and break your neck too."

"I am protected by an angel. By a host of angels that watch over the good people of this nation." His eyes were wide and he bobbed up and down like an insane bird but somehow he kept his balance.

Conrad let go of the wire and shuffled forward a few more steps. He nearly pitched forward and the crowd moved under him like a wave. They swayed with his movements, some with their hands high in the air as though they could steady him from down there.

"I'm your angel buddy. And this angel wants you to walk back here slowly."

"You are no angel, good sir. If you are one of them, one of those below, you are a devil to be feared and despised."

"Then I'm a devil. Just get the hell...heck over here."

The old man relaxed his eyes and his body. "I can't do that."

Conrad looked up from the crowd and met the preacher's stare. His long shaggy hair was actually a mix of light brown and white strands. He had large, brown eyes and a mess of a mostly white mustache and beard. What he really looked like was a modern-day Jesus Christ with a few years tacked on.

Conrad motioned forcefully with his hand. "Man. Just get over here. Now!"

The crowd was still tittering loudly but Conrad made out Melissa yelling at him to be careful. The preacher exhaled deeply and relaxed even more.

Conrad squinted, wondering, planning for, what might happen next.

The preacher turned his back to Conrad. "I can only pray for you my brother. That's all I can do. The rest is your responsibility."

The man went limp and began to slump. His left foot began to slide down over the edge of the beam as though a hook from below had attached itself to the man's heel with the sole purpose of dragging him down.

"Oh, shit!" Conrad dashed forward and grabbed at the man. He got him from behind, around the waist, before the man pitched forward. Conrad dropped to one knee, his knee banging loudly on the metal. The crowd gasped and pain shot through Conrad's leg. His right foot slipped off and Conrad found himself momentarily balancing all his weight on the one painful knee. Conrad gritted his teeth and refused to yell.

As the preacher slipped off the beam and pulled Conrad down, Conrad hooked the beam with his right foot, slid his left knee over the side, and then gripped the rail with his thighs. His lower back strained as he tried to hold on to the man. "Crap! Hold on will you?"

The man slumped forward and his upper body weight pulled him downwards over Conrad's grasp until Conrad was gripping the beam tightly with his thighs while holding the man upside down. Conrad had the man's waist against his chest while thin legs kicked and flopped over Conrad's shoulders.

"You motherfucker," Conrad yelled. His voice echoed through the hallway.

"Hold him there," a security guard said. A multitude of guards on the ground ran and disappeared around a corner.

The preacher craned his neck to look up at Conrad. His mane of hair and beard swayed with the platform. He smiled. "Perhaps you are an angel." He looked down again and spread his hands out. He began to thrash, forcing Conrad to hold on tighter.

The crowd yelled at Conrad to drop the preacher, that they would catch him. He ignored them. It seemed an eternity before the security guards returned with sheets. The guards and helpful members of the crowd held the sheets taut under the dangling men.

The muscles of Conrad's lower back felt like they were about to pop. In great pain, Conrad gradually relaxed his hold on the preacher so that the man slowly slid down through Conrad's grasp. When Conrad finally had his feet, he let the man fall the forty feet onto the stretched out sheet. Moments after he hit it, the crowd pulled the man off and held the blanket for Conrad.

Conrad released the grip his thighs had around the beam and dropped. He went limp and tried to turn himself as he fell so that he didn't land on his head or a joint. He looked up and felt like he was floating in the clouds. He hit the sheet without a sound and felt it sag under him. He was lowered gently to the ground.

Smiling and laughing faces swarmed above him. Someone cheered him and the rest followed. He looked left and found himself side by side with the preacher who had his eyes closed. He was mumbling incoherently, only now, Conrad smelled liquor on the man.

"He's been drinking," Melissa said. She and a couple of security guards towered over Conrad.

"Give them air," one of the guards said.

"Guess you saved his life," Melissa said. "Dibs my hero." She squatted down and vigorously patted Conrad on his arm. "Anything hurt?"

Conrad leaned towards the man and sniffed. "Damn it. Nothing but a Goddamn drunk."

The preacher's eyes snapped open and he looked at Conrad. The preacher smiled. "You," he said.

"What?"

The man smiled and nodded his head, keeping Conrad's eyes locked on his. "You are not convinced."

Conrad grunted. "What the hell does that mean?"

Conrad let Melissa help him up but he waved off the security guards who tried to assist him too. "I'm okay. Just see to this guy. Want to go back to the lecture?" he asked Melissa.

"Yeah right. How about a drink instead? "

Conrad nodded. He brushed his suit off and looked at his pants. "Crap. They tore."

Melissa threw an arm around Conrad's shoulders. "What the hell was that you're not convinced shit? What were you talking about up there?"

"I have no fucking clue and it's creepy as all hell too, " Conrad said. He slid a finger into the tear that ran along an inner seam near his thigh. "Damn it."

"Well, let's go get us those drinks. Maybe we can still catch the understanding religious guerrilla motivations, Christian and Muslim compared and contrasted, seminar at five."

"Yeah sure," Conrad said in mock agreement. He looked back at the preacher but the man was surrounded by security guards and the curious onlookers that had closed in on him.

8

T he sun above was just as angry as the people cursing DC's traffic. Neither cars nor pedestrians were spared the city's wrath. It was a carnival of bleating horns, furious voices, clanging construction equipment and the brash sirens of emergency vehicles attempting to drive obstacles out of the way. A nearly visible mass of humidity filled the empty spaces between.

In one corner of this turmoil, Conrad and Mary sat less than two feet apart, separated by a marble topped cast-iron lunch table. He was leaning forward, his forearms on the table's edge, while she sat back with her arm thrown over the top of her chair.

Mary looked at the street behind her, threw her head back and blew smoke into the air above. The sweet scent of her mint cigarette and the heat of the blazing sun beating down on his uncovered head made Conrad irritable. But the real problem was that he couldn't deny the incredible attraction he felt for his ex-wife.

Mary's hair was thick and wavy and in the humidity it lay heavily on her shoulders. That mane of blonde hair highlighted the perfect structure of her face. Her tanned skin tightly wrapped a muscular, athletic body. She was a petite woman who spent her free time running. Marathons, half-marathons, ten ks. Except that she hadn't run any of those in a year and it was beginning to show. Around this strong, thirty-eight year old body was a one-piece red dress with a modest v-neck cut in the front. The bottom edges of the skirt flowered out and hung down to her calves. A string of small pink pearls looped around her throat. Conrad scratched his left arm vigorously in protest of his own body's desires.

She looked away for a long time without speaking. He leaned back in his chair and folded his hands together across his chest. He would wait. Since the divorce, he had learned to force patience on himself whenever he was in her company. He turned his head slowly, carefully looking up and down the sidewalk and scanning his surroundings for the unusual and out-of-place.

They sat in front of the Metropole, a French restaurant that catered to downtown lobbyists like Mary, and to lawyers. It was set into the first floor of one of the many high-rise office buildings of downtown Washington, DC. The exterior of the restaurant was layered with dark brown paneling and four latticed windows that evoked the image of a French country inn broke the monotony of the building. The sounds of traffic did an admirable job of destroying the illusion for anyone sitting outside the restaurant, but a long row of potted hydrangea plants boxed the outdoor lunch area and gamely tried to aesthetically separate the Metropole from the rest of the city. The light blue flowers were thick on the potted plants and Conrad had an urge to break one off and hand it to this disdainful woman.

She had called at precisely eight a.m. on the second day of the conference and asked Conrad to meet her at the Metropole for lunch later that same day. She wanted to discuss the boys. Conrad had agreed to meet. He could skip a couple of talks and networking opportunities for the sake of Mary and his two children.

When he arrived at the restaurant, she had a half-finished gin martini in her hand. She seemed impatient and distracted at the onset and refused to speak. He had quietly taken his seat and, as they sat together in silence, Conrad's mind had drifted back to a day right before the war. A warm day in February 2017. The eleventh.

It was Karl's eighth birthday. Paul would be eleven in five months. He and Mary had taken the boys to the pony rides to celebrate. The boys were ecstatic, Mary was happy, Conrad was at peace. He could claim his own happy memories of learning to ride horses at an early age and he wanted to share that with his children. The boys often begged him to take them riding but he had been unable to because of his busy work schedule. It took a heavy dose of guilt from Jim Milway and others to get him to put his family first and chasing down terrorists second. For at least one day.

Paul chose a thin black pony to ride. Karl chose a stocky brown one. The horses went around and around in a tight circle within a wooden enclosure. His sons' happy faces were magical to him. The smiles they wore were like sunshine. Mary laughed when she prodded the boys to go faster and the attendant responded with a dirty look to quiet her rebellious suggestion.

Without warning, Karl had yelped and leapt out of his saddle onto Paul's pony. Both boys went tumbling down to the ground. For a moment, Conrad felt a dagger of terror in his stomach. He hadn't heard a gunshot but he looked for a sniper rifle. He calmed when he heard the boys laughing.

"It was just a bee," Paul had said. "Just a bee."

"Yeah but that bee wanted to bite me," Karl responded and all four of them couldn't stop laughing.

Conrad's mind came back to the present. Finally, fifteen minutes after he had taken his seat, Mary turned her head to glare at him. He dropped his eyes to the olive resting at the bottom of her glass and twirled his water glass.

He needed to break the ice before he broke something more delicate. "Starting early," he said.

"It's part of the business."

"So you always say. How are the boys?"

"Okay I guess. Like kids are supposed to be." She sucked on her cigarette and looked side to side. She blew the smoke out of the corner of her mouth. "Let's stopping pussyfooting around."

Conrad slid his chair back, scraping it loudly over the concrete sidewalk.

"Can't you ever move quietly?" Mary asked.

Conrad opened his mouth once, twice, controlled his rising anger and licked his teeth. A car horn blew and he turned his head slightly but sharply towards the noise. "Any feds try to interview you about me?"

She took her time to answer. "No." She closed her eyes and held her forehead with one hand. "Why would they?"

"I don't know. I had an FBI tail at the conference."

"I've been reading about spies." Her voice had lost its edge. She sounded genuinely concerned.

Conrad took a hold of his fork and tapped it on the table lightly. "That's a Midwest problem. Operations on the East Coast have been going well."

Mary dropped her arms down beside her so that they hung like two limp ropes. She arched her back and sighed. "So maybe they know something. Maybe something big is going to happen."

"Well, they put a pretty inept agent on me."

Mary raised her head lazily and looked at Conrad. "Do I have to move the kids somewhere? Are they in danger again?"

"You're not listening to me Mary."

She crossed her arms and the edge in her voice returned. "You deal with this, this violence everyday. You think it's normal out where you are. Out in bum-fuck Occoquan."

"I don't think it's normal."

Her voice rose and her head shook as she spoke. "Look at how you're talking. You're so blasé about all of it."

"Relax. You're causing a scene." Conrad looked around to emphasize his point but there was no one nearby. No one at the other tables, no one particularly close by on the sidewalk, only the waiter standing outside and leaning against the threshold of the restaurant's front door. He was a tall, thin man, pale, with a round face and thinning brown hair along the sides and back of his head. He had a gaunt, expressionless look that went naturally with the black pants and white dress shirt he wore.

Mary gulped down the rest of her martini. "It's just like it always is, isn't it? I ask you to lunch to talk about the kids and you tell me Feds are following you."

"You're blaming me?"

"Do you understand now why I left you?"

"I always understood why you left."

"For the kids. I left for the kids." Mary tapped the bottom of the martini glass on the table so strongly that Conrad clenched his teeth anticipating that the glass would break in her grip.

She stopped tapping the glass. Conrad spoke. "And for yourself too. Don't get so idealistic with me."

"What do you know about me?"

"When you fuck someone for twenty years, you get to know them Mary."

Pain shot across her face. He felt cruel having said that and lowered his shamed eyes to the ground.

"I didn't get to know you. I didn't get to know how much this job would absorb you."

Conrad gripped his forehead. "Jesus Christ, how did we end up on this topic again?

"It's you Rad. You bring this out in me." Mary pointed her face at the restaurant door and looked as though she were trying to conjure a spirit out of it with her chin and nose.

"You asked for the divorce," Conrad said. He turned his head when the conjured spirit in a waiter's uniform came out of the door with a tray and two empty tumblers. One had red lipstick on it.

"I had to didn't I. Waiter. Waiter!" Mary raised up in her seat, yelling at the man even though he was close by.

He hurried over. "Yes ma'am."

"Get me another one of these. It's a dirty."

"Yes ma'am. Beer sir?"

"No, no."

"Up tight as ever. Hurry," Mary said.

"Do you think you should have more?" Conrad was feeling uncomfortable. He felt too much in the open and they were making too much noise. He was sweating and the seat of his pants was becoming warm and wet from the humidity and heat.

"Oh, I certainly think that," she said.

"Since when do you drink so much during working hours?"

"Since I heard about you having a government tail."

"It's not a big deal. It could be a random check."

"A random check?" Mary sneered at Conrad and turned away from him in her seat. "When are they ever random now?"

"They do that sometimes. Anti-terrorism guys do it. Maybe C-I. That's probably all it is. No problem." Conrad paused. He didn't quite believe that himself but he said it anyway. "You can stop worrying."

"How many times have I heard that?"

"And how many times have I heard that from you. Look just tell me about the kids and I'll go."

Mary's face abruptly softened and her eyes gave a hurt look. A gust of warm wind blew and lifted the corners of their cloth napkins for a few tentative moments. "Aren't you going to eat anything?" she asked.

"You want me to stay and eat?"

"Why wouldn't I?"

Mary's response startled him. Her interest in his company seemed genuine. Confused, he looked around to avoid eye contact with her. He was bothered again by how empty the restaurant was.

The waiter returned and gently placed Mary's drink in front of her. He waited a moment before turning and disappearing again into the restaurant. Conrad followed the waiter's movements then turned his attention back to Mary. She was breathing heavily.

"Okay. This is a little too much drama for me," he said.

"Paul got caught smoking pot."

"So?"

"So? I don't want him drug addicted."

"He's just experimenting. Who cares?"

"You still feel guilty. You'll let him do whatever he wants won't you."

"Of course I feel guilty. But that's not the point."

"Letting him smoke pot won't bring his arm back." Mary lifted her glass to her lips but instead of taking a sip, she bit the edge and held it in her teeth.

"I know that," Conrad said. He twisted his hands together. Sweat coated his palms. His chest felt hollow as he thought back to the explosion. It still felt like a dream. His heart pumped rapidly against the back of his ribs.

Mary lifted her cigarette from a glass ashtray. "So tell him it's bad."

Conrad sighed and gave in to something other than Mary's request. "Fine. But I'm not going to stop him if he wants to continue with it."

"Of course not. You're never going to discipline him are you?"

"He's smart enough to make his own choices." Conrad realized that since Mary mentioned the arm, his son Paul's arm, he had been speaking quietly, softly. He could have been in confession again with the way he felt. Sitting in a dark space speaking to a screen, hoping for nothing but forgiveness.

"He's only fifteen. He's not experienced enough." Her voice got a little deeper, a little unsteady and she was beginning to slur.

Conrad looked at the hydrangea flowers. One was bruised with a few petals missing. "He'll be legal in three years."

"And that's okay with you?"

Conrad continued wringing his hands together and pulled at a knuckle. "No. But one thing I've learned is that the more you tell people not to do something, the more they want to do it."

"Paul's not people. He's your son."

"Oh I see." Conrad sat back and let his hands drop over his armrests. He and Mary looked into each other's eyes. He felt resigned to all of the misery. She looked just as ready to give up too.

She neither blinked nor moved her eyes from his. "I think we're going to move to Texas. El Paso."

His own eyes widened appreciably. "What? Since when?"

"Since now. Since you're being followed."

Conrad slumped back in his chair. "My God Mary. You're blowing this out of proportion."

"That's funny. Blow is a good word." Her voice was even thicker now and she sneered.

"You're away from me now aren't you? You won't get hurt again."

She nodded her head longer than necessary. "I want to be somewhere safe. Somewhere really safe."

"What you need to do is keep the kids here. Near me."

"I'll go. You can't stop me." She was talking to the table and nodding.

"What about your job?"

"I can do lobby work in Texas."

"At the federal level?"

"I can work state employee benefits. For the police associations or something."

"You'll miss DC money. I know you will."

"Fuck you." She paused. "I'm not shallow. You think I'm shallow but I'm not." Mary had stopped nodding and was now admiring her maroon high-heel shoes. Conrad looked at them too. His eyes crawled along the sidewalk to the empty table next to theirs. A few people in suits passed and looked at him. People with cell phones plugged into their ears stared straight ahead. A man coughed. They looked as lifeless as he felt.

Then something clicked in his head. He stared at her shoes again and felt heat rise up the sides of his neck. His heart pounded, demanded its freedom from his ribs. He gripped the edge of the table and savagely overturned it with a crash. "Fuck me? Fuck you! How about that! What do you think about that?"

Mary shoved her chair back and stood up. She looked horrified. "Stop it. Stop it. Please."

Conrad put his foot on the overturned table and pushed it away from him. The table screeched as it slid along the concrete pavement. Conrad opened his mouth to yell again but the fear on Mary's face drove the feeling out of him. His rage slipped back down from where ever inside him it had come. He was breathing heavily and stars flashed before his eyes. "I... damn it."

Mary's head dropped. She stooped down and picked up her small underarm bag. "I'm so sorry. So, so sorry."

But Conrad ignored her. When he had shoved the table, he also knocked over one of the potted hydrangeas. Behind it was an overstuffed black soft-leather bag on the sidewalk.

Conrad looked back at the restaurant door. "Waiter?"

The waiter hurried over from the doorway but stopped just out of arm's reach from Conrad. "Yes?"

Conrad pointed. "Why is that bag sitting there?"

"I don't know sir." The waiter looked around as though someone in the distance might know something. The seating area was empty. The sidewalk was empty. Conrad stiffened in fear when a thin stream of smoke began to escape from the top of the bag.

"Run," Conrad yelled. He lunged for Mary and grabbed her arm. She tried to pull away but he held tightly. He took two steps and pulled her with him. She stumbled forward but when he began running she ran with him.

The waiter stared at the bag without moving.

"Run," Conrad shouted. He pushed Mary ahead of himself, keeping his own body between her and the case.

The bag was still expelling smoke, a thicker stream now, when the waiter finally shook off his astonishment and followed Conrad. A moment later, the lunch area was rent by a terrific explosion. Glass shattered, the plants flew down the sidewalk, and a great ball of fire enveloped the spot where the bag had been.

Conrad dropped to the ground and fell on top of Mary. The concussive force of the explosion drove the waiter up and forward. His arms moved as though he were trying to swim through the air.

Tables slid towards the building and the windows of the restaurant blew inwards.

After an eternity airborne, the waiter hit the pavement, knees first, face second, and his bones made a sickening, cracking sound. Conrad shuffled over to look at the man. The clothes on his back were ragged. Streaks of blood and burn marks showed over the once-pristine white shirt. The waiter began to writhe in agony and clutch at the wounds across his back and legs. Mary rolled around on the ground and mumbled incoherently. People ran towards them, some ran away. All of them stopped and yelled when a tabletop crashed into the street. The shattered marble flew over the tarmac street in thousands of pieces. Conrad jerked away when Mary sat straight up and looked at him.

"Oh my God. Oh my God. Conrad!" Though pale, she looked unhurt. Conrad grabbed her hands in his.

"Call an ambulance Mary! Do you have a phone? Hurry up!"

Conrad reached for the waiter and tried to determine the extent of the man's wounds. He was bloody but none of his bones were at odd angles. "Don't move," he told the dazed man. "Stay still. You might have hurt your back." The waiter continued moaning and rolling back and forth with his eyes closed.

"That was for you. They were trying to get you," Mary said.

Conrad blinked. The surface of his eyeballs stung as though they were sunburned. He had briefly stared at the explosion as it happened. "Call 9-1-1 Mary."

"Do you hear me Conrad? Do you want the kids to die? Do you want me to die? Listen to me!"

Conrad focused on the waiter. "Mary, where's your phone? Call the ambulance. Stop thinking about yourself and just call it!"

9

T he words flashed in his brain. Woe to he who does me offense. For he will be punished. Conrad wondered if the old man had anything to do with the bomb. Should he have just let the old man fall and break his neck? He scowled at the thought of his bias against the man. There was no proof of anything except that the man was delusional and even that may have just been the alcohol. The screech of tires warned him! Conrad swerved to avoid a car carelessly pulling out into the street.

He had one hand on his steering wheel and the other on his cell phone as he sped down Route 123 towards his field station. A red police light flashed on the top of his furious black Mustang. His sirens screamed. He angrily snapped his phone closed. The nurse he had just spoken to confirmed that Mary wasn't injured, only shaken up. The old man's reprieve would last that much longer.

At the front entrance of the Occoquan Federal Compound, Conrad braked hard and cut his car towards the gate. The DHS guard jumped out of the sentry box and flapped his arms at him to stop. Conrad stuck his arm out and waved the guard away as he shot through the gate towards the Freedom Station.

Lina was outside, leaning against the station's front wall and peering into a handheld video camera. Conrad slammed his brakes and slid into his parking spot. Tires squealed again. Lina's head snapped up from the camera.

"Sir?" she asked when Conrad leapt out of the car but Conrad dashed past her and through the automatic sliding doors. The desk guard looked up but wisely said nothing as Conrad banged through the stairwell doors. He bounded up the stairs, through another set of painfully slow sliding doors, and into the main office. He immediately relaxed when he saw his two sons sitting at the common table with Blounts. Blounts looked up and smiled. The white end of a lollipop stick extended from the young officer's mouth.

Paul lazily raised his left arm when he saw his father. "Hey Dad."

Conrad took two steps forward and stopped in front of the security gate. With hands on hips, he took a very deep and weary breath.

"We beat you by," Karl, a chubby kid and short for a thirteen year old, looked at his watch, "seven minutes Dad." Karl smiled at his father.

Conrad's face was like plaster. "Why didn't you call me?"

Blounts leaned back in a plastic swivel chair. "We were talking. Lost track of things." Blounts let his chair drop forward and he pulled a purple lollipop out of his mouth. Conrad opened his mouth but Blounts spoke first. "Surfing. I was telling them about surfing."

Conrad closed his mouth and grunted. Blounts was ever the peacemaker, the one who could calm everyone down. Conrad passed through the common room gate and let it clang shut as he walked over to his sons.

"Dad you're getting a medal," Paul said. His teenage voice cracked as he spoke and he awkwardly smiled. "Sorry," he said in apology for his puberty.

Conrad looked at Blounts for an explanation.

Blounts shrugged and disengaged the lollipop from his mouth again. "The assault. Washington called and said they would be giving you a medal for the last couple of operations. They want to know when you want the ceremony." Blounts popped the lollipop back in.

Conrad's mind went back to the execution, to the three men and how their mouths moved as they prayed. But he couldn't recall the sounds of their voices. The guns popping, the flesh ripping, the blood's light splash on the wall. But their voices were beyond his recall. Soldiers, men not much older than Paul, watched him carry out the execution. Yet they only had the memory of the spectacle, not the act. Conrad nodded, grimly thankful for having spared his men that heavy weight of guilt. "Okay. I'll call them back."

Paul turned to face Conrad directly. "Dad, I really think I want to try surfing."

Conrad placed his hand on Paul's head and left it there for a long second. Then he made a jovial mess of his son's thick, dark hair and smiled for a moment, before the tenderness fell from his face. Apparently Blounts had made them move quickly because Paul was wearing a prosthetic arm that he often complained about. The straps were always too tight around his right upper arm. He'd thank Blounts later for emphasizing speed over comfort in getting his sons to safety.

Blounts stood. "Guess I should get back to work now."

"No, no. You guys talk. I need to see Dave."

Blounts agreed. "Yeah. He's got something for you."

"Dad?" Karl asked. "Are you okay?" Karl's face was expressionless. He was the calm, thoughtful one of the two boys. The organized stoic whereas Paul was the risk-taker and much louder in a crowd. Karl had on brown shorts and a yellow t-shirt that was too small for his fat belly. A pair of green canvas shoes completed the outfit.

Bright colors are too noticeable thought Conrad. Too easy for a killer to track. He put his hand on Karl's arm and squeezed it. "Yeah. I'm good."

"And Mom's fine too right?" Paul asked. He scratched the stump of his right forearm where the flesh was pressed against his prosthesis.

"Just shaken up," Conrad said. "The waiter is the only guy that suffered serious injury." Karl's chin dropped to his chest. "But he's going to be okay," Conrad added.

Karl shook his head and looked up. "They just shouldn't be doing that. I just don't care how much you don't like what someone else thinks."

Paul pushed Karl's arm. "It's a war! They got to do what they need to do and we got to do what we need to. We're all soldiers and we all have to be ready."

Karl pushed Paul's arm in return and his voice went up. "I don't like it at all!" Conrad and Blounts glanced at each other.

Conrad squatted down in front of Karl and lightly took hold of his son's arms to reassure him. "Hey kid, relax. We're okay. We didn't get hurt."

Karl's eyes were wide open. His dirty blonde hair was a mess and stood up at odd angles. He looked like a madman. "No! I'm tired of it. I'm tired! It's all over the internet. Blood, and body parts and blowing up things. I don't want to see it!" Karl tugged his arms backwards, trying to break out of Conrad's grip. Conrad squeezed tighter as his son wildly squirmed around.

"Stop that," Paul yelled. He put his prosthetic hand on Karl's shoulder and squeezed. Karl abruptly stopped moving and stared at

Paul's hand. Conrad looked at the synthetic hand too and, slowly, his eyes moved up the arm to the elbow and then the top of the arm. A chill went down his back and his head began to throb.

"Stop it," Conrad said. "Stop panicking."

Karl looked back at Conrad. "Ow. Dad, that hurts. Stop squeezing so hard."

"Stop yelling," Paul yelled.

"I'm not yelling anymore," Karl said.

Karl's voice had calmed and softened but Conrad felt something rise up through his own chest. His heart pounded in a familiar way and the heat rose in his neck.

"Just stop complaining." Conrad shook Karl. "Just stop complaining okay! Stop it!" His voice had risen to a thunderous roar.

"Okay dad. Let go."

"I said stop worrying. Just stop it."

"Dad?" one of his boys said. Conrad couldn't tell which.

Conrad's head was dense with fury. His temples throbbed. "It isn't helping when you complain! I have to do my job. Got it? Just let me do my job!" Conrad felt a heavy hand on his shoulder. His muscles tightened, in the ready to whip around and attack the offender, but he clenched his jaw and held himself in check. He turned his head slowly and saw Blounts' hand.

"Hey, hey boss, mind if I get in on the fun?" Blounts asked.

"Huh?"

"Can't I get in this wrestling match too? I've got some skills. Greco-Roman you know."

"Huh?" Conrad's muscles relaxed. The pressure in his body subsided and he looked at Karl and Paul. They were looking at him without blinking. There was fear in their eyes and they stood like statutes rooted to the floor.

Conrad shook his head and forced a smile. He let go of Karl and stood. He patted Karl's head and turned away. "Yeah, yeah. It's okay kids. Your mom and I are all right. We're all right."

Blounts spoke up again. "Hey guys. Let me show you some of my surf pics. How's that sound?"

"I guess so," Karl said. Karl turned away from Conrad in abject sadness and he and Paul followed Blounts to his office. Conrad looked at Blounts and their eyes met. Blounts gave a thin smile and nodded. The three walked into Blounts' surf and tiki kitsch strewn office and left the door open.

"Okay," Conrad said to himself. He rubbed the back of his neck. "They're safe. Bronson," he said as a reminder to himself.

Conrad walked to Dave Bronson's closed office door and tapped on the glazed windowpane with his knuckle.

"Come in." Dave pulled his nose from the computer screen when Conrad stepped into the office. "Sir, I forwarded some information to your terminal."

"Okay. So what do you think?"

"You didn't see anyone out there with you?"

"No. I was taking to Mary. Kind of got distracted."

"I'll say. He almost hid it in your ass."

Conrad stretched his mouth and rubbed his cheek impatiently. "And?"

Dave grunted and looked back at his screen. "What do we do now?"

"How about we examine any tape of the area?"

Dave frowned. "Will we get the videotape or is Internal Security going to step on our hands?"

"Probably step on our hands." Conrad shook his head. "Know what? Pull up Hawk."

Like an elephant exhibiting a moment of grace, Dave spun one-eighty in his chair and stopped his motion in front of a second computer screen. "I thought you didn't see the guy." He punched a few keys and Hawk, the global terrorist database, popped onto the flat screen.

Conrad leaned over Dave's shoulder. "I didn't. Search for detainees and prisoners."

Dave plugged the criteria into the search filter and the first twenty-five of 576,132 names found by the system popped up.

"Give me pictures only."

Dave hit another couple of keys and the screen was filled with pictures of terrorists captured on U.S. soil.

"Hold on," Conrad said. He walked to a locked filing cabinet, pulled a small belt pouch from his pant pocket and then a set of keys from that. He undid a small lock and opened the top sliding cabinet. He flipped through a series of large tan envelopes and pulled out a fat one sealed in plastic and labeled "Occoquan Patriot Committee".

He undid the seal, peeked in and removed a wallet size photograph from the envelope. The photo showed a young Japanese-looking man standing next to a pale, blonde girl, both from the waist up. They were arm in arm and smiling at the photographer. There was a large tree with white flowers behind them, maybe a cherry blossom tree in bloom. Conrad walked to Dave and showed him the photograph. Dave didn't take it. He looked at it and typed.

Conrad looked at the photo again. "Give me black hair, males. Try Japanese ethnic first."

"Yup," Dave said and the keyboard thumped under the jabs of Dave's index fingers.

Conrad scanned the new list of rebel prisoners that popped up. "'Keep going."

Dave scrolled to the second screen and pointed at the headshot of a young Japanese man. Conrad looked back and forth between the picture in his hand and the picture on the screen. "I think that's our kid," Conrad said.

"Good catch chief. Says here they were going to let him go in a few weeks. No actual proof of rebel sympathies. But why him?"

"Remember when that guy yelled at me 'He'll get you'?"

"He meant God."

"That's what I thought. But it didn't sound right the way he said it. I've been reading some of the documents we captured from the assault. I think the rebs are working on a new strategy. Political assassination."

"Really? So you think 'he' meant an assassin?"

"Maybe."

"The picture came from one of the rebels?"

"Off a body under the rubble."

Dave looked at the well-worn beige carpet on the floor and scratched at it with the tip of his shoe. "The blonde in the picture?"

Conrad chewed his lower lip. "Yeah."

Dave nodded. "So the kid might know something."

"Yeah."

Dave looked back at his computer screen. "That's weird."

Conrad slipped the picture into his shirt pocket. "What's that?"

"Kid's missing his arm. Says he got it blown off during an aerial bombing run of another compound he lived at."

"Oh? He had it in the picture." Conrad rubbed his shoulder and looked out of Dave's doorway. Paul and Karl were laughing at something.

"Blounts is good with your kids, chief."

"Yeah. He's always talking about getting married and having kids of his own."

"Too wild still. He's a bachelor type."

Conrad rubbed his chin. "How's your daughter doing?"

Dave looked at Conrad and frowned. A sharp vertical line formed between his eyebrows. "Huh?"

"Your family. Are they okay?"

"Yeah, yeah. Damn chief. Don't freak me out like that."

"So why do you do it?"

"What? This?"

"Yeah."

"The pay."

"Uh-huh."

"But really, it just comes natural I guess. What else can I do? This is my trade."

"You were kind of nervous out there. When I shot the picket."

"Haven't seen a clean head shot in a while. That's all. No biggie." Dave looked away from Conrad and focused on his computer screen again. "Just kind of chilling."

"It doesn't even make my heart speed up anymore."

Dave looked up. "What? Dead people?"

"I mean killing people. Not when I do it."

"Uh." Dave lifted the corner of his mouth and scrutinized Conrad. "Well I guess that's normal."

Cris Alvarez

"For me? Yeah. You're right Dave. I've been killing for a long time. Just a cold-blooded gunman. Doesn't even phase me to think about it anymore. Weird huh?"

"That's all right sir. You kill the bad guys."

Conrad shook his head and shrugged. "I used to feel a little adrenalin after the kill. A little nervous, a little guilt. Not any more. Not for the last couple of years."

"But your family. You feel for them. That's why you do it."

"That's what's strange Dave." Conrad moved to the door and peeked out. He closed it gently. "When I think about my family getting hurt, even Mary still, I shake a little. I lose focus. My heart goes crazy."

"Seems normal enough. I do the same."

"Not like this. Why do I feel for them and not for strangers? They have families too. They're people. I don't like it."

Dave shrugged and looked at Conrad quizzically. "Cause they aren't your family?"

"I. It just feels weird. I kill rebels like it's nothing but...I know they're dangerous, but still..." Conrad let his words fade. "It's like, like, I'm the gun. I'm nothing but a piece of metal now. Like the sniper rifle. I felt like I was part of it when I shot."

"You're good at your job."

"This isn't good Dave. It's not right to feel like this all of a sudden. Not after all these years. And now on top of that I keep losing control of my temper. It doesn't make sense. I wasn't like this before. I'm getting madder and calmer all at the same time.

Dave folded his hands together and looked down. Sweat beaded his temples. "You want to quit? Take a vacation? I can cover for a month or two if you need it."

Conrad kicked the bottom of Dave's desk lightly. "No. I have no reason to quit Dave. That's my point. I'm beyond being affected by the job. In my mind, I'm right there and committed to this. When I think about it, mentally I'm ready to take them all out without a second thought, and in my heart...I feel nothing when I kill. But it doesn't seem right. It shouldn't be that easy."

Dave touched his nose. "That reminds me. The department shrink's been trying to reach you."

"Oh shit. I keep forgetting to call her back."

"Three days left. They'll get on your ass if you don't talk to her soon. Especially with four personal kills."

"That's funny. I get a medal and a call from the psych therapist on the same day about the same damn thing I did."

"Huh. Yeah," Dave said. "Funny."

"So what am I? Crazy or a hero?"

Dave shrugged. "Both?" He typed on his computer.

"So, what the hell am I going to tell her?"

Dave looked up. "What you just told me."

Conrad narrowed his eyes and smirked. "Think I'm crazy?"

"No, no. Just that..."

Conrad snorted. "Forget about it Dave. I'll call her. Just keep what I said to yourself okay?"

"Hey, I never-"

"Just keep it to yourself Dave."

"Sure chief sure."

"Take my kids to their grandma's house in Bethesda okay. If anyone picked up Blounts' scent, I don't want them following him or his car back out of the compound."

"Roger that."

Conrad walked to the office door and opened it.

"Hey," Dave said.

"Yeah?"

"That kid you're gonna interrogate. What do you plan to do?"

"Hell. I'm not dangerous crazy yet." He made a gun with his right hand. "Just make sure," Conrad placed the tips of his fingers just behind his right ear and angled upwards, "when I do lose it, you shoot me right here. I think I've earned a quick one."

Dave shot up from his chair. "Let me go with you."

Dave's offer irritated Conrad. His face warmed over. "It's personal. Unofficial."

"That's why I need to go. Come on. I'll be good cop."

"What makes you think I want to be bad cop?"

"I sort of get that feeling chief. Something about the look on your face."

Cris Alvarez

"I'm getting the information I need. You know?"

"Okay chief. Let me just get my coat."

Conrad walked out the door and waited in the common area while Dave arranged the trashcans and some papers on the reception desk. Conrad glared while Dave puttered around. He didn't want anyone with him. Not now, not for this.

His heart pounded and his face got hotter. There it was again. The unnatural temper but he didn't fight it. At the moment, he liked that hot feeling, the lava flowing through his limbs. He was ready to get some payback from anyone connected to the person who had tried to hurt Mary. This wasn't police business, this was his business. But Conrad said nothing when Dave sidled next to him, smiled, and walked out of the office in front of him.

10

T
he gray room was twenty by thirty feet. Dust and small bits of gravel covered the floor. The low ceiling of the room was etched by spider-web cracks. One bare bulb hung from a wire in the middle of the ceiling. A roach scuttled into a dark corner and disappeared in the hungry darkness. A small, black video camera mounted in a top corner of the room eyed the space. A large one-way mirror set in the wall next to the single door in the room reflected the entire scene.

A steel table, six by three feet, was positioned precisely in the center of the room. Two silver, straight-backed chairs flanked either side of it. One chair was empty, on the other sat a young Japanese man in an orange jumpsuit.

The man was short with fragile limbs extending from a narrow torso. His neck and face were bare. His hair was short, straight and black, his skin a smooth, pale earth tone. His cuffed hands were folded together and resting on the table. His nails were chewed to the quick and the skin around them just as badly mauled.

The man's name was Maiku Hanama. Maiku had been an active rebel until his capture four months ago. He had been conducting surveillance on soft targets in the city of Washington, DC. This was the man whose picture had been pulled by Conrad from the files at the Freedom Station.

A shoe scuffed the ground and Maiku snapped his head towards the sound. Conrad stepped out of one dark corner holding a computer printout in his hand. Conrad crumpled the paper into a ball and shoved it into his pocket while he stared at the scared looking man.

According to the report so savagely compacted in Conrad's pocket, Maiku was twenty-two and a Christian idealist. It was for Jesus that Maiku had been involved in felonious activities but he hadn't admitted to the felonies, only his religious convictions.

Conrad glared and was happy to see the fear on Maiku's face. It satisfied, but only somewhat, his edacious need for revenge. An image of a demon Kabuki mask played in Conrad's mind and he smiled.

Conrad turned the smile into an evil grin for added effect and nodded. Maiku, more a boy than a man, slowly slid his feet back under the chair he was sitting on and lowered his cuffed wrists to grip the side of his seat with one hand. The other hand, the prosthetic one, was sandwiched uselessly between the chair and Maiku's good hand. Maiku shifted his eyes from Conrad to the edge of the table in front of him.

Conrad's malevolent gaze lingered on the plastic hand. Its skin tone was slightly different from Maiku's skin color. The lifeless thing looked cold and hollow. It wasn't as nice as Paul's arm. It was cheap. Something provided by the prison hospital for Maiku's use. Conrad wondered if Maiku's irritated his skin the way it bothered Paul's. He hoped it did. With impatience barking in his head like a junkyard dog, Conrad decided to lay it on thick. He swung his arms up over his head and, with all his weight behind them, slammed his palms down on the table.

The table shuddered under the loud blow and Maiku yelped. He fell out of his seat and onto his side. Conrad waited as he struggled to a sitting position using his one good hand.

"You can't do that," Maiku shouted. He sprayed saliva as he spoke. "They're watching." He pointed a finger at the camera, straining towards it from where he sat.

Conrad shook his head. "They're not watching. It's dead. Just like you'll be." He felt stupid for that last comment. It was idiotically melodramatic. He looked away from Maiku.

Maiku pointed at the mirror behind Conrad. "There are guards watching." His voice was high-pitched and fearful. "You can't hurt me," he said but he didn't sound like someone who believed that.

Conrad re-motivated himself into being a raging madman again. He pushed the table aside, its legs screeching along the concrete. He reached down and grabbed the cowering man by the back of his prison jumpsuit. He pulled Maiku to his knees and Maiku's shackled hands fell limply between his legs, the prosthetic hand bouncing on Maiku's thigh. He pulled his shoulders up and kept his head down.

"Talk!" Conrad shouted. A string of his saliva slapped against his lips. He roughly wiped his mouth with the back of his hand.

The one door in the room opened and Dave slipped in, his eyes betraying his agitation. "Boss, what are you doing?" He shut the door and entered the reflective view of the mirror.

Conrad grunted and released Maiku.

Maiku scrambled to his feet. "He's crazy," he said.

"We're just talking," Conrad said.

Dave came close and put his hand on Conrad's shoulder. "Maybe you shouldn't be so hard on the kid."

"Hard on him? I'm planning to kill the son of a bitch."

Maiku gulped and moved to the chair. He sat down and put his hands flat on the table.

"Let me talk to him," Dave said. He pulled a cigarette from his breast pocket and slid it between his lips. He lit it with a cheap, brown lighter. He looked up at Maiku. "Want one kid?" The cigarette wagged between his lips when he spoke and then both the smoke and Dave's face were still.

Maiku looked warily from Dave to Conrad. Conrad walked to the wall that faced the one-way mirror. He leaned his palms against its cool surface and dropped his head between his outstretched arms. He didn't want to keep up this act. That prosthetic arm was bothering him. He wanted to grab it and rip the thing from Maiku's jumpsuit. Then he would smash the mirror with it. He took a deep breath.

"No. No thank you," Maiku finally said.

Dave spoke softly but loud enough for Conrad to hear him. "This guy just lost someone and he's got friends here. They'll let him do what he wants." Conrad twisted his head and looked at the mirror and its reflections out of the corner of his eye. Dave pointed mysteriously into space and waved the lighter a little. "I wish I could calm the guy down, but I can't. So just answer his questions. Please."

Maiku raised his cuffed hands into the air. "What, what do you want me to say? You haven't asked me anything!"

Conrad spun around. "Just talk Goddamn it. Where are the headquarters?"

Dave raised his palm. "Now chief."

Maiku looked at Conrad. "I'm not talking. Get rough if you like." The rebel's face was suddenly a rigid cast of obstinacy. "You talk about freedom for everyone but you keep us prisoners here forever. You're liars."

Cris Alvarez

Conrad walked to Maiku and the boy recoiled. "Don't try to talk philosophy with me you punk. You know the difference. You preach violent opposition to American freedoms. Don't try to claim them as your own."

Maiku looked at Conrad with a face that seemed to show both great pride and disgust. It was arrogance. He jutted his chin out. "Do you believe in God?" His lips were pressed together and the muscles around his eyes were tensed. Conrad lifted his right arm high, held it there and crashed his palm against the boy's face. Maiku's head twisted sharply and the boy let out a hard grunt. His body slumped but he stayed in the chair.

Chief," Dave yelled. He grabbed Conrad's hand and gave a look that said Conrad was going a little too far.

Conrad wrenched his hand lose from Dave's grip. "Don't you fucking talk to me about God when your people lay bombs to blow up innocent people. Hypocrite motherfucker."

Maiku's voice was high. "You," he began but Conrad cut that short with another powerful blow against the boy's face. Maiku spun out of the chair and shoved the table along the floor as he fell. Conrad leaned down, grabbed Maiku's collar and shook him.

"Chief," Dave pleaded. Dave grabbed at Conrad but Conrad shoved him away with a powerful push. "For the love of," Dave said.

Maiku looked up with a face of terror. Tears streamed down his face.

"You fucking killers," Conrad said. He pushed the boy towards the ground and let go. He stood up straight and took a deep breath. "My boy lost an arm to one of your people's bombs. I'm glad you lost yours too."

"You aren't innocent," the boy said through sobs.

"You know someone tried to kill me don't you? What do you know about me?" Conrad looked at Dave, then the mirror. The room looked like a black hell.

Maiku rubbed his face and spit out blood with a large glob of saliva. It spread unevenly on the dusty floor. "You kill women and children and babies. Good God loving people. I'm not talking to you, you animal."

Conrad's mouth twisted into a smirk. "I knew you wouldn't talk."

Maiku looked down and his chest still shook from crying. "So what do you want from me?"

"Look, you're tired of being here right?" Dave asked. He held his hand out to Maiku.

Maiku tentatively accepted Dave's help and stood. He brushed himself off as well as he could and then gingerly sat in the chair. "I can take it." He crossed his arms and legs, curled in on himself and began rocking back and forth.

"Sure you can. You're tough," Conrad said.

"Hey chief," Dave said. He held out his hands towards Conrad, his eyes pleading for quiet.

Conrad nodded. Dave backed away and stood a few steps behind Maiku while the boy bit his lips in silence.

Conrad turned and squared himself to Maiku. "We're still hitting your people. They're pretty easy to find except for just a handful."

"So?"

"I can take it a little easy on the ones we get."

Maiku's face became stiff and long. He had stopped crying. "What do you mean can? You should be doing that anyway."

"No I don't. I can be as rough as I want."

Maiku stared at Conrad. He didn't answer but his crossed arms tightened against his chest.

Conrad continued. "Know this woman, Jessica Reinhardt?" He pulled the photo of Maiku and the blonde from his pocket and held it twelve inches from Maiku's nose.

Maiku's breath caught and his head twitched.

"I asked do you know her."

Maiku's head moved erratically and then he looked away.

"We have her."

Maiku looked at Conrad, his face soft now and his eyes becoming wet again. "Don't hurt her. She's a good person."

"I'm sure she is." Conrad concentrated on keeping his face was impassive. "I can promise to get her moved to a minimum security holding area, where she'll be treated," Conrad paused, "decently." He glanced at Dave but Dave was pondering the lit cigarette he held in his hand.

Maiku wiped the tears from his cheeks. "In exchange for what?"

"For information."

"You have to guarantee her safety. You'll do what you said?"

"I'll do my best."

Maiku leaned forward. "How is she?"

"Hurt but doing fine."

"Let me talk to her please."

"No."

Maiku looked away for a moment, then looked back at Conrad's eyes. "Tell me something special about her so that I know you're not lying."

Conrad thought back to the day of the assault. The prisoners they had caught were squatting together along one shattered wall. Bodies were piled up side-by-side one room over. He remembered Jessica's body - twisted, blackened and bent. "She has vertical whip scars on her back. Old ones. A large tattoo of a forest and unicorn covers them."

Maiku stifled a sob and looked down. "She got those scars from her father. He was a police officer too. Brutal, like you."

Conrad pulled his lips in on themselves and scratched his chin. "Keep talking."

"I don't know what to say. You can promise me anything you want and all I can do is hope."

"I keep my word."

Maiku nodded and frowned like he wasn't convinced, but Conrad knew that hope was more than Maiku had right now, which was nothing.

"I want to have a lawyer here when I talk. I want him to hear your promise."

"He won't hear nothing cause I won't be back."

Maiku lowered his head. He shifted his weight around in the chair and chewed the inside of his cheek. His chest shook and tears rolled down his cheeks. "You want to know about the bomb."

"Yeah. Who's doing the planting and the surveillance?"

"We have an agent in DC."

"Thanks for nothing kid. Jessica's going to like it in hard, stone solitary. Naked and cold. I'll make sure she knows to thank you for it." Dave was squinting his eyes as he sucked on his cigarette. Conrad shrugged and turned towards the door.

"No, wait," Maiku said.

Conrad drilled a hole into Maiku with his eyes. "Then talk!"

Maiku gulped. "He operates out of a hotel in Southeast. On the water somewhere."

"That's a lot of area. Keep going."

"He's foreign."

Conrad looked at Dave but his partner had slid into a shadow at the corner of the room. The tip of his cigarette glowed in the darkness.

"How so?" Conrad asked.

"Eastern Europe maybe. A mercenary."

"Okay, good."

"That's all I know. They keep things secret."

Conrad sucked his teeth. "That's all you know?"

Maiku nodded. Suddenly the door handle shook. Someone was trying to get through the locked door. Time was up. The table screeched as Conrad slid it back into place. "Okay kid. You bought Jessica a better place with that. If it holds up."

Maiku smiled without enthusiasm then dropped it. The door kept shaking. A voice came faintly from the other side. The shaking stopped. Conrad and Dave walked to the door. Conrad undid the door lock and both men stepped out into a dimly lit observation room. Bright lights snapped on and a dark screen lowered on the observation side of the one-way mirror. Conrad closed the door behind him.

A short, round and balding man in a powder blue suit glared at Preston, the interrogation room monitor. The round man did a double take at Conrad and spun towards him. He waved his arms madly and yelled, "What the hell is going on here?" He strode the short distance to Conrad and glared at him.

"Nothing," Conrad said.

The round man, Howard Bullow of the FBI, thrust his face up towards Conrad. "Nothing? That's my charge! No one interrogates him except me or who I say!"

Conrad shrugged. "Sorry Howie. Had to talk to him."

"What did you do to him?"

"Slapped him a couple of times."

Howie rose on the balls of his feet. "What?"

"Just kidding."

Howard turned towards the monitor. "What's on the camera?"

Howard shrugged. "Camera's broken sir. Well, batteries are dead."

"Batteries?"

"I was just a minute Howie. He didn't talk."

"I should hope not. He didn't have a lawyer present did he?"

"No."

"I don't even know if that's good or bad." Howie pulled a packet of cigarettes from his jacket's inner pocket. He tossed a stick in his mouth and used a lighter emblazoned with the FBI logo to light it.

Conrad stared at Howie's cigarette and the plain brown tie hanging behind it. Howie's yellow dress shirt was wet with sweat. "I'm going," Conrad said.

Howie slipped his free hand into a pocket and blew smoke at Conrad's chest. "Tell me what happened in there."

"Nothing. I need to go."

Howie nooded rapidly. "Okay, okay. I got you Greis. Fucking tough guy. Keep me out of it why don't you."

"If you say so. You're the boss." Conrad motioned towards the exit with his head. Dave walked ahead of Conrad and opened the door.

"How about you Bronson?" Howie asked.

"I was asleep Howie. Pretty quiet in there."

Conrad pushed Dave ahead of him through the open doorway. He didn't look back but he heard Howie ask the monitor, "And what about you?" Conrad wasn't worried about it. Preston could take care of himself. He always did.

11

Conrad sat on the concrete steps of the Centreville Detention Center, his shoulders slumped in dejection. A cloudy sky threatened to dump rain on him. He clasped his hands together and brought them over the back of his neck. Fear gnawed at him.

Paul's face and Maiku's face blurred back and forth in his mind. Their individual images became one person that looked vaguely like each of them but the figure was missing both arms. When Conrad closed his eyes, his imagination tortured him with an image of that hybrid person running at him, stumps stretched out, reaching for him with phantom hands. Guilt gnawed at Conrad for lying to Maiku about Jessica and for that he wished the thing he imagined could pummel him senseless.

"Fuck." What a ridiculous thought. Conrad opened his eyes and stood. The sound of footsteps came down from behind him.

Dave stopped at Conrad's left. "Paperwork's done chief."

"Did that kid make you think about Paul?"

"Don't kick yourself about it. Just a coincidence." Dave pulled his cigarette pack out. "Hey. Can you believe they hired a mercenary?"

Conrad hesitated, bit his tongue, and accepted the change in subject. "Sounds desperate. Maybe they ran out of homegrown talent to get the job done."

Dave nodded sagely. "That's a good thing. You're getting to them." Dave lit a cigarette and pocketed his lighter. He sighed in a relaxed way, then drew in a deep pull from his smoke.

"Yeah Dave. I'm doing such a terrific job, they gave me a personal assassin."

Dave slapped Conrad on the back. "We're close to them too boss. Come on. Let's get back to the office. I'm feeling good now."

Conrad and Dave trotted down the steps past three corrections officers coming up the stairs when a strange thought exploded in Conrad's mind. He stopped and grabbed Dave's shoulder. "Hey!"

Dave nearly fell backwards on the steps. He snatched the cigarette from his bottom lip before it fell out of his open mouth. "Jeez. What?"

"Where are their arms?"

Dave cocked his head. He was expressionless at first, then he furrowed his brow. "Arms? What in the hell are you talking about?"

"Where do they put the arms? When they come off. I don't know where Paul's arm is."

"Chief. Let's get some food or something. Pizza-"

"I've been thinking about it. When I was sitting there. Where'd they put his arm? They found it and then it disappeared again at the hospital. But that second time, I just forgot about it."

Dave stuck his palm out. "Gimme the keys boss. I'm driving."

Both men were startled when their cell phones buzzed simultaneously. The sound was that of the standard DHS emergency message tone. Dave pulled his cell phone from his belt and listened. Conrad reacted slower in drawing his phone from his belt and listening to the same message. Both men heard a recorded message transmitted by central dispatch to the phones of all officers who needed to hear it.

"Niner-three. All units respond to the intersection of Varney and Oakwood in Dale City. Rebel ambush in progress. Two officers under fire and stationary. Code 2." Code 2. The enemy was mobile and lightly armed.

Conrad and Dave hesitated for a moment and looked at each other in surprise before sprinting past a pair of officers hauling in a handcuffed and struggling prisoner. They reached the front parking lot and slid into their dark, unmarked DHS vehicle, Dave in the passenger seat, Conrad in the driver's. While Conrad started the car, Dave slipped an emergency light on the top of the car and flipped on the siren.

"What kind of weapons you have?" Dave asked as Conrad gunned the engine. The police vehicle shot through the parking lot and out on to the lightly trafficked main road.

"There's a light XMB rifle in the trunk. Not much ammo."

Dave pulled his handgun from the chest holster under his suit jacket and checked it and its magazine. Satisfied, he re-holstered it. "I guess that's what tactical teams are for. How long to get there?"

Conrad looked at the dashboard's electronic mapping screen. A blue pulsating light marked his car's current location and a stationary blinking red light marked the location of the emergency as mapped by the dispatcher. "Twenty-five minutes with the traffic remaining light."

"Two o'clock. You'll make good time."

Conrad raced on unimpeded but when he reached a nearly empty Prince William Parkway, three mid-sized cars, each one a deep maroon color and with tinted windows, appeared from around a bend behind them. Their engines roared loudly as they accelerated towards Conrad's vehicle.

"Check that out," Conrad said as he pointed his thumb backwards.

Dave looked to the rear. "I don't like it." Dave grabbed the dashboard radio. "I'm reporting this just in case."

Conrad grabbed Dave's arm. "No. I don't want to draw units away for this." Conrad looked at the rear-view mirror. The three cars were closer now and still accelerating. "If it's anything, we can handle it."

Dave drew his handgun and clicked the safety off. Conrad drew his own handgun, undid the safety too, and placed the gun in the space between the seats, grip up, barrel pointed at the floor.

The approaching vehicles were now four car lengths behind Conrad. Two of them accelerated rapidly. One passed and the other drew up parallel to him.

"Cocksuckers," Dave said low under his breath. "I'll get some fucking payback now."

"Let's see what happens," Conrad said. He moved his eyes rapidly between the three cars and then at his speedometer. He was going ninety miles per hour. The car farthest forward cut left into Conrad's lane and slowed. Conrad hit his brake quickly. Both cars slowed evenly, the tires squealing as they did.

The car to Conrad's right slowed too and pressed close to his car without making contact. The car behind them slowed and drifted into Conrad's lane. A narrow shoulder was all the space Conrad had between himself and the thick concrete barrier dividing the highway. As all four cars slowed, Conrad cursed himself for letting his car get boxed in like that.

"Braking," Conrad shouted at Dave. Dave immediately braced himself and Conrad slammed the brakes. As his car skidded to a halt, the car behind swerved to the right to avoid back-ending Conrad. The other two cars, after a moment's hesitation, slammed their brakes too. Eight pairs of tires squealed and smoked.

Dave's window began to drop.

Conrad grabbed Dave's arm. "Don't! They might be bullet-proof too."

Dave growled and his window went up again. He tapped his gun barrel against the reinforced glass. "Just you wait," he said.

Conrad kicked his car into reverse and pressed the accelerator as he turned his wheel sharply to the right. His car shot backwards in a half circle and he ended up facing the oncoming traffic. He gunned his car forward. Dave clutched the dashboard. "Shit!"

Conrad swerved around two cars as they hit their brakes. He slowed and quickly turned back in the right direction. One of the maroon cars had turned 180 degrees and was facing oncoming traffic now but the other two sat unmoving, facing the right direction.

"Just like a bull ring," Conrad said.

"Back-up?" Dave asked. He held the dispatch radio tightly.

"No. They want us to pull back-up from the ambush."

The traffic behind Conrad became tentative. Cars slowed down in their lanes or pulled to the shoulders. Conrad pressed on his accelerator. As he approached the maroon cars, they gained speed with him. Conrad stayed in the center of the parkway. "We're gonna pick them off Dave. Grab that rifle."

Dave unhooked his seat belt, lunged towards the backseat, and pulled down the back seat cushions. Dave fumbled in the back for a moment before he came forward holding the assault rifle. Dave snapped it into action. "Ready."

"Hang on." Conrad brought the car to ninety-five. He would go no faster through civilian traffic. The maroon cars took more speed and narrowed the space between pursued and pursuer. Conrad easily passed the few cars on the road ahead of him but his stomach clenched when he looked at his rear-view mirror and saw his pursuers pass the same cars. A high-speed collision involving civilians would have torn his mind and heart apart. They ate up the road for ten seconds more before Conrad began to ease off the accelerator. Dave lowered his window and stuck the barrel of his rifle out. "Okay."

Conrad double-checked the position of their pursuers. Two were side by side and the third hung back behind them. Conrad pulled his car to the right and slowed quickly. When he was abreast with the two cars, Dave rose out of the window and sat on the bottom of the frame. Conrad looked at the car to his left and two shots rang out. They ricocheted off the passenger window. Dave dropped back down into the car. "Shit."

"Yeah shit. Don't worry." Conrad jerked his car left, smacked into the left car and then pulled away. All three maroon cars moved to the left like a wave had hit them. They recovered and pulled up and past Conrad. The four cars drifted as they turned a sharp bend in the road.

"Fuck!" yelled Dave. A small, blue car loomed in front of the pursuers. Conrad pulled to the right again and slowed. The pursuing cars pulled to the left. The rear-most pursuer was too late. His car cracked into the back of the smaller car.

The struck car madly spun out of control towards the grass on the right side of the road. Conrad swerved around the blue car as it spun just in front of him. The driver sat unmoving, staring straight ahead in apparent shock through the spin. When the car's wheels hit the gravel of the shoulder, the car flipped over and landed top down on the grass.

Conrad looked away from his rear view mirror and smacked the steering wheel with his palm. "Fuck!"

Dave shot out of the window again and fired three times. The tire of one maroon car exploded. The rim of the car screeched as it cut into the road, the back end of the car swung clockwise, and then the car spun bottom over top. It made three flips before stopping. Dave dropped back into his seat. "Hah! Made for speed, not for bleed!"

"I have to slow down Dave. This is crazy."

"What's that?" Dave pointed forward, towards the sky. A Chinese Jaysing military assault helicopter flew towards them. It was the same kind of helo that had shadowed them during the assault on the rebel compound. When it was one hundred meters in front of their car, it turned 180 degrees and its 30 mm auto-cannon rattled off a second's worth of shots. The bullets ripped along the right of the car, chewing up the pavement.

"That was a fucking warning," Dave said.

"I'm stopping." Conrad pressed on the brakes.

"Where the fuck do they hide helicopters?"

"That's balls. Military helos? I can't fucking believe it. Better put that away." Conrad motioned at the assault rifle with his chin. Dave angrily threw it in the back seat.

When the car stopped, the two remaining pursuers pulled up behind Conrad. Conrad and Dave waited quietly as the helo floated fifty meters in front of them. Its pounding rotors swept the road clean of light debris and the grass along the road was lying down in abeyance to that power.

From the passenger side of one of the maroon cars, a figure clad in black, head and face covered in a white cloth, popped out holding an automatic rifle.

Dave held his handgun. "Say when."

Conrad realized their attackers could easily slide a bomb underneath the soft underbelly of their car. They would be blown up against the reinforced metal and glass of their police car and be ripped apart inside. Conrad took the radio. "Time for backup."

Another figure wearing the same black and white garb stepped out of the back seat of the other car. That person held a small girl by the arm and a gun to her head. She cringed and cried without moving. Another person in black came out of the passenger side of the same car holding a gun and a bullhorn.

"Get out of the car with your hands up," a deep voice said over the horn. "Come out or the girl will be killed."

Conrad didn't think twice. He dropped the radio and stepped out with his hands up. Dave dropped his gun and did the same on the passenger side of the car. Their hair and clothing flapped madly under the force of the helicopter's rotor-wash.

The other doors of the first car immediately opened up and four large figures in black charged Conrad and Dave. Two of them grabbed Dave's arms and pinned them behind his back. The other two did the same to Conrad.

"Chief," Dave said. One of the attackers brought a fist down on the base of Dave's skull. Dave slumped forward and the two people holding him dropped him, his body falling on the other side of the car and disappearing from Conrad's view.

"Dave," Conrad yelled. He tried to pull away from the two people who had him but they held on tightly. One of the figures on Dave's side of the car raised a pistol, looked at Conrad, and used an exaggerated motion when he pointed the gun down towards where Dave had fallen. Conrad fought harder and yelled, "Stop," but he couldn't break free. The figure pointing the gun down at Dave looked at Conrad again and smiled. A hail of bullets exploded around them.

The smiling figure's hands jerked up like they were attached to wires and his gun flew in the air. The little girl screamed and ran down the highway. Two cars had pulled to the side of the road and their drivers were raking the three cars with automatic gunfire. Concerned citizens trying to do their civic duty. They were done for.

The Jaysing helicopter swiveled towards the would-be heroes and chewed them up with its gun. The shooters literally blew apart in a mess of flesh and bone and the metal skin of their unarmored cars tore apart like paper. Tires exploded and the gas tanks of both cars caught fire.

The thunder of explosions drifted off and made way for police sirens sounding in the distance.

Two of the masked figures jumped into one car. Conrad's left arm came free. He pivoted right to free his other arm but something small and heavy, a blackjack he guessed in that split second of searing pain, cracked squarely on the lower part of his skull. His vision clouded and he pitched forward into the cold world of oblivion.

12

A long a dimly lit road, somewhere in the countryside, hazy figures ran past and ahead of Conrad. The air was misty and cold. In silence, an eagle the size of an elephant swooped down from the sky and snatched two of the runners, his sons Paul and Karl. Something black fell from the moonless sky and a wet coldness sheered across Conrad's face. Conrad bellowed and his eyes snapped open. His head swiveled from side to side in a frenzied attempt to see where he was.

He was on a chair in the middle of four concrete walls, each one ten feet from him. He sat under a cracked ceiling with his hands tied behind the back of the chair. Cold water dripped from the top of his head down his face and he had to blink his eyes tightly to clear them. A small piece of ice slipped down the back of his shirt and the touch of it against his skin straightened him up in his seat.

The chair he sat on was rigid, metal by the touch, and straight backed. Conrad tried to move his legs but his ankles were strapped to the chair's legs with thin rope. His boots and socks were gone, his blistered feet bare and cold on the floor, but he still had his business suit on. He strained to free himself but the straps held.

He shook his head and blinked again. His vision cleared. A tall, thin white man dressed in blue jeans and a black t-shirt stood in front of him holding an empty bucket. A red handkerchief covered the man's mouth and a black cloth cap was pulled low over the top of his head. Between the cap and bandana, a long, sharp nose jutted out and red puffy eyes glared at him. Another man, short, white, stocky and wearing the same garb was looking at Conrad with his arms akimbo.

"Should I do 'im again?" the tall man said. He spoke with a thick, Southern accent, maybe Georgian.

"No," the short man answered. "He's awake." The short man's words were clipped and he spoke with what seemed to be a Russian accent. He quickly walked his stocky form up to Conrad and raised an open palm over his head.

Conrad moved his head to the right, away from the anticipated blow, and felt a thin, wet rope bite into his neck. He moved his head forward. The rope allowed him only limited movement. Conrad relaxed and looked at the man.

"Speak," the man said with his palm still raised. "Who are you?"

Conrad realized they must have found his ID card but that only showed his face, an ID number, and a DHS emblem. The real information, name and the rest, was on an encrypted chip on the card, but they probably didn't have the technology to read the chip. Conrad tried to read the man's face and saw only stoicism. He shook his head. The short one brought his palm across Conrad's face and the sound of the slap filled the chamber.

Conrad's face pulsed in pain but he shook off the powerful blow. He looked away from the man's gaze and inspected the room. The walls, floor, and twelve-foot high ceiling were concrete. Light came from two places. The first source of light was two narrow, glazed windows set high in one wall through which a sliver of reddish sunlight peeked through. The second more immediate source of illumination came from two, long fluorescent lights that buzzed weakly over his head. A metal door, the one door in the room, was shut.

"You're not getting outta here," the tall man said slowly.

"Shut up," the short man shouted. "Get out."

The tall man looked at the short man's back and his eyes narrowed as if he were about to physically retaliate to the command. Instead, he slouched, turned around, and shuffled to the door. He cranked the thick metal handle of the door downwards and the door opened noiselessly. As the tall one left, the short one surprised Conrad with another hard slap to his face. "No looking," he said in his thick accent.

Conrad forced his eyes to stay open. A long hallway extended beyond the door, fluorescent lighting visible along its length. The door closed with a clang. The short man swept at the legs of the chair with his leg while pushing the back of the chair down. Conrad went backwards.

He pulled his head as far forward as he could to avoid smacking his skull against the floor. A cracking sound shattered the quiet when the metal chair hit the ground and Conrad's heart raced as he stared up at the man standing over him. The man pulled off the bandana and cap that covered his head.

Cris Alvarez

He had a hard, round face. His thick, dark hair and bushy black eyebrows were a mess and his face was covered with a layer of stubble. Crow's feet wrinkles extended from the edges of his eyes and his nose looked like it had been worked over a few times.

The man bent over and stared closely at Conrad. "Talk goddamn it," he said. The man's hot breath washed over Conrad's face. It smelled of liquor.

Conrad rested his head against the concrete. The floor was rough with the faintest of ridges and points over its surface.

Conrad rolled his head around to stretch his neck. He decided to be the interrogator. "Who are you? Where's the other officer?"

The man straightened and scratched his chest. "I am Darko. That's what you should call me. Your friend is," Darko paused and his eyes searched for a word. "Fine. Unless you don't cooperate."

Conrad wasn't afraid of Dave talking. He was a toughened veteran who knew better. Assuming Dave was still alive. "I've got nothing to say. What you're doing is a felony unless you turn me in to the authorities now."

Darko looked away and murmured almost to himself. "Well-trained probably. Lot's of time needed to break him. Okay. I have lots of time. This is my job."

Conrad took a deep breath. He knew what to expect. He had never been captured by the enemy, not in Iraq, not during the Modern-era Civil War but he had received extensive training in interrogation, both the right way and the wrong way. He had months of counter-interrogation training under his belt. Training might have been the wrong word. It had been a painful and terrifying experience.

Darko walked to the far wall and placed one hand on its surface. He turned and sprinted at Conrad. He stopped on Conrad's left, pulled his right foot book, and swung it at Conrad's head. Conrad twisted his head away but Darko stopped his foot short and simply tapped Conrad's skull with the tip of his steel-toed shoe. "Scared?" Darko chuckled.

Conrad looked at him and bit his dry lips. He was dehydrated. "Can I get the bucket one more time?"

Darko bent down, grasped Conrad by the front collar with one hand and began slapping him back and forth with his free hand. A metal ring on Darko's left ring finger kept hitting the bony edges of Conrad's face. He spit up saliva but he didn't react otherwise. After three minutes of the beating, Conrad began to feel dizzy. Darko stopped and shoved Conrad at the ground, releasing his collar. "I won't let you off so easily. You won't sleep on me."

The sound of a steady stream of water hitting the floor started up behind Conrad. It was out of his view so Conrad closed his eyes and concentrated on regaining his equilibrium. The sound was supplanted by the sharp tinkling of flowing water hitting the bottom of a metal pail and soon the sound was one of water splashing on itself. Darko chuckled and whistled a tune Conrad didn't know. Footsteps on the concrete. Cold water crashed against his face and Conrad snapped his eyes open.

The Russian bent his face down close to Conrad's again. "Maybe I fuck with your balls." Conrad winced when Darko placed his hand over Conrad's crotch and squeezed hard. Conrad gritted his teeth and howled behind them, the sound starting deep within his belly and up to his vocal chords. For ten seconds Darko squeezed before loosening his grip and standing. "I'm no fag," he said as though that would put Conrad at ease.

Conrad tried to slowly breathe away the pain that throbbed from his crotch to his gut. He tried to turn onto his side but the chair resisted his slight swaying.

Darko grabbed one of the chair's legs and held it tightly. "So maybe you talk? Where you from? What's you name? What station you from? You talk now and I give you a cigarette."

Conrad closed his eyes and thought of the questions he'd asked if their positions were switched. Was Darko actually Russian? Was he hired from outside or was he a religious immigrant? But Conrad didn't want to give the satisfaction of the sound of his voice. Worse, if Conrad started talking, he might not stop. That was the way of interrogations. Once you started talking, you were finished.

Conrad smelled smoke. He opened his eyes. Darko stood back among the shadows and a lit cigarette glowed. Conrad stared at the red tip of the cigarette and pushed the thought of Lisa out of his mind. It wouldn't do too well to think of naked women now. Darko walked close to Conrad and stood by Conrad's bare feet.

Darko squatted down and took the cigarette out of his mouth. He turned the lit end of the cigarette towards himself, looked at it, and smiled. He rubbed one of Conrad's feet dry with a sleeve and then pushed the cigarette into the flesh behind Conrad's left outer anklebone. Conrad yelled and began to thrash as the cigarette burned into his flesh.

Cris Alvarez

For a few seconds, Darko held Conrad's foot with one hand and kept the cigarette against the flesh. Darko pulled the cigarette away but the burn's sting lingered. Conrad kept kicking as though that would shake the burned skin loose from his foot but the straps around his ankles wouldn't give. Conrad clenched his teeth. At least the irritating feel of the leather straps around his lower shins helped distract him slightly from the new pain.

"Talk?" Darko asked. His voice had a soft and kindly tone.

"Nyet," Conrad said. Darko smiled. He poked Conrad's foot with the cigarette again and got the same result from Conrad. The yells filled the interior of the room. Darko pulled the cigarette away ten seconds later and stood. His face was impassive. Conrad breathed rapidly and heavily. Sweat poured from every pore in his body and his clothes felt warm and damp now rather than cold.

Darko looked at the burned out cigarette and tossed it into a thin layer of water that had pooled near Conrad. What heat remained sizzled to nothingness.

"I burn you, I beat you, I use water. I grab your balls and twist. All simple things. Maybe I use electric wires. Or maybe we hold your head underwater. Or maybe I break your fingers and toes. Or I pull your fingernails. You like all that instead? You think I don't do it? I do it. But not now. I'm hungry so I go eat. You hungry?"

Conrad stared at Darko, trying, hoping, that he was keeping his face expressionless. Darko stared at him for a moment before speaking again.

"I go eat. Maybe I bring you a little food. Some beef, some potatoes maybe. With butter. Think about the food." Darko shrugged and turned. He walked to the door and when he opened it, he let in a puff of cool air that Conrad didn't like. His clothing felt cold again and his heart was going a mile a minute. Darko closed the door behind him and the door lock clicked.

The ceiling lights went out. Only the dim light from the narrow windows kept the room from being pitch black. Conrad closed his eyes and tried to relax.

Ten minutes later, the door opened and Conrad opened his eyes with it. The door closed and the lights came on. A medium sized man wearing a dark jacket and dark pants stood by the door. His hands were tucked into his jacket pockets. He wore a black handkerchief around his mouth and he had a black kaffiyeh draped over his head. A dark blue baseball cap topped that and was pulled low over his eyes. Conrad waited for the man to speak.

Minutes passed as the man stared at Conrad. Conrad sighed, closed his eyes and rested his head on the floor.

"Quite a noble sacrifice Mr. Greis." The sound was metallic. The man was using an electronic distorter under the handkerchief to camouflage the sound of his voice.

Conrad opened his eyes and looked at the cracked ceiling. They had been playing a game with him. They knew his name and probably more than that. He didn't answer.

The man leaned against the wall and lazily crossed his arms and shins. "How's your family? Do they need to die too?"

Conrad smirked and said nothing. No need to give satisfaction. Talking would not save his family.

The man pushed away from the wall and slowly walked around Conrad. Step by step. Heel, toe, heel, toe. "You're a man of principles," he said. "I do admire that in you. You're also conservative which makes me wonder why you do this."

To protect freedom you asshole. Ever hear of that principle?

"You think you're helping the good guys don't you? The Constitution? It's just an excuse now. A piece of paper that liberals, wait you're a registered libertarian, that's right, big difference you think."

Right. A piece of paper. Just like your Bibles. Just pieces of paper.

"They use it to push an agenda Mr. Greis. Not justice or goodness. An agenda, a grab for power. Just like rulers have been doing for centuries."

Really you fuck? I'm with them and I don't see myself getting any power or fame or money out of this crap. But I still love my country and what it stands for.

"And just like the Christians of the Roman Empire Mr. Greis, we aren't free. We have these alien beliefs foisted on us. Forced on us. Drug use, abortion, gay marriage, the death penalty emasculated. Except for Christians of course. We get to die for resisting."

The death penalty is for rebels jerk off. Not Christians. Rebels and terrorist criminals.

"The country was better when we let strong Christian men with Christian values lead us Mr. Greis. Now it's a mess. But I'm not sure if you care. Regardless, we will free you and you will provide us with information on your activities. And you will do things for us that you won't like at first but you will learn to understand, respect, and even love."

"Kill his family." Darko's voice came from behind the closed door. It was clear but it sounded distant.

The man looked back at the door. "No. Killing his family gets us nowhere. He'll only hate us and try to have his revenge, if we let him live. It's a cheap useless method."

You're right. I will find you and kill you. I'll make you eat your own balls when I do.

"No. We'll take away his job. Then we take away his gun and power and his ability to protect and care for his family. He'll see what it's like to lose all that. You see Mr. Greis, do what we say, deal with us, or you lose everything you have earned to this point in your life. It's a simple deal."

Here's a simple answer. No. Conrad turned his head and spit on the ground.

The man stopped walking, pausing at Conrad's head, and squatted. He looked down at Conrad, their faces upside down to each other. "I want a Christian society Mr. Greis. It's a noble cause. The most important. It's one worth fighting for. It's worth fighting for at any cost. We do the Lord's work here on Earth Mr. Greis. There is no time out or second chance. This is it. When we are called, we will be ready to answer for ourselves and how we led our lives. I hope you understand. It's nothing personal."

Hey, I don't take it personally. Just don't take it personally either when I get you alone and show you how I feel about all this. Tyranny is tyranny bud. Whether you call it a Christian tyranny or a Christian paradise. It's all the same to me. The system is there for everyone's sake, not just yours.

"There's no getting to you is there Mr. Greis. Not only are you principled, you're stubborn too. You would make a good ally." The man stood. "Just think about it. Consider what's important to you. Pray a little for guidance. How about that?"

The man walked to the door, opened it and walked out. The door closed and the lights went out immediately afterwards. The light at the windows was gone. Conrad let the darkness carry him into a fitful sleep.

13

A sound came through the dead floor, soft footsteps on the concrete. That slight sound roused Conrad from his slumber. He opened his eyes to a grainy darkness.

The door opened slowly but no light came in. The lights in the hallway were off. Conrad turned his head slowly towards the windows set high up in the wall. No light came through them either. Everything was black. The world was unlit.

The footsteps approached. Conrad was still on the floor tied to the chair and he was lying on his right side, his feet and much of the rest of his body was numb. He wanted to move his limbs and shake them awake but he waited. Slender fingers touched him lightly on his left arm. The figure was petite and wore clothes that flowed around vapor-like. A woman.

The form of a small blade moved quickly in front of his eyes. A soft hand rested firmly on his mouth. The palm smelled clean, felt soft but firm. The other hand went behind his lower back towards his tied wrists. Conrad pulled on his straps but they held. The blade moved up and down on the straps around his wrist. He relaxed and waited. The cutting stopped and Conrad strained at the ropes again. They still wouldn't break. He shook his head and the dark figure went back to sawing. Outside of the room, footsteps sounded on metal.

She stopped cutting. In a few moments, the noise of steps quieted. She kept her hand on Conrad's mouth but only lightly. He felt moisture forming on the palm. His breath was making it damp. She didn't move. The noise, the sound of footsteps, began again but moved away. They faded into the distance. She began cutting again. She stopped.

He strained and the ropes began to give. He stopped straining. She cut quickly again and he pulled again. The straps slowly came undone and then broke. She backed away from him and he held out his hand for the blade. Point towards him, she handed it over.

First he cut the rope holding his neck and then he hurriedly cut the ropes around his ankles. He moved away from the chair quietly but the strain of sudden motion caused him to collapse on his stomach.

The blade clattered on the floor. Then everything was quiet. He rubbed and stretched his muscles and in less than a minute, he was able to stand. He moved close to the woman. She stood five foot six to his six feet. She faced him and lightly put her hands on his chest but she didn't speak.

Conrad took her wrist and moved to the door. He listened. Nothing. The door was still open but barely. He pulled it open a little more and looked out. The hallway was dark as far as he could see. She moved under his arm and stepped in front of him.

She grabbed his wrist and led him forward. The floor of the hallway was covered in linoleum and it was cold under his bare feet. The air was as damp and cool as that of a cave, but there was no breeze.

They passed several metal doors and at each one Conrad felt the urge to check for other prisoners, but he resisted. It was a difficult decision but he didn't want to raise any alarms or create a disturbance. He needed to rescue himself first and then bring back help.

He suddenly remembered Dave and reacted instinctively to the thought. He grabbed the handle of the last door and tried to turn it. It was stuck or locked. The woman grabbed his hand and shook her head. Her long hair shifted back and forth with the movement.

Conrad spoke as low as he could and close to her ear. "My friend. The man I came in with. Where is he?" She looked at him and shook her head.

"Is he around here?"

She shook her head.

"Did they bring him with me?"

She shook her head again.

"Is he dead?"

She shrugged and waited. Conrad nodded and lowered his head. "Let's go."

She led him a few more steps to a door at the end of the hall. It was set higher up in the wall than the others and two metal steps led up to it. The woman placed her hands and left ear against the door. She stepped back and nodded to Conrad.

He pulled down on the handle and the door opened. They looked into a long, dark hallway that ran perpendicular to the one they were in. They went in. The woman led Conrad twenty feet to the left and then pointed at the ceiling. Conrad looked up and saw nothing.

She pointed at the wall. Conrad moved to the wall and felt it. Small handholds were set into the concrete surface. Conrad climbed up the few feet to the ceiling. He felt along its surface until he found a metal latch near the wall. He pulled on it and something in the ceiling came loose. He pushed it open and saw moonlight. He stepped up the wall carefully and pushed the roof hatch further up. He climbed up as he pushed the hatch all the way open and let it down gently on the ground.

His arms and shoulders were out in the open. The air was warm. The ground around the hatchway was paved. He saw grass around the square of concrete and the silhouettes of three, small buildings close by.

He pulled himself out of the hole and got on his stomach to reach in. The woman had climbed towards him so he grabbed her under the arms and helped as she pulled herself out.

When they were both standing, Conrad looked her over under the quarter-moon. She was young and beautiful. Her eyes were wide and her blonde hair was long and straight down to the middle of her back. She wore a long dress and flats. Her figure was firm and curved and difficult to pull his eyes from.

Conrad shook his head clear and looked around. No one was in sight. He closed the lid carefully. A small handle on the outside was set in a recess in the lid. Conrad turned the handle to re-latch the lid.

"Show me the way out," Conrad said. She shook her head.

Conrad looked up at the yellow moon. The night sky was filled with stars. "All right," he said. He had no idea which way to go so he looked for the closest tree line. It was one hundred meters behind them. "This way."

When he took a step towards the trees, she tugged at his arm. Conrad took another step forward but she kept tugging at him to go the opposite way. Conrad looked at her quizzically. She stopped pulling and squinted her eyes at him. She crossed her arms, stood up straight and stared into his eyes, waiting for something.

"So you know the way out?"

She nodded her head.

He gave up. "Okay. Let's go your way."

She turned swiftly and crouched like an animal that had suddenly got the scent it was looking for. She went forward and Conrad followed close behind, scanning their surroundings as he did. He considered crouching too but he could see no reason to actually do it. Instead, he walked erect and watchful.

She took him through a thick hedge of un-cropped bushes and then through thick trees that grew tightly together. She walked as if she saw a path that Conrad couldn't make out. They walked that way for about three hundred feet, pushing aside thin branches, getting whipped in the face by other branches, stepping over tall heaps of vegetation, stumbling and slipping in the wet undergrowth.

Eventually the trees thinned out. The woman crouched lower but continued walking forward. Now Conrad had the feeling he should crouch and did. They stepped slower and more carefully now. The forest became a clearing and they stopped at the tree line. They knelt down in the wet dirt. It wasn't quite mud but it was slick and they had trouble keeping themselves steady.

In the field beyond stood the dark forms of multiple one story wooden buildings. Some of the buildings looked like long barracks and some like individual houses and offices. The grounds were quiet. There were no lights on. Only the moon made it possible to make anything out.

She tapped his shoulder and he turned his head. She pointed into the distance. His eyes followed her finger to a plot of land without any buildings. A low stick fence, maybe one foot high, surrounded a square of land. Near that fenced area were three large crosses fifteen feet high. A body hung from each cross, each head drooped on each chest.

"What the fuck is that?" Conrad said. He was embarrassed by the angry strain he heard in his own voice and relaxed. He looked around, saw no one, and in a crouch moved towards the crosses. The woman groped at his shirt but she made a weak attempt and her hands slipped away from his shirt as Conrad continued forward.

He had ninety-five meters to cover and he moved quickly. He looked side to side as he ran but didn't see anyone. When he reached the fenced area, he saw it was a burial area with small flat stones pushed into the dirt in intervals consistent with grave plots. A small stone cross was planted in the middle of one side of the fenced area.

Conrad glanced around again and, feeling comfortable that no one was watching him, moved in a crouch to the crosses. Three men were tied and nailed to them. Two wore torn dress shirts and slacks. One wore blue torn hospital scrubs. Conrad's heart jumped. These men were the three hospital workers that had disappeared from a Hagerstown hospital four weeks ago, men who worked in the abortion clinic of the hospital.

The feet of all three dangled at least two feet above his head. He could jump and tug at them but that would accomplish nothing. He touched the crosses. They were thick and made of a heavy wood. He pushed on one and it had no give. He guessed the crosses were buried deeply and securely in the earth. Conrad looked for something to get them down. A rope, a ladder, anything to either get him up or the crosses down. He heard footsteps and whipped around. She was running up behind him.

She shook her head wildly then stopped. She placed her hands, one on top of the other, over her heart, and then dropped her head and closed her eyes like she was asleep.

"They're dead?"

She opened her eyes, dropped her hands to her side, and nodded.

Conrad looked up at the men again. They were neither stiff with rigor mortis nor bloated. He looked at her again. "Did they die today?"

She nodded again with a grave look on her face.

Conrad looked long and hard at the crosses. He despised that visual insinuation that faith was incompatible with personal freedom. He imagined giant crosses sitting atop the Capitol Building and White House and shuddered. That was ultimately what the rebels wanted. One nation under God and Christ and no other. The crosses before him, bloodily adorned with the bodies of three law-abiding men, might as well be the red, clockwise-turning, broken crosses of eighty years ago. Nazi Germany loved Christ too.

A click and the beam of a flashlight lit them up. Conrad turned swiftly towards the beam and shaded his eyes. The light was only ten feet away.

"Who are you?" an excited voice asked.

The woman crouched in fear behind Conrad.

Conrad shrugged. "Oh, we were just admiring the executions. Couldn't sleep."

"You're supposed to be sleeping. It's curfew." The man's voice was angry but hesitant.

Conrad took a step forward.

"Hold it right there," the man behind the flashlight said. "Give me your name. I don't know your face. Drop your hand."

Conrad stopped walking and dropped his hands with his palms facing the watchman. Conrad assumed that was the man's role. The center point of the light moved towards the woman but she kept behind Conrad.

"Why's she so scared? This ain't right. I'm getting help. You stand right there."

Conrad's legs exploded towards the man. He sprinted like an animal about to die. The man stumbled back and his light pointed up at the moon. Conrad clamped his left hand over the man's mouth and grabbed him around the waist with his right. He dropped his weight on the tall, thin guard and they fall back onto the damp ground. The guard grunted when his upper back hit the ground. The flashlight fell one way and a gun fell the other.

Conrad got his right hand up to the back of the man's head and lifted his right leg up so that his knee rested firmly on the struggling man's left shoulder. He had to make a quick decision. He had nothing with which to restrain this man if he knocked him unconscious. He had one option.

He slid his left knee to the man's right shoulder to hold him down. Conrad held the thrashing man's head and chin tightly and savagely twisted it to the right. The man yelled and arched his back as much as he could but Conrad used his left hand to muffle the sound and keep the guard down. Conrad kept twisting until the man's neck audibly snapped and he went limp.

Conrad scrambled for the gun. It was an old style semi-automatic Beretta. The safety catch was still on. Conrad knelt near the body and felt sympathy for this timid, dead man who was too scared to realize he was trying to shoot a gun with the safety on. Conrad sat back on his haunches. His heart was pounding.

The woman ran to him and put her hands on his shoulders. Conrad looked at her and shook his head. She tugged on his shoulders, motioning him towards one of the barracks. He stood and moved away from the body. "Let's get the fuck out of here now." She shook her head and wouldn't stop. "What's got you so wild?"

She moved in front of Conrad and placed her hands gently on his sides. She held him like that for half a minute. She closed her eyes and rested her head against his chest. She held on to the sides of his chest and took slow deep breaths. Conrad held her waist with his left and put his right hand on the back of her head. Conrad liked how they felt together. Her warmth energized him. He looked at the crosses and thought about the dead guard.

"We'll have to move this body to the trees and then you can show me what you need to, but we can't stay much longer. They'll realize that guard is missing."

She raised her head and shrugged. Conrad gently moved her aside. He grabbed the dead guard by the waist and threw him over his shoulder. The body wasn't heavy for Conrad, maybe one hundred fifty pounds or so, but the dead man's length made him bulky and awkward to carry.

With the body over his shoulder, Conrad walked back to the trees. The woman followed close behind him. Conrad walked ten feet into the forest and dumped the body on the ground. He covered it with leaves and loose vegetation. "Now show me what you need to."

She took his hand and walked to the clearing again. She looked around nervously and, with Conrad in tow, dashed to a small brick building set among a cluster of wood buildings. When they got close to the wall of the building, she pointed at a window. Conrad cupped his hands and looked in.

Metal bars protected the inside of the glass. The building was one room, fifteen by fifteen feet, and was completely bare except for a chair and a hose. To his right, three people were sitting on the floor against one wall, their hands held over their heads with shackles and their ankles chained to the floor. There was a wooden door on the opposite end of the room. To his left, a large cross with a figure of Jesus nailed to it hung from the wall.

"Are they in danger?"

The woman shook her head slowly and shrugged.

"Are they with the compound? Is this a punishment for something?"

She nodded. She had tears in her eyes.

"Are they going to be killed?"

She shook her head.

"Good. Cause I don't have the energy to help them now. We'll get help tomorrow. Let's find a road."

The woman turned away and led Conrad back to the trees. They walked through the forest for half an hour. Conrad didn't have much of a clue whether they were moving in a straight line or were circling on themselves. His focus went in and out. His muscles became stiff again and he realized he was dehydrated and hungry. Tree branches whipped and pulled at his body and every so often his bare feet picked up a splinter or rock that pierced his skin. He realized he should have taken the guard's shoes. There was no going back now even if the could find the way.

They came to another clearing and saw the gray strip of an asphalt road. Conrad walked to its edge and looked up and down for street signs. He didn't see any.

"Okay, let's wait until dawn and I can figure out which direction we need to go. There. We can sleep in that thick clump of trees." He led the woman to a copse of trees and thick shrubs. Conrad chose to lay down in the center. He got on his back and the woman lowered herself down nearly on top of him.

He began to drift into sleep when he felt the woman move down his body. He tensed when he realized she was undoing his pants. He gulped but didn't say or do anything when she quietly and gently pulled his penis out and put it in her mouth. Conrad breathed deeply as she began giving him a blowjob.

He looked at the moon hanging over the tops of the trees. The air was lightly humid and still warm. His body was slick with a layer of dirt and sweat. A mosquito landed on his wrist and he felt a slight prick as it sucked some blood from him. He moved his other hand to it and may have squashed it.

The underbrush bit into his back and thighs. His body felt weaker and weaker. Conrad drifted away in the pleasure of what she was doing. It took him ten minutes to have an orgasm. She didn't move away when he moaned deeply and he didn't notice what she did afterwards.

At some point, he realized she had moved up to his chest again and had fallen asleep on him. He wrapped both his arms around her and drifted away into unconscious comfort.

14

C onrad sat in his chair gazing out of the large window of his office. The grass and the trees beyond were green with spring growth. Swathes of purple wildflowers dotted the wide field that stretched from his office building back to the security fence and concrete perimeter wall. The sun was overhead and bright in a nearly cloudless sky.

Dave's voice interrupted his calm. "So what's with you and the woman?"

"Huh?" Conrad swiveled his chair around. Dave, stuffed in dark pants and a white dress shirt, stood in the office doorway poking at his teeth with a toothpick. Conrad waited for Dave to speak.

The air conditioning buzzed on high and Conrad stretched the chill out of his body. It struck him that he should have been happier to see Dave there considering Dave was nearly executed just days ago. As it turned out, Dave had been left behind in the confusion. Conrad should have been happier just to be at the office himself. But he had bigger concerns.

Dave lazily pushed off the doorframe and straightened up. "So what's going on?"

"What in the hell are you talking about? Nothing's going on. She rescued me because she wanted to get out of there."

"Okay, got it." But Dave looked unconvinced.

"What about the surveillance?" Conrad asked.

"Yeah. Just got the report back. Everything abandoned."

"Any weapons?"

"Clean, clean, clean. They swept out of there. It was a registered religious commune. With a bunch of hardened underground spaces too."

"Guess they didn't conduct any live fire practice there."

"Naw. Just a convert collection site flying under the radar."

Conrad winked at Dave and frowned. "Interrogation center too."

"Glad you can make jokes chief." Dave made a fist with his left hand and bounced it off the side of his thigh a few times. "But what about that woman? Is she really staying with you?"

Conrad tilted his head. He felt a little twinge on the right side of his neck. He reached for the pain and rubbed it. "Ah, how'd you know about that?"

"Shit boss, we all talk. Everyone talks."

"Fuck," Conrad said low under his breath. "She's in the hospital now so don't worry about it."

"Yeah. I know. Can I rest the dogs?"

Conrad shook his head absentmindedly. He should have known the gossip would spread like wildfire. Who wouldn't talk? What he was doing was insane but at least it was the first time he had ever done something like this. Maybe he could talk his way out of the second-guessing everyone was doing. Conrad pointed at the chair with his chin. "Go on. Close the door and say your peace."

Dave sighed deeply. He closed the door behind him and pulled the chair out methodically. He sat down like he was testing the seat for the first time. Once he was comfortable, he leaned back and relaxed. "You really worried about her protection?"

"Someone's giving out secrets. Maybe someone here."

"But if someone's following you-"

"Maybe we got a mole."

"Maybe you're being followed. Sure it's nothing else boss?"

"What something else?"

"She's pretty and young. Looks like Mary a little too."

"Damn Dave. You can't be serious."

"When's the last time you got a piece of ass boss? Stress like that makes a man horny." Dave wasn't smiling.

"This is professional Dave. She's a great source, a damned perfect source, and we need to protect her. We have to protect her."

"Getting any info from her?"

Conrad looked at the wall. These questions were making him impatient and grumpy. "Not yet."

Dave nodded and the corners of his mouth went up. "FBI could protect her just fine couldn't they?"

Conrad's face got warm and his temples pulsed. "Hell no! They don't know what they're doing. She's scared and they wouldn't take that into consideration."

"They can pull her whenever they want boss. It's their prerogative."

"What do they know? They don't know what things are like for her."

Dave lifted his forearm from the armrest and planted his cheek on his fist. "You know how to treat her right chief?"

Dave looked too smug for Conrad's taste. "What's your problem?" he snapped.

"Not just me sir. Everyone's worried. Blounts, Lina-"

Conrad put up his hand to stop Dave. "Okay. What are they worried about?"

"You're stressed. You're focused on things other than the investigations and the operations."

Conrad was incredulous. "She's not part of the investigations?"

"Sir, stop BSing me and stop BSing yourself. You don't need to protect her like this. In fact, you shouldn't be protecting her at all."

"I'll put in an SF 19-578 and force the FBI to do an administrative hearing on this matter."

"What? That's for an entirely different situation boss. You know it won't fly."

Conrad pushed himself away from his desk. "You think you got it all figured out. Boss is tired. Boss is cranky. Must need some pussy. Hey. It's not as simple as all that." Conrad's chest tightened. He rose hastily and banged his left knee into his desktop. He grunted and swore and turned towards the window.

Dave capitulated. "Okay chief. I hear you."

Conrad crossed his arms and turned back towards his desk. His chest kept getting tighter and he pressed his crossed arms against his torso as he spoke. "You better fucking hear me. I'm going to watch out for this woman. If she gets killed because I didn't keep an eye on her... no. I couldn't live with that. Got me? I'm the one that got kidnapped, got smacked around, almost got killed."

Dave was hunched over now and looked nervously at Conrad. He clasped his hands together and kept glancing at the floor. Conrad continued. "I care about this investigation and I'm going to be front line on this. I'm not going to hand off responsibility for this source to a bunch of stupid glory-seeking suits who couldn't give a damn about her."

Dave leaned forward on the armrests of the chair. It creaked under his weight. "Sorry boss. Just speaking for the office."

"Well you spoke and I listened so we got it all straightened out now. She's staying with me and that's it."

"Yup. Got it." Dave pushed himself up out of the chair and left the room without another word. He left the door wide open. Conrad walked to the door and closed it with more force than he expected to. He coughed nervously and returned to the window to stare at the back lot. The pressure in his chest was still there but it was easing.

When the phone rang, Conrad looked at his wall clock. He had been standing and staring out the window for about fifteen minutes since Dave had left. He snatched the phone from its cradle. "Hello?"

"Chastey Presbyterian Hospital for Conrad Gries." It was a woman's voice.

Conrad pressed the phone tighter against his ear. "Speaking."

"The operation is done sir. Sort of."

"She's okay then?"

"We've checked her vocal chords but there wasn't anything wrong with them. We didn't have to do anything surgically speaking."

"So what's the matter? She hasn't spoken once since I, uh, met her. I thought she was mute."

"We think it's a psychological issue."

"That's," Conrad paused, not sure how to answer, "strange, isn't it?"

"Well yes. But we won't tell her all that yet. We'll see how she reacts to the fake operation. She's resting right now."

"Good. How late can I come in to see her?"

The woman on the other end of the line laughed for a moment and Conrad liked the sound of it. "Well, since it's official business you can come anytime. It's not a social visit sir." The woman laughed again.

"No of course not," Conrad said. He was smiling broadly and he rubbed the grin out with his right hand. "I, huh, I wasn't thinking. How funny I said that. Yeah, it's official."

"Well normal visiting hours are 9 a.m. to 10 p.m. if you'd like to know."

"Okay, thanks. I'll be there soon. Half an hour."

"Thank you sir." The line clicked.

Conrad looked at the phone then placed it in its cradle. He walked into the common area. It was empty and quiet and all the office doors were closed. He closed his door, walked to the low security gate at the front of the room and looked the place over but couldn't see anything unusual or out of place. Still unsatisfied, he left for the hospital.

15

The Chastey hospital was situated on the top of a broad, green hill in suburban Arlington, Virginia. It was a serene location surrounded by blocks of well-kept, detached, single-family houses. The area of the hospital and the neighborhood was quiet, ordered, clean and the sun still shined brightly overhead when Conrad arrived. There must have been an apple pie baking somewhere close by.

He drove into a covered parking garage attached to the facility and made his way to the front desk. A chubby, pleasant woman directed him to the wing of the hospital where his rescuer was recuperating. Conrad didn't have a name for her yet. He and the government simply referred to her as Janet Dower.

Conrad hurried past slow shuffling elderly patients to the elevators, waited an eternity to enter and exit the lazy machine, and finally found himself in a world of wide, sterile hallways. He saw Janet's wing and paused for a full minute before entering through the double doors. The attendants at the nurses' station glanced up at him but he passed them without speaking. He saw the room number. Two uniformed guards stood on either side of the open door. Feeling agitated, Conrad took the red baseball cap off his head.

One guard looked at him severely. "You can't stand here sir."

He felt silly holding his cap like a humble beggar before these men. He had exchanged his suit for a polo shirt and jeans and probably looked like some spectator off the street trying to figure out why the police were there. Shame and a sudden anger gave Conrad his courage back. "I'm Conrad Greis. DHS."

The officer looked confused. "Homeland Security?"

"Yes." Conrad took his wallet out of his pant's front pocket. He flipped it open and showed the badge.

The officer nodded and straightened. "Sorry sir. I don't know your face."

"That's fine. Can I go in?"

"Oh. Yes sir. Please."

The second officer folded his arms and looked straight ahead.

Conrad nodded at them and walked through the doorway. The tips of his nerves began to tremble again. What am I scared of? he wondered. He felt like a guilty child waiting for the principal to call him in. He nervously twisted the cap in his hand.

She was lying in bed with her eyes closed. She might have been resting only, not sleeping. He wondered if he should leave but he changed his mind. All he wanted to do was see her.

Feeling silly again, he looked around at the ordinary room laid out before him. Bed, chairs, desk, television. The curtains were drawn and only a small stream of sunlight entered the room. Janet turned her head towards him and opened her eyes. Conrad froze. Her face was neutral for a few seconds until the corners of her lips lifted into a smile. Conrad tried to smile back. He walked closer to her and put his hand lightly on the railing of the bed. "You all right?"

"Yes. How are you?" Her voice was raspy and lacking in strength, but however long she had been silent before Conrad thought she spoke well enough now.

He fiddled with his cap. "Oh, well I'm good. "You?" He shook his head in annoyance for repeating the question.

She laughed and the musical sound tore pleasantly at Conrad's heart. "Still good."

Conrad nodded. "Ah." He cleared his throat and decided to ask a real question. "Can I, uh, ask you your name?"

She smiled without opening her mouth. "My name." She looked at the ceiling and pulled one hand out from under the sheet that covered her from the chest down. She lightly touched her bare throat. "There are no bandages."

"They have new techniques. They just go in through your mouth." Conrad tried to smile but he felt guilty about lying to her only sixty seconds into the conversation. He reminded himself that the doctors felt it would help to lie about the operation, at first, to get her to speak again. But she was speaking just fine and lying seemed unnecessary to him. He wanted to change the subject. He put his hand on her bed railing. "Your name-"

"My throat is sore." She spoke to the ceiling. "That makes sense. I haven't spoken for, for," she paused and wrinkled her eyebrows. "I haven't spoken for ten years I think Conrad."

Cris Alvarez

His grip on the railing tightened. "How do you know my name?" He quickly relaxed. It could easily have been a guard or a doctor who told her.

"At the camp, they talked about you all the time. They hated you. They wanted you. And then they finally got you."

Conrad's chest tightened and a thickness filled his skull. Proper procedure would have been to interrogate her over this, begin with a little light questioning, go to heavier ones. He didn't want to do it. "But what is your name?"

"My name is Lydia."

Conrad searched for the appropriate remark. "That's a beautiful name."

"That's the name that used to be yelled at me. Whenever I yelled."

"I thought you couldn't speak."

Her eyebrows rose. She looked sad. "I spoke when I was a child. I screamed really. All the time. I don't know why. I remember being in the dark a lot. I was beaten all the time for screaming."

Conrad lifted his hand from the railing. He reached out to smooth her blonde hair but his hand hesitated in the air. She looked at it without expression. He reached forward and lightly touched her forehead. He gently stroked her blonde hair back. She smiled and sighed. She closed her eyes and he stroked her forehead twice more. He put his hand back on the railing and she opened her eyes. "I liked that very much Conrad. Do it whenever you like."

His eyes ran over the length of her lithe body. From her chest down she was covered by a sheet, but he could see the curves of her shape under the thin cloth. His eyes lingered here and there on her body and then he looked at her eyes again. He remembered his questions. "And then you stopped speaking?"

"Yes. I couldn't speak. I must have torn my speaking muscle or something. That's what they said at the camp. And since I couldn't make noise, some of the men and boys used to take me out back and play with me." She looked at the foot of her bed and frowned.

Conrad's throat tightened. He swallowed a lump that suddenly formed there. "So you didn't like it?"

She spoke softly. "I hated it. But they didn't care. They did it a lot but they always made sure I never got with child. Those boys would have been punished hard for that. Very hard. I would have been punished worse though."

Conrad lowered his head and closed his eyes. He wanted to be angry but now he only felt sadness. He realized he was gripping the bar too tightly with his hands. He relaxed. Lydia put one hand on top of Conrad's hands.

"I knew you were the one to save me when they brought you." Her voice was still raspy, her words spoken hesitantly. "They brought others but they didn't scare anyone. I could tell by how they spoke that you scared them."

Conrad tapped the bottom of the bed with his shoe. "I'm sorry they hurt you so much."

"That's okay," she said. "I knew God would save me eventually. So I waited patiently."

Conrad wasn't one to believe in coincidences or divine intervention. A worm of suspicion burrowed into his mind. "How did they know about me?"

"They said you made a mess of everything. That you were catching everyone in the area, finding all their secret places. They had to deal with you."

Conrad looked at the open doorway. The tip of one officer's cap bobbed in low conversation. He was feeling the old Conrad, the professional Conrad, taking over. It felt good. "Did they hire someone to get me?"

Lydia shrugged. "They brought someone I never saw before. I didn't know if he was from another church or commune."

"Did he seem religious?"

Lydia shook her head and pursed her lips thoughtfully. "No. He was drunk a lot. Some church members didn't like that but they were told to be quiet. He looked at me once in a way that scared me too. He grabbed me when no one was around and pressed me against a wall."

Conrad gritted his teeth and then took a deep breath to relax.

"He put his hand under my skirt and touched me. I tried to scream but..." She touched her throat. "I couldn't. But something scared him when he looked at me and he backed away. I ran and he never bothered me again."

"That's fine. Don't think about it." Conrad's neck felt warm and he became dizzy. He blinked tightly and shook his head to clear the rising heat.

Lydia nodded and pulled the blanket up to her neck. She smiled and opened her eyes wide as though anticipating something from Conrad.

"What was his name?"

Her face and voice dropped in response. "Alexander. You said don't think about it."

"Okay, okay," Conrad said. "When you're done here, you'll come back to stay with me, under my protection."

"Yes. I like how you hold me. I miss it already."

The old Conrad struggled to hold on. They had done nothing sexual since that first night. He had done only that in his bed, held her firmly to him. He had to remember his duties.

The words resisted coming out. "It'll be official you know." They mocked him with their dalliance. "Protective custody. Others will want to ask you questions."

"About the camp?"

"Yes. And the people there."

Lydia gave a thin smile again and slid her hands under the covers. She turned away from Conrad. "I don't want to remember any of that. I don't want to talk about the past." She turned her head, but not her body, back towards him. "I want to talk about good things now Conrad."

She let her head sink into the thick pillow. Conrad wanted, desired, to touch her thin shoulder but he didn't. He looked down at the floor and a minute later, having gotten no other response from Lydia, turned to the door and walked out.

Conrad paused next to the officer who had stopped him before. "Make sure she's completely safe," he said. "Keep someone under the window too. I'll give your supervisor those instructions as well."

The officer twisted his lips and his eyebrows came together. "Yes, sir, we're watching out."

"Good. Good, keep on it." And he hurried off without looking back.

16

H unching over his computer keyboard, Conrad typed as quickly as he could. He was incredibly frustrated and he took it out on the keys. The database he was using was not user-friendly and it wasn't providing him the assassin profiles he wanted to see. He had tried narrowing the search fields to country of residence, ethnicity, description, accent and whatever else he could think of but the computer was giving him nothing he could use.

He stopped and leaned back when he realized that he would simply have to search picture by picture to find Alexander in the database. He dropped his chin into his palm and leaned his elbow on the table. Outside the window, the wind had picked up. Tree leaves snapped furiously and dark clouds skidded across the sky. Someone tapped on the frame of his door. Dave stood there looking worried.

"What is it?"

"Have you been checking your e-mail?"

Conrad glanced at the tool bar running along the bottom of his computer screen. It indicated that he had new messages he hadn't checked. The message light on his phone blinked. He had turned the ringer off earlier to avoid interruptions. "No. Why?"

Dave held a sheet of paper out towards Conrad. "This came in the general mailbox." He moved tentatively towards Conrad's desk.

Conrad stood and leaned over his desk to take the paper from Dave. The official DHS seal took up the top of the sheet and his bureau head's signature graced the bottom. He scanned the letter's contents. 'Occoquan Freedom Station Chief Conrad Greis, you are hereby placed on temporary administrative leave pending counseling over your recent kidnapping.' Conrad glossed over the rest of the standard admin prattle. "What the fuck is this?"

Dave shrugged. "It's what it is sir."

"It says that you're to relieve me while I'm on leave."

Dave shoved his hands in his pockets. "Yeah. Effective immediately."

"Makes sense. Happy?"

Dave looked mortified. "What? No I'm not happy."

"You always wanted full control of your own station," Conrad said. He handed the sheet back to Dave and dropped back in his chair. He should have expected this. He had spent each of the last five days checking up on Lydia until her discharge from the hospital the yesterday. He had told the FBI he would keep her at the station in a protective house within the compound. At the last minute, he went with his original plan to keep her at his Georgetown apartment instead.

Dave pulled his hands from his pockets and tucked his thumbs into his belt. He kicked at the ground. "I'll need your badge, weapon and ID sir. The office keys and the patrol car keys too."

"I know Dave, I've done this to others."

"Shit chief. I didn't ask for this." Dave shifted his weight back and forth and tugged at his belt.

"You're gonna pull your pants off there Dave."

Dave looked up and quickly folded his arms across his chest. "Goddamn it. This isn't easy."

Conrad stood and walked over to his window. He rapped at it hard with one knuckle. "You're happy as a pig in shit to be taking over this office though."

"That may be but I don't like it done this way."

"So that's it? Out on my ass with no badge?"

"I...yeah I guess so."

Conrad looked past Dave at the common area. "Everyone know?"

"Not yet. They're all out."

Conrad looked out the window again. The trees were being blown back and forth by a strong wind now. Trash skipped over the surface of the grass. "What's the scuttlebutt gossip?"

"Still shacked up with that rebel?"

Conrad looked back at Dave "I've got official custody of her for now. Yes." A dark thought crossed Conrad's mind.

Dave still had his arms crossed. "Protective service sir?"

"Look, she saved my fucking life."

"She'd be safe with the FBI wouldn't she?"

Conrad walked past Dave to his thermostat. "What's wrong with the air conditioning in here?"

"It feels fine."

"Why do people mess with this thing? Seventy two degrees is what I like."

"Chief. Why do you have to be so close with this woman?"

"She saved my life."

"You said that already."

Conrad glared at Bronson and then hit the thermostat with his palm. "It's too damn cold in here. What're you gonna keep it at?"

"Don't you think it looks a little strange sir? Living with the enemy?"

"There's nothing to it Dave. And you can tell that to any anti-terrorism or CI guys the FBI is sending around here when I'm out of the office."

Dave wrinkled his forehead and looked down.

Conrad went back to his chair and sat down. He pulled his wallet out and dropped it on the table. "I don't think she'd be as safe as you think she would in government custody."

"They're professionals."

Conrad's heart twisted in his chest. "Are they picking her up now?"

"Uh," Dave's Adam's apple rolled in his throat. He folded his arms tighter across his chest. "No. Why?"

"When do I transfer her to your custody? "

"Just bring her to the FBI office at Penn later this afternoon." Dave stared at the floor again and stood there silently. Wet spots showed under his armpits.

"You're not cold. You're sweating up a storm."

Dave wrinkled his forehead and looked up at Conrad. He pulled the visitor's chair out and sat down.

Conrad leaned forward. "Dave. Maintain custody of her. Delay the paperwork. Let her stay at my place. You know she's safer there."

"No, I don't. And I can't do that. Not now."

"You signed the transfer orders already?"

"No. It's something else."

Conrad gave Dave a hard stare. "What is it?"

Dave grunted and then jumped out of his seat with a yelp. He was looking out Conrad's window at a uniformed officer patrolling the grounds outside.

"It's just the patrol. What's got you so damn nervous?"

"I'm not supposed to say anything."

"You think I need to know it?"

"Yeah. It's hard to believe."

"Goddamn it, Dave, talk."

"Someone up in HQ thinks you're not being square about your relations with the rebels."

The blood left Conrad's face and his spine dropped out of his back. He slumped in his seat and spit his words out like venom. "Those dirty motherfuckers. Who thinks that?"

"People. They say you seem to peg those rebel houses pretty easily."

"We're a good investigation house."

"Someone thinks that maybe you're playing sides."

"Meaning?"

"You know. Getting info from one rebel group on another one they don't like."

"So I let one rebel group go wild as long as they slip me info to keep me looking good."

"Something like that. I don't know. It's all bullshit talk." Dave shrugged. "What can I say?"

"It's not your place to say anything about idiots. Those goddamn fuckers sit in their DC offices and just make up wild ideas don't they?"

Dave smiled wanly. "All the time sir. They've got nothing better to do."

Conrad opened a large drawer on the right side of his desk and reached in. His heart was pounding as he gripped the handle of his official sidearm. He stared at Dave while he held the gun. Dave shifted his weight in his chair and wiped a hand on the front of his shirt. "Jeez, chief. You're looking a little pale there."

Conrad gripped the gun tighter and slowly lifted it from the drawer. His heart raced. Dave straightened in his chair and gripped his armrests. Conrad closed his eyes and shook his head. He relaxed the grip on his gun and placed it on the desk next to his wallet. He opened the wallet and removed his DHS badge and the official ID card that went with it. He dropped the badge and card on the gun. He closed the drawer and swiveled to face the window.

"Are you all right Rad?"

Conrad closed his eyes. "Just take the fucking things before I decide not to go quietly."

17

C onrad swirled his whiskey glass over the mahogany bar top, leaving small wet circles in its wake. He adjusted himself on the padded stool on which he sat and looked up at the long mirror behind the bar. Behind him about two dozen patrons flirted, danced and sat around in the reflection. Conrad smiled bitterly at himself.

He normally liked the atmosphere here. Every so often, when he had a few free hours after work, he'd drop by this bar, the old Georgetown Western Ranch House. It was a small drop of pleasure in the urban sea that was metropolitan Washington, DC. It tried hard to capture a country-western feel and did a passable job at that. Best of all, it was an easy walk of five blocks from his apartment building.

He turned towards the dance floor and reclined in his stool, his back pressed against the edge of the bar. Western trinkets and paintings of Texas and the Southwest decorated the place. Across a worn, hardwood dance floor, a five piece bluegrass band performed classic country hits on a small, cramped stage directly opposite Conrad.

Heads bounced up and down as dancing couples moved to the quickstep beat the band was playing. It was a tune whose title Conrad couldn't remember but which reminded him of the good years between his time in the sandbox and the Civil War. He'd have liked to be dancing out there right now. Maybe Lydia danced the two-step. That was one he could do just fine with the right tune.

"Still daydreaming cowboy?" Melissa stepped up to Conrad, pulled out a stool and dropped into it facing the bar. She wore a pair of blue jeans over her thick lower body and a faded, red t-shirt that read 'Bermuda Triangle Bar, North Carolina'.

Conrad looked into his half full glass. "Just feeling sorry for myself." He reached back to put the glass on the bar.

Melissa clapped Conrad on the back. "You must have some friends around here who actually like country music. But I suppose I can stand it for a night. Here's to Seattle." She smiled broadly at Conrad, lifted her beer glass once, and tossed it back, draining the entire thing in one go. She exhaled happily when she banged it down on the bar.

"It's beautiful music Melissa. Just got to let it in you."

"Okay Dibs. Maybe one day."

Conrad nodded. "Yeah. One day."

"So how're you doing buddy? Doesn't look like they beat you up too badly after all was said and done."

"Yeah. I gave worse than I got definitely."

"Not many people could do what you did Dibs. Not at your age."

"My age?"

"You ain't a young buck, wide-eyed and ready for action. You're a thinking man now. People our age have to live by our wits."

"Still a stone cold killer though."

Melissa waved towards the bartender. "Bad dreams at all?"

"Naw."

"Fuck Dibs. I haven't killed a person dead-on in three years just about. Damn desk jobs."

Conrad leaned his elbows back on the bar. "You ain't missing nothing Mel."

"Still thinking about Lydia?" Melissa asked.

Conrad looked back at his drink, snatched it off the bar, and polished it off. He banged the glass down on the counter top. "Yeah."

"You're in love with an idea Dibs, not a person. You want freedom. The personal kind."

"Aahh. What do you know? " Conrad glanced back at his glass and saw a filled shot glass next to it. The bartender, Sam, gave him a tight smile and a quick salute. Conrad lifted the glass to Sam in toast and then swallowed the shot. It was tequila and he groaned. "Damn that burns."

The bartender took Melissa's glass and filled it from the tap. She nodded when he handed it back to her and she took a gulp of the frothy beer. "Good stuff." She smacked her lips. "You didn't answer me."

"Ah Melissa, do you remember a time when the birds chirped and the flowers bloomed?" Conrad gave a hearty laugh. "Fuck me."

Cris Alvarez

"Now you admit it. It's a fantasy of what could have been."

"Melissa. I need this. She's damn hot, she likes me and she saved my life. What more can a man ask for?" Conrad laughed bitterly now. The quickstep ended and the band started up with a Cotton Eyed Joe piece.

"This isn't going to get you anywhere but into trouble. Keep work at the office. Know what I'm saying?"

"Fuck it. I've already lost my job. Goddamn system. To think I trusted them to know what's right and what's wrong."

"Stop talking like that Dibs. You haven't lost your job. They just need to look into things to feel comfortable about you again. Enjoy the time off."

"Fuck the system and fuck you Mel. Why the hell are you defending them?"

"Hey, I'm trying to save your hide buddy."

"Aaah, I don't want saving right now. People are trying to kill me left and right. I'll take what good things I can get right now. Nag me for it when I'm dead."

"So you think you can trust her?"

"The gut," Conrad poked his stomach with a finger, "says yes." The music changed rhythm mid-song. "Hey listen. It's a Cajun two-step. Bayou Buckeye. Come on."

"Aw shit Dibs."

Conrad shimmied out of his seat and grabbed Melissa by the arm. She stretched over her stool to grab her glass and get one more gulp of beer. She smacked the glass down and let Conrad lead her to the moderately crowded dance floor.

"Now come on," Conrad said. He grabbed Melissa by the waist with his right and held out his left hand. Conrad's boots gave him the few inches he needed to look Melissa straight in the eye.

She shook her head. "I'm two left feet." She put her left hand on Conrad's shoulder and took his hand with her own.

"Okay now," Conrad said. "Left, right, leeefft, slow on that one, wait, right wait, even. Good. Again."

"This isn't natural Dibs."

"What are you talking about?" Conrad kept dancing with his eyes moving up and down from his feet to Melissa's mortified face.

"My rep's going to be shot if anyone sees me doing this."

"Well I appreciate the sacrifice. Hey no. Right foot there. Then left. Okay. You're getting it."

"You better get a girl soon who can do this with you. Remind me to send her a bottle of wine when she does."

"You're doing just fine." The music kidded up a notch and they started to move a little faster.

Conrad and Melissa danced the floor, around and between the other couples, through the entire song. Conrad kept laughing at Melissa's reluctance to get into the mood of the dance. She shook her head and laughed boisterously with each misstep she made. When the song ended, they separated and joined the crowd in clapping for the band.

"Had enough?" Melissa asked.

"Yeah sure, for now," Conrad said with a laugh. They walked back to the bar and collapsed on their stools laughing.

Almost immediately, a young couple dressed western style approached them. "You looked like you were having fun out there," the young man said.

"One of us at least," Conrad said looking sidelong at Melissa.

The man held out his hand. "I'm Dwight."

Conrad took Dwight's hand and shook it firmly. "Conrad."

The young stranger was thin, a little shorter than Conrad, with a wild head of short brown hair and a smoothly shaven face. He wore blue jeans and a blue denim dress shirt emblazoned with a sunset and wild mustangs. He had dressed his feet in brown, stylized boots and his head was topped by a tan cowboy hat that made him look a little too stylish.

Dwight motioned to his smiling companion. "This is Sissy." Sissy was slight as well and shorter than Dwight by three inches. She had a full head of brown wavy hair that hung down just past her shoulders. Her face was pretty, not too sharp featured but rather soft and warm. She matched her man's western looks with narrow red boots, blue jeans and a pink blouse.

"This is Melissa," Conrad said. Dwight tipped his hat to her and Sissy shook Melissa's hand.

"Come here often?" Conrad asked.

Cris Alvarez

"Often enough," Dwight said. "Like to dance. We was resting when we saw you two dance. You were having fun. I like that."

"Thanks," Conrad said. "Can I get you a beer?"

Dwight nodded. "I will. Sissy's okay."

Conrad noticed the bartender's gaze linger on Dwight and Sissy as he drew a beer from the tap.

"Mind if we sit?" Dwight asked.

"Naw. Pull a couple up."

Dwight and Sissy slid a couple of stools close to Conrad and Melissa and sat. They both smiled broadly.

"I haven't heard these guys before," Conrad said motioning back towards the bluegrass band.

"I don't listen to country at all," Melissa said with a laugh. "He dragged me here."

"That's all right," Dwight said. "You two seem like good old Americans and that's good enough in my book."

Conrad smiled with one side of his mouth and felt a little heavy in his stomach. He sighed heavily. "What do you do Dwight?"

"For a living?" Dwight asked.

"Yup."

"Drive trucks cross-country."

"A little dangerous isn't it," Conrad said.

"It's all right," Dwight said. "I don't have much trouble."

Don't have much trouble? There were only two kinds of people who lasted long in cross-country truck driving these days. Rebels or people who the rebels liked. Not that rebels controlled all the roads but they controlled enough of the roads to make it necessary for a truck driver to be wary. You either expressed your sympathy to the rebels with cash or favors. That's how it worked outside the big cities. Conrad didn't feel friendly anymore. "So you pay protection money?"

Dwight shrugged and looked insouciantly at the wall. "You do what you need to. To survive. War took a lot of people out. Good people." The bartender dropped a beer in front of Dwight and Dwight took it. "What about you Conrad? Construction or something?"

Conrad glanced at his own arm. He was wearing a short-sleeved shirt and his thick biceps and forearms showed. He sensed

Melissa's gaze on him. "How about we say I do construction for the government."

"Yeah? What sort of facilities you work on?"

Conrad furrowed his brow. "Warehouses."

Dwight clasped his hands together in his lap and looked down at them. "I'm glad to hear it's not more freedom stations or forts. Damn government wants to kill every good person in this country."

"What do you know about good people," Melissa said. She scowled at the mirror.

Sissy lifted her chin and straightened her back. "Good family people. People who like the simple joys, like country music. People with values."

"You don't happen to be talking about the kind of values that lead people to hide out in the woods and kill people they don't like are you?" Melissa asked.

"Now take this," Dwight said, gesturing towards the dance floor. "A couple of faggots dancing together in a country bar. Can you believe it?" He sipped his beer. Conrad looked over at two pairs of men dancing to the latest song. He hadn't noticed them until Dwight mentioned it.

"This is DC," Conrad said. He looked at Dwight out of the corner of his eye. Dwight looked like he had just sucked on a sour lemon.

"Yeah, you're right. What should I expect from a country bar in the city? Everything's twisted around now."

"What else don't you like?" Conrad asked. He looked at Melissa. She was hunched over the bar and her beer and was still glowering at the mirror. "Don't break it hun," Conrad said to Melissa. She ignored him.

"Lots of it," Dwight said. "I don't like all this drug business, illegals having an easier time here."

"Lots of guns," Conrad said.

"Yeah, I like the guns," Dwight said. "I got twenty nice ones back home. Couple of automatic rifles too and a couple of grenades. But that's about all the good that came from the government lately. Still don't know if it's worth it."

Conrad nodded. "So what do you propose to do about it?"

"Well damn," Dwight said. "Them rebels are doing something about it aren't they." Dwight looked at Sissy and put his hand on her thigh. She smiled back at him and covered his hand with hers.

Conrad relaxed. Dwight was nothing but a simpatico who liked to talk a lot. Conrad's voice lost its grit. "Those rebels are doing nothing but making the situation worse. If you don't like the law, then just vote. Remember democracy?"

"Aw shit," Dwight said. "You're scared. You work for the government so you just plain agree with how they do things. It's all about the money ain't it. You like all this gay loving and drugs and all that garbage?"

"Look. I don't have a problem with who people fuck and yeah, people are taking too many drugs. But hell, at least now they're out in the open and they're getting treatment when they need it."

"Come on honey," Sissy said. "I'm getting warm." She slipped her arm under Dwight's and pulled closer to him.

"Hell no," Dwight said. "Junkies are out there getting into accidents and doing stupid stuff that gets innocent people killed."

"Look," Conrad said. He turned on his stool towards Dwight and emphatically counted on his fingers. "One, all those damn Mexican drug lords aren't making any more money. Two, you don't have crack whores stealing to pay for their shit. Three, ghetto kids aren't gunning themselves down anymore over drug turf."

Dwight shook his head. "Look mister. Good people weren't having problems with these things. It stayed in the ghetto where it belonged. Now drugs are legal and see how they crept into good homes? And then you have all these dudes," Dwight's face sucked on a sour lemon again, "running off left and right ass-fucking each other and getting married so they can adopt kids and teach them to be fags. It ain't right."

"So what's right? Born again?"

"I see where you're going. Well I ain't so religious at all. But I know what's right. I know how a community should be. We can't move ahead with this degenerate crap all around us. We gave in to everything wrong when we let those damn Democrats begin running things and win the war."

"Let's get out of here," Sissy said.

"Yeah maybe you two kids should run along," Melissa said.

"Now I don't fight women but you need to apologize to Sissy right now," Dwight said.

Melissa stood and took a step towards Dwight. She towered over the thin man and obviously outweighed him in the ways that counted. She clenched her fists and her face turned red.

"All right now. Let's not have trouble." Sam leaned over the bar and held his hand out as though it could form an invisible wall between the Melissa and Dwight.

Dwight shook his head and slapped his hat against his thigh. He stood and looked at Conrad and Melissa. "The two of you need to figure out what's right here. You looked like good old folks but I suppose a man can be wrong every now and then. But I'm charitable. Maybe you'll figure the truth out one day and figure out what you actually believe. I'll be seeing you." He took Sissy by the arm.

Melissa unclenched her fists. "Take your holier than thou garbage out of here."

"To hell with you," said Dwight. He and Sissy walked to the exit and left the bar.

Conrad tapped his aching forehead. "Shit." He wanted to slug the kid but he didn't operate that way. He let every man or woman have their opinion and their say as long as they didn't swing or shoot when they said it.

"Sorry about that Conrad," Sam said.

"Naw. It's all right. I've dealt with worse."

"I feel terrible about that Conrad. Vets don't need to get talked down to by a young punk who doesn't know what's what."

"Aw don't worry Sam. It was kind of fun. Thought I would see Melissa get into an old-fashioned brawl. Haven't seen that in a long time."

Melissa turned her gaze from the exit to Conrad. "Shut up," she said and sat back down on her stool.

Sam managed a smile. "Well not in here please." He straightened up and moved to the other end of the bar.

"What the fuck do they know?" Melissa said. "Assholes."

"Let's get out of here." Conrad pulled a twenty and ten from his wallet and slapped it on the bar.

"I want to finish my beer."

Conrad sat while Melissa fumed over her glass. It took her ten minutes to drain it and by then her demeanor had softened. "Okay, I'm done."

Conrad waved to Sam and walked out of the bar with Melissa. The dimly lit parking lot was empty of people but filled with cars. Conrad looked up and around at the lights of the office buildings that surrounded them, new buildings that towered twenty stories or more. Sixty feet away, the edge of the parking lot sloped down to meet the calm surface of the Potomac River.

"Boy, DC was nicer before all the skyscrapers," Melissa said.

Conrad shrugged. "Times change. When are you flying back to Seattle?"

"Day after tomorrow," Melissa said. She took out a marijuana cigarette from her chest pocket and lit up. She took a few puffs and offered it to Conrad. He waved it off and Melissa shrugged. "Good for the nerves."

On the opposite bank, the Rosslyn, Virginia side of the Potomac, stood more towering buildings. Conrad counted fourteen office and residential high-rises from where he stood, their countless window lights reflected off the river. Large searchlights mounted on top of some of them swept back and forth along the water while two small cigarette boats moved slowly and deliberately along the smooth liquid plain patrolling for terrorists.

"Nice and quiet here," Conrad said.

"You gonna be okay?" Melissa asked.

"Not exactly."

Melissa puffed on her cigarette. "No?"

"Lydia."

"Can you visit her?"

"No. I tried."

Melissa shook her head. "Sure you don't want a pull?"

Conrad stared at the cigarette Melissa held out to him. "I'm thinking about getting her."

"Getting her?" Melissa laughed loudly. "What does that mean?"

"Getting her out and running away."

"Jailbreak?" Melissa laughed again. "You're fucking wasted."

Conrad grunted. "Yeah. I'm drunk. But don't say anything."

Melissa frowned and looked at her cigarette. "Law and order, Dibs. That's our motto. You gonna stick to the plan?"

Conrad looked at his feet. "No crisis of faith Melissa. Don't worry."

Melissa patted Conrad on the shoulder. "I'll try to call before I leave."

Conrad nodded. They shook hands and hugged. "Okay. Get out of here," he said.

Melissa turned and walked up the street towards her hotel, a thin stream of smoke trailing her.

Conrad stood for a minute in the parking lot before walking to the edge of the river. A cool wind blew. He took a cigarette packet from his shirt pocket and pulled a cancer stick from it. He slid the cigarette into his mouth and popped a flame with a gray lighter. A gunshot exploded near him and a bullet whizzed past his head.

He dropped to the ground, the lighter snapping shut and clattering to the pavement. "Hey," Conrad yelled. He looked down the rows of cars. Another shot exploded through the quiet night.

Conrad could tell the direction the shot came from now. He drew a pistol from his ankle holster, leaned against a car, and considered his next move. The door to the bar opened, spilling music and people out into the night. From a row adjacent to where Conrad crouched, a sports car peeled out.

Conrad leapt up and ran to the other row. He stepped in front of an accelerating silver car and pointed his gun at the driver. He pulled his trigger twice. A spider web crack splashed over the windshield. The hood took the other bullet. Conrad instinctively ducked when he heard and saw the flash of a gunshot come from the driver's side of the oncoming car, but he straightened just as the car was nearly on top of him.

He dodged to his right and the speeding car's bumper caught him on the back of his left hamstring. Conrad spun completely around and shot at the rear of the car twice as he dropped to his back. The bullets hit, one tail light shattered, but the car turned a sharp right up the slight bank of the parking lot, its tires screaming, and it turned immediately again onto the main street. The silver car shot towards the Whitehurst Freeway entrance ramp and disappeared in the darkness.

Cris Alvarez

Conrad groaned and grabbed his hamstring. "Shit," he said but luckily it wasn't bleeding. Conrad clutched at a car to pull himself up. At the bar's entrance, three frightened looking couples were pressed up against the wall.

"Don't worry. No more trouble here," Conrad said.

Sam popped out of the bar door. "Conrad? You okay?"

Conrad limped towards the door. "I'll need to see your security tapes Sam. Seems like everyone has me on their shit list."

18

Something disturbed his sleep. His face was warm and a glaring light penetrated his closed eyelids. Conrad opened his eyes and immediately shaded them. Sunlight cut through his window and gave the room a bright sheen. His head throbbed with an intense hangover and, with difficulty motivating himself, he turned to look at his clock. The green digital numbering read 7:25.

He knuckled his eyes, kicked himself off his bed, and wandered into the bathroom. He spent three minutes rubbing his face with hot water and then headed for the kitchen. A whiskey glass holding a thin layer of liquor sat by itself on the counter top. He poured the viscous liquid into the sink and wished the sun and his body would have let him sleep a little longer.

After cooking himself a breakfast of eggs, meat and fried potatoes, he took a long, hot shower. He stood under the burnishing spray and let the previous evening wash off him. The steam opened his pores and he scrubbed himself vigorously with a rough washcloth. He cleaned the scabs and cuts that decorated his body and massaged his aching muscles as best as he could. He followed the hot shower with a long, cold one. Eventually he found himself in the bedroom, laying on his bed again, staring at the ceiling. His alarm clock finally went off at nine a.m.

He rose and went to his computer. He booted it up and opened a file showing the blueprints of the center where the FBI was keeping Lydia. He pulled up the building's security procedures and schedules. He got himself a hot cup of coffee and sat back down in front of the monitor. What the fuck am I planning? The rest of my life?

He went to his walk-in closet and dragged out a large metal chest. He undid the padlock and opened it. Inside the chest were a sniper rifle and an assault rifle. He lifted a body suit of lightweight armor that shared the chest space with the rifles and laid it on the bed.

Lightweight was a bit of a misnomer. The full suit weighed twenty pounds and was stiff around the joints and across its surface. It didn't even stop bullets that came in at certain angles. Neither he, his agents nor his auxiliary soldiers liked wearing the entire thing. But the vest portion served its purpose. He separated it from the limb and head sections.

The he removed a smaller chest from the closet and unlocked it too. That one held stacks of ammunition boxes and a blade. He pulled out the fourteen-inch military knife and laid it next to the body armor on his bed.

He stood in his white cotton robe and contemplated the equipment and what he might be able to do to rescue Lydia. He'd have to check on the transportation schedule they had for her. Maybe Blounts or Dave would be willing to get that information for him. He could always tell them that he simply wanted to tail Lydia's transport to provide extra protection for her. He could always abuse the trust of his close friends for the first time in his life. With a handful of words, he could throw away decades of loyalty and truth he had established with the people he knew.

Conrad squeezed his eyes shut and rubbed his face hard before looking towards his balcony at the busy city outside. The streets were crammed with cars trying to push forward to their drivers' self-assigned office buildings. Thousands of shoes pounded the earth of the city into further submission as though the asphalt layers stretched over it were not degradation enough. The city was filled with energy and exuberance and the sun bleached all of it into an efficient indistinguishability.

Conrad slid the balcony door open and was slapped by a wave of humidity. The day was hot, bright, and muggy. In the distance, the Washington Monument gleamed in the sunlight. About a half mile northeast of the Monument was the Department of Justice building where he had dropped Lydia off. He knew the area well and he knew the safe house where they would probably be taking her.

He fearfully realized his insanity whispered the possible to him. The fingers of fate caressed his heart. That small, powerful engine drummed faster when he looked back at the weapons and armor on his bed. He had the will, the ability, and the knowledge to accomplish what he should not. Life as an outlaw beckoned.

Conrad's cell phone rang. He shook his head clear and hurried inside to the bedroom bureau where it sat. The call was from a DC area code, 202, but he didn't recognize the number. "Yeah?"

A man's voice, smooth and tempered. "Conrad Greis?"

"Who is this?"

"Are you still a little angry about the attempt on your life?"

"Who the fuck is this?" Conrad stepped out on to his balcony and scanned the locations near his building where someone could watch his apartment. Nothing stood out.

"Don't worry Mr. Greis. I'm a friend with DHS."

"I don't recognize your voice."

"You're not meant to."

"You got an ID code to verify who you are?"

"One moment."

Conrad pulled the phone away from his ear and watched the screen. In about thirty seconds, a message flashed verifying that the voice on the other end of the line had sent an encrypted codeword that established the caller as a special agent within DHS.

"How do you know I got shot at?"

"Shot? I'm talking about the bomb Mr. Greis."

"Huh. Okay."

"Mr. Greis. We need to talk in person."

"Well, since you know about the attack, you might realize that I'm a little wary of stepping out somewhere that's not feeling completely safe for me."

"Where would you feel safe talking?"

The accent had been difficult to hear at first but Conrad realized the voice sounded British. Not a working-class Cockney accent but something educated and overly proud of itself. Public school. "I suppose this is official business that has to be done."

"It involves reinstating, well," a pause, "I've said too much already."

Conrad took a moment before replying. "You've said enough. There's a diner over in Annandale. The Cookery. I'll meet you there. It's out of my jurisdiction and sufficiently out of DC to be away from prying eyes and ears. I think."

"I know of it Mr. Greis. I'll see you there at say eleven a.m."

Conrad looked at his clock. He had an hour and a half. "That'll work."

The line went dead. Conrad closed his phone and leaned back against the wall. He didn't like being jerked around like this. If he was going to be reinstated, why not just do it the normal way. Why the subterfuge? The hairs on his neck rose and he scratched at them.

He returned to his living room and turned on the tv. The national news speculated on who did what in relation to recent bombings around the nation. Nothing but the standard. The shooting last night was so commonplace, it didn't even merit a blurb on the local news ticker running along the bottom of the screen.

With his remote, Conrad lowered the volume on the television and rose from his sofa. He got a blue button-down shirt from the closet and slipped it on. He put on a pair of comfortable dark pants and casual black leather shoes. He wrapped a holster around his right calf and slipped a small loaded gun into it. He stood and flapped his pants. They were loose at the ankle and the gun didn't show.

When he finished dressing, he sat back on the living room sofa and contemplated the city outside his window. He got some water from the kitchen faucet and gulped it down. He still felt thirsty and his head was heavy. He gulped down two more glasses of water, popped a couple of aspirins, and left the apartment.

Driving his black Mustang, Conrad took M street to the Key Bridge and crossed over the Potomac into Rosslyn. From there, he jumped onto a crowded I-66 West. Once he passed the Ballston exit, the subway tracks of the city's metro system rose from under the ground and paralleled the highway. He passed an orange line train going west and a few minutes later, he passed an orange line train headed east towards downtown.

Five miles further, he grabbed Interstate 495 South which was just as crowded with traffic. He exited at the Little River Turnpike and went east towards downtown Annandale. It had taken Conrad forty-five minutes to travel between Georgetown and Annandale and he was still encountering heavy traffic. His temper rose and he forced himself to breathe deeply to control it.

As he moved slowly along with the other cars and continued his meditative breathing, Conrad recalled the statistics that explained this pervasive crowding. Eighty percent of the U.S. population lived in urban areas like DC now. People were scared of the countryside. Not that it was lawless but, if a person didn't agree with their neighbors, there was certainly a higher likelihood of something undesirable happening. Police power had become provincial again.

The numbers rolled in his head. An estimated thirty-five million military and civilian casualties were sustained by the country through the twenty-six official months of the civil war. Sixteen million of those were fatalities, the other nineteen million were the injured and diseased. The U.S. still had a sizable population of three hundred and ten million citizens but everything was a mess now. Fear drove the survivors inwards to the safety of downtown skyscrapers and hopefully fair and balanced police protection. Overpopulated cities grew even bigger as a result.

Only now, nearly three years after the end of the Civil War, were people moving back into the countryside in large numbers but the rebels were resisting. They liked their open space and they didn't want any liberal urbanites polluting what they considered their God given right to the land. At least that's what the pundits were saying.

Conrad's opinion was that half the rebels were nothing but self-serving thugs and criminals taking advantage of the low level of law enforcement resources the country currently had at its disposal. That would change drastically in the next five years but until then Conrad knew he and other like him were there to hold the line. I am the line, he told himself. Am I still? He was having his doubts.

The Cookery's blue sign loomed ahead and Conrad snorted his worries out of his mind. He slowed to make the left turn from the busy street into the diner's parking lot. He checked his rear view mirror for tails but he didn't see any cars that he had noticed during his drive from Georgetown.

The parking lot, plain and gray, looked as homely as the building that housed the Cookery. The restaurant was a brown, plaster, rectangular block with a bit of dash added by a dark orange awning Despite its uninspired appearance, the place was popular for lunch. Cars filled its small parking lot and patrons entered and exited the diner at a steady pace.

Conrad parked illegally along a yellow curb, a spot reserved for emergency vehicles. He sucked on his teeth in anticipation of an ambush. He looked again at his rear and side view mirrors. Then he looked around, twisting his head back, to the left and right. The way looked all clear. He exited his car and strolled to the front entrance. A short, lean man in a dark blue suit and a gray dress hat leaned against a glass pane in the restaurant's front vestibule. His face was shorn of mustache and beard and his head might have been too. The man nodded when Conrad entered the small space.

Conrad looked the agent up and down. He didn't see any weapons on him, but they were there under the clothes. He was sure of it. Private citizens often liked to carry their guns out in plain sight. Government employees however - undercover law enforcement especially - still liked to keep their weapons out of sight. That habit had a practical purpose. It kept criminals from knowing exactly where the officer's weapons were.

Cris Alvarez

The man held out his hand when Conrad came close to him. "Mr. Greis?" The English accent was gone. He sounded Midwestern now.

Conrad nodded and grabbed the agent's hand firmly. The man's palm was dry and cold. Sterile. "That's me," Conrad said. "What happened to the accent?"

The man smiled. "Liked that? Opsec." He grabbed the inner door handle. "I've got a table for us already. Please." He held the door to the main restaurant area open and motioned for Conrad to walk ahead of him. Conrad passed through the door and saw the fruits of the protection he provided his country.

The people inside were smiling and laughing, joking around. Some were obviously enjoying midday drinks while others just a midday meal. Men and women sat together enjoying each other's company. Everyone looked carefree. Conrad's face felt like heavy lead compared to them, but he let it sit that way.

"This way," the man said. He slid past Conrad and sat down at a booth near a large window. Boisterous groups were seated all around them. "I like this place. It's easy to get lost in the crowd. Both your face and your voice disappear."

Conrad nodded and sat on the opposite couch. "Sure. Whatever you say." In the booth directly behind Conrad, a young man sat on the lap of another man. With them were a hetero couple and what Conrad supposed was a lesbian couple. All six were charmingly happy. Conrad nodded again but to nothing in particular.

"Still unhappy about the forced leave?" the agent asked.

Conrad scrutinized the man carefully now. He had bad skin laid over a narrow face. Small eyes, a small, sharp nose and a pointy chin. A razor-thin scar, three or so inches long, ran at a slight angle horizontally across his forehead very close to his hairline. "A crisis of faith."

"Huh?" The man was still smiling as he took a paper napkin from an aluminum holder and wiped the space in front of him. Unlike the presentation his face gave, his hand was meaty and stubby.

"I'm just noticing how different this place is from the places out in Occoquan."

"You mean the rear from the frontlines?" The man was still cleaning the table and smiling broadly. "We're not that far."

"You're sure damn happy."

The DHS agent removed his hat and slapped it on the tabletop. "Well of course. I'm about to give a good cop his badge back." A perturbed look crossed his face and he moved his hat from the table to the couch seat.

"Yeah, about that. What's going on?"

A loud laugh from one of the men behind Conrad startled him.

The man leaned forward and thrust his finger at Conrad. "The country needs men like you to protect its freedoms. Men like you shouldn't be forced to sit at home wondering what they did wrong when in fact, you did everything right."

"Well, I can see you're kissing my ass but if you know me so well, you should know that I do things by the book. If this is outside of regulations..." Conrad let the man finish the sentence in his own mind.

The waitress appeared next to them. She was an average woman in every way. Brown hair pulled back in a ponytail, pale skin with a touch of sunburn, body smelling of cheap perfume. "How're you gentlemen this morning?"

"Afternoon." The suit winked at Conrad. "Just fine, ma'am. How about some coffee for the both of us to start and, do you serve speed?"

"No license for that sir. We're still applying. Sorry. We've got some lighter stims if you want. Red Delight?"

"Naw. That's fine. Just the coffee."

"Food?"

"Give us a minute on that hun." The grin kept steady on the suit's face and followed her as she walked away. "You do speed?" he asked Conrad.

"I don't do any drugs. Just coffee and alcohol."

"Old fashioned kind of guy?"

"Guess so."

"I don't do speed much. Just every now and then."

"Even on duty?"

The suit smiled. "Okay, okay. I just asked her if they have it. Right?"

Conrad nodded and sighed audibly. But now he actually was content. He leaned back and put his right arm along the backrest. He surveyed the crowd again. Men and women, gay and straight, peacefully enjoying freedom. People enjoying alcohol and drugs in moderation. Not quite the chaotic mess some people were predicting seven years ago.

Conrad's spirits rose. The diner's blissful hustle and bustle reminded him of what he had spent the last twenty years fighting for. Absolute freedom enjoyed in moderation. He believed the U.S. was still a conservative country and, despite the law giving people free access to everything, in general people weren't going overboard. Still, he knew that despite the success of freedom in the cities, ignorant hate and fear endured in the countryside. He smirked and chuckled at the absurdity of that wasteful anger.

"What's funny there Rad?"

Conrad tilted his head and looked at the suit. "What's your name again?"

"You're wrong there buddy. I didn't say before. Zip Logan. Well, Zip's my nickname. I guess that's obvious."

"And you're with who?"

"Now we're getting down to business. Okay, I'm with DHS too you realize. Here. You'll want to see this next."

Zip pulled out his wallet and handed it to Conrad. Conrad flipped it open part way and looked at the gold and blue DHS badge inside. The ID card inside was printed with the name Michael Dunsany Logan.

"Okay, so what division do you work for?"

Zip leaned in closely and almost silently said, "CI."

Conrad leaned forward himself. "Mmm. I see." They both leaned back when the waitress brought two ceramic cups of coffee. She put a plate of creamer packets between them. "You fellas know what you want to eat?"

"Double cheeseburger and fries for me," Conrad said.

"Club sandwich," Zip said, nodding and smiling to the waitress.

"Coming right up."

Conrad leaned forward again. He was starting to feel even better now but he wasn't sure why. "I'm concerned about Lydia."

"The rebel who helped you escape. Yes, I'm sure you would be. You must be grateful." Zip winked.

"Well I am but I'm not sure I like how you said that."

Zip raised one hand with his palm facing Conrad. "Don't get testy. Meant no harm at all. I'd be grateful towards a woman who saved me from certain torture and death as well."

"Just say person, instead of woman, and you'll know where I'm coming from."

Zip had both palms facing Conrad now and he pushed them in concession towards Conrad. "Got you buddy. Don't worry about it."

The men behind Conrad laughed loudly at something but he didn't jump this time. He lifted his coffee and drank it black. "So tell me what's going on."

"Okay, here's the deal." Zip poured two creamers and two packets of sugar into his coffee as he spoke. "We've got an investigation going on. A possible irregularity within DHS."

"A smoke out the mole operation? Uh-huh. I only work a field office Zip."

"Yeah, yeah. We've been through your whole record. We asked around. You're tight. A loyal soldier. Time in the sandbox. Time in the Civil War."

"So counterintelligence likes how I look?"

"Yup. We're pretty sure you're not an, um, irregularity."

Conrad's voice raised without his realizing it at first. "Who ever suggested I was?"

Zip flapped his hand. "Keep it down Rad."

Conrad lowered his voice. "Where does anyone get off suggesting that?"

"Everyone's a suspect when the rebs are getting first rate information so quickly. But that's all I can say."

Conrad breathed deeply and angrily and took a big gulp of his coffee. "So I'm safe. Great. Now what?"

"Well, we think you can help us with the investigation. It's progressing, uh, slowly."

"It'll look strange if I just show up somewhere after having been put on administrative leave."

"Maybe not. We give you an assignment that takes you off the frontline and doing more admin stuff."

"Who in the chain is in on this?"

"The CI bosses, certain people in your chain. It's a pretty tight investigation. Black box."

Conrad hesitated. "Okay. Where am I going?"

"We're going to assign you custody of Lydia Mansfield."

Conrad's heart leapt. He tried to show nothing in his face. By Zip's smile, he could see he had failed.

"Like that?" Zip asked.

"The FBI. They won't allow it."

"It's out of their hands. DHS has taken over again. FBI had to give her back up to us. You'll be assigned to taking her to various prisons and rebel sites in the DC region. See what information you can get from her."

"Am I protecting her or interrogating her?"

"Interrogating? Interviewing her. She's a willing source isn't she?"

Conrad leaned back and twisted his mouth. "More or less."

Zip frowned and scratched his head. He sipped from his coffee cup again. "Oh?"

The waitress appeared next to them holding two plates of food. Conrad and Zip remained silent while she slipped them under their chins. "Here's some ketchup fellas. Anything else for now?"

Uh, no," said Conrad. He stared at the food, almost forgetting why it was there. He snapped himself out of it.

"So," Zip said before biting into his sandwich. "How's it sound?"

Conrad pushed his plate forward and stared at Zip. He couldn't tell if things were going well or not. He couldn't figure out the game. His stomach began to ache.

A soft voice spoke. "Hey handsome. Can I borrow that ketchup?"

Conrad looked back over his shoulder. A young man wearing a tight, yellow, button-down shirt held his hand out and looked at Conrad expectantly.

Conrad stared at the smooth-faced man. That interruption bothered him.

"I think they're cops," another one of the men at the table said. He looked groggy on alcohol.

"Can't you stop killing all those poor people?" one of the women asked. "I know they're crazy but do they need to die?"

The man who had asked for the ketchup frowned.

Conrad felt betrayed by their angry tones. Hadn't he just been admiring their happiness? Have you ever shed blood for your freedom? He wanted to ask the question but he could immediately tell what the answer would be. Conrad became even more frustrated looking at this frail man who had little ability to fight for himself, little ability to protect his own needs and well-being. Probably easily knocked down in a toe-to-toe fistfight, he thought. Conrad's temper rose. Paul didn't have the luxury of a real left arm to reach for anything.

A gold marriage band graced the man's ring finger. Do you know how many people bled and died for you and gay marriage? Conrad wanted to grab that hand and snap it at the wrist. Then the lot of them could all see how they would react to violence done directly to them. Would they still be so damning in their opinions? Would they then understand they needed tough people to protect their carefree happiness?

"Here, yeah, go ahead and take it," Zip said. He handed the bottle to the man.

Conrad made eye contact with the man. Whatever Conrad's face expressed, the man looked startled and then scared as he turned back to his friends. Conrad looked at Zip.

"What's with you?" Zip asked. "Want to pass on the assignment?"

"No. I was just thinking about the, uh, operational aspect of it."

"Okay, we can discuss all that later. I just want to know if you'll do it."

"Yeah, yeah. Of course I'll do it." Conrad gently took his burger with both hands and bit into it. It couldn't have felt drier in his mouth.

"Good because you start immediately. I have her in a van outside."

19

C onrad's face went blank as his mind registered what he had just heard. While Zip had been wasting Conrad's time in the diner, the one thing he yearned for was locked up in a van no more than sixty meters from him. For a searing moment, Conrad wanted to grab Zip by the collar and beat his head against the table. But that would have accomplished nothing useful.

Conrad rushed outside into the parking lot. He looked around wildly until he saw an unmarked white van with tinted windows parked in the rear of the lot.

Zip came up behind and put his hand on Conrad's shoulder. "Jeez, what's the hurry?"

Conrad swept Zip's hand off his shoulder. "Get her out of the van."

Zip's head swiveled left and right, looking for something. "She's watching a movie. Don't worry."

Conrad grabbed Zip by the collar and pulled him close to his face. "This isn't the center of DC. If anyone on the other side suspected she was in there, if you were tailed, they'd blow the van up. You realize that?"

Zip wrestled himself free of Conrad's grip and backed away. "I wasn't tailed. But someone might figure out what's going on if you keep acting like this."

"I'll have to pull my car up close by so the transfer isn't obvious."

Zip straightened his jacket. "Can we finish our food first?"

Conrad fished in his pocket. He pulled out his wallet and a ten from that and handed it to Zip. "This covers me. I want her now."

Zip frowned as he took the money. "I thought you play by the book Conrad. You do know you'll have to sign some papers first acknowledging your role in the operation and that you've taken custody of the woman?"

Conrad motioned rapidly with his fingers for Zip to hurry. "Where are they? Let's do it quick."

Zip shook his head in annoyance and walked to the van. He clicked the alarm button on his key and opened the driver's side door. He pulled a brown leather briefcase from the seat. Conrad stayed a short distance from the van and surveyed the area. There were too many trees close by, along the road and along the parking lot, for him to feel comfortable. Traffic was heavy. The enemy could be anywhere.

Zip held the briefcase flat with a small stack of papers resting on top. As Zip walked towards Conrad, a gust of wind forced Zip to clamp his hand down on the papers. He handed Conrad the case and a pen.

Conrad skimmed the papers with his eyes. They were standard government forms in triplicate involving confidentiality and secrecy and operational integrity. The important one gave him the right and responsibility to escort Lydia Mansfield. He rapidly signed and dated all of the papers and handed them back to Zip.

Zip gave yellow copies back to Conrad. "Damn, my food's getting cold."

"I'm getting my car. Get her out of there."

Zip went to the rear of the van and tapped on the back door rhythmically. Conrad walked to his car, got in and drove it close to the van. He jumped out and opened the passenger side door while Zip opened the rear of the van. It was dark inside but into the light stepped Lydia wearing blue jeans, a lavender blouse and a dark blue baseball cap emblazoned with a curly W on the front. Her blonde hair was tied in a ponytail pulled through the back of the cap. Conrad motioned with his hand for her to hurry in to his car.

She stepped down to the ground with Zip's aid and slid gracefully into the car without making eye contact. Conrad closed the door.

Zip handed Conrad a sheet of paper and a one-inch memory stick. "I was supposed to give you a briefing on where to take her but I guess you're in a hurry."

"Yeah." Conrad said as he took the goods.

"Just review this information and the sheet and you'll see what you need to do. Tape everything she says when you're interviewing the people listed and surveying the sites. Call me with questions."

"Got it."

"Where are you going to keep her?"

"My place."

Zip nodded. "I see. Okay. Good luck then. I'm going to finish my lunch."

Conrad grunted his farewell and got into the car. As he drove away, he looked in his rear-view mirror and saw Zip on a cell phone. Conrad turned right out of the lot and headed down Little River Turnpike towards the 495 North entrance ramp.

Conrad glanced at Lydia. She was staring straight ahead and her face was impassive. Her face was a stone mask - smooth, pink and unmoving. Her eyelashes dropped slowly and rose again. That was all.

His heart was pounding. "Did they treat you well?"

She stared straight ahead at the clot of traffic that forced Conrad to move slowly along towards the Beltway. "Why did you let them take me?" Her voice was strong, clear and angry.

"I didn't let them. I had orders to surrender you to the FBI."

"You didn't stop them. You didn't raise a hand."

"Lydia, it's a little different here. I have to follow the law." He tapped the steering wheel with his palm. "Forgive me."

"Law? I've heard of it. Usually it's the word people use when they force other people to do or accept something that isn't natural for them."

"What? What are you talking about?"

Conrad jerked away when Lydia thrust her face at him.

"Do you think I'm dumb?" she asked.

"Huh? No."

"Just because I'm a country girl and I couldn't speak."

Conrad's neck tensed and his temples throbbed. He concentrated on the crowded road ahead of him. The sky was gray now and the air around them was thick with an unresolved dampness that should have been rain already. "You're not dumb. You just don't know what life is like on this side."

"You let those other men have me. There's not much more to say."

"It's good here too Lydia. You should be happier about that. People have freedoms."

"I didn't have my freedom."

"Listen. You didn't let me finish. We have our freedoms because we live by the law. We live in peace because we let the law do our fighting for us. I..." He thought of his plans to kidnap Lydia from the FBI. "I have to respect that." Am I lying to her again?

"You didn't answer my question."

"You were free. You were just under the protective custody of the FBI. People want to kill you."

"I'm sure they do. I know things they don't want me to tell. But I didn't feel free Conrad."

Conrad merged onto the Beltway but traffic forced him to slow down again. "Damn." He leaned on his horn. His mind fumbled for a lie. "It was for your own good. I couldn't protect you like they can."

Lydia slumped back in her seat. "But you have me now."

"I guess I do. I don't really understand it or why."

"Are you unhappy?"

"No. I'm happy to help you."

"So we just do what? Sit around? I'm guessing you're not supposed to let me walk outside."

"We have things they want us to do."

"Like what?" She looked out of her side window and ran a finger along a streak of dirt that lined its outside surface.

"See some people, see some places." Conrad's cell phone rang. It was Mary's ring tone. "Shit. Hold on. Yeah? Mary?"

The voice on the other side slurred her words. "Yes. I need to talk to you. Can we meet soon?"

"No. Uh, are you at the hospital?"

"Yes. Where are you?"

Conrad looked around for signs. "495. I'm near Gallows Road."

"So you're not close. Never mind."

Mary sounded glum as well as drunk. The usual state. "What is it?"

"The boys. They haven't come by to see me."

"They're with your mother."

"I know who they're with. I'm going back to sleep." The line died.

"Damn." Conrad dropped the phone between the seats.

Lydia placed a gentle hand on Conrad's arm. He looked at her face and it struck him that that face was perfectly formed. The only blemish was a small, ragged scar on the side of her chin. He lifted his hand to touch it. Lydia lowered her eyes and her chin but she didn't pull away. He leaned towards her and kissed her lightly on the lips. She kissed back. Like a cat, she jerked away from him at the sound of several sharp cracks over the surface of the car.

Conrad tensed in his seat and looked around in panic for the gun that had shot at them. To his left, a mid-sized, dark blue car drove alongside. A rifle barrel was sticking out of the passenger side window. Conrad hit the brakes and was nearly back-ended by the car behind him.

Lydia screamed. She was looking at another blue car on Conrad's right. The back left side window of that car rolled down and a hand popped out. It held a volleyball-sized lump of clay that the hand flung at Conrad's car. It stuck momentarily to Lydia's window and then fell off.

"Clay bomb," yelled Conrad. He swerved at the blue car and pushed it towards a concrete barrier. The car's metal screeched and shot sparks as it slid against the concrete. Conrad hit his brakes and both cars slowed to an abrupt stop with Conrad slightly ahead of his attacker.

The traffic flowing behind them swerved around but didn't slow down. Conrad popped open his door. He grabbed a long knife from under his seat and pulled his ankle gun from its holster. He leapt out of his car and run around the back. The pinned car's driver's side window rolled down and a rifle barrel popped out. Conrad poured seven shots into the open window as he ran towards the car. Without having fired a shot, the rifle barrel rotated towards the sky.

The rear passenger side door opened in the narrow space between the car and the concrete barrier and a large person wearing a black shirt and black mask groaned as he tried to squeeze out of the car. The back driver's side door opened next and Conrad fiercely kicked it closed. He ran around the back of the blue car and kicked at the man struggling to pull himself out of the car's back door. The kick went low in the man's gut. When he bent over in pain, Conrad jammed his long knife down into the space between the man's neck and left shoulder. The man stiffened and gave a long, deep moan.

Conrad pulled the bloody knife out and let the body drop onto the pavement.

The back driver's side door opened again and Conrad spun to face it. A gun came out and angled itself towards Conrad. Two shots exploded from it and bullets tugged at Conrad's shirt. Conrad shot at the gun and heard a ricochet. The gun dropped to the ground and Conrad ran back around the pinned car, firing twice into it as he moved.

A foot kicked the door all the way open but didn't move again. Conrad crouched down and looked into the car through the open back door. No more movement or sound came from inside the car. Conrad looked down the length of the highway. The other blue car had pulled over to the shoulder about ninety meters ahead. A passenger door opened slightly and then closed without anyone stepping out. The car peeled away, a spray of gravel shooting out behind it.

Conrad moved closer to the remaining car and peeked inside again. The windows were darkly tinted and the car was nearly black inside. The driver was slumped forward against the steering wheel and the person Conrad had just shot was lying motionless across the back seat. Conrad moved back to the person he had stabbed. The body bled from Conrad's strike and from a bullet hole in the back. Conrad hurried back to his car. Lydia stared in shock at the scene without moving. Conrad grabbed his cell phone and dialed Dave Bronson.

"Boss?"

"Dave. I just got ambushed."

"Shit. Again? Where are you?"

"495 inner loop. Just south of mile marker...fuck if I know. I'm a little north of the Gallows Road exit. Two blue sedans. Tried to use a clay bomb on me but it didn't stick."

"Fuckin a. We'll get some units out there quick. They tail you?"

"No Dave. I watched for tails when I picked up Lydia."

"Lydia? What are you talking about?"

"DHS gave me Lydia back!"

"I have no idea what you're talking about boss. Let's get this ambush investigated first."

"Yeah, yeah. I don't want to sit here for long."

"We'll hurry. Just stay on the line."

Conrad heard the sounds of emergency vehicles approaching. He sat down in his car and leaned back. How the hell did they know how to find him? Lydia had closed her eyes and seemed to be sleeping. Conrad was dizzy. He got back out of the car and leaned against it. The adrenalin was quickly wearing off. He reached inside his car for a new magazine of bullets and quickly changed it out for the one he had just used to take care of the competition.

20

T he three of them, Conrad, Lydia, and the prisoner, sat in a room that looked all too familiar to Conrad. The floor was concrete and bare and in the center of the room was a functional and very plain metal table. Conrad and Lydia were seated on one side and the prisoner on the other. This prisoner, much like the one Conrad had interrogated only days earlier, was young, idealistic, and would not say a thing.

She was twenty-four according to the detention center's records. Tall and gangly with long, brown hair pulled back into a mess of a ponytail. She wore an orange jumper but the sleeves were rolled back showing thin, freckled and scarred forearms. Her face was long and stretched out, like a horse's, and she had twisted buckteeth. Freckles covered much of her face too.

Her lips moved nervously before she broke the silence. "I ain't got nothin to say." She directed her words to the edge of the table in front of her.

Conrad looked at Lydia. Lydia stared at the prisoner, one Jody Hines of Denio, Nevada who had been caught operating against the DC Capital Region. Lydia blinked once slowly and looked at Conrad with emotional pain showing on her face. She shrugged at Conrad's questioning gaze.

Conrad looked back over his shoulder at the one way-mirror behind him. He shrugged at his reflection too. He looked back at Jody. "You don't recognize this woman," he asked pointing his thumb at Lydia.

"Nope," Jody said to the edge of the table. She wrinkled her nose and slowly slid a finger along that silent table edge. "Jerk Fed," she added but this time she looked at Conrad. She stared below his eyes, maybe at his busted lip.

"Nice talk for a religious girl," Conrad said.

"Well they ain't nothing religious about this place, is there?"

"There was nothing religious about the explosives you were planting at the perimeter of your compound when they caught you either."

"That was to keep animals like you away. Guvment animals."

Conrad nodded and looked back at Lydia. Lydia subtly shook her head.

"You know, you could really do yourself a favor and get out of here quicker if you just started giving us names and locations."

"Why would I want to leave here? You got all my friends here don't you?"

"That's funny Jody. Keep joking"

"Cept the ones you execute out there on the fields."

"The one's who wouldn't surrender Jody. You know the law."

"There's only one law I know and it ain't yours." She was sneering as she continued looking intently at Conrad's mouth. One of her eyes was lazy. The brow and eyelid over that eye drooped. She scratched her pink neck with fingernails that had been bitten raw and left red marks on her neck.

Conrad looked at Lydia and opened his eyes wide when they made eye contact. He wanted her to say something that would shake this girl up into talking. He needed Lydia to be useful to the government or he would lose the assignment and her. A small wave of panic went through his skull.

Lydia responded by exhaling through her nose and looking down. She slumped in her seat and then raised her head to stare at the girl.

Conrad was bored of the assignment too and they were only on their first interrogation. He couldn't figure out what DHS was thinking with this plan. It wasn't usual procedure to bring a flipper, someone who came back to regular society, around to meet the rebels the government had incarcerated. It just wasn't done like that.

"Ever been to the Good Shepherd Camp?" Lydia asked.

Jody's eyes jumped. Then she squinted at Lydia and shook her head slowly. "I don't know what you're talking about."

"The one where they put abortion doctors up on crosses and punish members by shackling them up in a hot room," Conrad said.

Lydia spoke softly to Jody. "You ever kneel on the floor of punishment with your bare knees? You know the floor. The jagged one with small rocks and small rocks scattered everywhere under you."

Jody's flat chest heaved up and down as she began to breathe deeper.

Lydia continued. "You know the one where you kneel for so long on those little rocks that when you finally stand up, you got to peel the rocks out of your skin and watch your knees bleed."

Jody's hand rubbed at her knees. Her face went from anger to something pained. She slumped back in her chair and replied softly with a whimper to her voice. "I don't know what you're talking about."

"Let me see your knees," Conrad said.

Jody looked at him sharply. "No."

"Did you kneel much? Get many scars? Were you a bad one? Needed a lot of correction? I'm not surprised."

"Shut up," Jody yelled as she popped out of her chair and tried flipping the table at Conrad. Conrad slammed the table down before Jody had raised it very far. Dust jumped up where the table legs smacked down on the floor.

"So I know you're fucking lying to us. Thought we didn't know about the Good Shepard Camp?"

"You don't know nothin. You just made up a word."

Conrad pointed at Lydia. "Did she make up the punishment?" Lydia looked away and hugged herself as she leaned forward in her chair. Conrad's chest tightened.

Jody's head moved like she wanted to say something that would burst right out of her mouth. She clamped a hand on the back of her neck and looked down. "Shut up, shut up, shut up," she shouted in increasing volume.

Conrad walked around the table and turned Jody around to face him. He gripped her by the arms and her body went rigid. She looked down.

"Tell me the names of the people there at the camp. What did they look like? What else did they do? Did they live in the city?" Conrad didn't know what he would do if he got the names. Give them to his supervisors? Take his own revenge? His heart pumped rapidly. He shook Jody for an answer and Lydia gasped in response.

Jody shook her head and began crying. "No, no, no." Her body went limp and her weight sagged. Conrad stumbled forward as he tried to keep her from falling down. She dropped to her side and

Conrad bent over with his hand under her head so that she didn't smack it on the concrete floor. He slid his hand from under her head and let her head down softly on the floor. He stood up and looked down at her.

"Let her be," Lydia said. "She's an innocent girl. Just a tool. They lied to her and pushed her around."

Conrad shook his head. "No. It's not as easy as all that. She doesn't get a free pass just cause she was young and innocent and she's crying now. She was part of that machine that's still killing people and killing ideas." Conrad stood over the girl. She was laying on her side curled into a fetal position and crying into her clenched fists.

Lydia frowned. "She could have been me, if you caught us before I helped you."

Conrad walked around to his side of the table staring at Lydia.

"You would have been pushing me around and interrogating me night and day until I cracked. Even if I knew nothing, you would have kept it up until something happened."

Conrad nodded. "Okay Lydia. You made your point."

"Have I? How far would you go to win?" Lydia asked. She chewed her lips.

Conrad's chest got tighter. "I'd go as far as I was told to. As far as I was allowed to." That was a lie. He'd look at Lydia once and he'd have surrendered to her, even in an interrogation room.

"Trust your leaders to make the right decisions you mean?"

Conrad swallowed a hard lump in his throat. "More or less." He forced himself to stand up taller and straighter. Jody had quieted down a little but she was still curled up and hiding her face. "There's an order to this, even if you or I don't get it." Conrad's head throbbed as he spoke. He was repeating things he had said many times before, thoughts and ideas that came naturally to him but they felt like alien ideals now. He didn't think they were wrong but the old rules didn't feel like they applied to him anymore.

"You mean the way she trusted her people, my old people, to tell her the right thing to do?"

"They brutalized her," Conrad said. "Those aren't people to trust."

"They hurt her a little. But you're hurting her just as much here."

Conrad snorted and grabbed his chair. He turned it to face Lydia and dropped down heavily. "So is that it? We're worse than they are?"

"In some ways. From what I'm seeing."

"We're in a war. A civil war and everyone is beating down on us from all sides. We've got few friends so what do we do?"

Lydia shrugged.

"Don't know? I'll tell you then. We have to be tough." Tough against whom? He rubbed his temples. He had to remind himself who the enemy was, who his friends were.

"Tough for what reason?" Lydia asked.

"Tough to protect what we have. The American dream. And America is even greater now that we have so many more freedoms than the other countries on this angry planet." He believed what he said. He knew that to be true. Those ideals were true, ones he could trust in still.

"I see. No one brings down the right, white and blue."

"Exactly. But I think you're making fun of me now."

"You sound so tough, but I'm not sure what you're hurting people like her for."

Conrad placed his hands on Lydia's knees and softened his voice. "They won't let us live in peace Lydia."

"But they're Americans, and more importantly, human beings too. They just don't believe in all the things you allow now."

"But you rejected them and the way they live remember? Or am I wrong?"

Lydia shrugged and looked at the floor as she rubbed one arm.

"You didn't answer my question," Conrad said.

Lydia looked at the floor and continued rubbing her arm, slowly up and down.

"Goddamn it Lydia!" Conrad jumped from the chair and paced back and forth. "I didn't start this war. They did. There's laws that we passed. Just follow the goddamn laws. If you don't like them, use your right to vote to change it."

"Isn't it ironic that your new freedom laws gave them the right to carry all the weapons they have now?"

Conrad looked at the mirror. He wanted to yell and punch that mirror for reflecting every angry move he made. "It's every American's responsibility to use their given freedoms responsibly. And it's my job to jail those people who can't. Nothing will change just because a few people get out of hand. Freedom is a good thing. I don't feel stupid saying it. And Americans will fight to keep it. Understand?"

"Yes. I understand. We've traded in one form of repression for another. But it comes down to the same thing doesn't it. Might makes right."

"It's not our fault Lydia. But you're just going to refuse to understand aren't you?"

"I want happiness and peace Conrad. That's all I want."

A voice blared in through a speaker in the wall. "Are you done with her?"

Conrad looked at himself in the mirror again. "Yeah, we're done here for now." He shook his head in frustration. Lydia looked at him mournfully then she looked at Jody and went over to her. Lydia stooped down and stroked the girl's head while Conrad watched them. His body shook and he suddenly felt penned in by this room.

This interview is bullshit. These interrogations will all be worthless. That's what he believed. He realized the only thing that really came of this assignment so far was that he and Lydia had nearly been killed as soon as they got together. After the DHS gave him this new assignment, after they left Zip at the restaurant, after he talked to Mary, danger followed

Conrad became lightheaded and the floor shifted slightly under his feet.

"Are you okay?" Lydia asked.

"Are you done?" the speaker blared again.

The room started to sway. Conrad closed his eyes and many familiar faces drifted across the darkness in front of his pupils. A hand gripped Conrad's arm. He opened his eyes. It was Lydia. Her face showed concern.

"Let's go Conrad."

"We have two more interviews before we're done here."

"I don't like this Conrad. Let's go."

Conrad nodded and pulled Lydia closer to him. "I don't like this either. We need to go."

"Sir?" the speaker said.

Conrad walked to the door with Lydia. "We need to get out of here. Go somewhere safe where I can think."

"You don't like this either?"

"No. It doesn't make sense."

The door in front of Conrad clicked and swung out. A burly uniformed guard stood in the doorway. "Can I help sir? You look pale."

Conrad held out his hand. "No. No. We're done for the day. We're headed to the hotel. We'll be back tomorrow."

"I'll let the warden know sir."

"Good. You do that." The guard moved aside as Conrad led Lydia through the door. "We'll be back first thing tomorrow."

Conrad hurried to get himself and Lydia back out to the car and away from the detention center. He had to drive somewhere safe and he had a good idea where to go.

21

L ydia's hands were clasped together and tucked between her legs. She stared ahead at the dark asphalt street flying under her. The sun had dropped close to the horizon and twilight was coming on. A dense line of tall trees hung over either side of the two-lane road making the way even darker. "Where are we going now?" she asked.

Conrad turned his head to her. His eyes drifted from her profile to the trees and bushes they slipped past. Anything and anyone could be waiting in that forest. He looked forward and took in the speed of the car. He was pressing down too hard on the accelerator for a ragged road like this. He let his foot up a bit. "I'm not sure."

"What about the schedule?" Lydia spoke with a resignation, with a sadness whose background music was the drone of the engine and the violin sounds of thousands of cicadas.

The air in the car was damp and heavy. Something in the back seat, maybe a water bottle, rolled back and forth and the sound of it irritated Conrad. When they had left the detention center, gut instinct led him to tell Lydia he would be sticking to the itinerary provided by DHS. But the road they were on had nothing to do with the itinerary.

The two-lane passage they sped along wound through the backwoods of Virginia to the coast. It was a road prohibited for use by government officials because of the dangerous level of rebel activity that had been reported on it. Conrad knew the road had actually been safe for the past six months but he also realized the danger was still there. Rebels were mobile and nomadic. He was risking both their lives using this route but it was the danger this road presented that would temporarily isolate him from the reach of his people. This was the path to temporary freedom.

Lydia put one hand on the dashboard and kept the other between her thighs. "Why are you doing this to me?"

"What?" Conrad had a headache. He squeezed one eye closed and opened it again to help ease the throbbing in his head. "It's the job. I really don't want to do this."

"Why do you want the job then?"

He rubbed his aching head in frustration. "They'll let me have you if I do this for them."

"Have me? No one asked me what I want."

Conrad squeezed his eyes closed then snapped them open. He wanted a cigarette. He wanted to tell Lydia that she had no choice in the matter. He wanted to go away. That at least made him feel comfortable. He was doing what he wanted to do at the exact moment he wanted it. He couldn't remember the last time he had felt that sort of satisfaction.

"Did you hear me Conrad? I don't want to do this anymore. It sickens me."

Conrad felt his temper rising. It bubbled in his stomach, his back became cold. He wanted to stop lying to her.

The trees on either side of the road loomed larger and closer than they had a minute before. The sun dropped lower and everything around him was taking on a darker shade. Conrad suddenly wondered if he was lost. He feared coming across a rebel roadblock. He didn't fear death. He feared a loss of his privacy, the loss of this new freedom.

Lydia's hand touched his cheek. "Conrad? Conrad. Are you okay?"

He opened his eyes again without realizing that he had closed them. He saw Lydia's thin wrist from the corner of his eye. She stroked his cheek and his anger subsided.

"Conrad. Do we need to stop?"

"We can't stop. Not here. Someone could be following us."

Lydia looked back. "I don't see anyone."

"It's stress. Don't worry about it."

"I am worried Conrad. You know this is wrong. It's hurting you just like it's hurting me."

His voice rose. "Nothing's hurting me Lydia. I'm okay. Just a little tired and stressed."

"You need to clear your mind Conrad."

"When we stop, my mind will clear." He hesitated. "We'll get a hotel room near the next jail. I'll be okay once I sleep." The lying was hurting his stomach but he wanted no one to know where he was going, not even this woman he thought he trusted.

"Are you sure it's that easy?"

"Stop it Lydia. You're confusing me."

"Conrad?"

"Can you stop talking please? It's getting dark."

Lydia put her hand on Conrad's knee and stroked it. "Make love to me."

Conrad straightened up and his belly became warm. "Lydia, I'm driving."

"Do you know why I saved you?"

"You wanted out. You were sick of the place and the people." Conrad took a deep, hot breath as Lydia gently moved her hand up and down the top of his thigh. "I need to focus on the road."

"They brought other people in. Men and women who weren't tied up and jailed like you. I could have freed them and they could have let me out."

"I don't know why you picked me." Conrad took Lydia's hand and pushed it back into her lap.

She brought her lips close to his ear. "You looked beautiful. Tall, scarred, broad-shouldered, dark. Dangerous."

The pressure in his head eased and moved down through his body. "Where is this coming from?"

"You don't find me beautiful?"

"No. It's, yeah I do." Conrad squinted his eyes. His mouth was parched. He looked at Lydia. Her five foot two body was firm. Constant work at the camps probably kept her in shape. Her hair hung loosely on her shoulders.

Conrad looked at her full lips and the gentle curves of her body. His eyes ran over the milky smoothness of her skin. He thought of the physical and spiritual firmness that could be felt in the whole of her body. His body ached for all of it.

Conrad's mind went back to the night she made love to him briefly but sensually after the escape. They hadn't discussed it since then and hadn't made love again. It felt more like a dream that way and if he had nothing else, he had the dream.

He snapped out of his mental wandering and focused on the rear-view mirror. He needed to be constantly careful of attack.

"So you find me beautiful?"

"Of course." Tight frustration gripped his neck and his words sounded that tension.

"I remember how you touched me our first time. You touched me softly and gently. You took your time before you became more," she paused, "vigorous."

"Can we talk about this later? This isn't the safest area to be driving in."

She shifted away from him. "How can you be so cold?"

"We're in constant danger Lydia."

"Don't you think I realize it? I've lived my whole life in fear. Until now."

Her arm moved quickly towards him. He tensed when she clutched him between the legs. Not too hard, just right. She rubbed him softly.

"Oh shit." He slammed down on the brakes and pulled the skidding car over to the side of the road. The tires dragged at the gravel surface of the road's shoulder and the car shuddered to a halt. Conrad moved the stick to park but kept the motor running. Lydia was still massaging him between his legs.

Conrad grabbed her wrist and lifted her hand. "This is too dangerous."

"It's not dangerous. There's nothing here. I'm tired of this driving, of interviewing your prisoners. I don't want to look at old rebel campsites. I can't help you. I'm nothing, a nobody. Your government doesn't need me."

"You don't understand the process. They need you very much."

"They don't need me. You need me. Say it." Lydia leaned forward and pressed her hands against Conrad's chest. Her face was close to his, her lips near his ear. "Say it. Say you need me. Say that I give you what you've never had before."

Conrad gulped and stammered his words. "I need you. I need you badly." No woman had ever intimidated him like this before. He needed control.

"I know you need me. I could feel it in how your body moved when I made love to you. All those other men who took me were like animals. I knew there was something better than them. And when I had you, you proved me right."

Conrad closed his eyes and focused on the sensation of her warm breath against his ear. He felt the movement of her lips as they grazed against his skin. With his eyes still closed, he slid his arm behind her and pulled her close to himself. Her lips slid across his cheek and touched his mouth.

A vision of his ex-wife, of Mary, passed through his mind. As Lydia kissed him, he thought about how soft and full Lydia's lips were compared to Mary's thin dry lips. Mary, the mother of his children, would make love efficiently. As efficiently as she did her job at work. Lydia moved clumsily but free of worry. She kissed him with abandon.

He felt like a clod in comparison. He was nervous and stiff in response to her movements. But the more that Lydia kissed him and rubbed against him, the more he understood that she didn't care about his resistance. Resistance he wanted to shed. But he thought of the rebels, of ambushes, of bullets, of blood and opened his eyes.

Lydia languorously opened her eyes too. In silence, they stared at each other across the small space between them. Then, "In the grass. Now Conrad. Be quick if you're scared. But do it now."

Conrad pulled his door handle and pushed the car door open. He pulled her small body out of the driver's side with him. She moaned softly or she had simply said yes.

He looked around for danger but his vision was a blur. His body, his senses were focused on the warm, writhing body he held at his side.

"Quickly, quickly." The words might have been the wind for all Conrad knew. He moved around the car and into the soft bed of wet grass that extended beyond the gravel of the shoulder.

The bushes near them rustled and then were still. Conrad turned his head to one side. He listened for sounds, signs of danger. He only heard the high-pitched noise of insects all around. A bullfrog croaked. Lydia kissed him on the shoulder and slid her hand down his pants. He watched the dark bushes fearfully as he laid her gently on the ground.

He kept his eyes on the unlit space behind the trees as Lydia undid her jeans and pushed them down. Conrad kept one hand flat on the ground next to her head. He used the other to free himself. Lydia was breathing heavily and panting his name but he didn't look down at her while he rapidly undid his pants.

He finally glanced at her when he had his penis out. Her eyes were closed and her mouth was wide open. She pulled her knees up between them, her jeans and underwear pulled down to her shins. Another sound, a bird flashing off into the sky, jerked Conrad's attention away from her again. He had both of his hands on either side of her head now as she took care of guiding him to his mark.

He gulped and watched the bushes near them. She pulled him between her thighs and easily inside her. Warmth and a deep, soothing moistness enveloped him. She put her hands on his head and moved them roughly over his face and through his hair.

He thrust forward and back, over and over, while watching the bushes. The fear of the moment excited him and sent a chill down his spine. He was like an animal being chased by a throng of savage dogs. He felt the thrill of the chase and the fear of death. More sounds came from the bushes. Something rustled within them. Something tightened inside her. A vice of flesh and muscle gripped him like a tyrant.

He looked down at Lydia. Her eyes were open and she was mouthing the word yes over and over, but no sound came from her throat. Her hands clutched his head. The muscles of his entire body contracted in fury, his back bowed and arched. He lifted one hand and ran it over her chest. She followed the movement of his hand with her own hand.

He suddenly stopped thrusting and his whole body tightened. He let out a loud groan as he felt the wash of tension sweep away from his body and through that one piece of flesh between his legs. His orgasm lasted an eternity. From his pelvis outwards to his limbs, he suddenly relaxed and collapsed on top of Lydia. She gave a slight grunt. He gasped for air. "Oh shit. I'm sorry."

She pushed on his chest and he raised himself up on his hands. "No. It was perfect," she said. "You were...uninhibited. And scared."

He rose to his knees and looked into her eyes. She had her hands over her chest and she was smiling. Her face and neck were red. She dropped her bent legs down to the side and pulled her pants back up. Conrad stood while she squirmed to get her jeans back on.

Conrad breathed deeply, adjusted himself, and zipped his pants back up. He staggered a little as he buttoned his shirt. "I can't believe we did that."

"Now do you understand why I saved you?"

Conrad held his hand out and pulled Lydia to her feet. "How could you have known what I would be like?"

"I knew Conrad. After being silent for eleven years and doing nothing but listening to people and watching them, you begin to know them in other ways. I saw you and I knew."

Conrad heard the muffler of a car in the far distance. "Come on. Let's go. I had this crazy idea someone was watching us."

Lydia smirked as she walked over to her side of the car. "Maybe someone was."

Conrad stopped at his door and watched her disappear into the car. He looked across the expanse of bushes and trees along the road but he saw nothing except leaves and grass undulating in the light breeze. The unlit road both ahead and behind them was clear of vehicles. He climbed into the car. The motor was still running. He popped it into drive and hit the accelerator.

22

C onrad squeezed his shoulder blades together and dug their points into the wet sand. He was laying on the beach close to the edge of the water, letting the ocean lap at him. The water was refreshingly cool and the morning sun overhead hot. Linda lay next to him, her head and hand lightly resting against his chest. He folded his hands behind his head and gave a sigh that reached back through years of frustration and fighting.

He drew in a deep breath through his nose to fully smell the ocean. He and Lydia stank of a delicious sweat. They had spent the last eighteen hours driving to the Virginia coast, sleeping in the car, and making love three times in the ocean and on the sand under the moon. Conrad knew this stretch of shore south of the city of Virginia Beach well. It had been a comfortable place in the past and it was still a peaceful place now, generally free of the violence of guerrilla warfare.

Conrad closed his eyes and listened to the rhythmic flow of wave after wave sweeping across the shore. Memories of decades past floated in his mind. Headlines jumped to his memory.

The wave of change had begun years ago, in January 2010, when the federal government pressured state governments into instituting the draft for National Guard Service. Surprisingly, the change happened uneventfully at first. Liberals railed against it, conservatives found fault with various provisions and pundits jabbered on. It was all talk on both sides, with a few protests tossed in here and there, and life remained peaceful enough for the average person. But the war on terror got worse, the economy sank lower and U.S. citizens became anxious. More and more parents got tired of losing their children for two years to guard duty and the FBI even noted a marked increase of violence among American young adults as they returned from their tours. Bombs went off every few months within the nation's borders and some people began to wonder if all of them were actually planted by jihadis.

The frustration pushed the political pendulum the other way and the Democratic Party, led by Johanna Avery Reed, won the election in '12. Her first real test occurred a year after her election when the Supreme Court upheld a South Dakota law that virtually banned abortion in that state. Violent protests and counter-protests spread across the land over the South Dakota law. Other states passed similar legislation and finally, a conservative U.S. Congress passed federal legislation that severely restricted abortion rights. They overturned the President's veto of that law and the violence and bombings intensified. It culminated in the mysterious partial burning of the United States Capitol on February 11th, 2015.

Washington, DC was experiencing a huge blizzard at the time, a blizzard that shut down city services, and emergency vehicles were slow in coming to put out the mysterious blaze. Conrad remembered where he was when he got the news. It was a Wednesday evening and he was having dinner with fellow FBI agents at a restaurant in Boston. They had been discussing a bomb that had blown up prematurely near the Old North Church. He remembered the debate being whether the target was the church or a group of rich Saudi businessmen who were also in the vicinity at the time. His belief had been that the church was the target.

The federal government moved rapidly after the burning of the Capitol Building. On July 8th, 2015, President Reed issued Executive Order 15-2087, effectively telling her executive branch to stop enforcing federal laws that restricted American freedoms and which seemed to do little to stem the intensifying violence. Ironically, the order was more about the budget than with politics.

The E.O. specified the laws that the President didn't want law enforcement to investigate and prosecute. The federal and state governments began focusing on combating violence rather than moral issues. Conservative protestors suddenly became the new enemy. Jails began to empty as drug users finished their terms and new ones didn't arrive to take their place. Therapy and rehab became the new liberal cause, the goal being to educate rather than incarcerate.

It was on January 17th, 2016 that the Freedom Bureau of the Department of Homeland Security was formed. The new organization was tasked with enforcing the new comprehensive American Freedoms Law of 2015 that effectively made gay marriage a federal right, legalized all drug use, abolished all previous restrictions on abortion, allowed unrestricted ownership of guns, legalized prostitution, and which ripped away most of the restrictions on free speech. That was the day that everyone wondered when the really big powder keg would blow.

Conrad's attitude towards the law was a pragmatic one. He knew the federal government had to save money and he knew that some of the laws that this new law wiped away were in all events useless and practically un-enforced anyway. His own belief system was not based on religion. It was based on the belief that law, order and freedom were the keys to save the United States from its downward spiral. In his opinion, the American Freedoms Law, while not perfect, was something that needed to be enacted. But the November election approached.

One conservative candidate, firebrand Leo Treanor, alienated people, including many Republicans, but he created a fervor among his cadre of supporters. The slow, telling drip of a new type of violence started that May. It began with the lynching in Wyoming of a couple of gay men caught having sex in a gas station bathroom. The members of that mob were never caught. Then a black man was lynched in Texas and the secretly taken video of that heinous act spread like wildfire over the internet. Burned and beaten, the black victim's body had been left hanging from a tree to rot.

Three Central American teenagers were lynched in western Massachusetts by a group of Connecticut Aryans and then everyone knew this wasn't a North-South thing like all the media outlets were claiming. When they lost that fuel for the fire, they made it a race thing, a class thing, a sex thing. They made it everything they could. Conrad remembered being scared the day that the Aryans decided to torch a small black town in Florida. Something had given in parts of rural America and people no longer wanted to uphold the law.

Some conservatives who always preached respect for the law suddenly found that they didn't like the law that now existed and they turned against the government with their presidential candidate Thomas Freeley leading the charge from his pulpit. He had attacked Leo Treanor at first for being too much of a demagogue but then he later accepted him as his vice presidential candidate.

With the domestic violence came the terror of international totalitarianism. Russia, China, and many ex-Soviet countries turned again to the dark days of Stalinist repression. Liberal Americans saw it and they saw something in their own country, something evil gaining strength in every rural corner of the country. And something in the mind of those effete liberals, as Feeley enjoyed calling them, something in those soft-hearted "pussies" turned. Democratic leaders saw something too and they harnessed that energy, that energy that had fueled the Progressive movement, the Labor movement, the Civil Rights movement, the Peace movements.

"Are you all right?" Lydia raised her head and looked at Conrad.

Startled, he lifted his head. "Just thinking," he said. But Conrad knew she could feel the pounding in his heart. His body was stirred by the memories of the fights and blood that came.

Conrad voted against Reed. Not on any moral grounds but because he simply thought she wasn't doing a very good job of stemming the violence. Taxes had also gotten a little high for his taste. But he hadn't voted conservative, he went libertarian. But his vote didn't matter because people still only cared about the two main parties and Reed was re-elected. So called red state National Guard units protested her re-election by besieging federal facilities in their states.

The shooting started accidentally on April 3rd, 2017 when members of the Missouri National Guard besieging Fort Leonard Wood began shooting at each other. They couldn't agree on which side to take. An army unit in the base thought they were under attack so they returned fire. The news spread rapidly and fighting began everywhere. The 2nd U.S. Civil War had begun.

Like a dam breaking, that energy came suddenly and rushed forth and who honestly could have been surprised when those "pussy" liberals took a page from the conservative handbook. When the liberals turned to arms, conservatives began to die. By the dozens they fell. Then the hundreds, then the thousands.

Conrad shivered and Lydia moved a little in response. She coughed softly and shifted her weight on his chest but she kept her cheek down and her eyes closed. Conrad blinked and looked at a lone passing cloud.

Radical conservatives had started the Civil War with the lynchings and the fires but the liberals ended it. It took two years to wrap up. Two years for state militias from New York City, Boston, DC, Chicago, Seattle, San Francisco and Southern California to end the mess. It was a stalemate in the first year with the front lines being drawn where suburbs became exurbs and, deeper still in rural country. Then, with U.S. power ebbing on the world stage and countries like Russia and China and Mexico suggesting that they could send in their own troops to control the violence in the United States and help end its Civil War, then the conservatives wavered and the liberals sprang with a vengeance.

It was Sherman all over again but not just in the Southeast U.S. this time. Scorched earth happened in every rural part of the country. Farm towns went up in flames. Those who resisted were hunted down and shot or put to hard labor. For a short while, "Republican" became a word of disgust, of rebellion. During that second year, all international horrors came true, like dominoes falling naturally from the pressure of one little finger. Iran invaded Iraq, China took Taiwan, North Korea took South Korea, Israel was besieged. U.S. troops fled Iraq and were used by the U.S. government to instill order in the states and they did. Any soldier resisting the burning of the rural portion of America was put to twenty years of hard labor immediately. Few disobeyed orders.

On June 13th, 2019, the war ended. No one knew why the declaration was made on that date but it seemed fitting enough. The violence had petered out. It flared up again slightly next January when the mass graves of executed gays, illegal immigrants and minorities were discovered in out of the way parts of the country. But the violence died away again when it was quickly realized that the perpetrators of those crimes were long dead and sleeping in graves of their own. Overt conservatism had been killed in urban America.

It took two more years for America to heal and establish a semblance of life that resembled what existed before the war. Like the carpetbaggers of old, coastal liberals took over the governance of the major cities of America. For better or worse, America had rid itself of all concepts that involved the restriction of freedom. The country had re-embraced the spirit that some said existed in 1776. Now, 246 years later, it was time to rebuild. Though rebels still lurked in the countryside, just outside of metropolitan zones, the country healed.

Conrad heard something, faint noises that drifted over the sand dunes and along the ocean breeze. It was the sound of screams. His head came up sharply. Lydia lifted her head too. Conrad moved Lydia gently away and jumped to his feet. He heard the cries clearly now, coming from the south somewhere along the beach.

"Wait here." Conrad sprinted towards the commotion, his bare feet smacking on the wet sand as he ran at a full sprint for a quarter of a mile. Thick sea bushes on his right blocked his inland view and it wasn't until he turned a corner around a thick clump of bushes that he saw the source of the sounds.

Seven men wearing jeans and t-shirts and brandishing metal pipes surrounded three men and a woman wearing retro-1970s hippie garb. The four who were surrounded stumbled about in the sand while the seven men, all young and vicious, taunted their victims and prodded them with the pipes. One of the seven men, the shortest one, rapped one of the male hippies on the head with his pipe. The man collapsed to the ground moaning.

Lydia came to Conrad's side sweating and panting. She grabbed Conrad's arm and pulled him down behind the bushes. "Hide," she said.

Conrad pushed her off his arm. "Are you crazy? They're going to kill those kids." He peeked over the bushes and saw that five of the thugs each had a gun hanging on his belt.

Lydia grabbed Conrad again. "No Conrad. They'll kill you, then they'll kill me, then they'll kill those kids." Despair filled her eyes. Conrad could feel in her grip the horror she showed in her eyes, the violence of her past welling up in her memories. He shook his head and gently slid her hand off his arm. She sobbed as he rose.

Conrad drew his gun from his hip holster. He ran as silently as he could and it wasn't until he was nine meters from the men that one of them noticed him.

A dark-haired man pointed his pipe at Conrad "Shit! Watch out!"

The gunshot ripped through the soft sounds of the breeze and the waves. The man fell with a hole in his chest. The other six dropped their pipes and raised their arms. The wounded one squirmed and moaned as his blood flowed freely over his dirty white t-shirt. He gurgled and spit blood on the grass. A flock of birds shot into the air and flew towards the water.

Conrad barked his words at a man with a thin beard, the oldest looking of the half-dozen left. "What the fuck are you doing?" The man he spoke to shook his head and glanced at a younger, more powerfully built man.

"Well?" Conrad repeated to the larger man.

"Teaching them a lesson about using smack on our beach," he said. He sneered at the four on the sand. "Fags," he said. "You better shoot us all motherfucker 'cause you ain't getting away with that." He gestured casually at his dying friend.

"Luke," one of the other men said. "Shut the fuck up."

Luke slapped the one who spoke with the back of his hand. "Keep your balls out, bitch."

Conrad motioned with his gun to the hippies to move towards him. They didn't budge. Two of the men bled from cuts on their heads. The girl had a swollen lip and her skirt was torn open. All four looked horrified and confused. Conrad motioned again with his gun, vehemently this time.

They tentatively walked to him.

"Start walking that way," he said motioning behind him with his left hand. One of the thugs, more a teen than a man, charged Conrad with his head down and crashed into Conrad's chest. Both of them fell but in an instant Conrad brought the butt of his gun down hard on the back of the kid's skull. Something cracked. The kid went limp while Luke pulled his gun from its holster. One of the other young men charged Conrad but the last three turned and ran.

Conrad threw the unconscious man off him, jumped up and punched his second attacker in the face. Conrad aimed his gun at Luke.

"Move," Luke yelled as he tried sighting Conrad with his gun. Conrad shuffled his feet so that he kept the dazed man he had just punched between himself and Luke. Luke shot once and clipped the dazed kid in the shoulder. The surprised kid cried out in pain.

Conrad ducked and shot once. Luke's face showed surprise and he collapsed to his knees. His gun slipped from his hand and it made a thick sound when it hit the sandy ground. A wet clot of blood formed around the black mark that showed on the upper left leg of his jeans. Luke's eyelids fluttered and he collapsed face first into the ground.

The unarmed kid spun to look at Luke and then spun again towards Conrad with his uninjured arm raised. "Don't shoot," he said.

Conrad grabbed the kid by his shirt collar and smashed him in the face with the butt of his gun. "Are you fucking rebels?"

The kid howled in pain. Conrad's blow had broken his nose. It was a bloody mess that dripped red over Conrad's left hand.

"Let him go man," one of the hippies said. "You got him."

"Yeah we're okay," another said. "We don't want no trouble."

"Fuck you," the girl screamed at the two men. "They were going to rape me. Fuck that and fuck you. Shoot him. Shoot him." The girl had pressed herself against Conrad's back and held his gun arm.

"Come on Camille. Two of them are shot and this kid is fucking scared. That's enough isn't it?" One of the young hippies had started crying.

"I need a fucking hit," the third one said.

Conrad shook his head. "I'm the fucking law. I'm taking this one in."

"A fucking pig?"

Conrad smiled darkly. "I'm federal not state."

"What's the difference?" one of the hippies asked.

"Where are you kids from?"

"DC. What are you gonna do with those guys? They're shot."

Conrad pulled a thin plastic strap hand restraint from his jeans pocket and twisted the kid with the bloody nose around. He slipped the restraints around the kid's wrists, tightened them, and then kicked him into the sand.

Lydia ran up to Conrad and startled the four hippies. Conrad stared at her, unsure if he was happy to see her at that moment. The two bloody men, Luke and the first one he shot, were both alive but barely. They were quiet now. He could try to get an ambulance to the location – unlikely - let them die slowly or... Conrad pointed his gun at the head of one of the prone men.

"Wait, no," the girl yelled. "You're just going to execute them?"

The whine in her voice irritated Conrad. He bent his elbow, raising his gun to the sky, and looked off at the ocean. The waves moved smoothly across the blue surface of the water. He breathed deeply. Legally, he was not justified in shooting two incapacitated criminals since they had not engaged in rebel or treasonous activity. They had only been engaged in criminal activity of a lesser sort.

Conrad looked at the woman. "There's no medical help coming for them. Not out here."

"Can't you help them?" one of the men asked.

"No. I can't help them." Conrad looked back at the hippies. "You got a car close by?"

"Yeah, yeah. Right over the ridge there." The kid motioned abstractedly in the distance towards some grassy sand dunes further inland.

"Then go," Conrad said.

"Shit man. You got to help these guys." But they didn't wait for a response from Conrad. The four walked towards the dunes, supporting each other as they did and glancing back at Conrad until they disappeared from view.

"Fucking hippies," the bound kid said. He spit on the ground. "You Feds fucking let them do whatever the fuck they want."

"It's a free country. Drug use is legal."

"Fuck that. I didn't vote for that stupid president."

Conrad knelt and leaned close to the kid. Smooth-faced, he looked about seventeen. He was probably too young to have fought in the Civil War but he had certainly experienced it. A wave of disgust crashed over Conrad. He gulped and stared at the slowly dying men. The kid kept trying to inhale his dripping blood back into his nose.

"Fuck you outlaw." Conrad stood up, wrenching the kid up by the collar as he did, and then brought his left knee up under the kid's chin as hard as he could. The kid's head snapped back and he passed out immediately. Conrad dropped him on the sand. He took the kid's gun from his waistband and then picked Luke's gun up from the grass.

He was disgusted with all of them. Apparently no one could be happy and no one could follow the law. Screw them all. He walked past Lydia, his breath seething between his teeth. "Let's get the fuck out of here before those others bring back friends."

"What about these two?" The two were completely still, grotesquely painted by their own deep red blood.

"Forget about them. They lived by the sword, let them fucking die by it."

23

C onrad and Lydia walked north along the beach, side by side without touching. It was not yet noon but the sun floated high overhead. Its heat added layer upon layer of sweat to Conrad's body. From the ocean, a breeze blew across his skin in waves and the damp sand cooled his bare feet.

He stopped and waded into the water until it came up to the edge of his rolled up pants. Lydia bunched her skirt up and followed him in. They stood there for a few minutes, Conrad waiting for the rush of the recent fight to completely ebb from his body.

Dark clouds moved slowly from the east towards them. Conrad adjusted the two guns shoved in the front of his waistband and jerked his gun belt back and forth until it felt comfortable on his hips. He walked back to the shore, letting the sand slide between his toes at every step.

Lydia looked at him expectantly, a faint smile playing on her lips. Conrad returned the look and took a deep breath to calm his temper. Lydia was not to blame for the misgivings and doubts that haunted him and he needed to remind himself of that. He had chosen this life by himself.

A seagull's squall reminded Conrad they had lingered too long. "Let's head back."

Lydia nodded and dropped her head.

Conrad hesitated. He thought he was bringing Lydia to a quiet spot but instead he had found a place almost as violent as any front-line area he had worked. She didn't deserve this. Not when she had shown such undivided loyalty and compassion. For her sake, he swallowed the anger that refused to leave his chest.

They turned south back towards the car and Conrad began to recompose himself. Ten minutes into the return walk, the sound of automatic gunfire stopped them in their tracks.

They dropped to their stomachs and crawled towards a high dune. Conrad crawled all the way to its ridge and peeked over the top.

A little less than a quarter mile away, three pickups surrounded a yellow VW bug.

Black bullet holes and the red spray of fresh blood covered the car. The car windows were smashed. Four bodies lay crumpled along the bottom of the car. Three men with automatic weapons, M16s, stood shoulder to shoulder about six meters from the car. Eight other men also armed with automatic rifles ranged behind them, laughing and hollering with each other, smoking and drinking from gold beer cans. One of the eight, wearing a blue trucker's cap and chest armor over a denim shirt, didn't look so jovial. He surveyed the area carefully and ignored the rest of his group.

Conrad backed down slowly to where Lydia had stopped. She was pushing her face into the ground and clutching the sandy hill as though she would float away into the air otherwise.

"Come on," Conrad said. "We've got to get out of here fast."

Lydia raised her head with a look of sheer exhaustion on her face. Conrad had the feeling she would give up right there if he told her to. His heart steeled for action. His jaw muscles clenched and he gripped the butt of his holstered gun. He took Lydia's right hand with his left. They scooted back down the hill and then, in a crouch, ran south along the dunes. After a few hundred feet of running, they headed inland, southwest, at a forty-five degree angle from the water.

They ran for about four hundred and sixty meters and came over the top of a high hill of sand. One hundred and twenty meters away, a man with an automatic rifle in his right hand peered into Conrad's black Mustang. Conrad felt a quick sense of relief for having left the car locked and alarmed.

The man pulled a walkie-talkie from his belt and spoke into it. Conrad reacted by wrenching his gun out of his holster and pointing it at the man. He let go of Lydia's hand and jogged towards the car, his gun held out in front of him with both hands steadying it.

As he moved rapidly forward, he aimed squarely at the man's unarmored chest. The back of the man's white shirt had the phrase 'Where The Fun's At' printed in black letters. Conrad aimed at the space between the words 'The' and 'Fun's'.

The thin man turned and stood frozen for a moment when he saw Conrad. In a panic, he fumbled his walkie-talkie and dropped it. He backed up against Conrad's car and began raising his rifle.

To get a shot from as close as possible to his target, Conrad calmly waited for the moment right before the man had fully leveled his gun barrel at Conrad. As the man's rifle swept upwards, Conrad fired and simultaneously moved laterally to his own left.

Each bullet entered smoothly and exited the man's back in a gory mess, the projectiles slapping against the exterior of Conrad's car. With a shocked look on his face, the man slumped back and his rifle went off like a Catherine wheel, slowly spinning and spraying bullets at the ground in a circular motion. A few more shots exploded into the air as the man fell and then his gun barrel snapped straight towards the sky and he let loose one last shot at a disinterested, eternal sun.

Conrad continued walking towards the car. He pulled out his keys and hit the automatic ignition button. The dead man was on his back with his feet and shins twisted up underneath his hamstrings. His back and chest were spilling blood over the sandy paved parking surface.

Conrad looked back. Lydia had collapsed on the ground. Conrad stopped. "Lydia! Get up!" he shouted.

She didn't respond. Conrad looked back and forth between her and the car.

He looked north towards the far dunes but didn't see anyone yet. He ran back to Lydia. She was unconscious but had no visible injuries. He holstered his gun, hefted her over his shoulders, and ran back towards his vehicle. On the opposite side of the car, men appeared over the crest of a far hill. Away to his right, bullets splashed in the sand.

Conrad whipped open the passenger door and pushed Lydia into the car. A bullet ricocheted off the trunk. Ducking inside, Conrad slid Lydia into the back seat, head first. He slid into his seat from the passenger side and slammed the door closed after him.

He took a moment to consider his situation. He would have to do a one-eighty and drive past the men on the ridge. It had to be done. That's where the paved road went and his car wasn't built for sand driving. Conrad stepped on the accelerator and turned the wheel sharply to get out the way he had come. He was angry he had not thought to park for a quick getaway but his self-abasement slid away in the face of the immediate danger.

His tires spun uselessly over the sandy asphalt but, after a moment of fearful inaction, the tires gripped the parking surface and the car shot off. More bullets glanced off the face of the car. They were getting their range. The tires should hold thought Conrad but he readied himself for a blow out.

"Get my rifle from the back," he said to Lydia. The intensity of his voice filled the interior of the car and Lydia lifted her head.

"What?" she asked. She groggily touched her face.

"Pull my rifle and shotgun from the rear compartment. The backseat latches are unlocked. Pull the seat forward and get the guns out."

Conrad looked at the road in front of him and pressed down hard on the accelerator. His engine whined loudly as a hail of bullets cracked against the surface of the car. Lydia made a hellish racket as she tried to get the seat down and the guns out of the trunk. The barrel of the rifle bumped Conrad in the back of the head.

"Be careful!"

"I'm trying!"

Conrad passed the point closest to the men on the hill and the ricocheting bullets sounded like heavy rain on a tin roof. Moments later, the car began to pull obliquely away from the attackers. The car was still being peppered with gunfire but the distance was great enough that the force of the bullets was getting appreciably weaker. The tires held as Conrad crested a hill and the car raced down the other side. The rain of bullets ceased.

Conrad slowed down. In moments, they would be on the road that led back to the relative safety of Virginia Beach. He silently prayed, hoping the ambushers didn't have a roadblock up.

"How the fuck could they have known I was here?" Conrad asked. He didn't expect an answer from Lydia.

"Do you still need these guns?" she asked.

Conrad made eye contact with Lydia in the rear-view mirror. She had a calm expression on her face. "No. Put them back."

"Who did you talk to on the phone before we got here?"

Conrad looked again at Lydia's reflection in the rearview mirror. She wasn't looking at him now. She was trying to figure out how to put Conrad's dangerous possessions back in the trunk without accidentally shooting herself in the process.

Conrad licked his parched lips. A half-filled water bottle sat in the cup holder between the front seats and he took it. He unscrewed the top with his teeth and tipped it upside down to pour the water into his mouth. He sucked at the opening and then looked at the empty bottle. He threw it against the passenger door and it bounced harmlessly to the floor. "I talked to my fucking ex-wife. They must have intercepted the call."

"I thought you, ow..." Lydia shook her hand and stuck two fingers in her mouth. "Scramble those calls."

"Forget about the guns and climb up here."

Lydia reached over the front seat's headrest and balanced herself as she brought her feet to the front. She slid into the front passenger seat with ease. "Well?"

"Yeah. The message is encrypted. They might have broken the code."

"Maybe it was your wife?"

Conrad looked at Lydia, perplexed. Her expression was serious. Conrad burst out laughing, but Lydia's face remained stoic.

Conrad became serious too and shook his head. "It's not my wife. A rebel bomb blew my son's arm off a few years ago-"

She interrupted. "Is he alive?"

Conrad's chest tightened. He pressed his palm against his sternum. "Yes. He lived and he's doing okay. As well as possible without his right arm."

Lydia bit her cheeks. "So she wouldn't join them because she hates them."

Conrad was annoyed by her persistence. There was no use in Lydia trying to be a detective. What do you know about things like marriage and children? he wanted to ask. "Well, that's one reason. She's been cleared anyway. She doesn't have sympathies for the rebels."

"I see."

Conrad took his cell phone from between the seats. It was turned off. "They must have traced the signal. Knew it was a government call since it was encrypted. Must be."

"You trust her?"

"Come on Lydia. She has an active clearance." Conrad put his cell phone down. "They might have triangulated the signal. Encrypted message must have tipped them off to be on the lookout for someone like me. It was random."

"Must be," Lydia said. Her voice sounded sarcastic but she didn't say anymore. She looked straight ahead at the gray band of road they sped along.

24

He was close. He knew it. He felt it. He had laughed at Lydia when she had suggested that Mary had anything to do with the attempted assassinations. She had nearly been the victim of one herself. But there was something in that idea and he had mulled it over during the whole uneventful drive back to Georgetown. Mary wasn't the culprit but someone close to her was getting a hold of what she knew.

Conrad stood and stretched. His building's underground garage was not even half full and the sounds of the car repairs he was doing echoed through the small cavern. Most of the residents, many of them law enforcement professionals like himself, were still at work. He always hated the government's requirement that high-level enforcement managers like himself live in the safer parts of DC even if their field offices were an hour or more away at the edges of the city. He thought it best to work and live close to the action - if the government actually wanted results. Today though, it was good to feel the safety of the building.

Conrad looked down at his engine once more. The fluids were good and she was running well. He dropped the hood and it clanged loudly. Nothing and no one in the garage responded to the shocking noise. He walked completely around the car once more to triple-check for any bullet holes or tears in the tires he might have missed. The Mustang had numerous small dents but structurally she was still sound.

He lay down on the ground and ran the beam of his flashlight underneath the car. He didn't discover any new damage. He stood and peered through the driver window at the miniature motion-triggered surveillance cameras mounted on the dashboard and on top of the back seat. They were turned off but were set properly otherwise.

He popped his trunk and checked the equipment he had loaded. A small crate of a dozen grenades. Climbing gear. An assault and a sniper rifle. His repeating shotgun. Forensic investigative equipment. A standard tool set. Spare tire. Surveillance bugs and radio gear. A Nuclear, Biological, Chemical emergency suit and medicine kit. Fire extinguisher. He was prepared.

Conrad slammed the trunk down. He looked towards the elevators and thought of Lydia. He had brought her back to his apartment and told her to stay put. He expected she would follow directions. He had closed all the curtains and window blinds and told her not to look outside or venture out onto the balcony. She had meekly agreed. He wondered if he should check up on her again and decided against it. He was running out of daylight.

He slid into the driver's seat and got the Mustang going. He pulled out to the garage exit and just after passing the security gate, he stopped at the top of the ramp. The sky was empty of clouds and it was hot.

He pulled a panel on his dashboard down and flicked the power switch on a small pad. A digital map of a portion of the city appeared on the panel and a small dot indicating the current location of Mary's car flashed on it. The car was near a Bethesda mall. Nothing odd about that.

Conrad pulled up the recorded history of her car's location over the past 168 hours. He ran a program that determined whether a car traveled over the same, or nearly the same, routes during a given period of time. The five-second analysis of her car's movements revealed nothing unusual. That doesn't mean much, he told himself. Her information leach probably moves along the same lines she does.

Conrad kept the panel open and merged with the Georgetown traffic. He drove west for a few blocks and then north on Wisconsin Avenue towards Bethesda. He would catch here there.

When he finally approached Bethesda, her car moved from the one spot it had been occupying for the last fifteen minutes. He left the light traffic of Wisconsin Avenue by turning down a small side street. He stopped at the corner and waited for a moment. Mary's maroon Chrysler sedan passed across his front, right to left, and he turned into the street behind her. He kept a distance of about four car lengths from her. He maintained that distance as she got onto Wisconsin and drove south. She made a left on to Van Ness and about a dozen blocks down turned right onto Connecticut Avenue. She weaved a little as she drove. Conrad hoped that she didn't get pulled over for drunk driving.

Conrad closed the distance between himself and Mary to three car lengths. What am I doing, he wondered. He had to admit that she had been acting strangely for the last year. The drinking, the odd calls, the furtive looks and the nervousness. He always thought she had simply become sensitive to dangerous movements and sounds. The therapist had said she would probably be under great mental strain for years.

But all of that didn't condone what he was doing now. He had followed her in the past but only to determine whether she was being followed by someone. He always told her afterwards and she didn't mind it. But now he was following her not because she might be in danger but because she might be the danger. He felt guilty for distrusting her. He felt subhuman for being so callous to her problems, her fears. But he continued tailing her. It was time he knew what was going on.

Traffic was fairly heavy and only got heavier as they got closer to downtown. She wasn't driving defensively. Either Conrad was good, or she had simply forgotten the lessons he had taught her when they were married. His children came to mind. If nothing came of this, he would try to slide in a reminder to her of watching for tails everywhere.

Once they crossed the stone lions guarding Taft Bridge, Conrad hung back a little more. The slower pace of traffic would make Conrad easier to spot if he got too close.

She followed Connecticut into downtown DC and then headed east on K street. She was deep in her lobbying district now. She slowed and pulled into a parking garage. Conrad drove a block past that garage. He pulled into a handicapped parking space and hung his DHS parking permit from his rearview mirror. They might have taken his badge but the parking permit was still his.

He leapt out of his car and ran towards the garage Mary had entered. Near that entrance, he slipped into the front alcove of an adjacent building and peeked around the corner. He stood with his hands shoved in his jean pockets and a baseball cap pulled low over his face. Then he raced over to the parking attendant's booth and rapped on it vigorously.

"Yes, sir," a turbaned man with an Indian accent asked.

"How many exits are there in this garage?"

"Oh. Here sir and a set of doors around that bend." He pointed down the slope of the garage ramp to a point hidden from view. Conrad heard the sharp click of heels and quickly slid outside and behind the attendant's booth. He tried to look as inconspicuous as possible but he was no undercover detective. He probably stuck out like a sore thumb. The attendant squinted at him from behind the plate glass window and then lowered his head to work on a puzzle in the newspaper.

Conrad eased back a little more and pressed against the wall of the booth. The heels reached the parking garage exit and moved on to the sidewalk. Conrad held his breath until the steps moved in the opposite direction. Conrad peaked out and saw Mary's back. She wore a long blue dress and a wide-brimmed white hat that flopped up and down as she walked. A thin, white shawl draped her shoulders. Conrad let his breath go.

That had been clumsily carried out. He had gotten lucky she didn't go the other way. She would have spotted him immediately. He glanced at the attendant's booth. The attendant was staring at him, forehead furrowed, pencil in one hand, newspaper in the other. Conrad smiled and touched the tip of his cap. He hurried after Mary.

Conrad pulled his baseball cap lower down on his head and walked behind her about eighty-five meters. There were some vehicular traffic but only very light foot traffic. Conrad felt naked under the sun following her. One look back and things would be blown. If someone were watching if she had a tail, they'd spot him for sure. He glanced around but saw no one watching either of them.

Mary walked two more blocks, hurried across the street and entered an American style restaurant that had polished metal adorning its front. She had chosen the Flemi Café. Conrad crossed the street after watching the door for two minutes. If Mary knew what she was doing or was worried she had a tail, this might be where the shake would happen. She could clean herself of him by slipping out the back door of the restaurant and that would be it. Game over.

Conrad rubbed his chin, looked both ways and sauntered across the street, trying to avoid walking in a direct line of sight between the restaurant windows and the street. He debated entering the restaurant but finally decided to just wait.

Twenty feet from the Flemi's entrance, on the same side of the street, was a partially enclosed bus stop. No one was using it at the moment. Conrad grabbed a copy of the free city paper from a newspaper can, flipped the paper open and sat on a metal bench under the canopy of the stop.

He had a portable surveillance camera on hand but it was hard to hide in plain sight and it had a short battery life. He considered setting it up at the bus stop and checking for a back alley behind Flemi's, but he didn't feel ready to use it up just yet. He had a feeling

Mary was exactly where she planned to be and he forced himself to relax.

People - students, immigrant workers, some professionals, the aimless – came and went. Conrad stood for the elderly and the women. He sat when no one was around. Two buses passed and Conrad smiled sheepishly at each of the drivers.

Conrad killed forty minutes that way before Mary came out of Flemi's again. Conrad cursed himself for not having taken a peek in the restaurant and trying to determine whom she had met, but he had a good reason. The café's entrance was narrow and anyone watching whomever was entering and exiting would have seen Conrad with ease. There was nothing that he could have done if he wanted to remain inconspicuous.

Mary walked away from him, past an alley. Conrad adjusted himself on the bus bench to keep an eye on her, but he kept the newspaper in front of his face.

The Flemi's front door opened and she looked back. A man in a blue polo shirt, khakis and a casual dress hat stopped at the threshold. The open door was between Conrad and the man and Conrad could only make out that the man was average-sized and about five-foot ten.

Without breaking her stride, Mary smiled and blew a kiss back at the man at the door. The stranger darted back in to the restaurant. Conrad's heart raced for every reason. Mary seeing someone new she hadn't told him about. A secret meeting. Her happiness. His task at hand. Would the man come back out the front door in a few minutes, would he exit through a back way, or would he sit and wait for someone else? Now was the time.

Conrad pulled a video camera the size of a ring box from his belt. He turned it on, aimed the lens at the Flemi's door and adhered the camera to the glass surface of the bus stop paneling. He held a flat, four square-inch screen in his left palm. The screen showed what the small camera was transmitting – the Flemi's front door.

Conrad left the bus stop and walked around the block to see if an alley ran behind the high-rise office building in which the cafe was nestled. There was an alley and it led directly into an inner courtyard formed by the office buildings on that block.

Conrad leaned against the outer wall of the building and looked down the alley. He held the small screen low in front of him and glanced back and forth between the alley and the screen. Conrad

Cris Alvarez

straightened when the man in the blue polo exited Flemi's behind a group of four men and walked past the bus stop and the camera.

Conrad slipped inside the alley and leaned against the wall. He looked around the corner and watched for the man. The stranger crossed the street and disappeared past the office buildings on the next block. Conrad exited the alley, crossed the street at that point, and then moved up the block to the corner the man had disappeared past. He looked around the edge and didn't see him.

Conrad felt warm. This one might be experienced in shaking a tail. Conrad walked quickly down the sidewalk and looked through every door and window he passed. He saw nothing of the man. He walked back to a coffee shop he had passed. He looked inside. He didn't see the man. He went back outside and surveyed the area. He could have gone anywhere. Conrad went to the corner and crossed the street. He walked to the middle of the block, a vantage point where he could keep an eye on the entire length of the street block where the man had last been seen by Conrad.

Conrad waited five minutes, then ten. Plenty of people came and went but no one was wearing the polo shirt, the khaki pants or the hat. Conrad looked at his watch. He had been there for a fruitless twenty minutes now. He shook his head in disgust.

Carefully watching the people and the buildings around him, Conrad walked the one block back to the bus stop. A young man sat on the bus bench listening to his headphones. He looked at Conrad a moment and then stared straight ahead. Conrad pulled the camera from the glass and pocketed the device. He looked around one more time, saw nothing to worry him, and hurried back to his car.

Before he reached his Mustang, he walked into the garage Mary had parked in, ran to one of the other exits the attendant had pointed out, and exited. He was in an alley behind the building. He exited the alley and took a roundabout route back to his car.

Once inside his vehicle, he drove a few blocks and parked. He plucked the small screen from his shirt pocket and rewound what his surveillance device had recorded. The man exited Flemi's and walked by the bus stop. Conrad paused the video. The camera had caught a grainy but close shot of the man's face. It was someone quite familiar to Conrad. It was Nicholas Deevers.

25

The storybook neighborhood was dark, quiet, calm. It was a good, upper-class suburb of detached, single-family homes with a smattering of small garden style apartment buildings scattered here and there. Most of the homes Conrad drove past were dark inside with security lights illuminating the fronts. A dog barked and another briefly answered. Then the quiet came again to North Bethesda.

In due course, Mary's two-story, colonial-style home loomed before Conrad. The windows were dark and one bulb illuminated the front entrance. Conrad pointed his car's dashboard camera towards the front door of the house and the rear seat camera towards the gate that led to the landscaped backyard. Conrad slipped out of his car and looked around. Feeling comfortable that no one was watching him, he walked the pebble path to the front door.

He tattooed the door loudly with his knuckles and stepped back from the door, down two brick-layered steps. The peephole darkened. Someone slowly opened the door. Behind it stood Mary in a red satin robe tied tightly at the waist. Her feet were bare but her right hand was casually burdened by a whisky glass of ice and a clear liquid.

Mary blinked slowly. "What are you doing here?" Her speech was slurred.

Conrad reminded himself to stay relaxed. This constant drunken state of hers always infuriated him. Her hair was disheveled and her makeup had run down her cheeks as though she had been crying. He took a deep breath before speaking. "We need to talk."

She shrugged, turned with surprising grace on the balls of her feet, and took a gulp of her drink before walking away from the open door. Conrad tentatively entered the front hallway and turned to close the door gently behind him. When he turned again, Mary was sprawled out on a full black leather couch in the living room. The lights were dim and light jazz music drifted from wall-mounted speakers. Conrad, nerves on edge and unsure of the familiar surroundings, walked from the entrance hall, past a stairway, and into the thickly carpeted living room.

Cris Alvarez

"Where are the boys?" he asked as he looked back at the stairs.

"With friends. I'm alone." She stretched out the second syllable of the last word and said it deeply as though she were saying something humorous.

Conrad's heart pounded. He circled around the back of the couch and sat down on a leather love seat that faced both the couch and the front door. To his left was the dining room and the pass-through opening to the kitchen. Conrad knew that the kitchen had a sliding door that led to the back patio and it worried him that it might be unlocked. He rose to check it.

"Where are you going?" Mary asked.

Conrad waved his hand. "Just checking the patio door."

"It's fine."

Conrad ignored her and entered the kitchen. It was spotless and nothing was out of place. That was his Mary. Fastidious about everything except her own behavior. She used to be concerned about that too. Conrad stopped at the sliding door and looked the back yard over. The door was locked and the yard was empty. Satisfied with what he saw, Conrad returned to the leather seat and sat down.

Mary stretched her legs towards Conrad and yawned. "I told you didn't I?"

He could see that she wasn't wearing any underwear and it embarrassed him to have seen that. He looked at the blank television screen across from the couch. Old pictures of Mary and the boys adorned the entertainment bureau. His face was nowhere to be seen. Mary finished stretching and put her drink on the floor next to her. She smirked at Conrad and then nestled her face under her arm.

Conrad grunted. "Haven't you had enough already?"

"Go to hell," she said from under her arm. She pulled her legs up a little and reached down to flip the edge of her robe over her bare legs. She kept her eyes closed as she did that and she brought her arm back to cover her face.

Conrad leaned forward with his hands clasped. The smell of cigarette smoke lingered in the room. He dropped his head. "You seeing someone?"

Her arm and head jerked up but she looked at Conrad in a lazy manner. Her head didn't sit steady as she glared at him with narrowed eyes. "So what if I am?"

"Nothing. Just the boys. I want to know who's around them."

"No one who's going to get their limbs blown off." She sneered and slid her head back down under her arm. She squeezed her legs tightly together and stretched them out with her toes reaching for Conrad.

He stood and walked to the television. He lifted the picture of Paul and Karl from the bureau. It was a three-year-old picture taken before Paul had lost his arm. It had a gilded frame designed to look like oak bark bordering the picture. Conrad ran his finger along its grooves. Paul looked genuinely happy and carefree. He hadn't looked that way in a while.

Conrad's throat tightened and he rubbed it roughly with his left hand. He hadn't shaved in days and it bothered him to feel the stubble on his neck and chin. It made him feel, he searched for the right phrase, unpredictable. Out of control. He stopped rubbing the stubble and squeezed his neck instead.

"Keep squeezing," Mary said.

Conrad looked sharply at Mary. Her head was up and she chuckled. She dropped her head again.

Conrad growled at her comment. She was entitled to her anger but he was tired of her constant attacks. Did she think he felt no guilt about the accident? Was she the only one aggrieved?

"Who is he?" His tone expressed the anger he felt. He felt his share of guilt and she didn't need to make it worse. She blamed him one hundred percent for the accident. He blamed himself even more if that was possible. He had been the target of that bomb but it was his child who had paid for Conrad's successes. She never let him forget that.

Never one moment of forgiveness. Fuck it. He didn't deserve forgiveness. She was a deep scar in his memory and there was nothing anyone could do about the deep scars. You just carried them like a badge of honor, a scarlet letter of shame.

"Someone you wouldn't want me to be seeing," she said.

Conrad put the picture back in place without looking at what he was doing. "Why?" Instead of standing, the picture dropped flat on the bureau, but he didn't set it upright.

Mary shrugged. "Just a hunch."

Conrad wanted to draw first blood. Now was the time. He took a few steps towards Mary. "You're having an affair with Nick aren't you?"

Mary's body tensed and she stared at him, her lips pressed tightly together and her eyes wide.

Though the lights were dim, Conrad could swear the color slipped out of her already pale face. "So I'm right?"

She hemmed and hawed.

"Forget about us for a minute. If it's true, I need to tell you something."

"I'm sure you do, " she said.

"First I have to know if you're having an affair with him. How often does he come here?"

Mary rolled over on the couch and faced its back. Her legs and butt showed and Conrad turned his gaze from her. "I'm not married to you anymore. He's not married either. It's not an affair," she said.

A knot in Conrad's throat grew large. He lowered his head. He could deal with her seeing some random guy but to be seeing someone in his office, a new guy he supervised, someone fourteen years his junior, someone twelve years younger than Mary, was too much. He clenched and unclenched his fists.

On top of all that, Nick might be a rebel spy, the dirty mole everyone was after. He looked up. Mary had turned her head and was staring at his hands. As he looked at her, he felt the blood rise in his face. He hoped Nick was the mole.

"Do you need to leave?" she asked.

"No. But I have to tell you something."

Mary turned her head again towards the couch. "I'm sorry. It just happened."

"Where did you meet?"

"A function over in Rockville. Six months ago."

Nick joined the force five months ago. Six months ago, he was moving into town, just transferred from Orlando.

"We talked," she said. "A lot."

So it was even before he got here. A ready-made relationship for the guy. Great. Must have been an internet thing. Mary. A leggy knockout blonde with a high income, two kids and a DHS ex-husband. Did Nick even know who her-ex was when they met? His future boss? The pieces were starting to fit.

Conrad walked to the love seat and collapsed into it. "Here's the thing. Every time I talk to you lately, in person or on the phone, something happens. Something I don't like."

Mary lifted her drink and sipped it. "I don't know what you're talking about. What does something bad mean?"

"You know what I mean. Like getting shot at or attacked. Someone's tracking your calls or you're telling the wrong person where I am. I think it's Nick. Do you tell him where I am so you can meet without me finding out? That'd be a good cover story."

Mary put her drink on the floor again and turned onto her back. Below her waist she only had on panties but she didn't bother to cover herself. She crossed her arms over her face. "It's not like that."

"You've got to stay away from him."

She spoke from under her arms. "No. I'm crazy about him."

"So why is it a secret?"

"For his career."

The canned answer didn't surprise him. His temper rose and he jumped from the chair. "Cover yourself up. I have something to tell you about that."

"I don't need his fitness evaluation from you."

Conrad went back to Paul's picture and righted it. "He could be dangerous. He could be a mole for the enemy."

"Bullshit. You're doing it again Conrad." She got up from the couch and straightened her robe. She folded her arms and her whole face tightened around her pursed lips. "You'll make anything up to win the argument. You're just trying to drive a wedge between us because you're jealous. You were always jealous. Jealous of every man that ever talked to me. Or fucked me."

Conrad felt the knot in his throat again. "Bull," his voice caught, "bullshit." He felt like he might start to cry. The feeling shocked him. He had never felt so intensely unable to control a situation before. He had to convince her without seeming to be doing it for jealous reasons. He was jealous but that wasn't what this was about! He had to convince her for her sake and for the boys. There is no alternative. I have to win this argument.

He walked to her quickly in a panic. She held her hands out, palms toward him, trying to keep him away. He grabbed her right hand with both of his. She tried to pull away but he held her tightly.

"What are you doing Conrad? Let me go!"

"You need to listen to me Mary. Very carefully. This is real. This is vitally important."

She pulled and protested. He stared into her eyes while she struggled. She finally stopped moving and acknowledged his gaze with her own eyes. "Go ahead," she said with resignation.

"I don't care about myself Mary. Do you understand? I don't care anymore. I'll do anything to save the boys. I'll leave. I'll take all this violence away from you. Just tell me what's going on so I can stop it. And when I'm done, I'll leave."

Mary's face registered nothing. Conrad waited for her to respond but her lips didn't part. He needed to say something that would move her. "They might not stop with me. They might continue until you and Paul and Karl are dead. So I have to get them first. Do you understand Mary? Do you understand that?"

Her stony face abruptly morphed into a visage of sorrow. "Conrad." Mary threw her free arm around Conrad and pressed herself against his body. He released her hand and she threw the other arm around his neck. She kissed his chest and ran her hands over his head.

Conrad pulled her closer and held her tightly. He held the mother of his beloved sons close to him. He didn't want to let any of them go, ever.

She gently pushed back on him and he loosened his grip. She kept her hands on his chest. Her face had an angelic look of calm. "Lay down on the coach," she said.

Confused, he walked to the couch. He lay down on it with his feet towards the chair he had been sitting on. She knelt beside him and began to undo his shirt. His worries returned. It felt like the most inappropriate thing to do right then but he didn't stop her. For the first time in a long while, he was comforted by her presence.

She took his shirt off and then his shoes and pants. They both stared at the waistband holster tucked in his pants. She expertly undid the thin belt that held it secure and gently placed the holstered gun on the floor. She spread her robe open and climbed on top of him. She straddled his waist and bent down to kiss his bare chest. He placed his hands on her hips and let her do what she wanted.

She worked him up with her mouth and her hands, caressing the upper half of his body and then the lower. When they were both ready, she slid herself on him and closed her eyes. Nearly in terror of an ambush, he watched her as she undulated and moaned. He held her hips and felt more love than lust in the act.

He hadn't come for this and he certainly didn't want to do anything that she didn't want. The desire to make love to her had not crossed his mind for at least the last eight months. Where had this desire of hers come from? His mind rejected the reason that seemed most plausible.

She moved back and forth, slowly at first and then faster and with more purpose. She moaned louder and louder, the muscles of her body tightening and relaxing in rhythm. Conrad clenched his teeth and squeezed his eyes shut, hoping to hold out long enough for her to achieve the physical pleasure she presumably sought.

When she reached the final throes of ecstasy, he let himself lose control. They heaved and pressed against each other in that loud, final act for fifteen long seconds until she collapsed on him in a sweaty heap. She lay there without moving, he inside her, while her lips quivered on his skin and her breath passed over his chest.

Something shuffled in the darkness. Conrad jerked his head up and looked back at the front door. Was it closing? The lighting wasn't good and there were too many shadows for him to be sure. Had he seen something? He lowered his head and look down at Mary's hair. He stroked it lovingly.

A car engine started near the house and roared off into the darkness. Mary lifted her face to look at Conrad. She looked puzzled.

Conrad lifted her gently and they untwined their bodies. They sat side by side and then Conrad stood. He didn't know what to say or if he should even say anything. Would she admit to any wrongdoing or misgivings now? She squirmed her torso behind him to stretch herself on the coach. Conrad stood and picked up his clothes.

"Where are you going?" she asked

Conrad slipped his pants on and zipped them. He paused in the middle of buttoning his shirt. "I've got to check in at the office."

Mary touched her chin and looked towards the stairs. "Now?"

"Yes. Right now."

"Okay." She looked at the stairs again. "Are you scared?"

"For the boys I am. But when I find out who's after me and get them, then I'm through like I said. And they'll be safe."

Mary nodded. "I know they will be. Conrad?"

Conrad finished buttoning his shirt. He sat on the coach and pulled on his socks and shoes. "Yes?"

"I believe you."

"Oh. Just now you do?"

"Yes. I trust you and I believe you. You'll save the boys and disappear."

He attempted a smile but didn't know if it crossed his face as one. "That's what I said." He patted her bare thigh and took a hold of his waistband holster as he rose. He slipped the holster inside his jeans and tightened the belt.

"Okay." Mary rose and walked to the kitchen. She returned with her cell phone.

"Who are you calling?"

"No one. I'm just going to recharge it."

Conrad nodded. He couldn't force her to tell the truth. He'd have to accept what she said even if he had his doubts. He drew Mary close and kissed her on the forehead. "The boys will be fine."

Mary smiled. "I know Conrad. I know."

He tried to smile again and believed he succeeded this time. He walked out the door wondering what his car cameras might have caught.

26

T he compound was a ring of tower lights aimed outwards at a hostile world. Fixed patches of light encircling small street lamps partially illuminated the shroud of darkness within the ring. Not so much to reveal the secret, fragile curves of the buildings within but enough to guide the path of those whose official duties brought them to the Occoquan Federal Center during the witching hour. The unfinished war did not limit itself to regular working hours.

The black Mustang moved through the outer ring, stopped at a booth, started again, and approached the Freedom Station inside. It slowly rolled to a stop in a parking space just in front of the building. Two other cars sat in the Freedom Station's parking lot. Nick Deevers beat up gray Neon and Officer Allesandro Lippen's sky blue Taurus.

Conrad gnawed at his lips. They were dry and he wanted water. He pushed his hips forward and reached for the butt of his pistol. With his thumb, he slid off the piece of soft plastic that held the gun in place within the holster. He drew the gun from the holster and looked at it for a minute before opening the glove compartment and sliding it in there.

He didn't want to enter his own station as an armed antagonist. Since he was still officially on administrative leave, that's all he would have been to the guard on duty. It was bad enough that he had driven into the compound with a car trunk full of military equipment. For a handful of anxious seconds, Lou, the gate guard, had considered searching the car. Feigning a lack of concern, Conrad had gotten Lou to relax and wave him in. But Conrad's heart wasn't revving yet. There were more tests to come.

He opened the car door slowly and closed it quietly. He manually locked the door with his key instead of using the button alarm on his key ring. He approached the front entrance and, at the top of the steps, the building's tinted front doors slid open with a whisper.

A single desk lamp illuminated the reception desk. The uniform on duty, Allesandro, looked up from a crossword puzzle he was working on. His eyebrows pinched inwards in puzzlement.

Conrad put his wrists on the edge of the desk and drummed the surface lightly with his fingertips.

Allesandro's forehead remained tense. "Sir?"

"Just getting some stuff. I'll be quick."

Allesandro looked behind Conrad and then made eye contact again. "You have your ID sir?"

Conrad was impatient. He rubbed his left eye. He wanted to see what Nick was up to before the opportunity passed. "Ah, no. But I'll be quick."

"Lou let you in?"

Conrad folded his arms. "Yeah sure." He went for a minor pleading tone. "I'll be quick San. No worries."

Allesandro shook his head and shrugged. "I can't do it sir. Nick's up there. He'll have my ass and so will Dave." Allesandro looked around conspiratorially and his voice dropped to a whisper. "Maybe come back later. I'll let you in but Nick, he's a real asshole."

"I know." Conrad glanced at the stairwell and then at Allesandro's pained face. He didn't want to get the youngster in trouble. San was a good cop. "Okay." Conrad tapped the tabletop once more. "Maybe I'll just come back tomorrow."

"Okay. Cool. Thanks sir. Like I said. Nick's a real asshole."

"You see him much?"

"Yeah. He works this late a lot." Allesandro smiled. "You guys really lay it on the newbies I guess." Allesandro looked around, leaned forward and, still feeling conspiratorial whispered. "This a test?"

Conrad smiled back and shrugged but he was thinking about what San had said about Nick's work habits. Nick worked late sometimes. They all did but not necessarily this late or as often as Allesandro just suggested.

Conrad walked back out into the darkness. A faint light was still on upstairs. Conrad started his car and drove back to the front gate. Lou remained sitting when Conrad passed by and waved. Another good guy on the force. Loyal. I shouldn't be putting their heads on the line like this.

Conrad checked his rear-view mirror. Nick was still at work. Conrad turned right onto Route 123 and then made a right onto a side road that followed the perimeter wall.

Conrad drove for a minute and then went off road towards a section of trees growing along the wall. He parked near a grove of tall, heavily leafed maples. Apart from the heavy vegetation and the wall, there was nothing.

Conrad got out of the car but, before closing his door, he stared long and hard at the glove compartment. He decided he still didn't want the gun. He closed the door and walked to one of the larger trees. He felt around on the ground near it and found a metal ring that he slipped one finger through.

The ring was attached to a ten by ten-inch panel covered in dirt that came up when Conrad pulled. Underneath the panel was a small number keypad and an optical scanner. Conrad took a deep breath. He punched in a twelve-digit code and pushed his right thumb against the scanner. Ten seconds later, a small green light flashed and Conrad exhaled in relief.

Conrad reached into a space under the keypad and slid a larger and heavier panel, three by three feet, back. Below the panel were metal stairs descending down into a tunnel. Conrad entered the space and slid the panel closed above him.

There was a second keypad and scanner mounted on the wall near the stairs. Conrad entered a different twelve-digit code to lock the large panel behind him. He placed his thumb on the scanner and soon thereafter, another green light flashed. Conrad hurried down the twenty-foot length of metal steps. At the bottom of the stairs was a horizontal concrete tunnel ten feet wide by eight feet high with green glowing plastic strips running along the bottom length of the tunnel and dim lights running along its ceiling.

Conrad jogged down the tunnel back towards his office building. He ignored the many passageways that branched off from the main one until he came to one that he took. Fifty feet further, he came to another set of metal stairs. He climbed them and used another keypad and scanner to open the panel over his head. He emerged from the tunnel into a dark supply closet. He closed the panel underneath him but didn't use the security device to lock it.

He opened the closet door carefully. The hallway was dark and quiet. A stairwell entrance door ten feet to his left was closed. He walked softly to the door and opened it. Conrad breathed a sigh of relief when he got through the metal door without it squeaking.

He hurried up the stairs to the second floor and out into another dark hallway. He followed it to the double-door entrance of his division's offices. They slid open smoothly and quietly and Conrad entered.

The light in Nick's office glowed on the other side of the glazed pane of the closed door. Conrad looked around. His eyes were getting used to the low levels of light and he could see better now. The office looked a little different. The recycling bin had been moved closer to his office door and the coffee table had been moved to the opposite wall. Conrad wanted to laugh. Dave had always wanted the coffee table farther from him. He reasoned that would keep him from drinking as much of it as he did.

Nick's office door clicked. Conrad's face became warm and heavy and he no longer felt the humor in the situation. His hand instinctively went for his waistband holster before he remembered he had decided to leave his gun. At least he wouldn't be caught armed in a government office he had just broken into.

Nick's door opened slowly but stopped only six inches from its frame. A face peered out. Conrad didn't move.

"Who is it?" Nick asked. His voice boomed in the empty room. "Greis?"

"Is that how you address me now Nick?"

The door opened wider, just wide enough to let Nick slip smoothly and quickly through and close it behind him. "What are you doing? You're not allowed up here."

Nick was dressed casually. Jeans, dark boots, a collared shirt and his usual thin, dark green windbreaker that rustled when he walked. Conrad watched Nick's face and body language closely and he waited a moment in silence. Nick was nervous. That much Conrad could tell.

Nick stopped waiting for Conrad to answer. "If San let you up." Nick shook his head. "I'll have to report him."

"He didn't let me up."

Nick rubbed his right hand on his chest and the windbreaker rustled. "I can't let you go in your office. It's against regulations."

Conrad couldn't stop his face from breaking into a snide smirk. For a moment he was sorry it happened but when Nick blinked quickly and seemed more nervous, Conrad was happy he had done it. He pushed through the security gate and walked into the common area. As he casually walked left towards his office door, Nick stepped to him quickly. He put his hand on Conrad's chest.

Conrad looked at Nick's hand. He let his gaze move up the arm to Nick's eyes. Nick was about two inches shorter than Conrad and Conrad liked having the height advantage. Nick licked his lips nervously. A muscle in the young man's jaw twitched as Conrad looked him over.

"How long you been working tonight?" Conrad asked.

"I can't let you go in there."

Conrad moved slightly forward to test Nick. Nick applied more pressure to Conrad's chest and Conrad couldn't help but smile again. Yet his heart raced. He had been hoping for a confrontation and in his mind he had worked out how it would happen, all the possibilities and his reactions. But situations never worked out according to plan.

"Ever hear of common sense?" Conrad asked.

Nick glanced at Conrad's office and looked back at his own office door. The two doors were on opposite sides of the common room, nearly across from each other.

"Nervous about something?" Conrad asked.

Nick looked at Conrad and scowled. "What the fuck are you talking about?"

Conrad lifted his left forearm inside Nick's arm and knocked Nick's hand off his chest. Conrad simultaneously struck the side of Nick's face with a partially made fist. Nick's body turned with the blow and he stumbled back. He straightened up with a look of surprise and his hand went to his jaw. His face hardened and he reached inside his windbreaker.

Conrad dropped his weight, charged forward and drove his right shoulder into Nick's sternum while also wrapping his arms around the man. Nick shouted but couldn't hold Conrad's inertia. With a crash, they fell on top of the conference table in the middle of the room. It buckled slightly under the weight but didn't give. Nick's gun arm was pinned against his chest. Nick began punching and grabbing Conrad with his free arm while trying to pull his right arm from the windbreaker. The table moved under them and screeched as its metal legs slid inch by inch along the floor.

Conrad leaned his weight on Nick's chest and pushed his left forearm hard up under Nick's chin. Conrad used his right fist to punch Nick repeatedly in the ribs and kidney. His knuckles felt the hard leather of Nick's chest holster under the windbreaker but he kept hitting.

"Gah!" Nick barked in pain and twisted back and forth until he squirmed free of Conrad's hold and fell on the floor. He scrambled away on his hands and knees but Conrad leapt on to the back of Nick's legs and tried to hold them together. Nick got a leg free and cracked Conrad in his head with a heavy boot heel. Pain shot through Conrad's skull and he yelped. He grabbed his forehead with one hand and tried to hold on to Nick with the other.

Nick kept kicking Conrad with his free leg. "Cocksucker!" he yelled.

"You son of a bitch," shouted Conrad, trying to grab hold of Nick's jumpy leg.

"Fuck you," Nick said and kicked once more. Conrad lost his grip on Nick's other leg.

Nick scrambled to his office door. As Conrad staggered to his feet, Nick opened the door, slipped inside and slammed the door behind him. Conrad stood and shook his head. Each office door had an electroshock gun, an alarm button, short-term CBN equipment and a medical kit mounted next to it and low on the wall. The idea was that during an emergency, it would be easier to reach equipment from the floor.

Conrad bent down snatched the electroshock gun that hung near Nick's office. He twisted the door handle but it was locked. Conrad kicked the door but it only rattled without breaking.

He took a few steps back and launched his heel at the point of the door closest to the knob. The door exploded open under the impact and Conrad fought to keep standing as he stumbled forward into the office. Nick was banging away on his computer keyboard. He banged one more key before turning ninety degrees to his right to face Conrad.

Nick reached inside his jacket again and pulled a pistol loose. Conrad extended the electroshock gun towards Nick and squeezed the trigger. A wire shot out and hit Nick in the leg. The electrical current ripped into Nick's leg and he groaned in pain as his hair stood on end. His pistol jumped out of his hand as he straightened up. The gun crashed into a window but the glass held.

The electric jolt passed quickly and Nick collapsed to the floor in a heap. Conrad relaxed and walked over to Nick. The haphazard layout of his limbs made him look idiotic. Conrad checked Nick's pulse. It was racing but the man was alive. He wiped the sweat from his own forehead and looked at his hand. Streaks of blood decorated his palm. Conrad ran his hand over his head. A thin streak of sticky liquid, his own blood, extended from the now swollen point where Nick's boot hit him to his left temple.

Conrad folded a loose sheet of paper into quarters and used his left hand to hold the paper against the cut on his head. He shifted his focus to the computer screen. It showed a blueprint of the Treasury Building on 1500 Pennsylvania Avenue. Conrad moved the computer mouse and saw that the other open screens displayed blueprints of the White House and the Capitol Building. Yet another screen displayed Secret Service guard schedules and patrol routes for the government district areas of Washington, DC and Arlington, Virginia.

Conrad flipped through a sheaf of warm papers stacked on the printer tray next to the computer. The printouts included the same blueprints and schedules on the screen as well as other similar information related to the security arrangements used by the Feds in the city.

As far as Conrad knew, this information had nothing to do with Nick's official duties. It was possible but unlikely that Nick was working on some new assignment for Dave. Even if Nick wasn't using this information for an official assignment, the fact that these papers were sitting in Nick's office unmarked and unused meant nothing. This wasn't proof he was a mole. Every DHS agent printed out random security information for their own edification. Security was their career and hobby. Maybe Nick was only guilty of being more overzealous than most in the field. Maybe.

Conrad felt weak in the knees and looked down at Nick. How in the hell will I explain this? he wondered. He had just assaulted a federal officer in a federal building. Conrad was on assignment, albeit undercover, but would that fly? Or would the DHS cut him lose now for this and disavow any knowledge of the operation he was part of? It didn't seem likely that his bosses would forgive a fight that had resulted from a simple jealous rage.

He sat on the edge of Nick's desk and nudged Nick with the tip of his foot. "Shit." The paper he was pressing against his cut resisted a little as he lifted it up. The blood was thick on the makeshift compress. He touched the cut and felt a large tender bump swelling around it. Nick's cell phone was strapped to his belt. Conrad tossed the bloody paper on Nick's desk and stooped down to remove Nick's phone from its leather case. He flipped it open and turned it on.

Conrad went to the phone's address book and scrolled through the numbers saved on the phone. He knew some of the names and numbers but didn't recognize most of them. He plugged the phone into Nick's computer and opened the cell phone's number list in the computer's phone management software. He pulled a chair over and sat. Working quickly, he accessed a DHS security database and used it to identify the names and addresses associated with the numbers saved on the phone.

It took only a few moments for the entire list to be compiled and Conrad began reading through it. Mary's number was listed in the phone as 'sxy m'. A warmth rose up in Conrad's chest and he looked at the still prone form lying on the floor at his feet. He wanted to haul his foot back and release it into Nick face but he left that thought as an angry piece of imagination.

A couple of the numbers were listed to rural areas out beyond the city. A third number had no information associated with it. Conrad leaned back in the chair and rubbed his chin. The war had left the government lacking in some information and it was taking time to update and track certain items. The price of civil war included loss of database information and incomplete records. Conrad grabbed a pen and a small sticky note. He scribbled the three numbers on the small square of yellow paper.

He disengaged the phone from the computer and dialed the number with no associated data. It rang two times before being answered.

"Yeah?" said a thick Eastern European voice.

Conrad grunted without saying anything.

"Where do we meet?" the man said.

Conrad remained silent.

"I'm having fun drinking with myself fucker. Don't bother me if you're not ready."

Conrad gambled. He partially muffled the phone and tried to whisper in Nick's voice. He plucked a nearby location from the air. "Woodbridge. Train station."

"The train station again? Okay, fine. One hour."

The line went dead.

Conrad looked at the phone. The name for the number was 'Dax'. The time was 12:33 a.m. Conrad scrolled to 'sxy m' and pushed the call button.

The phone rang three times before it was picked up. Mary's slurred voice came on.

"Why are you calling me now? It's, oh shit, it's twelve-thirty. Are the boy's home? Wait a second."

Conrad heard the phone hit something hard. Nick began to stir. Conrad grabbed the electroshock gun. He stood and moved away from the desk. He looked at the gun and angrily realized it was a cheap model that needed a recharge before it could be used again. He threw it at the corner of the office.

Nick rolled around and made groggy noises.

Mary came back a little over a minute later. "Why are you calling? I told you he'd be here all night."

Conrad pulled the phone from his ear and stared at it. Who would be there all night? Was she talking about him? He ended the call with a push of his forefinger and slipped the phone into his pocket. Nick sat up and rubbed the top of his head. His face went from confusion to anger when he made eye contact with Conrad.

Nick looked back at his computer and then his hand shot under his desk. Conrad hesitated between running and charging Nick again. Nick pulled his hand back from under the desk. He held a small gun.

Conrad spun and ran through the office door. When he backed himself against the wall adjacent to the doorframe, the sound of a gunshot exploded behind him. That furious bullet ripped through the wall close to his shoulder. Another single explosion and a bullet smacked against the middle left side of Conrad's back.

The bullet laid an intense pressure against the skin, muscle and bone of his back ribs. He groaned and pitched forward, clutching behind him at the point of the bullet's contact. The slug was squashed against the thin body armor that Conrad had slipped on just after leaving Mary's house. Conrad still wasn't used to the new technology. At times he would forget that he had put it on simply because the armored vest only felt like an irritatingly stiff undershirt. At the moment, he was nothing but thankful for it.

Conrad popped the hot slug off the armor and turned towards the door. The butt of Nick's gun was coming down at his face. Conrad turned his face away from the surprise blow and instinctively raised his arm to defend himself. The butt of the small caliber gun cracked against his forearm and pain shot through that limb. Conrad went down to his knees.

Remembering an old martial arts move, he dropped to his hands and swung his legs around in a circle, slamming his shins against the back of Nick's legs. Nick fell backwards and his head cracked against the edge of a chair. Nick groaned and rolled onto his

Cris Alvarez

side. The gun dropped out of his hand and clattered to the floor. Conrad kicked the gun across the floor and ran for the office exit.

With each step, a dull pain traveled through his skull and down his back. He awkwardly jumped over the low gate at the front of the office and scrambled through the double doors that opened too slowly for comfort.

He heard Allesandro yell stop as he sprinted to the stairwell that led back to the supply room. Conrad took the steps two at a time, crashed through the stairwell's first floor doors, and sidled through the still open supply room doorway. He closed it as noiselessly as possible. Allesandro's and Nick's voices yelled somewhere beyond the door.

Conrad reached for the panel in the floor and wrenched it open. He descended the steps quickly, closed the panel over his head, and used the keypad and scanner to lock it. He ran a few steps and then leapt off the stairs down to the floor. He stumbled when his feet made contact with the ground and Nick's phone flew out of his pocket. The phone cracked against the concrete floor, breaking into a dozen pieces. Conrad swore loudly and held back from kicking the pieces across the tunnel floor.

He shook his head, collected his wits, and picked up what was left of the phone. He shoved the pieces haphazardly into his pocket. He swore again and both ran and stumbled in pain towards the other end of the tunnel.

When he reached the stairs that led back to his car, he took a moment to catch his breath. Voices echoed in the distance behind him. He swore again and ran up the stairs. He hurriedly unlocked the panel, got out into the darkness, slid the panel closed, and jumped in to his car. Without looking back, he gunned his engine and drove away from Freedom Station Occoquan.

27

L ife in negative. A heavy darkness surrounded him, the black canvas interrupted, painted, scratched, by points and patterns of a dozen different shades of neon. A tenebrous night overlaid by dreams of a shattered rainbow.

One car passed slower than the others had. Conrad raised his head and watched its double beams slowly sweep over and past him. The car was alongside him for a moment and then moved on to be swallowed by the night. Just a careful driver.

Conrad lowered his chin to his palm and leaned his elbow back on the armrest. He stared from inside the black of the abandoned and boarded up gas station in which he had parked. The strip mall on the other side of the street glowed under the yellow light of its security lamps. The illumination made the darkness in which Conrad sat that much starker. The traffic lights of Route 123 blinked from red to green, to yellow, and back to red. Time passed slowly while Conrad navigated his muddled thoughts.

After having survived multiple attempts on his life over the past two weeks, he was about to consciously step foot into a viper's lair. His physical strength was sagging. His body ached from top to bottom. Getting hospital care was more appropriate now than conducting surveillance form an old gas station. He thought of Lydia and his sons and the selfish pain receded to the back of his mind.

He shifted in his seat and adjusted his rear view mirror to get a view of a dark spot he didn't trust. He wasn't sure how to approach the railroad station meeting. The short conversation on Nick's phone only hinted at things, it didn't prove anything, barely provided probable cause in his own mind, and he knew a bit more than the average Joe off the street.

Go up to a man with a Russian accent who would probably look and speak furtively? Approach him and demand to know what he was looking or waiting for? Have him shrug and say I don't know what you're talking about and casually stroll away? Would it be unreasonable to chat a bit then knock him on his ass and find things out the old-fashioned way - with a bit of grit, a hard fist, and an irresolute will to get to the truth?

Conrad sucked on his teeth. He wished he had Dave there or Blounts or Angelina. Someone who would stake the place out before he got there, tell him the situation, and then stay hidden close-by to watch his back. For all he knew, he had a tail on him already. It would have to be a good one in this dark. Did they know he was close? He didn't have an electronic tracker on his car. He had wiped it for electronic surveillance and it was clear. Nick may have warned his man already. It might be another ambush. Or maybe Nick was still laid up dealing with a cracked skull. But Conrad was tired of running and there was no time for more preparation. If he was going to act, it would have to be now.

Conrad decisively slapped his leather steering wheel. He started the car and pulled onto Route 123. He headed towards the Woodbridge train station. Like many of the railroad stations along the rail line between Washington, DC and Richmond, Virginia, the Woodbridge station had been expanded in size to hold troops and heavy weapons. What had once been a simple two-room commuter stop had turned into a medium-sized military post during the Civil War. The stop's close proximity to the Occoquan River just down the ridge on which the stop was perched made it a strategic spot to collect and distribute supplies used for the defense of the southern edge of urban Washington, DC. But during the years following the war, the station had been left unused and abandoned.

Too much guard duty was required to get the trains between major cities now. Crime wasn't rampant along the tracks but it was there and any decent criminal knew how to slink back into the mountains, woods and swamps after a good heist. Commuter service no longer existed. Now the trains ran irregular schedules. They ran when they had enough cargo or passengers or both to make the expenses of a guard escort worth it. And they certainly didn't waste their time stopping in small suburban towns like Woodbridge anymore.

As he drove, Route 123 became Gordon Boulevard and Conrad followed the bridged road over the twelve lanes of Interstate 95. Just over the broad highway, the boulevard ended at Jefferson Davis Highway. Jeff Davis Highway was the name given to much of the stretch of Route 1 between Washington, DC and Petersburg, Virginia, which was located just south of Richmond.

The portion of the road Conrad drove on paralleled Occoquan Bay and part of the Potomac River. Conrad found it interesting that the capital of the Confederate States and the capital of the United States were only slightly over one hundred miles apart. He understood the claustrophobia those two sides must have felt during the first Civil War. But now the enemies were closer and the weapons ranges longer.

Conrad felt a kinship to the Union soldiers of one hundred fifty years ago. Both of them trying to save something they didn't quite understand or feel fully part of. Government for the people and by the powerful. Who was the U.S. government of? he wondered.

After less than a mile of driving south, Conrad turned left off Jeff Davis Highway on to a narrow road and drove over a bridge that spanned the tracks. The side road took him past the unlit rail station but he didn't slow down. A quick and casual scan and Conrad saw no one parked close by to the station. He continued down the road that veered to the right and ran somewhat parallel to a curve of the Occoquan Bay.

He was frustrated to be feeling nervous now. He didn't like feeling intimidated by the bay. All areas in a three-mile radius from his office, which included this rail station, should be safe for government employees. He was theoretically in friendly territory, in his territory.

Conrad made a series of turns that looped in tight circles and put him in an old subdivision of mid 20th century split level homes that sat very close to the rail station. Only a long, low ridge thick with bushes and pine trees screened the neighborhood from the station.

Outdoor security lights and street lamps faintly lit the roads. The homes were dark and quiet. It was coming on 1:30 a.m. on a work night and this was a neighborhood of working people. Conrad craned his head to find one house in particular. He found the house midway down a cul-de-sac and he pulled into its driveway. There were no lights around its perimeter or at the front of the house.

Conrad closed his door softly and walked to the front door of the red brick split-level home. The yard was a little messy but the lawn was cut and the bushes trimmed. Conrad looked back to make sure no one was watching him before he pushed a button doorbell set in the wall to the right of the front door. The muffled ring of a bell sounded behind the door and a dog inside barked. Conrad winced. That would be Fletch.

Conrad shuffled back and forth on his feet and glanced back again. Fletch scratched at the bottom of the front door and continued barking. The barking and the scratching abruptly stopped.

"What's going on?" a voice asked from behind the door. Steve Kilwain. From Steve's side, the sound of a pistol slide snapping into place.

Conrad pressed his face close to the door. Its surface was damp with dew. "It's Conrad."

"You okay?" Steve asked.

"Yeah, yeah, I need to tell you I'm leaving my car in front of your place."

"Hold on."

Locks came undone and finally the door swung inwards. Steve, dark-skinned, with a full beard, a mustache and a shaggy afro stood barefoot in a ratty, greenish-colored cotton robe. Steve squinted at Conrad and shook his head. He turned his lanky six-five frame and walked away from the door. "Come in," he said. Steve loosely held a nine-millimeter gun in his right hand.

Conrad paused to look at the small brown and white beagle that now quietly regarded him from a safe distance. Conrad smiled but Fletch looked nervously at Steve and back again at Conrad. The beagle stood his ground fearfully and silently. Then it moaned.

Conrad closed the door behind him, locked it, and followed Steve into the dark house. "Just for a sec, Steve. I've got work at the old station."

Steve walked into his living room and sat on the plush arm of a fat chesterfield coach. "Need help?"

Conrad followed Steve into the living room and smelled the stale scent of cooked fish. Steve liked fried fish as much as his ex-wife hated it. Conrad's mouth watered. He walked past Steve and dropped into the comfortable coach. It faced a large fifty-one inch flat screen television that made the living room look small and cramped.

"No. Don't worry. But if I don't get my car or come back here by morning, call the Freedom Station and let them know I was here and that I was meeting a suspect at the station."

Steve swiveled around on the armrest. "Sounds like serious stuff. Talk to me."

"Don't worry about it. Stay inside if you hear gunfire." Conrad removed a tube of dark green camouflage paint and a small mirror from his shirt's front pocket.

"Yeah right." Steve cocked his head. "Wait a minute. Where's your back-up?"

Conrad looked into the mirror and visualized the thick trees and bushes he saw around the rail station sans darkness. He vigorously rubbed the green camo paint over his face in a circular motion. "Special case. I'm on my own."

Steve's head bobbed up and down and he looked at Fletch. Fletch had ambled his way to Steve's feet. Steve bent forward and rubbed the beagle on the head. Fletch still seemed nervous and he eyed Conrad warily. He dropped to his stomach and laid his chin on the floor.

"You're dog doesn't like me."

"Fletch doesn't like many people at this time of day, uh, night. So what's the deal Rad? Special case with no back-up?"

Conrad paused from applying the camo paint and stretched his arms across the back of the sofa. "I was put on leave. For a little while."

Steve rose from the armrest and sat in the plush chair that went with the Chesterfield. "For what?"

"The kidnapping. That was me."

"No shit. So the leave is a psych thing? Normal stuff?"

"It's not about counseling Steve. I'm getting fucked with in a big way. Someone thinks I'm a mole." Conrad paused. "I think."

"Fuck. You? You're decorated like a goddamn pin cushion."

"Well someone is trying to kill me too." Conrad leaned forward again and resumed his task.

Steve looked around the room. "What? Like now?" He rose and left the room. He returned a moment later with the nine-millimeter in his hand and sat back in the chair delicately as though it might be wired to blow. "Shit Rad. Tell me these things quick, okay? Is that blood?"

Conrad looked in the mirror. A thin streak of dried blood extended from his hairline down his temple. "Yeah. A little." He resisted touching the lump on his head.

"Need something for it?"

"No. It's dry." Conrad began applying camo paint over the tops of his hands. "I don't know what the hell is going on Steve." He considered his next statement for a moment. "I'm in love, Steve. Can you believe it?"

Steve's forehead furrowed and he scratched at his bare knee with the butt of his gun. "I think I need a fucking drink Rad. You're wanted, you're in love. What exactly is on your mind?"

"Every goddamn thing Steve. Two weeks and my life is upside down. I get accused of having a security leak in my office, then I get kidnapped by the Christ cops. Some hot as hell, I don't know, rebel, she's real nice Steve, saves my ass. I get suspended cause some stick up his ass bureaucrat in DC decides I escaped too easy and I must be a traitor."

"Rad, seriously, you want a drink?"

"I'm not done." Fletch stood and walked to Conrad's feet. Conrad reached out and rubbed the dog's head. "My own agency brings me back undercover to interrogate the woman who saved me and take her around for a rebel tour and then I almost get killed maybe three times for it. Four times counting an hour ago." Conrad shrugged. "And here I am."

"Son of a bitch. Let me get that drink." Steve rose. He placed his gun on a white marble-topped lamp table wedged between the coach and chair and went to the kitchen.

Feeling energized, Conrad rose too. "Yeah. I'll have a drink. Make it a shot of whiskey." He put the camo tube and mirror on the lamp table next to the gun and stretched.

Steve shouted from the kitchen. "Is that it?"

"Not even. I freaking tailed my wife. Ex."

Steve came back out with two filled shot glasses. "You tailed Mary? What about when I asked to have Felicity tailed?"

Conrad took one glass from Steve. "Different." They tapped glasses and both men threw them back. Conrad smacked his lips. "Good stuff."

"Always. Okay. Keep talking bro."

"So I tail Mary and she's fucking rubbing up on one of my new guys."

"Shit no."

"Yeah. So I confront her and she doesn't tell me anything new and then I find the new guy an hour ago making copies of security documents that I don't even know if he should have."

"So he's the mole maybe?"

"Well we get into it and the fucker starts shooting at me." Conrad smirked. "I'm thinking he's the guy. But the kicker is he had the right to shoot at me cause I broke in. He could say I was the spy."

"Excessive use of force in my opinion." Steve put his glass down on the lamp table. "And Mary?"

Conrad shrugged. "I don't know."

"But you said she's boning the guy."

"Thanks Steve-o. That's not exactly what I said." Conrad shook his head. "Brother, I don't know women though."

"So what's the next step?"

"So now I set up a fake meet with my mole's handler, or at least the drop man."

"What's my job?"

Conrad shook his head. "Hell no, Steve. This isn't a software bug. Hell no."

"Man. I'm not a punk. Plus this is my neighborhood."

"Fuck that Steve. No. I've been losing everyone I know man. Everyone."

Steve tapped Conrad's chest with the back of his hand. "You can trust me."

"I know. That's why I don't need you getting shot on something like this. Help me how you can."

"Man. If something happens to you, how you think I'm gonna feel?"

"Steve. Fuck it. I said no. This isn't a game. It's the real fucking deal."

Steve picked up his gun.

Conrad nearly whispered it. "Fuck."

Steve rubbed his gun on the sleeve of his robe. "You said it was the train station right? I know the place."

Steve didn't notice Conrad's fist coming at his chin until a moment too late. Conrad twisted his waist with the blow and Steve's head swung to the side. The gun dropped on the sofa and Conrad grabbed Steve's limp body before it hit the ground.

"Goddamn," Conrad said low and through his teeth. He lowered Steve gently onto the coach.

"You're a stubborn motherfucker," Conrad whispered to Steve's unconscious form. "And loyal as hell. Forgive me Steve but I can't let you do this." Fletch was standing and staring at Conrad but he remained quiet and in place when Conrad rubbed his head. "Sorry you had to see that Fletch. Watch your buddy, okay?"

Conrad's heart was racing and his head throbbed. That moment of action had burned the bit of liquor out of his system. He had little time to waste and he knew Steve wouldn't take a knockout punch for an answer. He should have realized that before ringing the doorbell.

Conrad hurried through the front door. He stood at the threshold and pulled his handgun from the holster in his waistband. She was clean, fully loaded, and ready. He flipped the safety and slid it back into the holster.

He looked at his car. He had no time to cover it with a tarp. It was now or never. The bushes and trees of Steve's house would have to do. He walked then jogged towards the station that stood only four hundred and sixty meters away, up and over the ridge.

28

T he railroad station meant nothing now. It was only an empty husk of a building. Three years ago it was a symbol of many things. Hope, safety, danger, a harbinger of worse things or maybe better things to come. Its meaning was all in the eye of the beholder.

Physically, it was merely an organized pile of red bricks, a rectangular pile that measured three hundred and fifty feet by one hundred feet. Its many windows reminded Conrad of a bug. Long, narrow windows, stretching from waist level nearly to the roof, were spaced evenly along the wall that faced the unused parking lot. And like an old bug, its eyes were dark and dead.

A twenty-foot tall crane frozen in rust sat as a purposeless guardian on the opposite side of the building, on the side where the tracks lay. Ghosts of soldiers embarking and disembarking military trains flitted by in Conrad's imagination. His image was among them. The memories fled when a car engine came to life in the distance behind him.

He crouched in the bushes that lined the road he had driven down just fifteen minutes before. Across the road was a large parking lot and then the dead building. The windows were dirty but, having been made of high-strength glass, were unbroken. The window frames were cracked and scarred and were worse for wear than the windows they held.

Conrad looked right and left and saw nothing. Light came from only two sources. Behind, the faint glow of the neighborhood streetlamps. Ahead, a series of street lamps that lit the major road beyond the station. Route 1, Jeff Davis Highway, ran along the high ridge that rose forty feet above and parallel to the tracks. He didn't see anyone on that ridge but it was lined with bushes and trees and an ambusher could have easily hidden himself in the vegetation.

Conrad steeled his nerves and crossed the street. He moved quickly in a crouch to the left side of the building. Up two concrete steps was a rusted metal door secured by a keyed padlock. Conrad pulled an electronic lock pick from his pocket and inserted its thin metal shaft into the lock. He turned the pick on and saw in his mind's eye the device at work. The shaft mechanically morphed until it registered a shape that would undo the lock. A pinpoint of green light on the lock pick pulsed when the correct key shape formed.

Conrad held the lock while he turned the key. Rust held the bolt in the lock forcing Conrad to twist the key harder. The key turned and the lock came undone. Conrad let his breath out. He lifted the lock and pulled the rusted hasp away from the staple on the door. Conrad grasped the door handle and tested the push on the door. The door gave without much resistance and creaked as Conrad slowly pushed it inwards.

The door opened about a foot and a half before something blocked it from opening further. Whatever was in the way wouldn't give to a gentle pushing. Conrad slid through the doorway and shut the door behind him. He could barely make out the floor but he could feel that it was bare concrete. Black shapes cluttered the place. There was no smell of urine or rot which meant that the place actually had gone unused for some time.

A bit of light came through the dirty windows so he moved towards those. He stepped gingerly over and on top of large heavy things that rested on the floor. Chunks of metal, concrete and cabling that had been tossed inside when builders began using the station as a temporary construction dump and storage shed after the war. Conrad only hoped there was nothing flammable or explosive among the refuse.

When he reached the closest window, Conrad leaned on the wall next to it and peered through. He could see a portion of the empty parking lot but not the whole thing. The windows were set too deeply in the wall to give him a good view. He moved carefully along the wall stepping over rubble and broken lengths of two by fours. He considered using his pocket flashlight but he wanted to adjust his eyes to the darkness in here. A light would also warn others he was inside and waiting.

Conrad went from window to window trying to get the best view of the parking lot. Like the first window, the others were just wide enough to allow him to see a narrow portion of the old parking lot but not all. He wondered what side the contact would come in from. Both ends of the station area were well hidden by overgrown trees and bushes. Someone might simply drive into the lot from the side of the street closer to Route 1. Conrad decided to pick the best vantage point and wait.

The waiting didn't take very long. The door he had come through slowly creaked open. Conrad drew his gun and moved back along the wall towards the door as quickly as he could. The door opened as far as it had before, someone slipped inside, and then the door closed completely. Conrad stopped and crouched. He pointed the gun towards the door and swung his weapon slowly and deliberately from side to side, scanning the darkness. His heart pounded and he wondered if the other person could hear it. A pile of boards shifted abruptly and clattered to the floor. A man grunted and swore.

"Steve," Conrad hissed.

"Conrad," Steve said. "Shit. I didn't know if someone was in here."

Conrad moved towards the voice, taking high steps over piles of debris and twisted metal. When he got close to Steve, he saw the nine-millimeter in his hand. Steve smiled until Conrad gripped his arm tightly. "What the fuck are you doing here?"

"Man. You need back-up."

"Why did you follow me in here?"

"To back you up. Punching me wasn't cool. Let me go."

Steve had replaced his robe with jeans and a polo shirt and he had a baseball cap pulled tightly over his afro. A cell phone was clipped to Steve's belt and a faint glow came from it.

"What the fuck is that thing on for? No lights. Turn it off!"

"Fine, fine," Steve said. "Relax." He pulled the phone from his belt and hit the off button. It made a low electronic sound as it went dead.

"Shit," Conrad said. "Get down and stay still." Conrad looked at the windows and abruptly crouched down himself. A figure, a dim form darker than the surrounding black, moved slowly from the left side of the parking area to the center of the lot.

"They're here," Conrad said. "Keep still and don't move," he said in a whisper.

"My knees," said Steve. He stumbled backwards and crashed into a pile of boards that clattered to the ground. "Fuck."

Conrad froze and looked at the windows. The figure had disappeared from his view. Conrad glanced at Steve and wondered if the fall had been an accident. Maybe he was in on it too. With Mary and Nick. He looked long and hard at Steve. If he turned his back would he get a bullet in it? His fingers danced on the surface of his gun. The images flashed before his eyes - Steve shooting him in the back and he raising his gun and letting one go into Steve's belly. It seemed such an easy solution and the panic and anxiety would be gone. Conrad gulped hard. Steve's eyes were wide and he looked scared but he was still.

Conrad moved quickly towards the windows. The figure, Conrad could see now the person was short, had moved closer to the wall and was standing near one of the windows. He didn't seem to be looking in. The person outside swayed back and forth on his toes, gently and nervously. It didn't seem possible that he hadn't heard Steve fall. He might be pretending to play dumb.

Conrad inched his way closer to the wall. His heart raced. Beads of nervous sweat formed under his arms and on his forehead. It dripped into his eyes. He blinked and wiped his face. He had to keep looking down and forward to make sure he didn't walk into a pile of metal and stone garbage. He glanced back in Steve's direction.

He had chosen to go to Steve's house. Steve hadn't approached him. Steve couldn't be in on it. He was just clumsy. Mary was his ex-wife. She couldn't be in on anything but she was. What made Steve so innocent? Who brings a cell phone to an ambush? He should know better. Unless the phone was on and connected to Nick or the person outside.

Conrad wiped his sweaty forehead again. He put his hand on the brick wall between two of the windows. He balanced himself as he slowly stepped over a high pile of garbage. He carefully inched towards the window and cautiously slid the side of his face along the wall until one eye barely looked out the window closest to the figure.

He saw the back of the man's head and just a bit of the right side of his face. The man had a baseball cap on but Conrad could make out the closely cut hair on his head. His head, neck and back were broad. He was a short stocky man, perhaps five-six. He looked familiar. The man's head turned slightly more to the right. He had a long nose that pointed downwards at the tip. Conrad did recognize him. It was Darko. Proof positive that Nick Deevers was the mole.

Conrad abruptly pulled his face back from the window and his heart pumped even harder now. His head throbbed. He touched the bump on his skull but it didn't hurt. The endorphins were pumping.

Conrad's grip tightened on his gun. He was sorely tempted to pump the back of that man's head with a little extra thinking material. It would be easy if the glass gave. Darko's back was to him and he wouldn't be able to see a thing if Conrad aimed and shot. Conrad waited a moment before sliding his face out again. Darko was gone.

Conrad's jaw muscles tightened. He turned the other way, took two small steps to the window on his right, and slid his face to look out of that one. Nothing. He put his back to the wall and looked for Steve. Was he there? There was neither movement nor sound inside.

Conrad silently cursed. He gulped down his saliva and took a deep breath. Okay. There was no need to stay in here. He had identified the man and now he could concentrate on apprehending him. He crouched down and began moving away from the window towards the interior of the station. Steve seemed to have disappeared. Conrad looked to the windows again. Darko was standing in the center of the parking lot, his back towards the building.

Conrad kept his eyes on Darko as he moved towards the door. His shin swung into a broken concrete block laying on the floor. Conrad stifled a groan as he grabbed his shin and stumbled to his knees. A cloud of dust puffed up around him and small pieces of concrete and stone scattered from him like a colony of insects retreating. The metal door, only ten feet in front of him, was slowly opening inwards.

Conrad straightened up while still on his knees and pointed his gun at the door. He slid his left foot forward to brace himself, holding the gun with both hands as he did, and he aimed at a center point where this latest intruder might step into the room. Fingers, or at least what Conrad took them to be, slid around the edge of the door and pushed it open. The door stopped moving. Blood pumped in Conrad's ears. His gun felt slippery. The fingers slid away and nothing more happened.

Conrad rose to his feet and walked at an angle towards the back of the door taking care to stay out of the narrow opening's line of sight. He kept the gun trained at a point just beyond the open door as he positioned himself slightly behind it. Conrad glanced at the windows but couldn't see Darko.

A figure suddenly ran through the doorway, upsetting piles of garbage and startling Conrad. A nine-millimeter gun went off behind Conrad and the bullet loudly ricocheted off the metal door. The intruder ran towards the other end of the station and was followed by a much stockier and shorter figure who dashed in and spun to face Conrad. Here was Darko in front of him.

With as much force as he could muster, Conrad slammed the side of his gun against Darko's head and both of them fell down towards the ground. From the other end of the station, two guns cracked loudly and flashed brilliantly in the darkness. Conrad thrust his gun towards the figure whose silhouette stood out against the windows. He pulled the trigger twice and his gun cracked loudly. The sounds of the gunshots were followed by the thump of a body falling on a pile of construction garbage.

Conrad rolled off Darko and a gun blast went off under the position he held just a moment before. He shot at the gun flash and his bullet ricocheted off metal. Darko yelled and a gun clattered to the floor.

Conrad leaned forward and swung his gun down on Darko's face. The smack of flesh and bone being struck, another yell from Darko, and he waved his arms in the air. Conrad leapt up and pointed his gun at Darko who was now running his hands over the ground, presumably to find his own gun.

"Hands up!" Conrad yelled. "Hands up or I shoot." Conrad wondered if he should be worried about Steve. There was no other movement in the room.

Darko's hands shot up. "Okay, okay you got me," he said in a choppy voice. His accent had gotten thicker.

"Get up slowly, with your knees. Keep your hands up, not forward, or I shoot you in the stomach."

Darko slid his legs under him and clambered up with his back partially towards Conrad.

"Go out the door. No wait," Conrad said when Darko moved towards the door without hesitation. Darko stopped and turned completely towards Conrad. Conrad kicked the door to close it. The kick made a loud noise but the door barely budged. Darko chuckled. Conrad's vision was not good now. The gun flashes had reduced his night vision. He guessed the flashes must have done the same to Darko.

"Who are you meeting?" Conrad asked.

"I thought you were a thief going to rob me and my friend."

"Bullshit." The station house was silent. "I guess your friend can't confirm that anymore." Conrad wiped the sweat from his face. "Slice?" Conrad said using Steve's old nickname. There was no response.

"So you going to rob me or not? My car is outside. You want the keys?" Darko went for his pocket with one hand.

"Hands up!" Conrad yelled. Steve must be bleeding on the floor Conrad thought. Had Steve been trying to help? If it was help, why did he shoot at the door?

"What you want? You a faggot?"

Darko's voice irritated Conrad. He struggled to keep his cool. "You're here to meet someone. Who and why?" Darko's vision must have been reduced by the gun flashes too. How could he keep up this charade if he's seen my face already? Conrad wondered.

"I tell you I meet someone and now my buddy is shot. You won't even let me call an ambulance. You just let him die?"

"Okay. You can cut the crap. I," Conrad hesitated. He racked his brain. His head still pounded and he felt it even more so now that he had Darko. They were silent for a minute. Darko fidgeted and nervously moved back and forth, just as he had outside when he was waiting.

"What are you buying? You're not meeting someone here for fun. You're buying something illegal aren't you?" Where will that get me? he asked himself. Conrad wanted to clear his mind but the pain and the adrenaline and endorphins were screwing with his thinking. Maybe it was simply time to begin with some heavy interrogation. But there might still be someone outside. A sniper, perhaps waiting for someone tall and unrecognizable to walk out the door. If Steve really had wanted to help, he should have stayed outside. Conrad rubbed his head in frustration.

Darko shrugged. "Why don't we talk outside buddy? You can go outside with me. I give you my keys and you take my car."

Conrad shook his head in the negative and moved closer to Darko. Darko moved back a step, his arms in the air. Conrad still didn't feel completely in control. He would need to get this guy tied up but with what? He had no rope and he wasn't going to search for some now. It was an ugly stalemate. "Turn around," he said.

"Buddy you can just take my keys from the pocket." Darko turned his right hip to Conrad. Conrad kicked Darko in the calf and thrust his gun into Darko's side. Darko grunted and turned with the blow but he didn't go down. Someone groaned from the dark end of the station. Steve! I have to fucking help him.

"Your thief friend?" Darko asked.

"Shut up," Conrad said.

"You going to kill me, then kill me," Darko demanded. Conrad realized Darko was probing for an opening and he would act soon if

Conrad didn't. Conrad stepped behind Darko, grabbed him by the back collar, and pushed him towards the wall while tapping the side of his head with the gun.

"Okay, okay," Darko said, his heading pulling away from each tap against his skull. Darko smelled of alcohol. Conrad pressed closely behind him but Darko resisted walking forward. Conrad pushed and finally got him to the wall between two of the windows. Steve groaned again.

"On your knees."

Darko placed his hands against the wall. "What are you doing?"

"Tying you up. On your knees."

Darko slowly lowered himself to his knees. Conrad kneed the back of Darko's head and knocked his face into the wall.

Darko yelled. "Fucker! Tie me up then!"

Conrad slammed the side of the gun against Darko's head. Darko yelled again and dropped to his side. He grabbed his head and shouted in Russian.

"Who are you with?" Conrad kicked Darko in the back two times and Darko grunted with each blow.

"Okay, okay. I'm with the Grace of God."

Conrad kicked Darko in the back of the head getting more hand than head. "Uh-huh. Tell me more lies. Why were you meeting the policeman?"

"What?"

Conrad kicked Darko in the back near his kidney. Darko groaned and rolled around.

"He gives me locations."

"You're a rebel?"

"Mercenary. I work for pay."

Conrad backed up. "Keep talking. What was this info for?"

Darko turned his head a little towards Conrad. "Who the motherfucker are you?"

"Face the wall!"

Darko rolled towards the wall again.

"I'll shoot you like I shot your friend. I don't give a fuck. Locations of what?"

"People. Police."

"You're an interrogator aren't you?" Conrad asked.

"What?" Darko paused. "I'm a mercenary. A cheaply hired drunk of an operative. That's all."

"You torture people for information."

"No, no. I'm just a soldier. I do surveillance. That's all."

A gunshot shattered the window to Conrad's right. He ducked down and looked through it but saw nothing. "Fuck."

"You get out of here and you live. My friend he wants to kill you if he see me dead. You go now tough guy."

"I'll wait here for the sun. He can't stay until then. You'll wait too."

"Motherfuck."

Conrad rose from his haunches to look through the shattered window again. When he looked down, Darko was launching himself at his mid-section. Conrad tried to spin out of the way but Darko's weight and speed knocked Conrad back into a dense pile of debris. A board cracked under Conrad and something long and hard drove into his back without piercing it. Conrad's wrist flew back and banged against metal, causing him to drop his gun. Conrad rolled forward and grabbed at Darko but Darko jumped and Conrad caught nothing but air.

Darko crouched and dashed for the door. He wrenched the door open yelling "Nyet, nyet," as he ran out into the darkness. Conrad felt around for his gun and found it an interminable minute later in a pile of garbage next to him.

He went to the door and peeked out. A bullet glanced off the door near his head. He shot back once and then shoved the door shut. He ran for the nearest window and looked out. He saw nothing but he heard a car start up at the far right end of the parking lot and peel away. The sound faded into the night. Conrad slumped back against the wall and slid down to the ground. He remembered Steve and jumped up.

He pulled his penlight out and scanned the floor with it while he walked to where he had heard Steve moaning. Steve was crumpled on the ground with a pool of blood under him. He knew it was dangerous to move a shooting victim but the situation was not one where he could pick and choose where to keep Steve until emergency crews arrived. Conrad plucked the cell phone from Steve's belt and called a special law enforcement emergency number.

He told the dispatcher that he had a gunshot victim who needed immediate help and he provided the street name of Steve's cul-de-sac. Conrad ended the call and examined Steve. A bullet had passed through the front and back of his right side but there wasn't a lot of blood escaping the wound.

He pulled Steve's shirt off and wrapped his own around Steve's torso. He hoisted Steve over his shoulders and brought him to the door. He hesitated a moment, took a deep breath, and pulled the door open. Nothing happened.

A chunk of concrete blocked the door from opening wide enough to get Steve out. Conrad braced his one foot and used the other to slide the block away. With a great deal of difficulty, Conrad pushed the rusted door open with his leg and hip. He took only a moment to look around before he scrambled across the parking lot, over the road, and through the tree line.

When he reached the street he had named for the dispatcher, Conrad lowered Steve to the grass, right side down, and collapsed next to him. He applied pressure to both holes with his palms. Less than a minute later, Conrad heard the sirens of paramedic vehicles. Then his own body began screaming in pain.

29

F rom behind a window in Steve's house, Conrad watched the paramedics slide the gurney into their ambulance and speed off with the police close behind. The small crowd of local residents reluctantly dispersed. A few eyes turned towards Steve's house but no one approached. They headed for their beds instead.

Conrad let the curtain go. Fletch looked up at him. "It's not my fault," Conrad said. Fletch didn't respond. Conrad moved to Steve's sofa and dropped into it. He let his body relax.

A phone in the kitchen rang and Conrad snapped awake. The curtain at the front window was orange with the rays of the morning sun. How many hours had passed? Conrad hobbled to the kitchen and answered the wireless phone.

"How's Fletch?" It was Steve's voice.

"Fine. How are you?" Conrad noticed the coffee maker and proceeded to make himself a cup. Birds chirped loudly outside the window.

"Fucked up. I got shot."

"Uh-huh. But are you going to be okay?"

"Yeah. They have me in a room recuperating. They said the bullet went straight through. Nothing major."

Conrad opened a jar of coffee. "Good."

"I know."

Conrad took a few moments to collect his thoughts. "What did you tell the police?"

"That I was taking a midnight stroll and that someone rolled by and took a shot at me. Exactly what happened." Steve grunted. "So what now? How're you gonna get these guys?"

Conrad dismissed the question. "I don't know." Instead, he thought about what he had told the police. He and Steve had been walking the streets when a car rolled by, hit him, and shot at Steve. Random hit and run. Simple as that. The police had looked at him skeptically but one of them recognized Conrad from news photographs, Conrad the DHS hero, and they knew of his name in law enforcement circles, so they let it go at that.

"No security cameras there at the station right?" Conrad asked.

"Nope."

Conrad took an empty coffee mug from a cabinet. "Well, I have the guy's cell number at least. I can get a team to monitor that number and maybe trace any calls."

"You have the resources for that?"

Conrad sucked on his teeth. "No."

"Didn't think so. You gonna keep thinking out your ass on this?"

Conrad chuckled and felt a pain in his ribs. They weren't broken. Muscle pull. "I don't know. I played a hunch. It almost worked. Now I'm stuck with nothing. They won't use that location again for a drop. Neighborhood's safer." Conrad raised his cup in mock salutation.

"I was really worried."

"Jackass."

Conrad was feeling the full effects of the last few days. He became dizzy and lowered himself to a chair. "Fuck me. I need more rest."

"You can use my bed while I'm here. Take care of Fletch. His food's in the garage."

Conrad rose from the chair quickly. "I'm an idiot! I need to get my car covered up! They'll spot it!"

"Chill Rad. You're straight."

"What?"

"Think I'm dumb? Shit. I told you I did security back in Iraq. I picked up a little savvy."

"And?" Conrad reached into his pant pocket. His car keys were gone.

"I pulled your car in and put my car out before I followed you."

"My keys?"

"They were in the car Rad. When I saw that I really knew you needed some help."

"I didn't notice it had been moved. My brain is becoming mush."

Neither spoke for a minute.

Steve coughed away from the phone. "Why do you live this shit Rad? You did your time."

"My time?"

"Medals, respect. Do private security or investigations or something. There's plenty of Hollywood celebrities who could use a bodyguard like you. I want to meet some hotties."

Conrad laughed and grabbed his pained ribs. "I've thought about it."

"So?"

"You wouldn't know what to do with them."

"Come on. Really."

"Well what would happen if everyone left the tough jobs for the cushy ones. Who's left to keep the peace?" Conrad's temples pulsed.

Steve's voice went preachy. "Spare me the bullshit. The government will always have the people. Why you?"

Conrad rubbed his head. "It's not bullshit Steve. I'm happy enough. I mean, what the fuck do I need to make more money for? I have what I need."

"You make a compelling argument Conrad. What the fuck do we need more money for? You've convinced me buddy. I think I'm going to Africa and start networking computers for starving villagers. In fact, I might start today."

"If I wasn't so fucked up Steve, I'd go over there and kick your ass right now."

"Kick your sorry ass into my bed man. They tell me I've got to stay here for at least a week."

Conrad nodded. "Yeah."

"Hey Rad. What the fuck was wrong at the station anyway? You were acting real weird when I showed up. I've never seen you like that."

"I, uh, I didn't understand why you were there."

"I was there to help you."

"Were you?"

"Paranoid motherfucker. Are you listening to me? Get some sleep and dream about Hollywood."

Conrad blurted it out. "I was about to shoot you Steve."

"You what? What?"

"I didn't trust you. You came in, made all that noise. I didn't know what to think."

"You were going to shoot me?"

"I'm sorry Steve. What can I say?"

Steve's voice cracked. "That you're fucking joking."

"I'm not joking Steve. I was going to do it. Something got a hold of me. Something real bad. Something I don't understand."

Steve sniffled. "You were going to fucking shoot me?" He started to cry on the phone. "You thankless motherfucker. I was trying to save your life."

"What am I telling you Steve?"

"You're fucked in the head. That's what you're telling me. You're right. You're fucked in the head."

"I'm sorry." Fletch walked in to the kitchen and sat in front of Conrad. Conrad turned away from Fletch and hated himself for his feelings. He felt good telling Steve the truth though. It was a relief for him to admit to that and to apologize for it. Conrad listened to Steve cry for a couple more minutes.

"I only thought it for a moment. I was scared. They've been trying to kill me."

Steve blew his nose. "Okay Rad. Okay. But I'm telling you. I don't know. I don't want to see you any time soon. I can't believe this. You're losing it. You need help. You need therapy or something."

"I need to save my life first. When I do that, then I can get some of that brain healing."

"Feed Fletch before you go please. That dog doesn't need to be hungry today."

"Yeah sure." Conrad hung up the phone. The coffee was almost ready but he turned the machine off.

Conrad shuffled towards the bedroom. It was a mess. Bureau, bed and cabinets were covered with clothes. Steve had no one right now, he was divorced too, and Conrad felt another pang of guilt for having given Steve the kind of grief he just did.

Conrad walked to the bed and kicked off his shoes. He lowered himself on the bed, face down. He thought about Lydia and Mary, Darko and Nick. He thought about his sons and Steve and Melissa and the agents under his command. He shuddered in fear. He closed his eyes and he was gone.

30

C onrad's head snapped up. He rubbed his crud-encrusted eyelids and looked from side to side. A string of spittle extended from his mouth to the sheets.

He was on Steve's bed and Fletch was sleeping next to him. The light coming through the bedroom curtains was dim. He wiped his mouth and pushed himself to a sitting position. It hurt just to do that.

He stretched his sore muscles and looked at the digital clock. 5:27. He stretched again and stood up. It was time to get back to the city. He had left Lydia alone for too long and she would be worried.

The curtains in the living room were closed and the house was in twilight. Fletch followed Conrad out of the bedroom and stared at the front door.

"You need to eat don't you?" Conrad got his keys from the kitchen, poured himself an orange juice, and sucked it down. He shivered when the cold hit his stomach.

"All right boy." Conrad went through the door that led into Steve's garage. His car sat in the center. Fletch nosed his way behind him. Conrad grabbed a handful of dry dog food from a bag perched on a high shelf and dropped it into Fletch's empty food dish. Fletch ate as Conrad dropped another handful of food in the plate. A chunk splashed into the partially filled water dish.

"Okay." Conrad lifted the garage door and squinted at the late afternoon rays that dribbled in. He blinked a few times to adjust to the light before looking up and down the street for anything untoward. He got into his car, started it up, and rolled slowly out. He again cautiously looked around as he got out of his car to close the garage door. Fletch stared at him from inside. Conrad was forgetting something. "Shit."

He pulled the car back inside and closed the garage. He found a leash for Fletch and one of Steve's baseball caps. He pulled the cap low over his head and left the house with Fletch, heading towards the train station. It was a nice area in the daylight. The trees and bushes were lush and green. The air was clear and smelled fresh and the houses whispered with the sounds of suburban living.

At the tree line near the station, Conrad stopped to let Fletch relieve himself. Conrad took the opportunity to scan the area for cars and people. The only traffic was that moving along Route 1 up on the ridge. In the light, the train station looked safe and pedestrian now. It really was nothing but an old, useless building.

With Fletch in tow, Conrad went to the side door of the station. It had been re-locked. He walked to the opposite end of the building and found another door padlocked like the first. He tied Fletch to a tree, inserted his electronic pick into the lock, and turned it on. In seconds, the lock was off.

He walked around the corner to the closest window and peered in. He couldn't see the door well but it didn't seem to be booby-trapped. Apart from the debris, the interior was empty.

Conrad went to the door and pushed. It resisted. With difficulty, he pushed it partly open. After taking one last look around, he went inside and looked for a body.

All he found was dry blood where the man he had shot would have fallen. He took out his wallet and removed an old receipt. He scraped some of the blood from the floor and smeared it on to the paper. He carefully folded the receipt and put it back in his wallet.

He checked the other door for booby traps and found nothing. He walked through the rest of the room and saw only the dumped materials he expected to be there. Wooden boards, warped plastic, aluminum siding, concrete blocks and loose wiring. Pieces of old electronics and discarded personal item was scattered here and there but he found nothing else of use. He considered trying to get fingerprints but chances were that the rebs had either used gloves, wiped possible prints clean, or, most likely, had simply not left any usable prints behind.

Conrad exited and locked the door behind him. Fletch sat quietly by the tree. "Okay boy. I'm done here. I hope you are too."

Conrad hurried back to Steve's house, taking care to avoid being watched or tailed, and scooted Fletch into the house. Fletch wagged his tail wanly when Conrad waved to him. "I'll tell Steve to have a friend see to you Fletch. I have a woman to take care of." Conrad pulled his car out of the garage, walked back in to close it and then left by the front door, locking that behind him.

He drove back past the train station and on to Jefferson Davis Highway, north to Washington, DC. Traffic was moderate. Conrad checked the time again. 5:52. It was rush hour and traffic would get heavier as he got closer to the city. He debated whether to take Route 1 or I-95. He chose I-95. It was a slower but safer route.

It was just after Conrad had crossed the Occoquan River and jumped on I-95 at exit 161 that he tensed up. He had forgotten to check whether any cars had been sitting on the street or entrance ramp shoulders. If the rebels were watching the traffic that passed along Jeff Davis or at the highway entrance, they would have seen his car, assuming they knew what it looked like. Conrad didn't think that was a bad assumption to make. Now they would know whether he was headed west to the station house or north back to DC.

Conrad smacked his steering wheel. "Fuck." He was making mental mistake after mental mistake. He was still fatigued.

He checked his rear view and side view mirrors and got to know the cars that were immediately visible around him. The traffic going north was lighter than traffic coming south but it was heavy enough for a pursuer to hide in.

He checked and double-checked his mirrors as he drove. The less he saw to worry him, the more his anxiety increased. Minutes later, he took exit 166 on to the Fairfax County Parkway. He was about sixteen miles south of DC and his Georgetown apartment.

He pulled into a gas station and stopped at a pump. He exited his car from the window and scanned the station carefully as he got a pump and filled his car with gas. None of the cars at or near the station looked like any he remembered seeing on the highway with him. If someone were following him, the pursuer might have passed him off to another tail he hadn't seen already.

DHS had trouble determining the number of operatives the rebel groups had in the city and surrounding areas and how coordinated these various groups were. The FBI didn't do a good job of sharing what information they had either. Hell if Conrad could get anyone outside of his station to help him determine how many enemies were conducting surveillance on him and his people on a daily basis. Maybe Conrad was lucky and it was just good old drunken Darko on his case.

When he finished pumping, Conrad walked to the cashier's window. He was low on cash so he pulled out his electronic payment card for the attendant.

"Sorry sir. System is down. Another cut cable."

Conrad shook his head. "I'm with D and M Bank of DC. Do you have a dedicated line to their systems?"

"No sir. Just a general line. And it's down." The attendant had a lazy look on his face and he stared at Conrad blankly.

"Right. You said that already." The rebels liked to cut fiber optic cables when they could find them. That tactic helped disrupt everyday activities and kept the average citizen frustrated by the war. Feeling frustrated himself, Conrad pulled a twenty from his wallet and slid it into the attendant's metal security drawer. The drawer slid inside and then back out. Conrad took the twenty-three cents change for three and a half gallons of gas. "Thanks," Conrad said without meaning it.

Conrad glanced at the mirrors around the cashier's booth for any strange activity behind him or near his car. Nothing. He walked casually to his car and scrutinized the other drivers pumping gas.

At one end was a young woman in a brown business suit pumping gas into her purple Dodge. Closer in were some retro-hippies in an old black Subaru mounted with bike racks and a kayak. Near Conrad's black Mustang, A gray haired man in a blue seersucker suit was washing the windows of a charcoal Cadillac. The hippies looked at Conrad and seemed agitated. They whispered amongst themselves and moved quickly into their vehicle.

Conrad knew he looked like a stereotypical rebel who liked to beat on hippies and hipsters. He was muscular and grit-faced, with cropped hair and wearing working clothes rather than the soft, silky threads many people in the city wore. He shook his head at the irony of their mistake. He wanted to tell them that as long as they didn't do anything criminal he was on their side one hundred percent.

Freedoms were greater than ever before and yet here was America, on its knees and wracked by crime brought on by an improbable enemy - violent conservatives. That's one for the history books. The barbarians brought down Rome, egalitarian and nationalist revolutions eventually brought down the English and French empires, and now conservatives were taking down America. But who was he to be so naïve? Fear of change wasn't so easily eradicated. It was fear that would keep people fighting both for and against freedom until the end of time.

Conrad swung his legs through his car window and slid into his car seat. He looked in his glove compartment and took out the spare gun and a box of magazines. He drove away from the gas pump and pulled into a parking spot alongside the station to check that the gun was in good working order. But he was still thinking angry thoughts.

Cris Alvarez

If those close-minded fools would just lay off, America could get back to the business of rebuilding its infrastructure and economy and settle back as leader of the free world. Yet it was the year 2022 and the country was no better off than post-war Germany and Japan in the late 1940s and 50s. Things were arguably even worse considering the number of arms dealers that were trying to flood the rebel insurgents, the purported Christ cops, with surplus armaments. The U.S. was reaping the harvest of all the international enemies it had made over the years. Maybe not everyone hated the U.S. but enough were gleefully supplying its violent internal components with arms and sitting back to enjoy the show.

It was yet another grand irony that communist and Muslim states were making sure that American Christians were armed well enough to take down the government of their own homeland. The maxim was, "Don't battle your enemies, have your enemies battle each other." Well, maybe it would take ten or twenty years but the U.S. would give some payback to everyone involved in the destruction – here and abroad. No doubt about that.

There was a tap on the glass. Conrad jerked in his seat and swung his loaded gun at the window. One of the Subaru hippies yelped and jumped back with his hands in the air. A piece of paper floated from his hand to the ground. Conrad twisted left in his seat as the kid dashed to the passenger side of the Subaru. The car was running and, even before the car door was fully closed, it shot off into the main street, forcing another driver to slam his brakes and mash his horn.

Conrad opened his door and dropped out of his seat into a crouch on the pavement. Nothing else happened. The other drivers at the station were looking towards the spot of the near accident. None of them paid Conrad any attention.

He leaned forward and snatched the white piece of paper. It was a small piece, torn along all four edges. Written on it in pencil was, 'We have Lydia. We also have Mary. You will wait for a call at your apartment.'

A pall settled over Conrad's face. His shoulders slumped and a phantom snake wiggled up his spine. He slowly crawled back into his car. He wanted to cry, bellow, and tear someone apart all at once. His limbs ached and a vice tightened over his temples.

Both of them held by the enemy. He put his spare gun back in the glove compartment. He backed his car up without looking where he was going and someone honked a horn at him. He pulled out of the station lot and took the road to DC.

he sun sat low on the horizon when Conrad finally
reached the Francis Scott Key Bridge that connected
Rosslyn, Virginia to Georgetown. He was almost
surprised to see the towers of the University. He had driven from the
gas station in a near daze. He had an intense headache and his back
hurt. The late spring sun was mercilessly overheating everything in
DC and even the multitude of trees along the Potomac wilted under
the onslaught. The many boats anchored up and down the river
bobbed lethargically in the water, their occupants moving just as
slowly on the decks under the shade of canopies.

Conrad rolled his window up when traffic slowed on the bridge
to keep out the exhaust of the cars that surrounded him. He and the
cars around him pushed onwards from the bridge to M street. Once in
Georgetown, he drove east towards his apartment building.

The rebels worked the outermost edges of metropolitan areas
and real-estate developers knew it. A few years ago, their lobbyists
had DC's building height restrictions removed for neighborhoods
outside the National Mall and government district areas. With the
restrictions removed, high-rises were built with a vengeance in DC.
Physical security in Georgetown improved. Guards and police officers
of the highest caliber were assigned to this part of the city. The area
was littered with security cameras.

Yet all of the safety precautions didn't help as much as they
should have. Electrical and technical equipment problems arose all
too frequently and sometimes the rebs got a small bomb through or
shot an innocent bystander. But Georgetown was still the safest and
most popular neighborhood in DC.

Conrad would have preferred living in his territory, out by
Occoquan, but federal regulations prohibited officers at the
managerial levels from living in the outlying areas and these
regulations were strictly enforced. The government didn't want their
best people blown up or otherwise assassinated in their sleep. Safe
accommodation was the requirement for off-hours.

Mary had preferred it that way too. She hated Conrad's job, or
at least the danger of it. She told him often enough but she was madly

in love with him so she accepted the situation. Conrad always found it strange that so many women, Mary included, were both strongly attracted to him for the same reason they were repelled by him. Violent work apparently bred both lust and fear in the women he met.

Mary was, or had been, a grounded woman. A businessperson turned lobbyist, who liked the stories Conrad told about his war days and who drew closer whenever he described the action of those times. But she became unhappy with the coming of the Civil War and Conrad's involvement in it.

He was a decorated soldier before the Civil War and earned even more recognition during the conflict. Mary and many others in the rear only heard hints of what the guerrillas and federals did to each other on the battlefield. There were reports of inhuman barbarity, that they had used chemical and biological agents against each other. Mary grew distant and scared.

It was ironic that she didn't experience the terror of war first-hand until after the Civil War ended. A bomb planted under Conrad's car detonated early and blew the family back towards the restaurant they had just left. Paul had been closest to the explosion so it was Paul's arm that went past them.

The horrific event was burned into Conrad's mind. The car lifting into the air almost silently, perfectly spinning one hundred and eighty degrees. The smoke, the movement, the people running. The sight of the end of Paul's forearm, a bloody stump twitching like a hyperactive broomstick. While Mary cried and held the children close to her, Conrad yelled at the waiters.

He remembered yelling, "Goddamn it, it's a fucking arm. How hard can it be to find?"

The arm was lying behind a large potted plant, a Superman watch still around the wrist. It had been sheared through by a random piece of metal destined, apparently, to change a young boy's life forever. Conrad rushed the arm to the paramedic team that had responded but he could see that it was too late. Thanks to dad and his work, Paul would have to live without one of his limbs for the rest of his life.

Conrad reached the parking entrance of his building and he slipped his ID card into a security machine. It beeped, a bulb flashed green and he pulled his ID out. A metal wall rose slowly, gears and chains grinding and squeaking. Conrad drove down into the garage while the security door slowly rolled back down behind him.

Mary asked for a divorce soon afterwards. Conrad didn't argue. He saw the danger too and he refused to be the cause of any further injury to his children. He helped her get an apartment for the three of them, one far from him and in the safe environs of Bethesda. Georgetown was safer in terms of implemented protections, but it also attracted a lot of undesirable attention that Bethesda didn't.

Once she moved to the new house, Mary lost it. She had been understanding at first, right after the accident, and rationalized that it wasn't Conrad's fault. It was the rebels who maimed and killed. Conrad protected. But she drank more and more and swung her arms around more and more and answered the phone with slurring speech more and more. She had just become a slightly eccentric lobbyist she would say. "Hey, we have parties all the time so it's only natural for me to drink." Yeah right.

Conrad stepped into the elevator. It was small, narrow, and slightly worn. A black streak cut across the lower part of one plastic panel. Conrad stuck his finger in his mouth and then vigorously rubbed at the stain but it wasn't coming off. His inability to rub off the discoloration angered him. He slammed the dirty panel with the side of his fist. "Can't they keep this damn place clean?" The elevator rose without answering.

Mary was always hostile now but she kept insisting they meet for lunch or some such thing to discuss the kids. She was usually a little tipsy for those meetings. Conrad would give her money if she needed it and give his approval to anything that she wanted the kids to do as long as it wasn't too wild. He was a good father. He cared. He put up with the crap. As hot as it all got, he put up with the crap.

The elevator stopped and the doors slid open. Conrad left the elevator and walked the carpeted hallway to his apartment door. He unlocked it and entered. He touched the light switch to his left and the lights came on. He stared at a room that was unfamiliar to him. The days had changed so much, it seemed like another person had put the sofa in its place, had adjusted the height of his tv, had tossed a football in the corner of the room. He looked down at his brown carpet and stared at a faded spot. He closed the door and still felt out of place.

He pulled off his shirt and removed his waistband holster. He saw the phone and it seemed to him an evil instrument. It always brought the worst news. He couldn't recall the last time he was happy to hear it ring. He walked around his apartment and checked the rooms. She hadn't answered his frantic calls to the apartment so he assumed the note was accurate. She was gone. Everything was in place but she was gone.

He sat on his sofa and thought. He looked at the phone, stood, and walked to his living room bay windows. Conrad pulled the curtains open. A semi-circle of nearly floor-to-ceiling windows provided a commanding view of DC, the Potomac River, Roosevelt Island and Rosslyn, Virginia.

The lights of both cities were snapping on in the advancing dusk. From across the Potomac, the lights of Rosslyn blinked at Conrad. The activity in those offices represented life that moved forward either not knowing or not caring that it was always in danger. Ignorance is bliss.

Conrad rubbed his chin thoughtfully. Someone must have called her and convinced her to go outside where she was nabbed. Or she went out of her own volition and was snatched by someone scoping his residence. He took his phone from its cradle and plugged in the wire that converted the phone from a wireless line to a more secure landline. A cheap protection against someone listening in on his wireless signal assuming the landline itself wasn't tapped.

He called a friend at DHS HQ, an old buddy who owed him his life. A lot of people owed him like that but he wasn't the type to take advantage of debts. This was different.

It was a short conversation. He asked for a report on all the calls that had been made to his number over the last 48 hours.

"Give me thirty. I'll have the numbers," his buddy said.

Conrad hung up the phone and walked to his refrigerator. He pulled out a cold beer and twisted the top off. He tossed the cap at the garbage but it missed and bounced off the wall. He walked back to the living room and sat.

He let the lights be his focus. He took a long swig of his beer and then breathed slowly and deeply. He relaxed his body and kept his mind active. He watched the lights on the buildings become brighter and he turned his head to look at them with the corners of his eyes. His peripheral vision was good. He stood and stripped to his underwear. He stretched his arms, flexed and relaxed. He took another gulp of beer and got down to a push-up position.

He began to think of ways to kick the shit out of Darko, Nick and the others rebels he personally knew. He dropped from the ready position and he held his push-up two inches from the ground for five seconds. He pushed back up slowly, exhaling evenly as he did. He continued his push-ups this way, lowering and rising slowly, exhaling to the top.

He continued for a long time until his muscles burned. He ignored the other pains in his body and focused on the right ones. Then he flipped on his back and did crunches, slowly and with measured breaths. He did two hundred, five hundred, perhaps more. He stopped when his muscles refused to lift him again. He remained on his back and grabbed the beer. He wiped his sweaty forehead with the bottom of the bottle. He jumped to his feet and took another drink.

He hunched into a boxing stance and began a slow and regular jab, jab, punch combination. He shadowboxed with the wall for the next ten minutes until the phone rang. He grabbed it before the second ring.

His friend told him to get a pen and pad and he did. Conrad heard seven phone numbers, six familiar and one that was not. The unfamiliar call was from a payphone located at 20th and M street. There were security cameras there but it might take a few hours to catch an image from the video assuming the authorities would even help him. Conrad didn't care about the camera. Anyone pulling this kidnapping would have covered his face well enough to avoid identification.

Conrad thanked his friend and asked another favor. Conrad told him he'd be getting another call and asked him to monitor the line and call back as soon as he had a fix on its location. The friend agreed and hung up.

Conrad took one hundred and eighty seconds to shower and another one hundred and twenty seconds to get dressed. He went to his bathroom closet. In the back of the closet was a latched box out of which he pulled a sheathed stainless steel bayonet knife. He strapped it to his left calf. He removed an eighteen-inch wire with wooden handles attached to each end. He rolled up the garrote and slipped that into his front pocket. He took his holstered gun from the bed and stuck it into his waistband. He slipped more camouflage paint into his pocket, returned the box to the back of the closet, and went back to the phone.

He stood over it and watched it as though someone had told him it would actually move on its own. The phone rang thirteen minutes later. Conrad lifted it robotically. "Yes?"

"Good. You're there." It was the Russian voice, Darko's voice.

Cris Alvarez

A smile crept across Conrad's face. Special rewards for this one. "Yes."

"You must go to the large parking lot in Vienna. Near the community center."

"Why?"

"I will kill both your women otherwise."

The snake in Conrad's back returned and stiffened. Why would he kill Mary? Doesn't she help you whether or not she knows that? he silently asked. Is she expendable or is it a bluff? "Then I'll be there. Will you let them go once I arrive?"

"Of course. It's you we want. But do not take long. Or they will die. First one, which I don't know, then the other." The line went dead.

Conrad hung up. Thirty seconds later, the phone rang again.

"Yeah?"

Conrad's friend provided the number and its location. It was another payphone located near where Darko told Conrad to go. Good. Darko would be with the women or close by.

Conrad touched the butt of his holstered gun and turned off the lights. The darkness felt right to him.

32

More parking lots. Conrad leaned on his car and chewed his cheeks. He spit on the asphalt and looked around with a pair of night vision goggles. The city lights reduced the effectiveness of the goggles so he adjusted the visual settings to compensate for the heavy amount of ambient light. The adjustment didn't do much good. Objects still appeared unclear.

Conrad was parked four blocks from the meeting point, next to a grove of oak trees, and he was pissed. He wondered how a rebel, a kidnapper at that, could feel comfortable operating between two relatively well-patrolled neighborhoods like Tyson's Corner and Vienna. Being a center of government contractor activity, Tyson's was only slightly less guarded than his own Georgetown neighborhood. But regardless of what the rebels thought, he had put in a call for DHS reinforcements and he would soon have Darko in hand. Still, his priority was keeping Lydia and Mary from getting hurt.

He pushed off his car and touched the gun in his waistband for reassurance. The butt was ready for his grab if it came to a quick draw. He slid it out partway as he walked and then slid it back into the holster to test the smoothness of the draw. He wore a dark blue shirt that was becoming damp with sweat. The night was hot and his nerves were kicking. He would have preferred wearing an assault outfit but that gear was at the office. He was stuck rescuing his loved ones in jeans and a long sleeved t-shirt.

He paced back and forth in anticipation of action. Light and fast footsteps suddenly sounded behind him. He spun and dropped to one knee in a smooth motion while drawing his gun. He gripped it with two hands and aimed. The person running towards him skidded to a stop and raised his arms.

"Whoa. Whoa chief," Dave said in a whisper. "Relax there."

Dave dropped his hands and walked slowly towards Conrad. He was geared up in the all black urban night assault gear Conrad would have liked to be wearing. Dave had his night vision goggles on and he looked from side to side as he approached Conrad.

Conrad stood and lowered his gun. "Why'd you run up behind me like that without warning? Where's your backup?"

"That's why I ran up. There is no backup."

"What?" Conrad's voice was a touch louder than it should have been and he reflexively looked around for reactive movement.

"Shhh." Bronson said touching his finger to his mouth. "Yeah. We got an order to disregard your request for backup."

"From who?"

"The opcenter in Langley. They nixed it."

"Why?"

"Who knows? They just told all units to stand down from the request."

"So why are you here?" Conrad looked at the trees in agitation. He didn't know this area well which meant he didn't know the best approaches and exits for an operation around the community center.

"Well, I ignored the order. So did Lina and Blounts. So they're backup if you want to call it that. But no heavy weapons, no riot foam, and no helos." Dave frowned and adjusted the goggles. "I have no idea where Nick is. He's been out of touch since yesterday afternoon."

Conrad nodded. "Naturally." He thought they could have surrounded Darko and any other rebels present and hit them with foam and gas to immobilize them. Now he was faced with the prospect of a gun battle in the middle of the night. But if anything happened to either of those two women he would find the person at the operations center who cared more for rebels than his brother DHS agents and that person would pay dearly.

Conrad dashed the thoughts of preemptive revenge from his mind. He had to focus on the hostages and the safety of his own agents. "You could lose your badge," he said.

Dave shrugged. "Fuck it."

Conrad liked the answer. "That wonderful supervisor job that was mine?"

Dave smiled broadly. "Not as great as I thought."

"You might even get yourself killed." Conrad laughed low under his breath.

Dave did too. "That I don't like so much. Listen boss. I'll try to get on the low roof to your right and cover you from there."

"You know the location?"

"Yeah. Don't you?"

"Not really."

Dave nodded. "I'll have Lina stay to your left rear behind tree cover. About as close to four o'clock to you as she can get. I'll put Blounts at seven behind tree cover too."

"Where are they?"

"Nearby. Don't worry."

Conrad nodded. "Roger that. Just be careful. They'll have two innocent civvies there. My ex-wife and Lydia. Treat it like a hostage negotiation."

"Lydia? The rebel?"

"Yes."

"No shit. How?"

"Nick's in on it."

"Nick Deevers? Are you sure? I thought that was all power politics bullshit."

"No. It's Nick."

"Hm." Dave looked into the darkness and nodded. "So how are you gonna work the rescue?"

"I'll have to wing it. I was planning on the backup." Conrad looked at his watch. Green numbers glowed in the darkness. "I gotta hurry. They're expecting me."

Dave looked around. "They must be using a small crew. I haven't seen or heard anything."

"Yeah. Be careful." Conrad waited for two sedans to pass and then crossed the street. He walked the four blocks until he was close to the community center parking lot. Bushes and a mix of poplar and maple trees ringed the lot and the center itself. The neighborhood was well wooded and provided an abundance of cover for anyone sneaking around.

He thought about how many people in the neighborhood could get hurt if something nasty started. Moreover, if the rebels thought they had free reign this close to the city they could really start a nasty terror campaign, but that didn't feel like his problem anymore.

Conrad shook the thought out of his head. Every day it was getting worse and worse. He was thinking more and more about himself and less about the people he was paid to protect. But he wasn't doing it for money was he? he asked himself. He had been doing it out of mutual respect. And who now deserved his respect?

Conrad positioned himself behind a thick bush of medium height and pulled a small metal box out of his side pocket. He took a small earpiece from the same pocket and placed the small bit of metal and plastic in his left ear. He tapped one side of the box and he heard the tapping through the earpiece. He adjusted his goggles and scanned the area.

A fifteen-foot wide swathe of grass lay between the tree line Conrad was in and the asphalt. The community center's parking lot was about two hundred by one hundred feet in size. Beyond the lot and past forty more feet of pavement and grass was the wide, one-story brick community center. Conrad was positioned opposite the middle of the building, across from the center's front entrance. Smaller one-story buildings sat on either side of the lot and other buildings were spread out behind those. A half-dozen street lamps barely managed to light the empty lot and the community center grounds.

Conrad removed the earpiece. He pressed a button on the box and then threw the box towards the wall of the community center. The box didn't reach the wall. It clattered on the pavement about fifteen meters short. Conrad put the earpiece back in his left ear.

"Is that you?" It was Darko's voice calling out from behind the main building. Conrad took a small metal cylinder from his front pocket, held it near his mouth and pressed a button.

"It's me," he said softly into the device. His voice came from the metal box he had thrown.

"Remote speaker," Darko said. Darko's voice was barely audible but the box transmitted the sound to Conrad and the earpiece amplified it for him.

"Naturally," Conrad said.

"I don't blame you." There was a long pause. A chuckle floated over the air. Conrad readjusted the optics on his goggles. A soft breeze blew a bit of garbage over the surface of the parking lot.

Darko spoke again. "But it's useless. Come out."

"I have no reason too."

"I see." The voice was resigned.

Conrad's anger rose at the thought of Darko feeling comfortable in this situation. What made that scumbag feel so calm? He tightened and relaxed his grip on his gun. He wanted to shoot something. He could fire at the sound of the voice but would probably end up hitting the hostages. He swallowed his surging rage and considered what Darko could be thinking. Either Darko was very stupid, foolhardy, or someone was protecting him. Conrad decided on all three in equal amounts. "Show me what you have to bring me out."

Darko laughed. "Yes. Of course. Don't shoot."

There was motion along the left side of the building. In the darkness, someone moved forward in a jerky motion. Conrad clenched his teeth when he saw his short stocky nemesis drag a woman out by her hair. She struggled to walk behind him but could only stumble forward with her head bowed down. Darko stopped at the outer edge of the circle of light from one street lamp. He and the woman were between the shadows and the light.

"Who is that?" Conrad asked.

"Your friend Lydia of course."

"I can't see her face."

Darko looked at the metal box. "Where are you?"

"Lift her face you cocksucker."

Darko's head bobbed up and down. With great effort, Conrad kept his ground when Darko pulled her head up and lit her face with a flashlight. Grabbing her chin roughly, Darko twisted her head back and forth. It was Lydia and her left eye was bruised. Conrad's heart pounded and adrenalin shot through his limbs. He forced the next words out of his mouth. "So what? Why risk a DHS agent for her?"

"Tough guy eh?" The Russian turned towards the side of the building he had come from. He motioned with an outstretched hand towards someone unseen. "Come on Mary. It's your turn."

Enraged, Conrad pushed the top of his gun barrel against his closed mouth. He rubbed the barrel against his lips but kept his eyes focused on Darko. A woman in a blue blouse and dress, wearing light blue pumps, took tentative steps into the light. From what Conrad could see, she was disheveled but not beaten up. When she turned her face towards him, he saw it was Mary.

"Conrad?" Mary called.

He nearly responded by yelling from the bushes. He caught himself and spoke into the microphone. "I'm here. Are you all right?"

"Conrad?" She spoke softer than Darko did and Conrad had a difficult time hearing her through his earpiece.

He was tempted to walk out into the light but he held back. "Mary, are you all right?"

"Give yourself up Conrad, " she said. "They plan to kill the children."

"Fuckers." Conrad pulled the microphone from his mouth.

"That got you, you son of bitch," Darko said. "I should have stayed and killed you at the railroad you lucky bastard. Then I would be done with this fucking contract."

"Contract?" Conrad asked.

"Fuck you," Darko said.

Mary spoke again. "Conrad, please. Quickly. They want to kill my children. Just give them what they want already."

"They want me Mary. They want to kill me."

"Give them whatever they want Conrad." Mary sobbed lightly. "You're not so important as the children you asshole. Stop thinking about yourself."

Conrad rubbed his throat. A muscle in his neck was cramping and twitching. She didn't mean it, he assured himself. Darko pulled a gun from his jacket.

"First I shoot her," he pointed the gun at Lydia who was kneeling on the ground in front of him, "then I shoot her." He pointed the gun at Mary who stood at his side like a ghost. Darko waved the gun abstractedly towards the sky in front of him as Mary began crying harder. "Then I find your fucking kids and I shoot them."

"I could kill you asshole," Conrad said.

"Then someone else kills them all. It don't fucking matter to me. Believe me. It don't fucking matter." Conrad was sick of hearing that clipped English. He ripped off the goggles and dropped them on the ground. He stepped out from behind the bush and walked into the light with his arms raised.

"Fucking good finally," Darko said.

He pointed his gun at Conrad.

"Who else is here?" Conrad asked as he walked forward.

"People, you cocksucker. Don't you worry."

When Conrad was five steps from the Russian, he stopped. Darko had a glazed look in his eyes, the eyes of a drunk alcoholic. A professional in every sense.

"Now what?" Conrad asked as they stared at each other.

"Drop that fucking gun."

Conrad lobbed the gun towards the grass and it hit the ground without bouncing.

"Kneel down here in front of the woman."

"Thank you Conrad. Thank you," Mary said. She was still crying. Conrad ignored Mary and scrutinized Lydia as he knelt in front of her. She wore gray sweats and a gray sweatshirt, clothes that Conrad had bought for her. She was on her knees, hunched over and looking at the ground. She didn't raise her face to Conrad. He placed one hand on her shoulder but she didn't respond. Her wrists were bound together with plastic strips, her hands resting between her knees.

He looked up at Mary. She didn't have a mark on her. Lines of mascara ran down her cheeks and some lipstick was smeared across her lips. Conrad felt like spitting at her feet.

"They didn't rough you up too much did they?" He felt guilty for the sudden words. She was trying to protect her children the only way she knew how. Hadn't he warned her before that they never do what they promise? When they want to kill someone, they kill everyone they say they wouldn't.

Mary was still. "What do you mean?"

"They're your people."

"They were going to kill the children if I didn't help."

"This is fucking touching," Darko said. "Confession, hope for absolution. Will there be forgiveness?"

"So you helped the rebels find me?"

"Oh Conrad." Mary knelt down next to him. Conrad recoiled from her touch.

Darko snickered. "The bitch betrayed us. Can you believe it? At the last fucking minute, she thought she could win it all. She got greedy. She tried to save your life and fuck Nicholas. Now she loses everything."

"Kill him now," a voice said from the dark. It was as though a snake had hissed the venomous words. It was hate and disgust.

Conrad tried to see who had spoken, but he couldn't see anything beyond Darko and the women.

"Fuck you. I'm having fun," Darko said. "He'll die soon enough."

Mary put her hands on Conrad's shoulders. "I wanted you dead. I met Nick. He was a policeman so when he told me he knew people-"

"After you fucked him?" Conrad asked.

"Conrad, it got complicated. We didn't really..." Mary looked at the ground. "He told me he knew someone if I was really serious."

"This idiot over here?"

"I guess so. I didn't know they were rebels."

"Would you have cared?"

"Kill him," the voice in the dark said with greater insistence.

"Fuck you," Darko said. "I am loving this."

Mary didn't speak for a few moments, only rubbed her nose and sniffed. "No, I wouldn't have. They wanted to get you. They would have hurt my children. So I just gave you up instead. Now they'll be safe."

Conrad's pressed his balled fists into the asphalt. "Don't fucking bet on it," he said.

"Kill him," the voice from the darkness said but closer this time.

"God's ass, fine," Darko said. He took three steps to Conrad and lifted his gun to the left side of Conrad's head.

Conrad didn't move. "Lydia," he said.

Lydia raised her head. She had a dark bruise on her face. Her eye was swollen and she looked dazed. From her expression and the movement of her eyes, Conrad assumed she had been drugged. She stared blankly into his eyes without making a noise.

Darko pushed the tip of the gun barrel against Conrad's temple and then pulled it back a few inches. "Don't want to fuck up my gun," he said.

Conrad still didn't move when a gunshot exploded from behind them. He maintained his stoic stillness when Darko's hand jerked up. When Darko's gun spit lead and fire near his skull and jarred his eardrums, Conrad instinctively dropped his head. He instinctively pulled Lydia and Mary down towards the ground. Finally, instinct drew his ankle-holstered gun for him and shot into the darkness.

Darko staggered back clutching his side. He pointed his gun at Conrad and pulled the trigger. A wedge of lead crashed into Conrad's armor-vested chest and knocked him backwards.

More shots exploded behind Conrad and Darko. Darko stumbled forward and fell on his face. There were two dark holes in his lower back and one in his left arm. A man tall and thin and wearing a dark suit ran into the circle of light. He was eagle-faced, with angular features and a thin hooked nose. A vague sense of recognition teased Conrad. The man grabbed Lydia by the ankles and pulled. She fell to her face and screamed and clawed at the pavement as he dragged her back into the shadows. Bullets whizzed at Conrad from the far right end of the building.

Conrad lurched forward on his knees while gunfire flew back and forth around him. He lunged at Lydia but he only managed to brush her fingers with his own as he fell on his chest. He rose to his hands and knees and crawled forward into the darkness after her. Another bullet sounded in front of him and clipped his side. He aimed his gun where the shot had flashed and, thinking of Lydia, held his fire.

A stream of gunfire moved steadily closer from behind Conrad, raking the two ends of the building. Dave rushed into the light. Behind him came Blounts decked out in black assault gear. Dave lifted Conrad by his arms and Blounts lifted Mary's limp body over his shoulder. Someone in the bushes, Conrad guessed it was Lina, continued peppering the building with covering fire.

The three men staggered towards Lina's location at the edge of the parking lot. Halfway across, they all flinched when they heard the thunderous sound of a helicopter shooting past them but, they kept running. Conrad shielded his eyes from the rotor-wash as the dark form of a military helicopter dropped behind the community center.

"You okay?" Lina asked over the din.

"Yeah, yeah," Dave said as he was lowering Conrad to the ground. "They have a damn helo! I'm calling the opcenter."

Conrad grabbed Dave's arm. "No," he shouted. Pain shot through his chest and he clutched at his side. The blood coming from his wound was warm and fluid. He pressed down on his side to stem the flow. "They'll trace your location."

Dave let Conrad's head down gently. "So?"

"Just don't. Someone will want to know who was here. Get it?"

Police sirens sounded in the distance. Sixty seconds later, the helicopter rose and flew off in the opposite direction from which it had come. Lina took four shots at it.

Conrad reached his hand out to Lina and tugged the bottom of her pants. "Lina, stop. Those bullets are gonna drop on someone's head."

Dave leaned over Conrad "How bad are you hurt?"

Conrad lifted his torn shirt and began undoing the thin protective vest underneath. "Mary. What happened to her?"

Blounts laid Mary gently on the ground. When he pulled his hands from under her, he collapsed to a seated position. Dave snapped on a flashlight and swung its beam over Blounts and Mary. Blounts' shoulder was covered in blood and a tear in his pants along his outer right thigh oozed blood. He looked ready to faint.

Dave let the flashlight linger on Blounts wound. "Fucking hell."

Blounts gripped his bloody thigh with his right hand and used his left to tap on the small radio mounted on his left shoulder.

"No." Conrad said. Searing pain shot through his chest again and he clutched his side. He panicked. Blounts was about to reveal himself to the opcenter mole who must have been waiting for just such a communication. "Stop," he struggled to say, but it was too late.

"Agent fiver, two, seven requesting three ambulances to Vienna community center. Critical gunshot injuries to civilian. Repeat. Three ambulances to Vienna, Virginia community center. Critical gunshot injuries to civilian."

"Huh?" Dave swung the light to Mary. She was covered in blood.

Conrad rolled on to his knees. "Mary?"

He ignored the pain that screamed at him to stop moving and instead dragged himself across the ground to his ex-wife. He reached for her hand. It was cold and limp. All of the color had left Mary's face. She didn't move. A wave of cold terror shot through his body. Conrad bellowed out all the hate and fury bound up inside him and then he threw up.

33

He became conscious that his eyes were closed. For a moment, he wanted to keep them that way. He moved his hands. He might be on a mattress. It was firm without being stiff. Adequate only. He lifted his hands and felt his body. His torso was wrapped in bandages, as was the top of his skull. His head throbbed and he decided to open his eyes. He did and saw a blinding white.

Conrad blinked out the incredible brightness that surrounded him and stared at the silver-domed light bulb that hung over him. A white ceiling floated above that. He stretched his legs and squeezed the bed with his hands. He looked side to side. The walls of the room were white and the television, a square black eye reflecting his bed-ridden image, hovered in the far upper corner. A wheeled food tray stood off to the left side of the bed.

Conrad lifted his right arm. A tube fed him nutrients from a clear bag hanging on a straight rod next to him. A small clip on the middle finger of his left hand was wired to a machine monitoring his heart rate. He took a deep breath and it hurt his chest to do that. He raised himself on to his elbows and that hurt too but he stayed in a propped position. He looked around for a gun but didn't see one. There was nothing that didn't normally belong in a hospital room.

Gathered curtains hung motionless along either edge of a window frame. Morning sunlight streamed through the window glass. A click and a door opened. A gray hat with a thin black band around its base preceded the head and face of a pale, middle-aged man peeking in. The man made eye contact with Conrad and his smoothly shaven face offered a thin smile that suggested business formality. "Feeling awake Mr Greis?"

Conrad narrowed his eyes. He was tired of surprises. "Sure." Conrad lifted the blanket that covered him. He wore a loose pair of boxers and small pillows of bandages covered his thighs and shins. His last waking moment was coming back to him. Darkness, flashes, guns, death.

Cris Alvarez

"Who are you?" he asked though he really didn't care. His body hurt, his thoughts were muddled, and he simply wanted to be alone.

Apparently that was too much to ask. The man gingerly stepped into the room with a smile still on his face. He wore a gray two-button suit that went with the hat and a white dress shirt graced by an indigo tie.

Conrad frowned. At least he could comfort himself with the thought that he had taken care of the assassin hired to kill him. He assumed that there wouldn't be a new contract in place so soon after Darko's death, but he steeled his body and mind to be ready to leap on this smiling stranger if necessary.

The man removed his hat and tossed it on the bare food tray. He appeared to be in his late thirties. He was a generic, plain-looking white man. A big business or government type. Athletic by the hardness of his face but undistinguishable. The man smoothed a layer of thinning brown hair to the right side of his head. A fat gold ring encircled the index finger of his left hand. Bluish veins bulged out from the back of that hand. He thrust his right hand towards Conrad and the smell of heavy cologne came with it. "Carl Flannery."

"Carl? That's my son's name. With a k."

"Ah, yes." Carl looked at the wall and furrowed his forehead. "You're right."

"Of course I'm right." Conrad firmly shook the man's hand and held it. "Conrad. Did you know that?"

Carl's eyes widened. "Pardon the interruption but we had to see you as soon as you were awake."

Conrad maintained his grip on Carl's hand. He thought it an interesting coincidence that Carl had shown up immediately after he had woken up but he passed on mentioning it. Why antagonize his keepers? "We? Who's we?" he asked instead.

Conrad released his grip and Carl slid his right hand into his pant pocket. Conrad kept his eye on Carl's hand. Nothing was bulging in the pocket and he didn't see weapons anywhere on Carl.

Carl smiled. He hunched slightly as he stood next to Conrad's bed and he raised his left hand as though silencing Conrad. "Here, put this on and you'll see." Carl's right hand shot out of his pant pocket and it slid into the inner pocket of his jacket. Conrad bent forward just as quickly and grabbed Carl's left wrist with one hand and his collar with the other. No pain at the moment meant they were filling him with painkillers.

Carl froze. "Whoa there Mr. Greis. Not a weapon okay?"

Conrad relaxed his grip slowly and hesitated before finally releasing Carl. Carl took a deep breath and pulled a pair of thick, silver glasses from his jacket pocket. The right side of the glasses had a five-millimeter memory stick attached vertically to the rim.

"Good job by the way on that Russian mercenary, Vladimir Tushkin." Carl smiled broadly. "Who says dead men don't talk?"

"Dead huh? I thought his name was Darko."

Carl shrugged. "Darko, Alex, Vlad. It's all the same to me."

Conrad sat up. "Mary! How is she?" He grabbed at a sudden, dull stab of pain that pulsed through his side.

Carl moved back a half step. "Mary?" He scratched his chin and glanced up at the ceiling. "She's stable."

"I want to see her."

Carl laid his hand gently on Conrad's bare shoulder and gave an ingratiating smile. "In due time. You have to let her rest."

"Rest? Okay." Conrad leaned back again. Sweat beaded his forehead. He warily eyed the glasses before taking them. Both lenses were completely clear. He unfolded the glasses and slid them over his eyes. Small video images were projected over the inner surface of each of the lenses though Conrad could still see his hospital room through the glasses.

"Here, you'll need these too." Carl pulled a pair of thick hearing pieces from his jacket. "We keep the audio and video tracks on separate devices for security reasons. And here." He pulled out a thin silver hood with a cord sewn around its base.

"I slip this around my neck?" Conrad asked.

"Yes. The shielding in the hood dampens the residual electronic waves coming from the two devices. Maybe a little security overkill but..." Carl tapped his nose with his right index finger.

Conrad nodded. He didn't relish the thought of slipping a hood over his head. He supposed there were easier ways to kill him though. He put the audio devices in his ears and slipped the hood over his head. He used the cord to tighten the hood until its open end was completely snug around his neck. The hood didn't completely obscure the room's light but Conrad was edgy about having it on.

"Now just tap the small button on the memory device attached to the glasses and tap the left hearing aid at the same time. They'll synchronize tracks automatically."

"Watch it," Conrad said. Carl stepped back as Conrad slid his legs over the edge of the bed and sat up straight. The movement hurt his abdomen but he felt more comfortable and safe sitting like that. As instructed, he pressed on the glasses and the earpiece. There was a short delay while electronic scratches, hisses and tones sounded in his ears. Then it began. A square image appeared in the screens. A static image of a government seal. The National Security Council's emblem.

"Special Agent Conrad Greis," a deep voice said, "you have been selected to serve the U.S. government on a mission of vital importance. The National Security Council has been monitoring suspicious activities within the FBI, DHS and other government agencies for some time and has determined that there exists a hidden enemy presence within one or more of these government entities.

"Yeah? I could have told you that." As soon as Conrad spoke, the presentation paused. "What day is it anyway?"

"It's May twenty-fifth. Wednesday Mr. Greis."

"What time is it?"

"Eight forty-seven a.m."

Conrad thought for a moment. Fuck it. I have time for this garbage, he decided. After three seconds of silence, the presentation began again. "For security reasons, these agencies have not been specifically alerted to this danger beyond standard procedure counterintelligence and anti-terrorism warnings."

"You're with these guys?" Greis asked. The presentation stopped again.

"Please Mr. Greis. I am with the NSC. Don't say anything more. Just listen and watch."

As the presentation continued, graphics showing the branches of the government splashed onto the lenses of the glasses. Following that, pictures of people and places appeared and disappeared. It was a miniature power point presentation made specifically for Conrad.

The brief explained that all levels of these various agencies were at risk of infiltration. The enemy, the domestic rebels trying to take down the government, blended easily into the normal population. They spoke the same way, looked the same way, kept the same habits as the average citizen. They knew what to say to successfully integrate into lawful society and operate undercover.

"This is ridiculous," Conrad said. "It's a civil war. Of course they're hard to find. They're our neighbors and friends." Conrad shook his head. The presentation was standard government bullshit. Little useful information and lots of talk.

"I'm sorry if it seems so obvious to you Mr. Greis. This presentation is slightly generic. Not all of our recruits have the training you do."

"But you make me sit through it anyway?"

"Procedure Agent Greis."

Conrad shook his head again in frustration. After three seconds, the presentation resumed but Conrad immediately interrupted it. "I've already been assigned to one undercover mission and look where it got me."

"Yes, that mission."

"Lydia and I didn't get any info. We screwed the pooch on that one." Sharp pains went through his temples.

"Oh, the mission was to lure the rebels to you."

Conrad loosened the hood and removed it. He stared at the expressionless face of the NSC agent. He didn't know whether to laugh or to strangle the man that stood impassively in front of him. He considered doing the one after the other. The order didn't matter.

Carl's face broke into a frown. "I can freely tell you this since that mission has been completed." Carl's head danced side to side. "So to speak. Someone from the FBI will do a close-out interview with you and, uh, on that operation."

Conrad lifted his legs back on the bed. "DHS versus FBI versus NSC?" He laid his head on the pillow. It felt cool and soft. He could just close his eyes, go to sleep, and disappear and it wouldn't matter a whit. He clasped his hands behind his head and closed his eyes in preparation for a long nap.

"But we have a new mission for you," Carl said. "A slightly different one."

Conrad opened his eyes. For the first time during the interview, Carl appeared nervous. He looked at the far end of the floor as he spoke. "This is a much more delicate mission but my superiors have reviewed your record and your actions during previous missions and they consider you a very strong candidate for this assignment."

Conrad removed the glasses and folded them. He rested them on the edge of his bed. "You know I'm done with all this shit."

Carl crossed his arms. "What does that mean, 'done with this shit'?"

"Sorry to waste your time and watch your dog and pony show but I'm done with the killing., the chasing, the revenge. I killed Darko. Well someone did but he's dead. Now I'm going to put the boys and Mary somewhere safe and disappear. The government can find another patsy now. Maybe I'll go to Hollywood. Who knows? But my revenge days are done."

Carl raised an eyebrow. "Oh really? Nothing more to avenge? Must be nice to feel completely secure when the rest of the country is still at war."

Conrad closed his eyes and rubbed his temple with his palm. He was forgetting something important. "Yeah. I told you I'm done."

Carl's voice took on a nasty tone, a mocking one. "Why don't you just watch the rest of the presentation and then give me your decision? Maybe your family isn't so safe as you think."

Conrad's eyes flashed open. He pushed off the bed and grabbed Carl by the collar. The heart rate monitor jerked forward.

"Hey," Carl shouted. Carl's hands grabbed Conrad's wrists and he tried to pull away but Conrad was too strong for him.

Carl was about three inches taller than Conrad and Conrad was able to use the height disparity to get a better grip on Carl's shirt. Carl grunted and tried to step back., but Conrad pulled Carl in so that they were nose to nose. He was done with being pushed around by people he didn't know, people he had never met. "Listen now. I'm sick of this little fucking g-man game. I used to think it was worth something, you know? I made a difference in people's lives."

Carl continued wrestling with Conrad's grip but to no effect. "You do Greis."

"Fuck all that Carl. I kill people and people try to kill me. That's all it fucking amounts to. Do you get shot at? Or do you just go around designating who the fuck is going to get shot at?"

"I don't bring this on us Greis. I have a job and I do it. You have a job too and you should do it. Use your skills."

Conrad released his grip and Carl stepped back gasping. He savagely wiped his face clean of Conrad's spittle. Conrad smiled evilly. "You mean the skill I was just using? Kicking the shit out of people and maybe killing them too."

Carl wiped his hands on his pants. "You track people. You find people. You do the dirty things other people won't."

"And what happens when I stop doing the dirty things? Then what are you left with?

"You make a perfect point Agent Greis. What are we left with? What do you think we're left with? Why am I here trying to convince a disheartened agent to do this? Because there is no alternative. You are the line Agent Greis. In front of you is the enemy and behind you, I hate to say it, there's nobody but sheep."

"Nobody to do your killing? I can't believe that."

"Nobody who can kill well."

Conrad sat back down on the bed and lowered his head. His heart was still racing but he was beginning to calm down. He could just say no. He didn't want a return to the violence. That's what got him into this mess in the first place. The violence around him and the violence he delivered in retaliation. That was my old life, he told himself.

He looked up at Carl. "I don't want to be the grim reaper anymore. It's...I'm done with the killing. I cleaned up my mess and now I'll walk away." The top of his skull began to ache. "I'm just one man. I don't amount to all that much. You can easily find someone who can do what I did. Find someone young, someone eager to kill. But it's not me. Tell your people it's not me."

Carl sighed. "Please watch the next power point presentation Mr Greis." He pulled a low chair out from in front of Conrad's bed and sat. He removed a packet of cigarettes from his outer pocket and shook a stick loose. Then he surprised Conrad by taking a lighter from his jacket pocket, a black lighter with a small metal eagle emblem on it, and lighting the cigarette. He held the cigarette between thin fingers and thin, pale lips and took a long draw from it.

"You can't smoke in here. It's a hospital," Conrad said.

Carl's face hardened. "Who's going to stop me?" He looked to the ceiling and blew a stream of white smoke upwards. "Enough talking. Just watch the brief Mr. Greis and you'll understand."

Conrad watched the smoke spread along the roof of his room. "You're all the same. Every one of you. You're not human beings. You're all about a process and that's it. Here's the task and do it."

Carl nodded. "Okay. I didn't want to show you this but I guess I'll need to." Carl took another memory stick from his pocket and held out his hand. "The glasses please." Conrad shook his head at the

Cris Alvarez

man's obstinacy and handed Carl the glasses. Carl replaced the one memory stick with the other and handed the glasses back. "Watch this."

Conrad took the glasses and stared at them. Is this what I've been a part of for twenty years? he asked himself. A machine that just moves along regardless of where any of its creators want it to go? Conrad put the glasses on, slid the hood over his head without tightening it, and laid back in the bed.

The small screens showed a grainy video of an empty interrogation room. A door opened and a woman wearing gray sweats was pushed into the room. She stumbled forward and fell on her hands and knees.

Conrad's heart jumped. His mind had betrayed him. He glared at the nutrient bag and angrily wondered what sorts of drugs they were pumping him with. The memory of the night, of Lydia and the eagle-faced man, came back to him in a rush and the pain in his head returned.

The woman, Conrad wasn't sure if it was Lydia, was on her knees and crying. Conrad wanted to look away but he didn't close his eyes. He was frozen by the fear of shutting her out of his mind again.

A man walked into the room. It was the same man who had dragged Lydia away and he was wearing the same suit he had on at the community center.

For the next three minutes, the man swore at the woman and kicked her around. Conrad caught glimpses of her face but he couldn't tell if it was Lydia. Conrad impatiently moved his head around as though he could get a better look at what he was seeing. The woman didn't speak, she only yelled and cried as she was beaten. The man kicked her, punched her, slapped her, and berated her for treachery. Blood dripped from her mouth.

Finally the woman's face came into focus and a great hand squeezed Conrad's chest. It was Lydia, the woman he loved. Then Conrad realized he knew the man's voice. It was the same man at the Christian compound who had tried to convince Conrad to become a traitor.

Conrad tore the hood off his head and pulled the glasses from his face. Carl was still sitting casually and smoking.

Conrad crushed the glasses in his hand. "Where the fuck are they?"

Carl smiled and raised both eyebrows. "So you're in? I thought you'd want some revenge. Mary, Lydia. Those rebels have no respect for you."

Conrad jumped from his bed. "Wait a minute. What happened to Mary? You said she was okay." Conrad took three quick steps towards the door and stopped abruptly. He impatiently pulled the feed tube out of his arm and undid the clip on his finger.

Carl rose from the chair. "Mary? I said she was stable."

Conrad grabbed the door handle and turned it but the door was locked. "What do you mean stable?"

Carl rubbed his chin. "Relax, Mr. Greis. We've taken care of everything. Just focus on the mission at hand."

"Taken care of what?"

Carl blew a stream of smoke from the corner of his mouth. "Everything."

34

T he day was sunny and warm and it shouldn't have been. It should have been raining and it should have been depressing. Conrad kicked the ground with the point of his shoe. He folded his arms tightly and looked up the slope of a low hill.

His family and friends were gathered on the crest of the hill, soberly talking together. Dave, Blounts and Lina were grouped together near Conrad's other law enforcement friends. Across from them, on the other side of the grave pit, Paul and Karl stood silently under their grandmother's comforting arms. A thought flashed across Conrad's mind and panic struck him. His hand went into his hip pocket to touch his gun.

He looked over his shoulder. Anyone could come by and lob a bomb into the group and destroy everything Conrad had left in the world. He forced that fear out of his head and turned his face back towards the group. The priest and others were watching him.

He stopped hesitating. He walked up the hill and joined the funeral party. He took his place next to Paul and Karl. They looked up at him with eyes that were puffy and red. He put a hand on Paul's shoulder and smiled at their maternal grandmother Denise. She gave a slight smile back and dabbed her eyes with a handkerchief.

Conrad's gaze swept over the rest of the scene. Mary's coffin sat on a low platform next to a large pit dug in the ground. A white marble headstone graced one side of the fresh grave. A mound of fresh black earth graced the other side. Karl sniffled and the priest waited for Conrad. Conrad nodded and the priest began speaking.

The words were like the wind to Conrad. He only listened to the quiet around him as the priest recited sermons and prayers. Conrad's mind went over the years of memories, replayed in static motion, and he disappeared inside himself. Twenty minutes passed and at the end of it the group murmured thanks and amens and crossed themselves. Conrad walked to the coffin and helped lift it from the platform and lower it into the grave. Something thick stuck in his throat and he forced himself to swallow. There was pain in his abdomen and back but it was dull and seemed trivial to him.

The coffin touched the bottom of the pit. Conrad put the lowering strap on the ground and backed away. He took a handful of earth from the dirt pile and tossed it over the coffin. He stood aside to let others do the same. Karl and Paul seemed bewildered when their turns came but they threw the earth too and moved back to their grandmother.

Conrad watched each of those attending the funeral file past, each saying some word of sympathy or grief and perhaps adding another pile of earth on to Mary. Is it over? Would it be over? What remained of his family might be safe for now. He could move away, leave his children behind and do it publicly, and the forces pursuing him would be drawn away with him. Would they leave his children alone after that? Possibly.

He could allow his desire for revenge to disappear. He could refuse the gratification of killing the man who had tortured Lydia to death. Killing that man would serve no practical purpose now. It wouldn't bring Lydia back. Nothing could bring her or Mary back. He had to protect his children. That's all that mattered.

The last person in line returned to the assembled group. All eyes were on him. He looked at them all and nodded. They turned towards each other and exchanged hugs and words of comfort. Conrad walked away from the grave and the assembled mass. He stared at the trees of the cemetery. Maples and oaks, thick with leaves, stretched their limbs skywards towards the sun. Someone tapped Conrad on the shoulder.

Dave was looking down the hill and pointing. Conrad shifted his eyes to follow Dave's gaze. Agents Yablount and Ridenauer were striding with purpose up the hill towards Conrad.

Conrad looked at his sons and his hand went into his hip pocket. "I'll talk to you guys soon," he said but they didn't react. He had spoken too low for them to hear.

Conrad took two steps towards the agents. Dave followed and Conrad swept his gun hand through the air to stop him. "Stay with my kids Dave. I'll handle this."

Conrad continued forward to meet the two DHS agents. They wore their unofficial uniforms - gray suits, felt hats and sunglasses. When they were ten feet from Conrad, they unbuttoned their jackets in near unison without breaking stride.

"You're coming with us," Yablount said. He reached out and grabbed Conrad's upper left arm with his right hand.

Conrad stopped. "What's this about?" he asked. But he knew they might be working for him, Lydia's killer.

Ridenauer looked over his shoulder. "Not here. Come with us."

"No."

"No?" Yablount asked. He squeezed Conrad's arm but Conrad refused to be baited into the fistfight Yablount was obviously agitating for.

Conrad raised his palms. "Can I say goodbye to my family properly?"

Yablount released Conrad's arm. "You'll have time for that later."

"Come on Ronnie," Ridenauer said to Yablount. "Give him a minute."

"We have our orders Mike. No minutes, no nothing. We have to talk to you now."

Conrad shook his head. "You heard me before. No," he said as calmly as he could. He needed to maintain his composure. He wouldn't make a scene at Mary's burial.

Yablount turned and grabbed Conrad's arm again. "Come on."

Conrad changed his mind. He raised his right arm and brought it down hard on Yablount's right shoulder. Yablount buckled under the blow, releasing Conrad's arm as he went to his knees. He grunted and grabbed his shoulder.

"Agent," Ridenauer said. He reached under his left arm and fumbled for his pistol. Conard cocked back his arm, lunged forward and propelled his fist at Ridenauer's face. Ridenauer's eyes widened and he barely dodged a full blow. Instead, Conrad's knuckles raked along the side of the stocky man's face and Ridenauer bent backwards.

Yablount rose and reached for his gun. Conrad swung his foot up and caught Yablount squarely in the lower gut with the point of his shoe. He drove his foot all the way up.

"Unh!" The cry of pain exploded out of Yablount's mouth. He doubled over clutching his belly and groaning. His gun fell out of its underarm holster and hit the dirt.

Ridenauer drew his gun and two people screamed. Conrad threw a left roundhouse into Ridenauer's right shoulder. Ridenauer turned with the blow and stumbled. He slipped and went down on his hands and knees.

"Conrad," Dave yelled. Conrad didn't look back. He swung his foot into Ridenauer's stomach and something cracked under the blow. Ridenauer moaned softly and grabbed his chest. He collapsed and rolled on his side.

Yablount reached for his gun but Conrad deftly pulled his own out of his pocket first. Yablount took hold of his gun and drew it at Conrad. "You piece of shit," he said.

Conrad pumped his trigger once. Yablount's face turned into a pale grimace as the flesh of his left thigh ripped open. Yablount dropped his gun and grabbed at the bloody wound.

Dave crashed into Conrad from behind and wrapped him in a powerful bear hug. "Stop! What the fuck are you doing?"

Conrad twisted his head back. Blounts was hobbling towards them on one crutch while Lina sprinted. The funeral guests were yelling and dispersing in all directions. Denise, Karl and Paul, as well as a handful of his other law enforcement friends, stood motionless watching the commotion.

Conrad tried to wrestle free of Dave's grip but he couldn't break lose. "Shit Dave. Let me go."

"Drop the gun. Drop the gun."

With his forearms pinned against his sides by Dave's hold, Conrad used his wrist to vainly wave his gun. After mere seconds of futility, he gave up and let the gun drop to the ground. Lina swooped in and snatched the weapon.

Dave relaxed his grip. "Keep it cool boss."

"I've got to go."

"Yeah. I think you're right," Dave said.

Conrad looked back again at his children. It would never end unless he did something about it. Looking at Yablount and Ridenauer, he was glad he had told Carl yes. "Dave, look after my boys." The he shot off like a racehorse for the parking lot.

"Stop," Ridenauer yelled.

"Rad," Blounts said. But no one followed.

In moments, Conrad was in the car and had it running. He hit the accelerator and peeled out of the parking lot.

On the street, he sped through a red light, nearly hitting a car as he went. His mind raced. The eagle-faced man was pulling the strings. Were Ridenauer and Yablount traitors or innocent dupes?

Those maniacs tried to shoot him at Mary's funeral. Did his family have to see that violence? He could have gone quietly but he didn't. They might have taken him straight to the man.

Conrad pressed down on the accelerator. The engine screamed in his ears and his head throbbed. He came to a thick line of traffic and slammed his brakes hard. His tires squealed like banshees and smoke rose up from behind his car as it skidded to a stop. He stopped inches short of the car in front of him. The driver of that car opened his door and stepped out. He had the look of a man ready to beat the shit out of someone.

He took a step, made eye contact with Conrad, and got back into his car. Conrad opened his window. The stench of the burning tires wafted inside and Conrad inhaled deeply. The smell reminded him of the battlefield.

He hadn't spent twenty-two years of his life devoted to the protection of the United States just to have his family endangered by scum hiding in his own government, to have his children put in fear of his employers. His mind seethed with thoughts of murderous rage and retribution. He thought of everything he had done with his life. The awards, the praise, and now the treatment he had been subjected to over the last three weeks.

Someone was going to pay for this insanity, someone deserving. And that was it. There would be no peace.

35

H e looked like he belonged there, standing alone at the bus stop, but little clues gave him away. If anyone were inclined to look for them.

Conrad cleared his throat and tapped the tip of his shoe on the ground. His hands were stuffed in his pants pockets and his arms were close against his sides. A breeze, a little cold and a little depressing, blew across the streets of the government district of Washington, DC and Conrad shivered.

Spots of dirt, grease and grime blemished the gray sidewalk. He tried to remember how many times he had walked these streets but couldn't come up with a number. Countless was all that came to mind. Many times with Mary, but that was a finite number now.

Conrad noticed movement in the area he was conducting surveillance on and looked up. He moved away from the bus stop and pulled an unread newspaper from under his arm. His heart beat quickened. It was time.

He had spent two days laying low, sleeping in his car away, avoiding his regular haunts. He had called Carl Flannery once and got the information he needed. Carl had sounded happy to hear from him but warned him to keep a low profile. "You're undercover now. No help from us," was what Carl had said.

The target exited the security doors at the front of DHS headquarters. The man, Donald Rygan, Deputy Assistant of Civilian Control, a man appointed to his position by the President of the United States and confirmed by the Senate, marched confidently across the brown concrete plaza in front of the DHS building towards a line of cars parked in tandem along the opposite curb.

Should have used underground parking today, Conrad mused. Should have, could have, didn't. Conrad walked three steps to his car, a new dark-blue midsize provided by Carl and the NSC, and got in. He started the engine at the same time that Don did and he pulled away from the curb slowly after Don had merged into traffic. Three car lengths of distance separated them and Conrad left it at that. It was 2:13 p.m.

The two cars drove slowly through the DC traffic. The air was cool and the sun was out. Clouds peppered the blue sky. Off to the west, thick clouds were turning dark gray and scudding east.

Conrad easily played tail in the stop and go traffic, easily followed this man who appeared oblivious to his tracker. Conrad turned on the radio and switched the dial to a country station. He wanted a little cowboy music. Something that was too much of a ballad and too focused on lost love crooned through the speakers so he switched from station to station until he came to a driving rock song. A new pop rock tune. The lead kept singing "gut check" and Conrad nodded to the music.

After ten minutes of driving north through downtown DC, Don pulled into an underground parking garage. Conrad drove just past the garage entrance and pulled to the curb opposite the garage. Conrad looked at the reflections in his rear-view mirror and watched as Don exited his car and handed his keys to the valet.

Don crossed to Conrad's side of the street and walked in the opposite direction from Conrad's car. When he turned the corner, Conrad hit his emergency blinkers and got out of his car. He jogged to the end of the sidewalk where Don had turned.

Conrad went around the corner carefully and just caught Don stepping into the foyer of the Jefferson House, an expensive and established restaurant built in 1833. Conrad ran back to his car and drove to a self-parking garage two blocks beyond the one Don had used. Conrad pulled a blue baseball cap low on his head as he paid for his parking ticket.

Conrad parked, grabbed his lock pick tools, double-checked the weapons he had strapped to his body, and made his way back out of the stomach of that concrete enclosure. The air was getting thicker, the wind was moving faster, and the clouds looked angrier.

Conrad briskly walked the two blocks back to Don's garage. Conrad asked the attendant how much more it would cost to keep his car there until eleven p.m. The attendant reminded Conrad that the garage closed at ten. Conrad smiled sheepishly and cursed lightly. Then he apologized to the attendant and walked down the sloping driveway into the garage.

The garage was filled with cars, mostly middle class sedans. Conrad walked down to the first level and down again to the second, glancing at each car. On the third level below ground, he found Donald Rygan's black midsize.

Conrad crouched down in between its driver side and the car next to it. He scooted back to the passenger side rear door of Don's car and pulled out a lock pick instrument that looked like a car alarm device. Conrad peeked around the car. The lighting in the garage was dim and no one was around. He didn't think he was in the line of sight of any security cameras. He pressed on the electronic lock pick device and let it cycle until Don's car alarm beeped off. He looked around again but saw no one. He opened the unlocked driver's door and slid into the car, closing the door quietly behind him.

The interior of the car was lined with supple black leather. The strong odor of a coconut freshener filled the car. The car was devoid of junk, nothing was out of place. Conrad arched himself over the front seat and reached for a latch that held the back seat in place. Conrad pushed on the latch and the seat came down to reveal the car trunk.

A stab of pain reminded Conrad of what he faced for the next few hours. He took a small syringe from his jacket pocket, uncapped it, and punched the needle through his shirt into his chest muscle. A morphine-derived drug mixed with a light stimulant flowed out of the small needle and into his body. He re-capped the needle and put the syringe back into his pocket. He pulled himself over the front seat and into the cavity of the car's trunk.

His pain ebbed as the injected liquid flowed through his body. The trunk was dark but as Conrad moved around, he could tell that it was empty. He curled himself into a kind of fetus position until he was facing the back seats. He had twisted himself so that his head was directly behind the driver's side front seat. He pulled the seats up until they were firmly back in place. He used his lock pick device to re-alarm the car and he heard the driver's door lock click.

Conrad pulled out a penlight and flashed it on. The inside of the trunk was standard and, as he initially thought, free of garbage. It was uncomfortable but Conrad adjusted his knees and arms until he felt as unrestricted as possible. He turned off the penlight, removed his waist-holstered gun and waited. After ten minutes, he closed his eyes and relaxed. The drug would keep him awake.

In about an hour, the car alarm beeped. Conrad's eyelids lifted. His heart raced and he was sweating. He felt groggy. The abrupt transition from calm to excitement disoriented him slightly.

Someone climbed in the car and turned it on. Soft rock played on the radio and the driver softly sang along with it. The car moved backwards, turned, and then moved up towards the garage exit. Nothing more than a cursory thanks and farewell was said between

Don and the valet as the two exchanged places. The car pulled out of the garage.

Conrad itched to begin his revenge. At the first stop, he carefully pushed the seat cushion down and slid forward. It was his man. Conrad pushed his gun forward into Don's side. Don jerked forward and stopped singing. He looked down at Conrad with a face that could have been made of chalk. His lips slowly spread open and he sucked in air. "You," he said in a soft voice.

Conrad looked carefully at the angular face he had seen only a few nights before. Don's gray hair was a little messy and he smelled faintly of whiskey This was the man who had pulled Lydia into the darkness. It was the man he had seen on the video. Conrad's emotions raced like frantic lizards through his gut. He clenched his teeth and loosened them.

"Yeah, me. Try anything and I'll blow a hole through your side." One side of Don's mouth twitched up. A look that seemed like doubt to Conrad flashed over Don's face. "Try me," Conrad said. "I've got nothing to lose."

Don looked forward. "I'm sure you're right," he said.

Conrad stared for a long hard moment at the back of Don's head. "Drive to Constitution Avenue, get on the Sixty-Six, and start driving west. Slam on the brakes and I shoot, speed up unexpectedly and I shoot. Talk to someone or do anything funny and I shoot. In fact, if you're hands come off that steering wheel, I shoot. Notice a theme?"

Don accelerated the car normally when traffic started moving again. "What are you going to do with me?"

"Prisoner exchange."

Don glanced back with the tips of eyebrows pinched together. "What?"

Conrad pushed the gun into Don's side. "Just drive." Conrad was already tired of the conversation. He was tired of Don's voice. He hadn't thought through to the gab that might arise, only the physical possibilities. He took his finger of the trigger and rested it along the length of the gun barrel.

The car moved but slowly. Don's hands quivered as he drove. His lips and chin trembled too. Conrad got a quiet satisfaction from that. The video of Lydia's torture played in his mind and steeled his nerves. He had to be careful that the memory didn't make him lose control. He had a task to accomplish which would change his life forever. He had to do it right.

It took Don almost ten minutes to get to I-66 West. Once on the highway, the car picked up speed. Conrad pulled himself out of the trunk and slid himself to a seated position in the driver's side of the back seat. He kept his gun pressed against Don's right side while he looked over Don's headrest.

Don met Conrad's eyes in the rear-view mirror. "Who will I be exchanged for?"

Conrad's throat tightened and he looked out the window. Large, full-leafed maples and oaks waved at them from the edges of the highway. They were thick, venerable trees that lined much of the length of the highway. Behind them, residences, single-family homes, condominium complexes and twelve-story apartment buildings were piled together in the small neighborhoods of Virginia. The tops of these houses made the late afternoon seem serene. Conrad sighed. "That's not up to me."

Don's hands slid up and down the steering wheel as he drove. Sweat beaded on his temples. "Where do I exit?" His voice shook.

"Exit fifty-two onto Lee Highway West. We're going to Cub Run Park."

"Oh? Near Manassas?"

"Hurry it up."

After thirty more minutes into the drive, Don appeared to relax. Conrad realized they were entering an area where things became a little iffy for federal agents like himself. Conversely, Conrad knew that rebels like Don felt slightly more at home away from the big cities, in areas like Manassas.

"Getting comfortable?" Conrad asked.

"No, no."

"Good." Conrad barked out more directions and he led Don off Lee Highway. They didn't use the normal park entrance. Conrad had Don drive off the road, past a line of tall tress, into an open area of the park that ran along the highway. The open field was in the neighborhood of four acres in size. The clouds overhead were thick and black and the weather was colder now.

Conrad poked Don in the side with his gun. "Get out."

Don opened his car door with his left hand and as he stepped out he leaned a little too far forward and down for the movement.

Conrad lifted himself over the front seat and brought his weight down as he clubbed the back of Don's head with the butt of his gun.

Don groaned and something thudded on the ground. Conrad scrambled to the front seat and pushed Don all the way out of the car. Don stumbled forward and grabbed the back of his head with both hands.

Conrad leapt out of the car and saw a small handgun laying on the ground where Don had dropped it. Conrad felt surprisingly exhilarated and happy. "I'm not playing games," he said.

But he didn't feel threatening when he spoke. He felt joy about being so close to finishing off a problem that had plagued him for so long. But the feeling went as quickly as it had come and he was angry at his cockiness.

He couldn't deceive himself. He had always been devoted to his sense of fairness. He had always been committed to the lawful process. That's how he had dealt with the enemy many times over and never had he felt guilty for the consequences of his actions. Now he felt nothing but guilt. But he couldn't stop now. There was little point in that. What was happening had to run its natural course.

Don turned around still holding the back of his head. "Where are the others?"

"There are no others."

Don's eyes widened and he looked straight at the gun. His body straightened up and his head turned side to side. "What are you going to do?"

Conrad shrugged. "Don't know yet. Tell me about Lydia."

"What about her?"

Conrad bent down and lifted the right cuff of his jeans. He slid his hand up and pulled a military knife from the leather sheath strapped to his leg.

Don took a step back. "What are you doing with that?"

Conrad moved forward and Don took another step back. His face was ashen.

"What are you worried about Don? Feel guilty about something?"

"I won't bother rationalizing with a crazy man."

"Oh, I'm not crazy Donald. I'm just mad. Slight difference. Now start talking."

Don looked around. "I don't know any Lydia."

The field behind them was large and Conrad knew what Don was thinking. Any dash for freedom would give Conrad ample time to aim and shoot. Precisely the reason Conrad had chosen this location.

Conrad used his thumb to pull the hammer back on his gun while he aimed it at Don. "I'll just shoot now, how about that?"

Don waved his hands at Conrad. "She was, she had to be dealt with. She would reveal too much."

"Did you need to torture her?"

"I didn't torture her. She was with us. She..."

"She what?"

"She was spying on you for us." Don's head dropped and his shoulders sagged. He glanced up at Conrad.

Conrad sprinted at Don. Don stumbled backwards and fell. He raised one arm to ward off the anticipated blow but Conrad stopped short without tackling him. He crouched and shot his knee up into Don's sternum. Don groaned loudly and clutched at his chest. "Leave me alone," he yelled.

"Don't lie to me." Conrad yelled. "Why lie now?"

Don coughed and his face relaxed. His eyes narrowed but he didn't answer.

Conrad pushed Don back at the ground. "Why are you a fucking traitor?"

"A traitor? A traitor to whom?"

"To your fucking government. To the position you were appointed to. To the President and Congress."

"Those aren't my leaders."

"Yeah, yeah, I know who your leaders are. The fucking rats who run through the forests and the mud proclaiming a holy war in Christ's name, killing innocent people along the way."

"Innocent you say? We aren't just your run of the mill religious nuts Agent Greis. We're people who are sick of the government telling us what godless things they'll allow in society." Don stood and straightened his coat. "We represent a day when people could live out beyond the suburbs and not completely suffer the outrageous edicts and proclamations of a degenerate group living within the Washington Beltway. My people reject the hedonistic and

Cris Alvarez

bohemian lifestyles yearned for by the dirty masses living in the cities. If living is the right word."

"Bullshit. You wreak your violence on law-abiding people for one reason only. You simply don't like their laws."

"They deserve it. Their laws are not laws. They are animal desires fulfilled and guaranteed on papers topped with federal letterhead."

"So you hurt people like Lydia so that you can return to some goddamned golden age?"

"You can make it sound romantic and childish if you want, but that time existed. And not more than two decades ago it still existed to some extent. Don't you remember?"

Conrad lowered his knife and gun. "Yeah. I was twenty, living on MTV and computer games and wondering why the hell we spent our time outlawing every innocent thing that people wanted to do when we had real problems to deal with. Guess what Don. I may have been young and stupid but civics class taught me a little something about constitutional freedoms."

"Don't you lecture me about constitutional freedoms Greis. I'm a lawyer. You're nothing but a punk with a badge and a gun who doesn't know how to think about the laws he's promised to enforce. You're nothing but a brainless foot soldier for the government."

Conrad grunted. "Maybe so. Maybe so. Kind of funny though don't you think?"

"The collapse of America is not funny at all Greis."

"We're rebuilding, slowly, fitfully, but it's happening. Despite your efforts to drag us back down."

"We're rebuilding a Sodom and Gomorrah for our children. I'd rather my children die standing than live in that. All we have now is nothing but a godless, witless Christian-hating communist state."

"We still have a free market. We have freedom of speech."

"Really?" Don adjusted his tie and stood before Conrad as though he were addressing an assembly of his peers. "This government you love so much uses violence crudely, like the socialists and communists did. To uphold your ungodly laws and hurt whoever strives for real, pure, morally correct freedom. We fight for the right kind of freedom."

Conrad turned and threw the knife at the ground behind him. The blade sunk almost to its hilt into the moist earth. Conrad held his gun horizontally and began rubbing the barrel. "Your people use violence too. I've seen it first hand."

"Our violence is applied rationally, properly. We use it in a different way and for a different purpose. We use it to free people from tyranny and we apply it sympathetically and fairly. We strive to make sure that only the deserving," Don raised one finger, "if they refuse to yield to the one truth, suffer their due."

"And right now, people like Lydia deserve to suffer and die, right?" Lydia loved Conrad and he loved her in return. He knew this to be true. To hell with Don and his self-serving lies about her.

Don spat on the ground. "Pretty or not, the dangerous and destructive deserve it."

Did Don want Conrad to rip him apart? No. He was trying to goad him into losing his self-control, into losing his grip on what he knew to be the truth. Conrad lowered his gun.

Twenty years of the violence that he had been a part of and which he had endured stoically for all that time flashed before his mind's eyes. His body tightened up as the painkiller began to wear off. He was tired of anger. His head throbbed and his body ached. He wanted to expel this hate that had grown in him during the twenty years of brutality that both sides, right and left, had wrecked on each other. The gun in his hand felt heavy.

He only just noticed that a slight drizzle had started and the earth felt softer under his feet. He wanted to drop his gun and let the earth suck him down. His temples pulsed harder. No. He didn't want to drop his gun, he wanted to fling his gun away. He wanted his rejection of violence, chaos and killing to be an active action, not a passive one. He wanted to do something good for the world. He wanted to bring world peace, not world war. That had been the dream since his youth but somewhere, he had walked a different path to his goal. "I want this violence to end," Conrad said to no one in particular.

Don smiled. Away in the distance, over the treetops, something thumped rhythmically in the western sky. Conrad turned his head slowly until he saw it - the expanding image of a Jaysing 732 military helicopter. Probably a surplus piece shipped to the rebels across the Mexico-United States border. Shipped along the Mississippi and then brought over by truck to be stored and hidden somewhere in the Appalachian Mountains. It came closer and when it was a third of a mile away, its electrically charged machine guns belched lead at him. As the guns ripped up the earth in front of him, Conrad dashed behind the car.

The bullets followed him, splashing dirt into the air and clanging off the reinforced metal of Don's car. Conrad peaked over the hood. Don was waving at the helicopter and yelling at them to stop shooting. The helicopter did stop and Don ran close to the car on the side opposite Conrad. Conrad dropped his head back down.

"Greis," Don shouted. "I have my gun and the helo has its sights on you. Stick your head out and it will get blown off."

"I know that."

"And you definitely will be a wanted man now. You're dead. And how ironic it will be when I have the government's best agents are out there tracking you down."

"I'm sure it will be."

Conrad kept his head down as the helicopter hovered about forty-five meters up and twenty meters beyond the car on Don's side. When it began to descend, Conrad saw what he had been waiting for. From the line of trees at the eastern edge of the field, a four-foot long Spiker surface-to-air missile sailed through the air and smashed into the descending helicopter. Don bellowed as the Jaysing helicopter exploded in mid-air. What was left of its fuselage spun wildly and crashed to the ground about sixty meters north of the car.

Conrad popped up from behind the car. Don ran screaming to the flaming wreckage. Dave Bronson came sprinting out of the eastern tree line holding an automatic rifle. Conrad ran around the car and dashed towards Don.

Don turned and backed obliquely away from Conrad and the helicopter. "You got me! You don't have to kill me. Just arrest me."

"Arrest you? Hell. On what charge?"

Don backed up quicker, turned and sprinted for the tree line at the far end of the park. He slipped and stumbled on the slick grass but he kept moving desperately forward using his hands, knees and feet to get away from Conrad.

Conrad raised his gun slowly and gripped it with both hands. The rain splashed lightly on his face and obscured his vision but he took his time to aim. He adjusted his position as Don tried to put the wreckage between Conrad's line of sight to Don. When Don was ninety meters away, Conrad pulled the trigger. Don stopped and raised his arms to the sky. He stood frozen in place with his gun in his right hand.

"I was supposed to kill you," Conrad shouted. Don didn't move. "I was supposed to kill you by instruction from the federal government." Don stood and quivered under the curtain of thickening rain.

Conrad squinted his eyes. "But I'm not going to kill you for them you filthy piece of shit."

Don's dropped his arms and turned. He was smiling.

"I'm going to kill you for my own fucking self!"

Don dropped into a crouch and swung his gun upwards. Conrad pumped his trigger twice. Two bullets tore through Don's chest. He howled and collapsed to the ground.

"Conrad!" Dave yelled. He was sprinting to reach Conrad.

Conrad ignored Dave and ran up to Don. The man who had killed Lydia and caused Mary's death was writhing in the mud and clutching at his chest but he wasn't bleeding. A protective vest had stopped the bullets.

"You scum," he managed to spit out at Conrad.

Conrad lifted his gun and pointed it at Don.

Dave finally reached them and froze, his eyes staring in horror at Conrad. "Don't do this Conrad. We have him. I got it all on tape."

"Find Christ in you, " Don said. "Have mercy. Walk away from evil and join me."

Conrad gritted his teeth and his finger danced on the trigger.

"Your children, " Dave said. "Remember them."

Conrad looked at Dave with wildness in his eyes.

"Please," Don said. "I'm a good man. I have a mission to complete."

Conrad slowly swiveled his head back to Don. "Woe unto you, scribes and Pharisees, hypocrites, for ye make clean the outside of the cup and the platter. Cleanse that which is within the cup and the platter. Woe unto you hypocrites, for ye are like whited sepulchers, which indeed appear beautiful outward, but are within full of dead men's bones, and of all uncleanness. Even so ye also appear righteous unto men, but within ye are full of hypocrisy and iniquity."

Conrad lowered his gun and turned away. He looked to the sky. The rain was heavy now. He looked back at Don. "You deserve to die," he said. "But I won't do it."

Conrad walked back to the car and stuck his head inside. He took a handful of papers from the glove compartment, pulled a lighter from his pocket, and lit the papers. He threw the flaming sheets on the floor mats and watched the blaze grow.

Don watched Conrad for a moment and then ran for the trees. Dave looked back and forth between Dave and Conrad before deciding to join Conrad.

"He's getting away," Dave said.

Conrad shrugged. "So what. He can't be in public anymore. He'll stay in his caves from now on."

"What was that anyway? Those words."

"Matthew twenty-three," Conrad said and followed his answer with a deep and tired sigh. The smell of the burning helicopter and car - the rubber, the fuel, and the bodies of the helicopter crew - was overwhelmingly strong and he wanted to vomit. "I'm getting the hell out of here. What about you?"

Dave looked at the burning vehicles. "The same I guess. I'll see you later boss."

Dave walked back towards the tree line he had come from, slowly and with his shoulders slumped, like a man with the weight of the world on his back. You're a good man Dave Bronson, Conrad thought as he watched his friend disappear into the tree line.

Conrad left the park in the opposite direction. He crossed the street and walked two blocks to a yard thick with bushes. His black steed was parked behind them. He climbed into the car and drove back to Washington, DC through the pounding rain.

36

He opened the door slowly because the place wasn't completely dark. A crack between the curtains allowed some light into the quiet apartment. Peeking in, he saw shadows dancing on the wall across from his bedroom doorway.

Conrad instantly drew his gun and softly closed the door behind him. Holding his gun with both hands, he tiptoed to the threshold of the bedroom door. Once there, he dropped the gun to chest level. He slid into the room, pointing his gun where he looked.

She was lying on the bed, her eyes closed, her hands folded under her head, and her knees drawn partway to her chest. She wore a thin, light blue teddy and it was spread out over her and the bed. Candles of various colors and smells - vanilla, cherry, apricot - burned from various spots in the bedroom.

Conrad lowered his gun to his side and stood there for a full minute, taking in the luminescence of Lydia's beauty. He knew he wasn't dreaming but he didn't believe that this could be reality. She shifted slightly and opened her eyes. A smile spread over her face and she stretched her arms to him.

Conrad looked around apprehensively as he approached her. He tentatively sat down beside her. With one last look around, he put his gun on the dresser and took her in his arms, first gently then tightly. "I thought you were...gone."

"Ow," Lydia said. "Not so tightly honey."

Conrad eased his grip. "What's going on?" He was beyond being surprised by anything now. His mind felt drunk, in disarray. Thoughts spun in his head and he didn't know which one to reach out to and have faith in.

"I'm not sure," Lydia said shaking her head. Her hair fluttered behind her, grazing Conrad's forearm.

"What do you remember?" Conrad kept his voice low, as though he were speaking in a dream and any sudden motion or loud sound would banish it in an instant.

"I was being slapped around, kicked, burned by something, wires, I don't know. I kept my eyes closed most of the time. Then I was gone and then I was here. Not in the bed yet but here in the apartment."

Conrad nodded and looked down at the skin on her chest, her arms and her legs. She showed almost no signs of torture. She had little bruises along her body. Hidden under the sheer nightgown were small dark blue and gray splotches on her skin. The marks of an experienced interrogator. Conrad knew the methods. Give a taste of harm and injury but not too much to incapacitate one's charge. But the marks were not as intense as what she had described. No burns, no cuts. He was confused. "That's all? You don't know anything else?"

Lydia shook her head and her smile almost but did not quite disappear. She took Conrad's hand and lifted it to her mouth. She kissed his knuckles lightly and let her lips linger on the bruised, calloused skin. "What happened to you?"

"Nothing much. But we have to leave here, for good. Can we do that?"

She nodded. "Yes."

"Gone from here forever?"

She looked at Conrad. Her eyes, her face were relaxed. "I have nothing here Conrad. It's you who'll lose something."

They gazed at each other for a minute, maybe two or three, before the phone rang. Conrad's heart jumped. He took a deep breath and relaxed. He forced a deceitful smile to his lips. "Let me get that."

Lydia released Conrad and dropped breezily to the bed. Conrad rose and reluctantly turned his back to her. He went into the living room and lifted the receiver.

"Are you locked into an encrypted landline?" It was Carl Flannery.

"Yes."

"Sorry about this afternoon."

"What do you mean sorry?" Conrad looked out of his high-rise window.

"It was a little messy. I like how you got agent Bronson involved."

"Yes."

"But this always happens."

"I don't understand." Conrad's voice was measured and calm. He did understand.

"It gets messy. Others are drawn in. Recruited. Maybe forced to do something that seems morally outrageous."

"Uh-huh."

"So I apologize. For the mess. But I'm also proud of you. Every provocateur in your position, well almost every, lets the first one or two go. It's human nature to not want to kill. In cold blood I mean. We always let that slide and give you guys a second chance. You did pretty good Greis, considering."

Conrad walked to his window and looked out at a city going through its normal, blissful motions. "A second chance?"

"I mean essentially we are all good human beings. Righteous before God and all that. None of us wants to go to hell."

"No, I guess not."

The other end of the line exploded in laughter. "That's funny Greis. That's choice."

Conrad waited for a moment and neither spoke. Conrad watched the minute counter on his digital clock advance one digit.

Carl coughed away the rest of his laughter and hummed a moment. "Well this is how it goes."

"Who am I working for again?"

"For the American people Conrad."

"You said the NSC before."

"You're correct Conrad. And the American people."

"Carl." Conrad took a moment of silent reflection. "I don't want to do this anymore. I've done my part and I'm through."

"Conrad. There's really no discussion to be had on this and I refuse to become unpleasant. You're a smart man and I know you realize the consequences. You're a marked man too and, in my experience, you can't survive without protection of some sort."

"In your experience?"

"Don't get smart Greis. See. I'm becoming unpleasant already. Damn."

"Sorry bud."

Cris Alvarez

"But look, no one is protected for free. I mean imagine if everyone expected someone else to take care of their lives for them. Nothing would get done. It'd be bad. And messy.

"Messy. I got it." Conrad walked away from his window and looked around for the room for hidden surveillance devices.

"Good. Just relax for a few days. Take a week. Rest up and maybe vacation somewhere. Not too far. How about Hagerstown? We've got people there."

"Okay. Hagerstown."

"You'll be fine kid. All of you always turn out fine."

"Gotchya. Thanks."

Carl continued speaking but Conrad put the receiver in its cradle. His hand lingered on the phone. He returned to the bedroom.

"Let's pack."

Lydia smiled and rose from the bed. She had nothing underneath her teddy and the candlelight illuminated her body perfectly. Conrad hesitated. "We'll have to get you dressed."

They spent the next twenty minutes packing clothes, toiletries and various sundries into two large suitcases and a military duffel bag. Then Lydia put together some sandwiches while Conrad packed a hardened carrying case with knives, two guns and ammunition.

Conrad carried the luggage to the front door and waited. He looked over the room for the last time. Lydia came up to him and put her head on his chest. He hugged her tightly and then gently pushed her away. He took out his cell phone and dialed. Dave's voicemail kicked in.

"Dave. Sorry about getting you involved but there's nothing I can do now. We're in a fucking rat's nest. Only thing to do is to get out of the cage." He killed the call and tossed his cell phone onto the sofa.

"Don't you need that?" Lydia asked.

"They'll trace me with it." Conrad gripped the doorknob tightly.

"So where are we going?"

Conrad canted his head. "Hagerstown honey."

"What's there?"

Conrad looked at the case of weapons he had prepared for the trip. "Hell if I know, hell if I care."

He lifted their luggage to his shoulders. He left the case of weapons on the floor and walked out of the apartment. "I've got everything I need," he said more to himself than to Lydia.

Lydia followed him out and closed the door shut. It automatically locked behind them.

37

T hey cruised south and east, down the Virginia coast, past towns and beaches tainted with fear and blood. They continued on until they found a short stretch of pristine coastline lined by a half-dozen sturdy but empty wooden houses built on raised foundations. The earth there was rich and clean.

Conrad tore the boards off one abandoned home and spent two weeks under the sun making it livable. Lydia helped with the work and together they planted a small vegetable garden behind the house and raised a chicken wire fence around it to keep out the wild rabbits.

In a large shack further back from the beach were fishing nets, rods and a long rowboat. Conrad spent another week fixing those. When the boat was fully repaired, he put to sea in the morning and returned home with fish that evening. It became his daily ritual.

Three months passed. They endured a hot summer and the occasional traveler who came in for a night's rest and a bite to eat. The salty breeze and the sun browned and hardened their skin. They went to bed when the darkness came and woke when it left. They spent the evenings wrapped together, their bodies as one in a primal embrace. Nightly, their bed became a place of sweat, dirt, sand, flesh and unbridled love. It was their new rhythm. They embraced nature and nature embraced them.

It was near the end of August that Conrad woke from an afternoon nap to find a group of young men, much like the ones he killed so many months ago, wandering through his garden and around his boat. They weren't the same men though, only the same breed.

He pulled on a pair of jeans and a t-shirt and told Lydia to stay inside. He came out the back of the house and startled the men. They relaxed when they saw he was unarmed. He didn't speak as he approached the five of them.

"Well what's here?" one of them said. That one had a long blonde ponytail pulled back behind his head. A long mustache and a short, dirty blonde beard covered his face. A tattoo adorned the left side of his neck and extended below his t-shirt neckline. The other four men with him spread out around Conrad.

"Nothin," said Conrad.

"Nothin? No one else is livin here? You the landlord?" The others laughed and they all shifted their weight from foot to foot furtively. They seemed ready to pounce but not quite courageous enough to do it yet.

"I don't own anything," Conrad said. He stood with his bare feet shoulder length apart. His toes gripped the sea dirt.

"You got a garden, a boat. Fishing. You own something."

"You looking for money? I don't have any money. Just food." "You got any guns. We need guns."

"No guns. Just me."

The man stepped closer to Conrad. "Damn. No guns?"

"Come on Dee," another man said. He was of medium height and thin, but he had a paunch. Angry tattoos covered his bare arms and he wore a tank top t-shirt like the rest of them. He was clean-shaven and his dark hair was short. "Let's get going. We need to get some real supplies."

Dee looked back at the man who had spoken and looked back at Conrad. "He says he got nothing but I don't know."

"If he had something, why the hell would he come out here without no gun?"

"I said I got nothing," Conrad said. "If you want some food-"

"We don't need no food," Dee said. His face dropped and his mouth squirmed. He looked back at the other man. "Let's have some fun Mack."

"Let's get the fuck outta here," Mack said.

Dee spun and pulled his gun. Everyone including Conrad jumped when he blew three large holes through the hull of Conrad's boat. Dee and one other man who hadn't spoken laughed.

"Goddamn it," Conrad said. "What the hell?" Dee spun around with his gun in his hand. Conrad raised his palms. "What do you want?" he asked.

One of the other men, a darkly tanned short and thin man, rushed to Conrad's fenced garden and kicked the gate down. He ran through the plot of ground ripping at the shrubs and pulling the vegetable plants out of the ground.

"Damn it," Conrad said. He turned and walked towards the garden but stopped when he heard a gunshot behind him.

"No, no," Dee said. "You let him have his fun." Dee laughed again.

Conrad looked back. The silent man who had laughed when Conrad's boat had been shot pulled out his gun and began shooting more holes into Conrad's boat. Dee joined him. Mack shrugged when Conrad made eye contact with him and he walked to the garden with the fifth man. Those two watched the tan one rip up the garden.

"Conrad." Lydia, wearing a long thin skirt, ran down the back stairs.

"Well what's this?" Mack asked. He walked towards Lydia, but she ran past him to Conrad.

Lydia grabbed Conrad by the arms. "That's our garden," she said. Conrad saw the worry in her eyes. That look was there. Ten years of fear drilled into her brain.

"Inside," he said. He gripped her arm and moved towards the stairs. Something came down on the back of his head, near his nape. He went to his knees.

"Inside," he said again to Lydia.

She turned and dropped to her knees next to him. "Not without you."

"I don't think so," Dee said. He stood near Conrad with his feet apart. "I think she stays here with us." He pressed the barrel of his gun against Conrad's left side and reached down for Lydia. When he got a hold of her shoulder, Conrad twisted left and reached under Dee's left arm with his right hand to grab Dee's wrist.

Dee said "Huh?" and pulled the trigger. The gun exploded and the bullet clipped Conrad's side but Conrad had Dee's wrist and he didn't let go. He stood and slammed an elbow into Dee's nose. Dee grunted and tried to pull out of Conrad's vice-like grip.

Someone shot a gun at them and Dee yelled, "Don't shoot! Grab him."

Dee dropped his gun and wrestled with Conrad. Lydia stumbled back as the others tackled Conrad from different sides. Conrad writhed in the grasp of ten arms. They were all smaller or leaner than him but he didn't have the strength to wrestle with them all. Each time he got a leg or arm free from one hold, a new hand would grab the limb.

He twisted and squeezed anything he could get his hands on but they moved with as much desperation as he did. Lydia screamed for help and she hit one of them with a piece of wood. Dee punched Lydia in the face and she went down unconscious.

Conrad became furious but he lost his focus. He lashed out without thinking. They gripped him tighter and his strength began to ebb. He went to his stomach and their weight pressed against him. A piece of metal pressed against his arm and may have entered his flesh. His adrenalin was pumping too hard for him to be sure.

They moved away from him, panting and coughing, and he crawled towards Lydia. He could barely get to his knees. A man kicked him in the gut and he kept going. Another man kicked him in the ribs and he kept going. Someone grabbed his hair, lifted his head and punched him in the cheekbone. He kept going. He collapsed on top of Lydia. A hand twisted him around. He looked up. Dee had him by the hair and was yelling at him.

"Do you believe in God?" Dee yelled. "Do you believe in God?"

Conrad gritted his teeth and said nothing. I know you sure don't believe in God, he said to himself. But I guess it's easy to pretend you do since that's what the side you're on now preaches. "Is God what you salute to now punk? Out in the wild pretending holiness."

"What the fuck did you say?" Dee pointed a revolver at Conrad's face. His thumb pulled the hammer back and the cylinder turned.

"Get some balls," Conrad said.

There was an explosion. Dee's head opened up over Conrad's face. Soft flesh and blood sprayed over him and both Dee and the gun dropped on top of Conrad. The others yelled and scattered.

There were more explosions, quick, timed, precise. The men, the boys, went down one by one. Conrad could at least see that much. He pushed Dee's body off him and turned on his side towards Lydia. He put his arm around her and closed his eyes. He thanked nothing in particular for this unexpected salvation.

38

C onrad woke in his bed next to Lydia. The temperature was cool and the sun was on the west side of noon. His arm, the arm he thought had been stabbed, was wrapped in blue cloth. Lydia had a black eye but looked well otherwise.

Conrad got out of bed. He only had his boxers on and he saw how badly bruised he was. He walked quickly but carefully to the bedroom door. Someone moved in the living area. They could have killed him already. He opened the door.

Carl Flannery, wearing military fatigues, looked back at him from the open kitchen area. A sniper rifle leaned against the wall near the front door, barrel up.

"Good morning," Carl said. "Want some coffee?"

Conrad hesitated, looked around and closed the kitchen door quietly behind him. He walked close to Carl before speaking. "What are you doing here?"

Carl lifted a cigarette from a wooden saucer Conrad had carved weeks ago. "Protecting an investment."

"We don't smoke in here."

Carl smiled and opened his eyes wide. "Aaah," he said. He nodded, looked at the half-finished cigarette and put it out in the saucer. "Sure, sure kid."

He moved away from Conrad towards the makeshift stove. "I was about to make some lunch. Fish actually. You've got some good stuff here. Smoked triggerfish?"

Carl had some of Conrad's most recent catches on the countertop. He was using his fingers to pluck at the stash of smoked fish.

"Yeah. Triggerfish," Conrad said. "You want to stop picking at my food and have a decently prepared meal?"

"Don't get testy now. I saved your life didn't I?"

Conrad looked out an open window. He couldn't see any bodies from this angle or any scavenger birds in the sky.

"I buried them," Carl said. "Not too deeply. It was a rush job."

"Did you send them after me?"

Carl smirked. "Did I need to? People like that were bound to show up sooner or later."

Conrad nodded. From the moment that he and Lydia had discovered this place, he had known it was simply a dream waiting to end. Who could possibly escape the life that he had led? "Okay. Now what?"

"You know why I'm here. You can't just leave."

"You won't let me escape will you?"

"You're government property Conrad. Twenty years of service made you that."

Conrad walked to the fish that Carl had pulled out. He used two fingers to scoop some of the flesh from the body of the smoked fish. He stuck the food in his mouth and rolled it around his mouth. He had learned to love the taste of it more than any other food he had ever eaten. "What if I said I'm not going back?"

Carl shrugged. "You have to." He glanced at his rifle and so did Conrad. They both flinched towards the gun. Then, they both sprinted for it. Conrad got it first and swung its butt into Carl's stomach. Carl grunted and doubled over.

Conrad stepped back and pointed the rifle at Carl.

Carl looked up and smirked. "What? Kill me and more will be here."

"So? Maybe I just want to kill you. I owe you don't I? For your lies. For making me a pawn."

Carl's mouth gaped opened like that of the fish he had been eating. He straightened. "Now wait a minute buddy. You got me all wrong. I saved your life out there."

Conrad smiled. "Got you, you bastard. I'm not gonna kill you. I'm just going to tie you up. Sit down or I will shoot." Conrad waved the rifle barrel towards a chair.

Carl nodded and sat. His eyes narrowed. "This isn't a game. Dave disappeared."

"Dave? What do you mean?"

"We think the rebels got him. That's what happens when you don't kill them, they kill us."

It was more manipulation. Lies on top of lies. Conrad lowered the gun. "Is Dave really dead?"

Carl looked off to the side and stretched his mouth. "I...uh...that's what I was instructed to tell you. That's all."

Conrad went to the bedroom door and knocked on it lightly.

"Yes," came from the other said. It was close. Lydia must have been eavesdropping. Conrad gently opened the door and Lydia stepped back.

"It's okay," said Conrad. "Come out here and tie our guest up please."

"Who is he?" asked Lydia.

"Just a friend who's made himself unwelcome. Nothing I can't handle. Can you get some rope from the shed?"

Lydia nodded. Wearing only a long gown, she shuffled barefooted to the back door. She opened it, glanced back once, and walked out.

"And then what?" asked Carl.

Conrad shook his head. "Please Carl, just shut up. You're like a fucking car salesman."

"Look Conrad," Carl said. "I'm just trying to tell you how it is."

"Goddamn it," Conrad said under his breath. The man couldn't stop.

A scream made them both jump. Conrad ran to the open door and out onto the steps. A bearded man in ratty clothes was jogging from the tree line towards Lydia and the house. He was waving his arms in the air and shouting something Conrad couldn't make out.

Conrad lifted the rifle and looked through the telescopic sight. He was looking directly at the face of the old preacher whose life he had saved months before at the DC Convention Center. Conrad lowered the rifle and watched the man approach.

"Lydia, come up here," he said. Lydia ran back up the steps and into Conrad's arms. The old man unexpectedly stopped and pointed towards the other side of the house.

Carl was running along the beach away from the house. He was making his way towards the trees but away from the old man. Conrad shot once into the air. Carl kept running. Conrad peered at Carl through the rifle sight. Carl looked back and forth frantically but kept running. Conrad shot once into the dirt in front of Carl. Carl kept running. Conrad let him disappear into the trees.

"Come on old man," Conrad said. "Get in here." He carefully watched the preacher amble to the house, but he also kept an eye on the trees to make sure the man had no one else with him.

"Okay stop," Conrad said when the man was twenty feet from the foot of the back stairs.

"People been messing with you a whole lot," the preacher said. He had a forest green backpack on that he shrugged off his shoulder and let drop to the ground.

"What do you know about all that?"

"I've been here watching you."

"Oh really?" Conrad asked. He took another cursory look around and led Lydia into the house. He stuck his head out the doorway. "Come on in and explain yourself. We've got fish if you're hungry."

"Damn right I'm hungry," the old man said. Conrad went to the kitchen and took the fish to the dining room table. Lydia sat as the old man tentatively entered. He slid his palms on his thighs nervously and looked around the sparse room. "Not much here," he said.

"Nope," Conrad said.

"I'll get plates," Lydia said. She rose and went to the kitchen.

"Sit down," Conrad said. He leaned the rifle against the table. Lydia came back out with three wooden plates and placed them. While Conrad and the old man stared at each other, she walked back to the kitchen and returned with three wooden cups filled with water. She put them next to the plates and sat.

"Come on," Conrad said. He took a gulp from his cup.

The old man sat. He took a piece of fish and put it on his plate. He ate slowly and methodically. "I came by maybe two weeks ago," he said. "I laid low for a few days not sure what to make of this place."

"Why here?"

"Just walking the coast. Meeting people who have run away, like you did."

"I didn't..." Conrad swallowed the rest of the sentence with some fish. I did run. Why deny it? he asked himself.

"Well, as you say," the old man said. "But I looked and saw it was you. I remembered you at the big hall." He ate some more fish and chomped on it with his mouth open. Lydia raised her eyebrows towards Conrad. He only nodded back. "Go on."

"So I didn't know how you'd take to me. So I slept in the trees. Ate what I had. Then that fella in military clothes snuck by. He didn't sense me but I sensed him. I watched him for a week watching you."

Conrad looked at Lydia but she didn't respond. She just looked at her fish and picked at it. "A week you say?"

"Something like that. Then finally those kids come by and the fella shoots them down once it looks like they were really gonna kill you. Then he comes out and helps you. I couldn't wait no longer while you was inside bleeding. I had to help. So I came when I did."

"Kind of lost me the guy."

"He wasn't a friend of yours I guess. But why'd he save you and why'd you try to kill him?"

"Just trying to scare him old timer. He was trying to sell me something I wasn't buying."

The old man smiled broadly. "Like religion?"

"Exactly like religion," Conrad said. He laughed loudly and ate a big scoop of fish.

"I guess I'm sort of done with it too. Religion I mean. It's just too much pressure."

"How so?" said Lydia. She was looking intently at the old man now.

"All those rules. Havin to hate so many people, and distrust so many people, and always having to worry about whether you done right in the eyes of God and men. I decided I'd be happy enough just making God happy and not all of those fools at the church happy too. It shouldn't be that God wants so much blood on his hands in order to spread his word."

Conrad chuckled. "You could say the same damn thing about the government too old man. Know that?"

"That man that run off was a government man?"

"Sure was." Conrad rose and took the rifle. "How long you plan on staying?"

"How long'll you have me?"

"Long as you want."

"Good. Things are getting pretty bad near the cities. More blood, more bombs. Some of em started calling it an offering to God. Gives me the creeps."

"I don't suppose the feds have shown any restraint."

"M-wave weapons are comin back," the old man said.

Conrad was a little surprised. "You know some Army?"

The old man nodded and grinned. "Yup. Green Beret out in South America, little bit of the Gulf Wars."

"Regular woodsman," Conrad said.

The old man chuckled. "Yeah. Know my way around a hidden trail but try to get me to walk a straight path through life and I don't know where the hell I'm going."

Lydia laughed and stood. "Let me clean this up." She took the dishes and walked outside.

Conrad glanced back at the empty doorway. "You know these roads?"

"Oh yeah. I've been walking them all my life. Up and down the coast. Know how to walk em, eat on em, hide on em. Everything."

Conrad bit his lips thoughtfully. "Then I have a heavy question for you."

"Heck. You saved my life didn't you? Just ask brother."

Conrad nodded. "I can't stay here. That government guy'll be back soon enough with others."

The preacher nodded. "True."

"Maybe I need to hit the road, keep moving."

"It's a tough life, I won't lie. You can stay one step ahead of them for sure, but you'll always have to. There's no rest. I'm not sure if two can do it together. I mean you and the woman."

"I don't know what else to do."

Lydia stepped back through the doorway and closed the door. "Looks like that man is out there watching the house Rad. What're you gonna do?"

Conrad glanced at the old man. The old man coughed and rose. Lydia frowned and watched the preacher suspiciously as he walked out the back door. She looked at Conrad. "What's wrong?"

Conrad stared at her then pushed a wooden chair out. "Sit down honey. We've got to talk."

39

F irst Conrad took down the bug Carl had placed above the threshold of the bedroom door and broke it. Then he spent the rest of the day trying to convince Lydia to agree to every conceivable plan he could come up with. Nothing made sense to either of them.

The sun dropped below the horizon. With the preacher sitting outside watching for danger, Conrad and Lydia spent the night making love over and over until their bodies were exhausted and their minds clear. Conrad pulled a blank writing journal from a drawer, a journal that should have been a record of his day-to-day life in seclusion with Lydia, but in which nothing had been written.

Now Conrad lit a candle and he wrote. He recapped his recent history with the DHS, NSC and the rebels who had tortured him. He wrote about the duplicitous nature of both the rebels and the government, of their mutual propensity towards torture and violence, and about the fact that leaders of both groups were simply involved in the pursuit of power over others. The problem wasn't the ideals they professed, the problem was the people who claimed them as their own. But people never actually live for an ideal, Conrad reminded himself, they live for the flesh.

Conrad had thought he could live in peace. He thought that by running he could escape the cruel vortex his life had fallen in to. But it was a fantasy. He realized now that using violence to end violence perpetuated violence. He also realized that he couldn't escape something that he had made. He was part and parcel of the machine that was chasing him down. It was a child come of age, grown up and looking for its father.

Conrad had helped mold a society that needed men like himself to function and now it demanded his return. The machine had become more powerful and influential than its makers intended. Its ideals were strong, its beliefs good, but the machine had stopped understanding why it existed and now it only adhered to a desire for self-preservation at the cost of all other truths.

Conrad wouldn't go so far as to say that the machine was evil, because its enemies were not good. But the machine and its enemy were two rocks clashing against each other, blind faith on both sides, and between their sheer walls dripped the flesh and blood of the happy and innocent. Conrad was the product of that clashing, a cold-hearted survivor who saw the truth.

He knew that rock could be brought down in time by the wind and the sea. Or it can be brought down in a moment with dynamite. At forty years old, Conrad didn't have a long time. In fact, he had a short time. And both gore-covered cliff faces had let him know that each was itching to be brought down and brought down quickly. He could think of only one man with the ability and the will to do that.

Maybe the government could have what it wanted. Conrad could find Carl and profess that he finally understood that the NSC was right. "I need you more than you need me," he would say submissively. Once they took him back, he would become the best damn assassin they ever had. He would hunt down rebel traitors within the government and dispatch them himself. He and his masters would bypass what they obviously considered an onerous and corrupted legal system and bring justice swiftly and efficiently.

Conrad would become an executioner and a busy one at that. He could envision himself moving up in the organization by earning the one currency they respected – blood. He would elevate himself and gather his loved ones close so that he could protect and enrich them on the government's dime. He would become intractably enmeshed in that illegal and underground world of the powerful and he would rise up the ladder until the time he could control it. He wouldn't be the boss but he would learn the machine's pressure points and manipulate it as it will have manipulated him. And he would not be kind.

Conrad smiled with grim satisfaction over his plan. He could give in and he could break the machine. He could become the rolling juggernaut that neither side wished to acknowledge was coming.

Conrad saw the light of the sun lifting high above the ocean. He put down his journal. He was hungry but he did not know for what. Lydia woke and she smiled. She took his hand.

Silently and together, they walked into the kitchen and then outside down the back steps. The preacher was just waking up and stretching the sleep out of his bones. The rifle was lying on the ground next to him.

Conrad picked up the rifle, pondered on it, and then flung it towards the trees. It landed somewhere in the dark vegetation. There was a sudden rustling of leaves. Something moved along the ground in the underbrush. Birds and squirrels scattered.

Moments later, Carl stepped out of the tree line grinning. He had a gleam in his eye and the rifle in his hand. He walked towards the three, holding the rifle by the barrel, the weapon outstretched towards Conrad. A shiny, sleek offering of peace.

Conrad stood on the threshold, balanced precariously on the edge of the future. Peace and war each beckoned. On his left stood Lydia, the responsibilities of uncompromising love, to his right stood the preacher, the rigors of enlightened pacifism. Approaching him came confidence, power, fire, obligations, society, law and order.

In the far reaches of his mind, he heard the juggernaut approaching, a rumbling train of overwhelming power and finality. The time for decision was at hand. The machine cried louder. It yearned to be broken, reordered, rebuilt. Freedom called out to be free. Conrad took a step forward.

www.ingramcontent.com/pod-product-compliance
Lightning Source LLC
Chambersburg PA
CBHW031113030726

47496CB00002BA/522